The Shattered Truce

Donna Brown

First published by Starling Wood Press Ltd in 2024.

www.thestarlingwood.co.uk

Print ISBN 978-1-0685086-1-5

Ebook ISBN 978-1-0685086-0-8

Cover design by Matisse Luisa Designs

For my father

Contents

Map

N
W
E
S
BERRY DRUM
FOREST
ERUTHIN
VADENSCROWN
BOTHY
CLOUDWATER RIVER
MARCH SETTLEMENT
STONE HOUSE
STARLING WOOD
FORD
RISE
TO THE BARROWS
CLEARING
DEAS HOWE
GROVE
FOREST
RANGERS PATH
RIVER EVERLODE
THE HARTS HORN
RUMBLING CRAGS
SPIRAL COVE
NETHERMORE PASS
WATERFALL
← TO ERUTHIN
LAKE EVERLIS
ELDEN DEAS

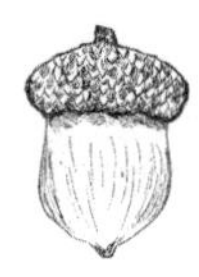

Prologue

Negotiating a marriage is never an easy thing. Ebba struggled to keep her expression neutral as she eyed the thin-lipped woman across the table. The son, however, was comely enough, and it would be for the best ...

Hilda bristled. "You may sneer, but my son will be chief one day; he can pick and choose. Your Elsa's a pretty girl, I grant ..." The raking glance swept Ebba head to foot.

Pretty, yes ... beautiful even ... at any rate, more than good enough for a man grown so tongue-tied and awkward. Ebba straightened, keeping her voice even. "And Gareth's a fine young man – old enough to know what he wants himself."

"Indeed," retorted Hilda.

Beyond the half open shutter, dandelions clothed the hillside, but winter's half-forgotten chill crept back in, settling between them.

"And we may be isolated, but March has its share of fine young women. Your daughter isn't the only one worth having," Hilda added.

Stone-cold creature. But she was right, the plain of March was vast, and they were a lonely outpost. New blood was scarce. "You could fly across the mountains and scour the length and breadth of Eruthin for better." Ebba gritted her teeth; she knew her own daughter's shortcomings all too well. *Pretty, yes ... but small. A little strange. At times ... vacant.* Sometimes the girl's expression reminded her of a sheep, and often she just wanted to shake her.

"Well, obviously we don't have that luxury, but she's a pretty girl, as I said ..."

Ebba's gaze returned to the dandelions. *Oh, to see a stranger again ... More chance of seeing a ...* She pushed the thought away, focusing on Hilda's fireside and the empty cauldron at their feet. *Time to end this conversation.* "Of course, she's yet a girl – as you say – but she'll be seventeen summers' old at harvest. Gareth obviously admires her, and perhaps a young wife will suit him. Why, he could've wed any time these last ten summers, but he hasn't. Let him make his own choice now." *Enough. No more.* Ebba's hands encircled her cup. Sunlight flashed through thatch. Outside, she could hear laughter and the clatter of hooves, and clanking buckets and the careless young. She sipped cold tea.

"He's always been free to make his own choices ... although that's not something you'd understand."

It was a well-aimed retort, but Ebba ignored it; she had what she wanted now.

CHAPTER 1

TALES FOR TELLING BY FIRELIGHT

Fran stopped, and moved so his back was against a tree. The presence grew stronger, like the deepening stillness before prey broke cover. He almost caught its scent, but sniffing again he could only smell the mellow freshness of oak and beech, newly unfurled, bright and downy. *What do you want with me?* No answer. He took a deep breath and strode homewards, the late sun glancing through the high canopy. When the forest began to thin, the caw of a rook, flapping amid the high branches, rent the air. Fran's heart skipped a beat; they were not alone, he and the rook, both fluttering to reach the light, neither looking back.

At the trees' edge, with the broad clearing leading to home and the evening sun warming his face, his misgivings faded, replaced by a more familiar ache in the gut. He stopped, peering up through broad oak branches. Nothing, but they wouldn't be far away. He flopped down, stretching out and resting his head on the bundle of wood he had collected.

Moments later, he jumped as an acorn bounced off his forehead – then another. He heard giggles, then two familiar tangles of curls bobbed into view.

He went to catch Elsa, but before he could reach her, she dropped from the lowest branch and turned to him, smiling. Dappled light flashed around her, and the moment stretched. She wrinkled her small, freckled nose and stepped back.

"Enough firewood for two, is there?" she asked as he lifted her younger sister, Maya, down from the tree.

"Yes, me and my mother."

Elsa darted away between the trees, emerging a short time later with a bundle of branches. "Some of us don't make it all day of a job."

"Fast work. You'll make a great wife for somebody one day."

Her face froze.

Fran fought back a smile. *Typical Elsa.* "Joking."

"I know."

A cloud drifted over the sun and their shadows vanished. Maya slipped between them, taking some of the wood from Elsa.

With the bundles rearranged, they moved down the clearing until they could see the smoke from Fran's home – a tiny stone-built dwelling standing alone, adjacent to the main fording point on the Cloudwater River. Beyond it, spirals of smoke from the settlement of March drifted skyward.

Fran's heart lurched when he caught sight of a figure approaching and recognised Elsa's cousin, Cader, coming to walk the girls back to March. *So soon*. But perhaps Cader would stay – they hadn't seen each other in days; they were due a hunting trip.

"Empty handed, are you?" Fran asked.

"Nice to see you, too."

"Not even a brace of rabbits. Your mam will be overwhelmed."

"There's a surprising lack of wildlife in the wood today." A shadow flitted across Cader's broad face, and he shook his head.

Fran recalled the solitary cry of the rook. *Not surprising at all.* He felt Maya's eyes on him, and Cader's flashed a question, but it was not one he wanted to answer.

"Cader." Elsa cocked her head and stepped aside. Her cousin followed, stooping to hear what she said.

"Family business, is it?" Fran called over.

"What's the matter?" Maya asked, frowning as she peered up at him.

"Nothing, Maya. It's just ... it's just been a long day."

Cader, towering over Elsa, gave a helpless shrug.

"Well, you're all welcome to take tea with me and my mother." Fran moved away, feeling hollow inside, kicking at the path. "You know we like visitors." He forced himself not to look back, then he jumped across the stepping stones at the ford, stopping on the last to watch the water eddy. Away to the left, a dragonfly flashed over a pool by the bank. He closed his eyes, sun on his back, the familiar rush of water over pebbles surrounding him.

He was across the ford when he heard Elsa and Maya running to catch up with him. He turned, trying not to let his smile betray him.

"Cader will take a message back. I've told him to say we're taking our meal with you and your mother, if that's all right," said Elsa.

"Of course it is, but ... will your parents mind?"

"No. We're to be back before dark, that's all."

"You didn't mention spring cleaning," said Fran, ignoring Maya's giggles as he followed his mother, Annerin, around the side of the house to where a table and chairs, a cupboard, ironware and pottery lay strewn across the grass.

"Well, I knew you wouldn't rush back if you thought there was work to be done." She smiled, cutting her eyes to Elsa. "You're joining us for supper, then." As she spoke, his mother's hand smoothed Maya's curls, but Fran caught the hesitation in her voice. "You're welcome, of course," she continued, "although it's already getting late, and you'll be missed."

"I've sent word back with Cader," Elsa answered. "We won't stay late, but with a clear sky and near full moon, it scarcely gets dark, in any case ..."

"You've convinced yourself, Elsa, at least." His mother looked away. "But Fran will walk you both back before sunset."

Fran nodded, then he sat down on the grass next to an old cauldron and a pile of pots. Amid the chaos, his father's sword immediately caught his attention; it lay in front of him, silver against the black of fire irons, tongs and ladles. In its usual home, mounted on the wall, it dominated their little house, but now, with the hilt almost touching his foot, it seemed to have grown even larger. The sight of it, lying carelessly on the grass, transfixed him, and he started when a sudden breath of wind moved the branches of a nearby silver birch, making shadows flicker across the blade. He leant down, fingertips tracing the familiar outline of the silver rose embossed on the hilt, and goose pimples stood out on his arms.

Fran and Elsa busied themselves returning things to the house until his mother called them for supper. They ate, and afterwards, with the fire glowing bright in the fading light, his mother brought out three shawls while Fran followed, carrying a jug of ale and four cups.

"It gets cold so quickly," commented Elsa.

Fran sat down next to her on the rug and watched her wrap the coarse grey fabric about herself, covering her delicate shoulders and pale blue dress and tucking her hair away beneath its heavy folds. She slipped her hand into his.

"As night follows day," his mother answered, nudging a log with the iron.

"Will you tell us a story, Annerin?" Maya asked. "About the sword or about Arete."

His mother flinched. He knew she did not like talking about Arete, or the witch, as most of March called her.

"I love hearing about the sword," Elsa added, peering round Fran to check on it.

His mother hesitated. "There isn't much time ... but let's see."

Fran passed the sword to her. She turned the blade in her hands and the familiar wheel of conversation turned, and with it the endless questions about the sword's origin.

"It's the only one of its kind we've ever seen," said Elsa, speaking across the fire to his mother and slipping her hand away from Fran as she did so. "But my father does always say the sword that once hung in the longhouse – Vaden's sword – had a black rose."

Maya leant forwards to trace the outline of the flower with her finger, then she asked his mother what she thought. Fran watched the exchange, unsure whether to be amused or irritated by Maya's unerring bluntness. The question should not have been so contentious – legend told of many similar swords – but given the state of their relations with the chief of March, it always struck a nerve.

When his mother answered, she wore the thin smile he knew so well. "We live here alone, me, Fran … and this sword. So, yes, sometimes the old legend preys on my mind, and yet …" She trailed off, catching his eye. Her face brightened.

"Mother?"

"I don't believe this is March's lost sword. I never really have." She held it aloft over the fire. "Your father treasured it. It belonged to his father and grandfather before him, so it's more likely this rose was once red."

Fran nodded. That would make more sense. Legend had it, ancestral swords from Glendorrig, his father's old home, had red roses on their hilts.

"I asked him about the colour once, but he never really answered me," his mother continued. "I think owning the thing weighed heavy on him. Sometimes I'd catch him lying awake, staring at it … It's old, after all, and was probably often used."

"Oh, Mam, it's only a sword. It can't answer for its deeds." The exchange was familiar. Bittersweet. Fran often wondered about their family in Glendorrig, the kingdom on the far side of the mountains that was part of the province of Eruthin. The sword might one day return there with him … Now, however, it remained here – both a treasure and a symbol of exclusion – a trigger for both anger and pride, hanging over them both in the most literal sense, the only ornament adorning their tiny house.

"No, indeed. But sometimes it looms," his mother answered.

"True, and it always draws my eye." *Reminding me how different life might have been.*

"Mine too, despite the blood it's spilt." She watched the flames reflect off the blade, and Fran, watching her face, saw that rare glimpse of hope ignite. It reminded him that, for her, the sword embodied the spirit and strength of the father he'd never known. It put paid to those darker moments when he thought the chief of March could have it, and be damned, if it meant he could have Elsa. His mother would not allow that, and pride would not allow that. Not now. Not ever.

She passed him the sword, remarking on its crafting, as she always did when they took it down from the wall. Fran thought of Farran, March's smith; he spent his days mending axes and sharpening hoes. Well, perhaps Farran was no great smith, or perhaps the legend was true and regular iron swords were transformed by dragons into weapons such as the one he now held.

Fran admired the sword while Maya nudged his mother into recounting how the swords were made, two hundred summers ago in Eruthin on the eve of a great battle – red for Glendorrig, blue for Bywater and green for Tiroren.

"Why did the prince of Ranoc attack the other three kingdoms?" Maya interrupted.

His mother shrugged. "He had a great army and wanted to rule all of Eruthin."

"Power," said Elsa, "he wanted to be high king."

Fran stole a glance at her, but it looked like her thoughts took her far away, back to March, he wagered, where her own father perennially fought to maintain his standing, sharing power uneasily with Lukas, the chief.

"But our king stopped him," said Maya. "Our King Vaden and the black sword."

"Yes, the missing black sword," quipped his mother, watching Fran as he spun the blade. "The legend doesn't say where that one came from."

Stolen from the prince of Ranoc was one version, Fran recalled, as well his mother knew, but unsurprisingly that version of the story held no currency in March. He caught her eye.

"Yes, and I wonder how Vaden came by it," said Elsa, noticing the exchange. "And where it went after he died."

"If it ever existed, it's probably in Eruthin with all the others – except this one, of course," said his mother. "The colour's probably chipped or worn off most of them by now. They've probably all been polished to silver like this one."

Hmmm. Polished to perfection by a better blacksmith than Farran. "If we could get to Eruthin," said Fran, "we'd see other swords. One in each family, probably." He looked up, catching sight of the mountain ridge known as Vaden's Crown rising above the woods, with its summits stark against the evening sky. From that summit, as the elders would have it, all of Glendorrig was visible on a clear day. Maybe even his father's old home ...

"You know the rest," said his mother, setting a finger on Maya's lips before the next question came.

Her tone pulled him from his reverie. As she said, perhaps the whole thing was a myth – just another of the winter tales they all told to pass the time – just one of the many stories Elsa and Maya would have heard when they were huddled together in the longhouse with everyone else aside from his mother and himself. With their mother and father, Cader, Liselle, Frey, and even the chief's son, Gareth, a silent man whose eyes were forever following Elsa; those were times he hadn't shared with her, and perhaps never could.

"I know some people think a sword very like this was March's greatest treasure, but it disappeared so long ago that it's wicked to still call my husband a thief," his mother added, speaking almost to herself.

Wicked and convenient. Fran clutched the hilt. *Just let them try. Let them say it to my face.*

"It's because it just reappeared ..." Elsa's voice faltered, and she chose her next words more carefully. "I mean it's the only one anyone's ever seen. Like you say, Fran, if we could see others, no one would listen to ... to him, but Eruthin's like a legend now, never mind the swords. My father says the same."

So, he speaks up for us still, just not to us.

"Exactly. It's just an heirloom now, although ..." A shadow passed over his mother's face. She stood up. "It's getting late. You two need to be going home."

She took the cups, leaving Fran to admire the sword. It felt light in his hand, firelight and ale guiding his arm. When she came back out, she offered Elsa her hand, pulling her to her feet as she proffered Fran a lantern. Reluctantly, he swapped it for the sword and set out to walk Elsa and Maya home.

Later that night, Fran sat alone outside the stone house watching the light fade over the mountains. The world grew still, trees black against a mauve sky. Then, in the distance over the fringes of the forest, a flock of starlings took fright, their grating cries carrying through the night air.

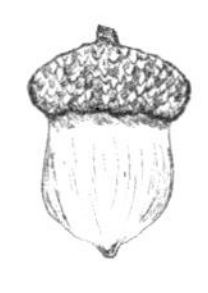

CHAPTER 2

I SAW THE DRAGON

Several days passed. Fran and his mother spent them alone. Even Cader did not venture the short distance from March to visit them. As the time slid by, Fran struggled to shake the feeling that all was not well.

"I meant to ask you, Fran, did you see anyone when you walked Elsa and Maya back the other night?" his mother asked one morning, as the silence threatened to drown them.

"Elsa's father met us part way along the path."

She nodded. "They stayed too late. Did Galos speak to you?"

"No, but then when does anyone ever go out of their way to speak to me? Or to you?"

She raised an eyebrow but said nothing.

Fran glanced at the sword, now hanging on the wall again. "No, he didn't say a word. He just looked at me, same as he always does."

"Galos is a good man. It's just—"

"It's just that he's married to Ebba. I know, Mam. Your old friend, Ebba."

"He was very fond of your father, Fran."

"I know. You've told me a thousand times."

"And that's because it's true."

"Not fond enough of me to want me in his family though, is he?"

"Oh, Fran, we've been over this too, and I don't know. Perhaps you should ask him. I ... I haven't seen him since before winter."

"That's because you don't go out. When did you last go to March?" The words were out before Fran could stop them. The last time his mother visited March was to break the news of his grandmother's death. Galos and his brother, Tom, built the pyre.

She rose, and without meeting Fran's eyes, she went outside.

A short while later, Fran went outside too and discovered his mother had taken her basket and gone – presumably to gather kindling in the Starling Wood, which was the name given to the section of forest demarcated by the river and clearing. Here, the trees grew less densely, with the undergrowth well-trodden and criss-crossed by paths.

He decided he would go south into the forest and hunt, find something good for their supper. She would have forgiven him by then, and they could cook together and talk of happier things. Perhaps he would bump into Cader. Sometimes they met when they hunted, both having taken to wandering deeper into the forest to avoid ending up with one of the villagers in their sights. The residents of March were a timid bunch – frightened of their own shadows once they lost sight of the clearing – except for Cader, of course.

But no, he had not forgotten who their friends were, despite what his mother might think. Galos, Elsa, Maya, Cader, and Cader's father, Elsa's Uncle Tom. Then there was his and Cader's friend, Frey … No, they were not altogether alone, although often it felt that way.

Fran took his bow and followed the path to the ford, crossed it and headed south into the forest. He walked for some time before a movement off to his left caught his eye. It was something small, small and unusually bright, weaving through the bracken. Fran lowered the bow.

Maya flashed back a grin before putting a finger to her lips and making her way towards him.

"What are you doing here? You don't usually go on patrol with your father … or hunt."

Maya shuffled.

"Well?"

"I'm not with my father."

"Oh, who did you come with then? Cader?"

"I … I was with Elsa."

"And now you're not." Fran spun, scanning the forest.

"It's all right, Fran. Elsa's not in the forest."

"Then what in the name of the good green earth are you doing here, Maya?" She looked at the ground, so Fran dropped down to better see her face. "Maya, explain." He plumped down, his back to the beech trunk and a thicket of nettles, set aside his bow and waited.

"What are you hunting?" she asked eventually.

"I'm following deer tracks, but never mind that. Why are you here on your own? Elsa will be looking for you. She'll be worried."

Maya studied him, biting her lip. "I saw something in the wood. Not a deer."

It was his turn to look away.

"Fran, I think it was a dragon." Her voice trailed off and a flush spread across her cheeks.

Not this. Not now. Elsa, where are you? "You've been spending too much time with my mother." He stood up. Beyond the bank of nettles, dappled sunlight brightened the forest, and overhead, the to and fro of bird chatter filled the canopy. "She thinks there's a dragon in the woods too. She says that's why no one ever comes to March over the mountain pass." He ran a bracken frond through his fingers, weighing his next words. "I've not seen one. There's no unusual tracks in this part of the forest, and I've never found a carcass with teeth or claw marks from anything much bigger than a fox. We're the only ones who hunt here now. The last wild boar was killed many winters ago, and the wolves hunt the northern forest – they don't venture as far south as March unless they're starving."

"But why is there nothing else hunting here, Fran? The forest stretches north and south for many leagues, and it grows all the way out until it meets the marshes. My father says so. And no one ever takes a patrol far in – not even to the river Everlode. He says he always stops when he hears the Rumbling Crags."

"That's because Spiral Cove and the falls are half a day's travel away. Go any further and you need to camp out overnight."

"There may be other creatures in the forest. The men from March keep watch, but they can't see into the forest, only out across the plains."

The truth, as always. In her blue check dress and brown apron, she might resemble her mother – darker, but the same curly hair and blue eyes – but, like Elsa, she remained honest and true, infuriatingly so at times. *No match for Ebba.* The thought slipped in, unbidden, but it was true, none of them were a match for the wretched woman. He heard it in Cader's descriptions of the little goings on in March. Ebba clicked her fingers and Galos jumped—

"Fran, what are you thinking?" Maya asked.

"Nothing, Maya."

"I don't believe you," she retorted.

"What?"

"You've seen something too. I can tell by your face."

Damn it, Maya, why not leave the forest alone? It means no harm. "Can you, now? I didn't know I was so easy to read," he countered.

"You're not."

"Well, you're right, as usual. There is something ... but if it wanted to kill me, I'd be long dead by now." *Instead, it watches me. Watches and waits. And now it looks as if it means to be seen.* And yet, he felt less safe in March. The forest felt like home, and he was never afraid to go there.

Maya stared at him, her eyes growing round, then she jumped when a bird broke free of the high branches overhead.

"You know all the stories, Maya," he began. "You know my mother's tales and the stories the elders tell. I don't know about magic water and streams leading to who knows where. I don't know much about Arete either, but, well, I go to the forest every day ..." He trailed off as something caught his eye, darting through the undergrowth.

Maya followed his gaze. "My mother says you spend a lot of time in the forest."

"What?"

"My mother. That's what she says."

Your mother. Fran tugged at a frond, then he stopped himself, letting go before he ripped it. He clutched his hair and closed his eyes.

"Sorry." The voice was tiny.

"Why does she say that?"

"I don't know."

"Yes, you do." Fran fixed his gaze on Maya, fighting back a smile, despite himself. Above their heads, another bird took off, wings batting.

"I think it's because she doesn't like you," said Maya.

He picked up his bow and made to tighten the string.

"I already guessed that, Maya. She never so much as speaks to me. Not now, anyway. Maybe she did when I was small."

Maya weighed a handful of beech mast, rolling the prickly casings between her hands until they fell, then she stooped to retrieve them. "She was angry because we missed the start of a supper in the longhouse."

"Oh. You and Elsa didn't mention that." *Nor did Cader.*

"Elsa didn't want to go."

Maya pressed the casings until they stuck to her palms.

"What about you?" Fran asked.

"I like visiting you and Annerin."

"Put those down, they're sharp." Fran brushed the debris off Maya's hands.

She stepped back. "Fran, I'm trying to tell you something."

"I don't know what's going on in the forest, not really."

"It's not about the forest."

Fran took a deep breath. *Elsa, where are you?* He listened, but the only sounds around them were bird calls and the crack of the beech casings underfoot. "What then?" he asked eventually.

"It's about Elsa."

Of course it is. Cader, you've not warned me. Fran squatted down, putting aside the bow again. "What?"

"Mother sent her out with Gareth. She sent us both out – to collect wood."

Now his hand dug down, clutching a fistful of the beach mast and earth. "Why?" His heart lurched, and he grew numb.

"Because she wants Elsa to marry Gareth. He'll be chief one day."

"And what does your father say?"

Maya pulled his hand free. "It's arranged ... but not yet done."

So, he says nothing ... and does nothing. But nothing's done yet. "When you say ..."

"My father says nothing yet, and ... and *he* says nothing yet."

Fran met Maya's eyes. So, the women arranged it, and the men held back. It spoke of a grudging arrangement, at best.

"He sent Cader with them," Maya continued. "My mam met Gareth's. They decided, and Gareth came with us today, but Cader's not really friends with Gareth, so he walked ahead ... and I left them to find you."

Fran let go of the fistful of dirt, got to his feet and wiped his hands on his trousers, while Maya dusted her hands off on her apron. He picked up the bow, setting aside his plan to hunt, and they headed in the direction of the ford.

When Fran and Maya reached the house and saw it was empty, Fran raised his hunting horn and gave three short blasts before hanging his bow back on the wall inside and fetching some bread and a drink for himself and Maya.

"That should bring your sister back here. We'll see who comes with her. Hopefully, it'll just be Cader."

The two sat together on the grass. Maya unwrapped her cloth bundle and handed a piece of cheese to Fran. "Gareth'll still be somewhere around. He can't go back without me and Elsa."

Fran stared down at his bread.

"Mother wanted everyone to see," Maya added.

"And did they?" Fran struggled to keep the anger from his voice.

Maya recoiled. "We met him on March hill."

"But Cader's with them."

"He went on ahead."

Fran set aside the bread and took a slug of ale. *Damn it, Cader.* "Does Cader ever speak to Gareth?" Fran seldom went to March, but when he did, he stayed close to Cader and Frey. Galos was usually around, nodding distance away.

"Sometimes, but ... well, Gareth's strange."

Coming from Maya, Fran took a moment to digest this.

"What are you smiling at?" Maya asked.

"What do you mean by *strange*?"

"He doesn't speak much. He's not like his father, or his horrible cousin, Wyntr."

"Wyntr ... he's the dark-haired man." Cader continually warned Fran to keep well away.

"Yes, Gareth's not like Wyntr. Gareth's ..."

"Strange?"

"Yes, I don't know what else to say. I think he's unhappy. His mother's not ... I keep away from her. Gareth's father's grumpy, but Hilda ... even Father says nothing nice about Hilda."

Fran nodded. *Grumpy.* That was one way to describe such a wicked man. Lukas was, undoubtedly, both ill-tempered and morose. He was a great bull of a man with a face set permanently somewhere between a scowl and a sneer. Hilda, meanwhile, was stick thin and as cold and unyielding as pond ice in mid-winter.

"Do *you* like, Gareth, Maya?"

Maya shrugged.

"Does he speak to Elsa?"

"No." Maya thought for a moment. "We walked here quietly."

"Oh."

"I think he doesn't know what to say. And Elsa didn't know what to say to him."

"Didn't he speak at all?" Fran asked.

"He pointed out how well the barley was growing."

"Oh." Fran finished his ale. Patches of sunlight flickered across the grass as the branches of the silver birch swayed in the wind. He didn't want to leave Maya alone, but news of Gareth's awkwardness emboldened him, making him want to find Elsa and rescue her from her silent companion, if Cader hadn't already done so.

"I wish we lived here, out by the ford and the wood ... but maybe you wish you lived in March with everyone else," said Maya suddenly, fixing him with one of her questioning looks.

Her comment knocked Fran sideways. Maya was the only person who would speak so openly about their estrangement from the settlement. Even Elsa avoided the subject when she could.

"Your father was called Edwyn, wasn't he," she added – a statement rather than a question.

"Yes, Edwyn." Fran played with the empty cup. "Do they still talk about him in March?"

"No." Maya spoke slowly, carefully cutting a wedge of cheese. "No one talks about any of you."

Fran went to stand beneath the silver birch. In the shade at its foot, he kicked at the fallen branches, snapping them beneath his boots. *Edwyn.* That was his father's name; his poor murdered father. But no one said it. No one ever said his father's name. Not even his mother. But far from his being remembered as a victim, it felt like people recalled only some shadowy character from an out of favour fireside tale. Edwyn seemed to be remembered as either a thief flaunting a stolen sword or, worse still, as a man who had consorted with the witch, Arete, who lived in the mountains in a cave beside Lake Everlis. Fran just pictured a young man who'd wandered haplessly into March, carrying his own father's sword, then stayed because he fell in love. And now, here they were – Edwyn's family. Alone. Trapped by the past like insects in amber.

Putting aside his thoughts, he returned to the house while Maya turned cartwheels on the grass. He put down the cups on the table, but on turning to leave, he glanced upwards and froze at the sight of the empty space on the wall where his father's sword always hung, and Maya's words rang in his head. *A dragon*. Could the creature have shown itself? His stomach churned. Cader knew about it, too. Lurking in the forest, it approached, slowly and steadily, circling from the south, tracking beneath the mountains. And now it was here.

Fran ran from the house and out into the lane, checking each way as he always did, then he headed towards the ford and the clearing, Maya following. Before long, a figure came into view, running towards them. *Elsa. Elsa alone.* She slowed, skirt hitched up, and when she caught sight of him she stopped, hands on her hips and chest heaving.

"Thank the gods, Maya's with you," she began. "You need to go after your mother. We went to look for Maya. We were in the forest just south of the clearing and then we heard you sound the horn, but there was a scream straight after it. It came from the direction of the crags, and it sounded like Gareth, so your mother went to look."

"You heard a scream, and you think it was Gareth." Fran's vision swam. What nightmare was unfolding? "What about Cader? Where is he?"

"He met Frey, and they went hunting. I don't know which way they went. Has Maya told you ...?"

"Your mother's plan. Yes."

"She sprung it on me. I don't know what to do." Elsa hung her head.

"Don't worry about that now. But what happened?"

"Maya disappeared while we were walking down. Cader had gone on ahead, and I thought she'd gone across the field to get to the stone house. I went over, but only your mother was in." Elsa hesitated, her face flushing. "I told her what had happened – about my mother, I mean. She went in the house when she saw Gareth following me, and ... and he just stood in the garden looking at the herbs. I don't think he realised she was there."

Elsa's look was apologetic. Fran thought of his poor mother; she hated the chief, Lukas, with a passion, and Gareth was his only son.

"When your mother came out, Gareth said he'd go and look for Maya, and he hurried away towards the ford." Elsa turned to Maya. "We looked for you, Maya, but we couldn't find you. Where were you?"

"I was—"

"Never mind, I found you, didn't I." Fran tousled Maya's hair. "So, then you both went out to look for Maya as well."

"Yes, we went to the clearing together. I assumed she'd be there. We looked around for a bit, but we didn't know where Gareth had gone, and then we heard you sound the horn ... and the scream."

"So, my mother headed from the clearing towards the crags."

"She said she'd head for the new fallen beech tree first. Do you know the place?"

"Of course."

"The scream sounded a bit further away, though."

Fran's heart sank. Finding someone out there would be an exhausting and thankless task. Beyond the fallen beech, the tracks petered out and tangling darkness grew. Tame woodland gave way to forest, which continued for many leagues, framing the edge of the mountains before sprawling away across the plains, only giving way to tufted grass where seedlings met mire.

"Don't let Maya out of your sight. I'll be back soon." He tucked a stray curl behind Elsa's ear then set off at a run to find his mother.

Chapter 3

Seeing Monsters

Annerin unsnagged her cloak from a patch of thorns and moved deeper into the forest, beyond the vast fallen beech to where the forest grew wild and dark. She fought through tangles of branches and nettles, trying to maintain her bearings, the iron chape of the scabbard dragging over the forest floor behind her. After what seemed an age, she stopped at a small opening in the trees, took a long draught from a half-full skin of water and checked for tracks or signs of disturbance. She was convinced the scream had been Gareth's. Her mother's instinct told her it wasn't Fran – knowledge that sent a wave of relief washing sidelong across the horror she felt when they heard the cry. No, the horn blast would have been Fran finding Maya, she was sure of it.

The forest was quiet now. No birdsong. Listening hard, she began to tune into a faint shuffling sound, intermittent and infuriatingly quiet, but each time she paused it seemed to stop. This stop-start went on for a while – a shadow dance with her own fears, perhaps

– but then Annerin caught it, just for a split second, the unmistakable sound of something large moving with stealth. Her heart froze, and she instinctively moved her hand down to meet the hilt of the sword. Gauging the direction of the sound, Annerin slipped behind an oak, her back against the trunk. Blood thundered in her ears. Slowly, she peered round to the right. Everything remained still. She almost looked away, but the slightest flicker of movement coming from behind some low-growing shrubs caught her eye. Annerin forced herself to keep looking. *Nothing.* Then a sickening fog of realisation hit; there was an instant where time stopped and the air around her slowed to a thickening soup. She gasped for breath, letting out an almost silent scream, then she froze as she stared into the blackness of a large, cold, amber-ringed pupil. Annerin's hand numbed on the leather grip as, helpless, she watched it dilate and bring her into focus.

Her heart froze mid-beat and the hair on her head prickled. A long-suppressed impulse to cry welled up inside her. She could not move, and she could not look away. Instead, she registered the image of herself, small and pathetic, reflected in the eye. But then a spark – What was it? Courage? Hope? Life? – lost in her for so many seasons, reignited. She remembered Edwyn – not the shadowy figure who inhabited her memory, his face now blurring into an older version of Fran's, but the way he had truly been. She pictured him, and her fingers, which were still gripping the hilt of the sword so tightly, loosened their pressure slightly. She felt, again, beneath them, the rough leather of the grip. Annerin focused on the sword, recalling it casually propped against the wall when Edwyn lay beside her. The same sword he carried that first day he came to March. The same sword she'd hidden in a wooden trunk when, grieving, she carried his child. The trunk Fran balanced against as he learnt to walk and, later, climbed on to reach for the sword, which by then hung proudly on the wall by the doorway. Frozen time stuttered, and Annerin, after so many weary summers and winters spent alone, raised Edwyn's sword aloft, and never taking her eyes off the huge one staring back at her, stepped out from behind the tree.

The great head turned to face her, bringing the creature into clearer view. Two massive front feet crashed down, trampling the undergrowth, and a limp bundle dropped from its jaws, hitting the forest floor with a sickening thud. *Gareth.* Registering blood on his shirt, she faltered. She was face-to-face with the creature now. Claws, with a short talon at each heel, planted themselves amid the bush, flattening stout branches like mere twigs. A reptilian head covered in golden-brown scales, with a tapering snout set in front of arched eye sockets that fell away into a ring of spikes and fans, bent down to look more closely at her. A long, segmented neck curved away to a sturdy body covered by the same glimmering golden-brown scales that faded to white on its underside and changed back to gold on its short legs. Wings were folded at its sides, and its tail, which writhed and curled as it surveyed Annerin, was long and tapering, with a spade of shimmering gold at its end.

Annerin and the creature weighed one another, the forest silent around them. Annerin's courage flared. If she were to die today, she intended to do so facing the enemy with the sword in her hand. She would die bravely, like Edwyn, and in courage they would be equals, standing together in the halls of their ancestors – but no, something in the creature's movement seemed wrong. It was so still, as if contemplating her. Then she realised its gaze rested not on her but on the raised sword, and its eyes held ... What was it? Recognition? Or fear? And all the while, Gareth's prone body lay between them.

Annerin, rigid, clutched the sword, hope flickering. Whatever happened, she would not run. She wanted to look at Gareth. *Perhaps he tried to run but fell, pinned down by those great front claws.*

The moment hung like a rip in time. Annerin raised the sword higher, both hands on the hilt as the cold, alien gaze switched from the sword back to her, and the head lowered. The creature took a step back and let out a noisy puff of smoke from its nostrils. Annerin flinched but remained rooted to the spot. Relief and confusion flooded her in equal measure as she watched the creature turn and melt away into the wood.

Annerin took a few cautious steps to follow but caught only the crackle of trampled twigs unfurling. The creature had gone, leaving only Gareth behind. She watched the forest for what seemed an age, her heart slamming in her chest.

Then she heard birdsong.

Her hands loosened marginally on the scabbard, and she bent down to check Gareth's body for signs of life. His skin was warm, and a steady pulse beat in his neck, but he'd been dropped from a height and he was out cold. She raised the sword again and patrolled in a wide circle around where he lay. Finding nothing, she scanned for tracks, but the forest floor was dry. *Safe for now, but what could vanish like mist could surely return just as swiftly.* They needed to get out of the forest.

Just then, a breeze shook the leaves, cooling her sweat and making her clothes cling. She returned the sword to its fur-lined scabbard and took a sip from the waterskin. It was close to empty, and she wasn't sure how far they were from the clearing and river. Ducking down beside Gareth, she raised his head slightly and pressed the skin to his lips. Water trickled away down his neck, and when she released him, his head slumped.

They were going nowhere imminently, so she gave three short blasts on the horn before sinking down among a sprawl of moss-covered tree roots. Gods, she felt weary. She leant back against the oak, staring after the creature. The sun was low, and she needed to find water, and then there was Gareth. She didn't want to leave him alone, but she needed to find one of the many streams running down through the forest, breakaways from the Everlode, the tumbling river fed by Lake Everlis, high above on Elden Deas. She strained to catch the sound of running water. *Nothing.*

Forcing herself to her feet again, she returned to Gareth – to the son of the man whose hatred and loathing made her an outcast. She looked down at his face, but anger did not come. She recalled him stammering and hesitant at the stone house, eyes darting from her to Elsa and settling nowhere. Instead, when she looked down at him, Edwyn came to mind – Edwyn dying, accompanied, like that memory always was, by the ring of clashing swords. Then by emptiness, black and endless.

Tears prickled, but as she wiped them away, Gareth's eyelids flickered. Annerin put the waterskin to his lips for the second time. This time he managed to drink, and when Annerin propped up his head, his eyes opened and locked onto her, widening as recognition dawned, then they flashed to the surrounding forest.

"What happened? Why are we here?" Gareth pushed himself up to sitting using one arm, rubbed the back of his head and winced.

"I don't know what happened, only that you went looking for Maya."

Gareth glared, ignoring the waterskin proffered to him.

Annerin went to lean against the oak. Her back ached and she was in no mood for an interrogation. She let her head fall back and exhaled, tracing patterns in the canopy of branches and leaves. High up, new growth shone translucent where sunlight filtered.

She had no idea what happened, or why the creature was carrying him away. Perhaps it was taking him to its lair in a cave at the foot of the mountains. And it had been keeping him alive. Annerin shuddered, then she fought back a smile when she noticed Gareth staring at her again, this time with a petulant look redolent of Fran.

"Do you know what happened to you?" she asked.

Gareth rubbed at his mop of brown curls, then he gingerly felt the back of his head. "Maya got lost. We came to your house to look for her."

"Yes, and then you went off to find her on your own. I followed with Elsa. We heard three blasts on a hunting horn coming from the direction of the ford, and then straight afterwards ... well, we heard screaming, and we thought it was you."

Gareth's brow furrowed. "I heard the horn too, but then ..." He shivered. "I don't ... something awful happened. There's blood on my shirt and I've hit my head." He pulled at the stained shirt and grimaced.

Annerin looked him over, noting the blood stains on his back and the matted blood clumping the hair on the back of his head. He must have a mass of cuts and bruises, but at least he was conscious. "You must be thirsty, and I have precious little water left. I'll go and see if I can find a stream."

She returned a short while later and passed Gareth the skin of water. He took a long drink, blinking in relief as the cold water met his dry, cracked lips.

"There's a tiny stream not far away," Annerin explained. "I couldn't hear it, but you can almost smell the water."

Gareth nodded, watching her intently. "It's going to be dark soon. I don't think I can walk. It's my head. I feel so dizzy."

"You've had a shock, and you've obviously hit your head quite hard." Annerin wanted to ask him about the creature. She imagined he'd seen it too. *Perhaps it had unhinged his mind.*

"Will you go back and get help?" he asked. His face was pale and drawn, the pain clear.

"I won't leave you. I've sounded the horn, so Fran will find us. I know he will." Fran spent half his life in the forest. He must have seen this creature too; this silent watcher, prowling so very close to their tiny, isolated home. She knew the truth of it now. Long ago, when Fran was a little boy resting on her hip, she'd walked in the clearing with her father and glimpsed the creature through the trees, away in the distance. Today she knew it wasn't a figment of her sleep-deprived brain. She recalled Fran laughing, pointing a chubby finger and saying "draygon, draygon", while her father, avoiding her eyes, smiled down at Fran and told him it was a stag.

"Well, I hope he's quick." Gareth's voice recalled her to the present.

May the gods grant him speed. Annerin surreptitiously fingered the rose embossed on the sword's hilt. Why did the creature retreat? And if it had been lurking in the forest for so many seasons, doing them no harm, why attack Gareth now? None of it made sense, but she was glad she carried the sword. The beast surely recognised it. And what did that mean? The sword was special – everyone knew it – especially the father of the young man sprawled on the leaves in front of her.

"I don't remember what happened. I think maybe I fell, but something startled me ..." Gareth searched her face for an answer.

Annerin weighed how much to tell him, wondering how much he would believe. "Very well," she said, after a long pause. Then she told him as much of the encounter as she dared, although describing the creature made the blood rush to her face. Gareth's brown eyes held no derision, but they grew wide, and he looked around nervously while she spoke, flinching at the eddying of starlings preparing to roost on the branches above them.

He said little in response to her story, only checking again and again the cuts he could reach, and continually scanning the surrounding forest. She could see the shadow on his face that would be a growth of stubble by morning, but the eyes were those of the little boy, afraid of the growing dark, and becoming more afraid, as time went by, because his legs refused to bear his weight.

"Do you think you can walk yet?" she asked. "Come, you must try."

He struggled to stand, clutching her hand and leaning against her, but immediately slumped back down, dragging her with him and making her stumble.

"I'm sorry. It makes my head spin," he muttered.

"No matter. You can't walk and I can't carry you, so here we will stay." Annerin dropped down next to him, her stomach growling.

Turning to him, she was met with an uncertain smile, something she'd never expected from Lukas' son. *How unlike his father he is – and his mother*. Her thoughts flashed back to her youth in March, and she remembered Gareth's grandfather, Luwain – a good man and a friend of her own father, who had always blamed Lukas for hastening the old man to his grave – and Lukas, and his actions eighteen winters before.

"What is it? Have you seen something?" Gareth asked, trying to move again.

Annerin looked away quickly.

"The way you look at me ... I am not my father, Annerin."

Annerin stole a glance back at him, weighing how to answer. "I look at you and see your grandfather."

"Ah." Gareth fell quiet, his gaze resting on the middle distance. "My grandfather."

"I didn't mean to ..."

"No, Annerin, I remember him well."

"As do I."

"Do you?" Gareth turned sharply back. "And yet ..."

The birds rustled in the tree above. Annerin did not want to answer the question in Gareth's eyes.

"But all our memories lead back to the same place, do they not?" he added.

Annerin sighed. "Yes, always to that night. But you were only a boy."

"I was ten summers old, but I remember ... I remember the snow ... and how the witch came down from the mountain. And I remember what happened to my poor cousins ..." Gareth's voice caught, and he looked away.

And I remember your father killing my husband.

"Poor Elin and Roe. Their deaths sent my father mad with grief. He ... he nearly killed Elsa's father the next morning ..." Gareth's voice became tiny, and he looked away.

Annerin crushed the dry leaves with her hand. *Better to be devoured by the creature than sit here like this.* She moved herself to the far side of the oak. *Their deaths sent his father mad with grief ... So, he doesn't know the truth. He was only a boy, and he doesn't know the whole truth of it. In the name of all the gods!* After all the long summers and winters, here she was with Lukas' son, and he did not even know.

She stood for a long time, her mind blank. The shadows grew and Gareth called out her name. She walked back to him, and his face brightened.

"I thought you'd gone."

"No, I said I wouldn't leave you."

"I'm sorry."

"Why, there's nothing for you to be sorry for. You're to marry Elsa and make everything right." She heard the acid in her own voice and did not care.

No answer came from Gareth. *Indeed*, Annerin thought, *for there is none to give.*

She recalled Fran's words that morning about Elsa's father, Galos. He was right; Galos might be their friend and protector, but he danced to Ebba's tune, and now Ebba brokered peace – peace in March. The prize was the chiefdom for Ebba's future grandson, and the cost was Fran.

Chapter 4

Fading Light

An unnatural quiet enveloped March as evening fell. Ebba sat alone, staring into the embers beneath her cooking pot, where a stew of barley and turnips was keeping warm. She ladled yet another spoon of water into the pot and stirred. A loaf of rough brown bread waited on the table – a table set for four. Ebba went to the door and looked out into the square. The longhouse sat on the far side, and behind it, March hill – a small, conical rise sheltering the eastern side of the settlement and enclosed by the encircling stockade.

Cader and Frey sat a short distance away in the square, still intent on skinning the young deer they had caught earlier. Ebba walked over to them, carrying a small bundle of herbs to season the meat. They nodded when she placed the herbs on the table between them.

"Everyone's late returning," Ebba remarked, watching Frey cut skin away from the flank.

Neither Cader nor Frey replied. Eventually, Cader raised his head and looked at Ebba. "I walked with Elsa and Maya this morning like

Galos asked, but I'm afraid I lost track of them. They were walking very slowly. Elsa and Gareth were near the ford when I last saw them. I couldn't just hang around, but I saw Frey, so we decided to track this deer. I'd assumed they were back, but you say they're not."

Ebba waited, sensing he was holding something back, but Cader returned to work on the deer's neck, the head, with its downy antlers and dead eyes, watching from the bench behind them. Then a dart of panic shot through her. "You last saw Maya near the ford too, surely."

It was more statement than question, but Cader looked up sharply, his mouth dropping open.

"Cader?"

"She must have been there." Cader ducked his head, avoiding Ebba's eyes. "Then again, she might have stopped by to see Fran and Annerin. She's very fond of them."

Ebba stared at the top of Cader's head for a few moments but decided to let the remark pass. There were more important things at stake here. She sensed something amiss, and if she was right, she would likely need their help.

Glancing up, she noticed Ileth, Lukas' closest friend, asleep outside his hut on the far side of the square. She checked the sun – still visible, but it was now lower than the summit of Elden Deas. It was unusual for Galos to be this late. He and his men ranged to the south of March each day – an easy enough area to control because the rise, a small hill directly south of March, granted views for many leagues in every direction. Lukas, meanwhile, hunted north of the line between March and the old bothy down by the riverbank. This was a convenient arrangement given the rivalry between them, but it meant if anything happened to Gareth south of the line, Galos would be held responsible – Ileth would make sure of that.

"Both your fathers went out with Galos. They're late too," Ebba remarked.

Cader and Frey exchanged glances but ignored her and continued working on the deer. Ebba waited. Cader frowned, looking past her and around the square. Ebba maintained her silence. Cader was her nephew, and Frey's mother was distant kin, so both young men recognised her as family. Eventually, they set down their tools. Something was wrong, and now they sensed it too. Little more than boys, neither had ever needed to worry unduly about the safety of their fathers before, and now, when they looked up at her, their faces betrayed a little of the trepidation of the child – fear, ripe to be hidden behind the weight of a wooden shield and the balance of a spear. Ebba hoped it would not come to that.

"Do you want us to go and look for them?" Cader asked, checking the sun as he spoke. "We can go to Annerin's house. If anything has happened, it's the nearest place for anyone to go."

Ebba made a snap decision. "I'll go with you."

Cader and Frey looked questioningly at her, then Cader cleaned the knives in a pail of water set beside the table and Frey reached for a pole to convey the carcass to one of the stone huts for hanging.

If anything was amiss, she needed to be there. Galos and Elsa were both too caught up with Annerin and Fran, but she would keep the peace, whatever the cost. The arrangement between Elsa and Gareth was a precarious thing, brittle as the dry shell of a bird's egg. It had been secured by steady, painstaking steps, beginning when she saw Gareth watching Elsa across the square, then growing as she noticed Gareth shrink from his obligations, and his cousin, Wyntr, find favour with Lukas. Hilda saw it too, she was sure, and she understood that Ebba's plan offered a way out, an alliance that would make her son strong again.

Steeling herself, Ebba moved around the longhouse and approached Hilda and Lukas' home. Hilda – a gaunt, cheerless woman, with dark rings around her sharp brown eyes, and a scarf over her greying hair – looked up warily from her seat at the table outside her door as Ebba approached.

"Gareth hasn't returned yet," she stated, her eyes never leaving Ebba.

Ebba took a deep breath and sat down opposite. "No. Neither have Elsa and Maya, or Galos. I intend to go with Cader and Frey to check all's well, although I expect they're on their way back as we speak. I wanted to tell you before I went," she added, returning Hilda's unflinching gaze.

Hilda stiffened. "Gareth is rarely late. I'm sure his father will want to accompany you." Without waiting for an answer, she stalked away, presumably to find her husband.

Ebba watched Hilda's retreating back and hoped whatever made them late wasn't down to Elsa.

Hilda returned, then Lukas strode over, his face stern as he looked Ebba over from her head to her toes and back again. He was a burly man – thickset, with a neck the width of his head, hostile brown eyes and greying, patchy stubble. *His eyes are like Gareth's,* Ebba thought as she returned the glare. Without speaking, he went into his house to collect his sword.

"Are you ready?" Without waiting for an answer, Lukas moved towards the southern opening in the stockade. This formed the main entrance to March and was the quickest way to the lookout point called the rise, an outcrop far smaller than March hill. Light permitting, from there they would be able to see across the fields and most of the way down the path leading to the ford. If there was no sign of anyone from the rise, it would indicate they had crossed the Cloudwater at the ford and gone into the clearing or the woods.

Ebba remained seated for a moment, head held high, then, with a curt nod to Hilda, she returned home to quench the fire and to collect her bread and a skin of water.

Cader and Frey waited with Lukas at the gate. Neither met her eyes as she approached.

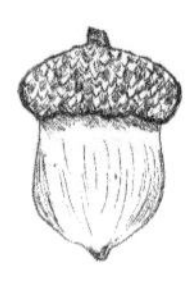

Chapter 5

Shadows and Birdsong

Fran's heart pounded as he clambered over the trunk of the fallen beech tree. On the far side, he stopped to listen. The starlings were singing, but it grew late, and he sensed all was not well. He blew three sharp blasts on his hunting horn, making the rooks caw in protest and take flight from their roosts. Then he waited.

The reply came quickly, faint but clear, coming from the southeast. He set out, noting broken branches and flattened undergrowth as he went. *Yes, this was the trail.* He stopped himself from thinking about what might have happened. Part of him had already guessed. *Maya's dragon.*

Fran followed the tracks until he saw an oak that he recognised up ahead. It stood at the edge of a small break in the trees. He knew this tiny clearing well; it made a useful staging point on his trips – a marker amid endless thickets that could baffle the sense of direction of even the most seasoned hunter. He always tried to keep it clear by tearing up the saplings that sent their strong white roots delving down through the fallen leaves. It was a place where he often sat, resting his back against the trunk of the great oak at its edge ... and now here was his mother – and Gareth. Fran contemplated them, relief mingling with surprise. Both slept, their backs against the oak's trunk, as if some magic prevailed over the tiny glade.

Fran, hardly sparing Gareth a glance, knelt by his mother and nudged her. Her head bobbed forwards, jolting her awake.

"Mother, are you all right?"

She took a moment to bring him into focus, then she smiled.

Fran turned towards Gareth, who remained slumped. "What's happened? He looks injured."

"He is, but I don't know how badly," she replied. "He's cracked the back of his head, and he's got quite a few cuts and gashes. He tried to walk but couldn't." Fran waited for her to continue, but she looked away, grasping for the hilt of the sword. "Some sort of creature was carrying him in its jaws, but I scared it away."

"You used the sword." His question was only half serious, the sword being far too big for his mother to carry, let alone wield.

She raised an eyebrow in response. "You don't believe me."

Fran shrugged, and she turned to Gareth, grimacing as she looked at the back of his head.

"As it happens, I do believe you. Did he see it?"

"He didn't exactly say so, but I think he did and it's half turned his mind. It had him in its jaws ..."

"Really?" Fran tried to picture it and shivered. "Well, we can talk about that later. We need to get him out of the forest now."

"Yes. It's good you found us so quickly. I knew you would."

Fran moved to Gareth's side, noting the matted hair and the patches of dried blood staining the fine grey wool.

"You might believe me, Fran, but it's likely no one else will. I'll say I found him this way, but what everyone else will make of it, I don't know."

"They'll probably send hunting parties into the forest," said Fran.

"Yes – and they'll find nothing, then blame us."

Fran turned and stared at her. This was a new and unwelcome thought. "Mother, Elsa was with you, and Maya with me. Besides, surely no one thinks we would ..."

"I don't know. I haven't been to March for a long time." A sob choked her voice.

Fran went back to his mother and put his arms around her. "He'll be fine. He's not dead."

The two of them regarded Gareth, the evening song of birds piercing the silence of the darkening wood.

"Mother, when I said I believed you, I meant it. I've seen the dragon too."

Her eyes widened.

"I've seen it too," he repeated, "but you're right, some people might not believe us. Galos and Tom must know about it, but no one will want to talk about it. No one ever wants to talk about anything."

"Fran?"

"I'm sorry, Mother, it's just that everyone ignores us." Fran stopped, looking round the small clearing. "The dragon ... I always know when it's there. It watches and it follows me, but I feel safe here – safer than I do in March. Maya's seen it too now, and she hasn't collapsed unconscious; she was picking daisies and doing cartwheels around the garden."

She turned away abruptly, pulling Fran up short. He snatched the horn from his belt and gave three very sharp blasts, then he moved to

Gareth's side, grasped him under the arms, raised him to his feet and lifted him over his shoulders.

Without a word, his mother walked ahead, leading the way and retracing their steps out of the forest.

Fran struggled through the trees behind her, the weight of Gareth making his knees buckle. Eventually, they reached the track that led back to the clearing.

"I can see someone ahead, Fran. I think it's Galos. Yes, he's seen us."

"Thank the gods. He can help us. Mother, help me put him down."

She held Gareth under his shoulders while Fran dropped his legs then spun to help her lower him down between tufts of grass.

"He's a dead weight, isn't he?" She gasped as they leant him against the wide trunk of a beech.

"He's surprisingly heavy." Fran stretched his arms and flexed his back. "It's lucky Galos is here."

His mother gave him an appraising look. "Yes, and Tom, Jake and Willett are with him."

"That's good." Fran made a show of circling his arms and pacing back and forth while they waited. Despite sharing the southern forest as a hunting ground with Galos and his men, they rarely met, largely because Fran, being fleet of foot, preferred to go deeper into the forest to avoid ... to avoid Galos. This was the truth, but it was inconvenient, so he tried not to think about it. Tom, and Frey's father, Jake, were always friendly, though, and Willett was a quiet man, but he was unfailingly kind.

"Yes, we're among friends, at least." Her voice corralled his thoughts. "They'll have heard the horn blasts, and most likely seen Elsa. They wouldn't normally be out here so late."

"I think Elsa's sent them. She's good at finding her father."

"I've noticed that too." His mother gave a wry smile. "It makes a mockery of Gareth accompanying them. They only ever followed their father, if truth be told, and Cader usually followed them."

"I know," said Fran, whipping around to check Gareth remained unconscious.

She walked to meet Galos, who ran ahead of the group.

"Annerin, forgive me; I've been a stranger." His eyes flashed to Fran and the prone form of Gareth as he spoke.

"You're never a stranger." Fran's mother hugged him then went to greet Tom, Jake and Willett.

"Fran." Galos approached, his expression strained. "Good to see you."

"And you, Galos. Timely too." Fran nodded down at Gareth. "Mother found him like this." Unaccustomed to lying, Fran felt the blood rush to his face, and he felt unsure what else to say. Did his mother intend to take Galos into her confidence? Had Maya told her father she'd seen the dragon?

There was a pregnant pause before Galos spoke. "Elsa sent us after you. She and Maya are at the stone house."

Fran nodded as his mother, Willet, Tom and Jake joined them.

"What's happened to him? Is he badly injured?" Willett asked, frowning down at the prone form of Gareth lying at the foot of the tree.

Galos bent down beside Tom to take a closer look at Gareth. "He's out cold. Has he fallen or something?"

"He's hit his head, and there's quite a few cuts and grazes on him. I'd say he's taken a tumble." She kept her voice even. "Elsa and I heard him scream. That's why I took the sword."

Remembering she'd set out with the sword to look for Maya, Fran gave his mother a sharp look, which she ignored.

"Yes, Elsa told us what happened," said Galos. "He went out looking for Maya. Is that right?"

"Yes, he came to the house with Elsa, but ..." She shrugged. "He set out alone to look for Maya, but as it turned out, Fran had already found her. It was right after Fran sounded the horn at the stone house that Elsa and I heard Gareth's scream coming from deep in the forest. I just followed the direction of the sound, and I found him a bit on from the fallen beech."

"What could possibly ...?" Jake's voice trailed off as he gingerly lifted Gareth and looked at him. "You're right, it looks like he's fallen, onto rocks, maybe."

"Yes."

Galos looked at Fran's mother, then he turned to Tom, their eyes locking for a beat.

"This is unfortunate. Most unfortunate." Jake looked up at Fran, his face full of concern.

"I was with Maya ..." Fran began, not knowing what else to say.

Jake rose and patted him on the shoulder. "She tried to tell us about it before we left. We'll get the whole story as soon as we're back, no doubt. It's a shame she wandered off. She's normally so sensible."

"Yes, it's not like her," Fran agreed, looking away – the warmth of Jake's gesture too much. Hot tears prickled, and when he turned back, he couldn't look at Galos.

"You've carried him far enough, Fran. We'll take over from here." Tom winked at Fran and signalled for Jake to help him. "Big enough fella, isn't he?"

"Big lump probably fainted and fell off a log," Jake quipped back.

"Fainted without Elsa to look after him." Tom aimed this at Galos, whose face remained grim.

"Shut up, Tom, he could wake up any time," Galos snapped before turning to Fran's mother. "You found him near the beech, you say?"

"A short way on from there. He regained consciousness for a bit. We talked, and I gave him water. He couldn't tell me what happened, and he couldn't stand up without getting dizzy, so I sounded the horn and we waited for Fran to find us."

"Let's get him back. Can we bring him to the stone house first, Annerin?" said Willett. "We might be able to get a message back to March from there if we can't revive him. If—"

"Yes, we can't just carry him back to March," Tom agreed. "Things might turn ugly. We need to wake him up. He must have fallen, but—"

"He must have done." Galos shrugged. "I'm not sure it wouldn't be better to go straight back to March with him, though. If Lukas finds him at the stone house ..."

"It all depends on what he remembers," added Jake. "If he can't recall anything ..."

"Then we're best keeping Fran and Annerin out of it."

"He'll remember speaking to me," she reminded Galos.

Galos gave a shrug of resignation. "Then let's hope he comes round on the way."

Tom and Jake lifted Gareth, who winced when they put a shoulder under each arm and hoisted up his legs. Willett followed close behind.

"So, he'd got as far as the fallen beech, then carried on into the forest," Galos asked his mother as they made their way towards the clearing, following Tom, Jake and Willett.

"Yes. Elsa and I weren't far from here when we heard him scream." She turned to Fran. "You blew the horn at the same time, so I presume you were at the house with Maya."

Fran nodded. "Maya wasn't lost. She found me, in fact. I was hunting, and she was in the forest alone – not far from here either – so I took her back to the house."

"Ah, so she left Elsa deliberately," Galos mused.

"It's unfortunate." His mother turned to Galos with an appraising look.

Galos said nothing, then he trudged on, his head down.

The shadows were growing long as the group approached the ford, and the rush of the Cloudwater bubbling over the stones was the sound of welcome home. Above them, starlings whorled, and rooks and crows called out from the treetops, warning that dusk approached, rolling in from the high moors to the east and across marshland and plain.

Fran walked a short way behind his mother and Galos. He could see she was too tired to talk, although Galos continually turned to her, as if he wanted to say something but couldn't quite find the words. His own feet dragged against the stones of the path, and twilight gave the whole bizarre scene in front of him the quality of a dream. At the ford, he followed Tom, who now carried Gareth across his shoulders. Tom moved slowly across the flat stones of the crossing before putting

Gareth down on the far side, then he removed his boots and sat down to cool his feet in a pool of eddying water.

The other men filled their waterskins and drank. Fran turned towards the lamp at the stone house – lit, no doubt, by Elsa – which shone brightly in the distance, before slumping down beside his mother, who, unconscious of Galos' curious stares, knelt at Gareth's side and tried to make him drink. Fran made patterns in the dirt with the heels of his boots. He wanted to tell her to leave Gareth be ... or to drop a skinful of cold river water over the man's head and be done.

Through the branches, he could see the orange glow of the sun sinking behind the mountains, and the final trills of the birds sounded overhead as they returned to their roosts in the treetops. The day had been long and hot, but now he shivered in the fading light. The fireside called, old forgotten words echoing. *Stone walls, bolted door, hearthstone and peace. Warm ale and blankets to chase away the cold. Red embers and the shroud of night. A sword for luck and a dragon standing guard.* He glanced at his mother again. The scabbard stretched out behind her as she knelt, and Gareth's head rested on her arm. The scene flickered in front of him – his mother sometimes becoming Elsa – as he struggled to keep his eyes open. Stupid with sleep, his head bobbed while he watched Tom forcing his boots back on.

"Look out now." Jake's whisper brought him back sharp.

Running feet approached. Fran forced himself up. Galos peered in the direction of the stone house. The path was empty, which could only mean one thing – whoever approached did so on the track from March, which met this one at a fork about halfway between the ford and the stone house.

A figure turned the corner and sprinted towards them at full pelt, blotting out the light of the lamp at the stone house and filling the path like some shadowy demon. Fran staggered back, fighting the urge to grab his mother and melt away into the woods until all this was finished and they could go back home in peace.

Galos, however, acted more quickly. "Annerin." Bending down, he caught her sharply by the arm and pulled her away from Gareth.

Lukas. No! Fran only had time to register the burly figure of March's chief before Lukas was upon them.

Lukas caught sight of Gareth lying bloodstained and unconscious, and his hands went to his head. Wild-eyed, he mouthed something that Fran could not make out.

"What's happened? How can this be?" His face darkened as he glanced towards Fran's mother.

"He was found like this ... in the wood ..." Galos began.

Lukas stared at Galos, uncomprehending, then he scanned the group, paling as he straightened himself, taking in the scene. Fran, holding his breath, scarcely dared look. The atmosphere grew charged. Lukas' jaw hardened, rage replacing confusion.

"You—" He turned to Galos. "What did you say?"

"He said we found him." His mother's voice was brittle as pond ice in the thaw. "We found him like this. In the wood."

Fran felt his heart contract. Only bird calls broke the silence.

"You ... why him ... what have you done to him?" he demanded of Fran's mother, his voice choked. Without waiting for an answer, he took a step towards her, veins bulging in his neck and his arm raised as if he would knock her down. She recoiled, and Fran saw spittle fly from Lukas' mouth as he let out a curse.

Galos caught Lukas by the arm as Willett pulled Fran's mother clear. "It's nothing to do with her. Wait. Let me tell you—" Galos spluttered.

"Get out of my way. She'll answer for this, not you," Lukas spat at Galos, his face growing purple.

"We found him unconscious. We were bringing him back to you. Listen to me, you stupid ..." Galos shouted.

Fran stood and watched as if he were one with the earth beneath his feet. The man generally avoided him when he visited March, only once glaring and spitting in the dirt before shrinking away into the shadows, but seeing his mother reach for the sword acted like a dose of icy water hitting him full in the face. He sprang forwards, closing his hand over hers on the hilt, then he looked down into her stricken face before taking the sword from her.

Meanwhile, Lukas struggled with Galos, and Galos began to lose ground.

Fran hardly knew what he did, only that some imperative took hold – a lodestone pulling together all those bitter thoughts, all those sharp moments of anger, the rage for the father he'd never met, and directing them like a flight of arrows at his murderer. He took a step forwards and quietly brought the point of the sword to rest in the folds of fat beneath Lukas' chin.

Lukas let go of Galos suddenly. Galos staggered and fell. Lukas turned, gaping, as if Fran were some new species of being completely unknown in the world. His eyes followed the sword down to the symbol on the hilt clasped firmly in both of Fran's hands.

Fran stood braced, waiting for the tide of hatred flowing from this man to wash towards him, but instead, Lukas' eyes seemed to dull, disbelief giving way to an emotion that Fran could not read. He stepped back carefully, all the time watching Fran.

Fran followed, keeping the sword pointing at Lukas' throat. "What quarrel do you have with my mother?"

Lukas' mouth opened and closed, but no words came out.

Fran stood immobile, waiting for an answer. The birds, it seemed, held their breath too, as no sound broke the silence. He felt the strength of the sword, and the blood sang in his ears as he recalled Lukas' hand, moments ago, raised to strike his mother. Then he thought again of his poor father, dead and forgotten, but still hated.

"What quarrel did you have with my father?" he asked.

At these words, Lukas took another step back, his eyes flashing to Galos, pleading almost, then back to Fran.

Fran's thoughts turned red. He took a step forwards, but Tom and Willett grabbed Lukas, pinioning both his arms before spinning him around and attempting to drag him away. He fought to get back to Gareth, but with assurance from Jake and Galos that they would be right behind him with Gareth, and a final stricken glance at Fran, he let them lead him away.

Fran stood transfixed, watching them go. A breeze rustled the leaves around him, brushing cool against his skin, then his mother and Galos appeared, one at each side of him. His mother touched his sword arm lightly. Fran felt the pressure of her hand, alongside the thumping of his own heart, and slowly lowered the sword as he turned to look at her.

No one spoke, but they watched the receding figures moving away towards the stone house. Lukas shouted for Gareth now, while Tom and Willett continued to drag him. The man struggled and fought, craning his neck around every so often to look back at his son, who still lay unconscious by the side of the path.

Fran turned to Galos, retaining his grip on the sword.

"Fran." His mother stepped in, the flat of her palm pushing gently on the blade. When he relaxed, she stepped back and untied the scabbard and hanger from her belt and handed them to him. "It's yours now. Use it wisely."

Fran felt Galos' gaze on him. He turned to the older man, looking for he knew not what.

"You hold it well. I'll teach you ... soon." A pained expression crossed Galos' face then he went to help Jake lift Gareth.

Fran clipped the hanger to his belt and sheathed the sword. He turned to his mother, his heart still beating hard. They walked home together, guided by the lamp at the stone house, which shone brightly in the dying light.

Chapter 6

The Stone House at the Ford

Dusk became night, and the first faint traceries of stars appeared, rising above the moors. Fran trudged on, following the men back to the stone house, his mother at his side. Looking up, he saw Elsa outlined in a puddle of yellow lamplight, Maya, Cader and Frey at her side. *Family.* The tightness in his chest eased at the sight of them, replaced by heaviness of heart and limb.

Ahead, Lukas looked calmer. He walked with Tom and Willett, turning repeatedly to check Galos and Jake were close behind and carrying the still unconscious Gareth. When they reached the stone house, Ebba appeared in the doorway and told them to bring Gareth inside.

"Come, Lukas ... your son." Ebba ushered the chief into their tiny house as if it were her own. "Galos, set him down carefully."

Fran stopped short of the doorway, instead turning to his friends, who followed him to the bench beneath the lamp at the side of the house.

"Here, Annerin. A chair." Elsa ducked back out of the house and set an extra chair down for his mother.

"Thanks, Elsa." Fran surprised himself with a smile.

His mother nodded to Elsa, her face relaxing as she sat down. "They'll be on their way soon, so I'll let your mother sort this out. I've done all I can."

Fran held his tongue as Cader rolled his eyes. *Yes, let Ebba sort out it out. It was her stupid plan that started this mess.*

From inside, Ebba called out to Elsa and Maya to come and help her. Elsa pulled a face and stretched out a hand to Maya. Cader and Frey beckoned to Fran as they slipped to the back of the house, to a small, high opening through which they could listen, unobserved. Fran followed, but his mother wandered away, towards the foot of the silver birch, where she set herself down in the shadows, hugging her knees to her chest.

Fran, Cader and Frey crowded together by the corner of the opening to watch. Galos sat by the bones of the fire, with Maya at his side and Elsa lighting straw over the glowing embers. Lukas, fortunately, had his back to their vantage point. He fussed over Gareth, all the while pointing out yet another cut or scrape, hounding Tom for an explanation. The two remained in heated discussion for a while, with Galos a weary onlooker. Tom's voice grew high pitched as he explained for the third time what had occurred.

"Here." Ebba thrust a cup of nettle tea towards the two men. "This might revive him, and he can tell us what happened himself."

Lukas snatched it from her. "It's obvious what happened; that's what I keep saying. He's been attacked from behind – by someone. Hit over the head, and he probably didn't see them coming because he was too busy looking for your daughter. Probably didn't hear them either because they're so used to creeping about in the forest all day."

Tom threw his arms in the air in exasperation and looked to Galos.

"Oh, yes, I know they've got their convenient excuses," the chief snarled, turning to Galos too. "They heard him scream at the same time that the lad's horn sounded – from the house ..." His voice trailed off, but the curled lip spoke volumes. Cader set an arm around Fran's shoulders.

"We did hear him," said Elsa, just loud enough for Fran to hear.

"Oh, you did, did you?" Lukas muttered, sounding, Fran thought, a bit deflated. "A scream's a scream, girl. Could have been anyone. And what about the little one, eh, did she hear it too?"

Elsa's chin shot out in defiance, but Ebba set a hand on her arm, and she said nothing more.

Maya slipped over to Galos and whispered something.

"What's she saying?" Lukas demanded.

"Nothing ... just that she saw something in the wood—"

Lukas threw back his head and gave a horrible, mirthless laugh. "Oh, here we go. What was it? A goblin or a dragon? Or let me guess, maybe a bear."

Fran followed the chief's gaze as he scanned the various furs on their hooks.

"Leave her alone," said Galos, his voice dangerously quiet.

"I'm not saying it to the child." Lukas aimed a rough pat towards the top of Maya's head, but Maya withdrew behind Galos' chair. "What does she know, she's ..."

The silence deepened. *Poor Maya.* Fran's heart twisted and he wanted to scoop the little girl up and run.

"I said, leave her alone," Galos repeated, iron in his voice this time.

Behind them all, Gareth stirred and groaned.

Fran hardly dared breathe. For a few moments no one spoke, then Lukas ventured, "If you didn't want this arrangement, Galos, you should have said so."

Fran waited to hear Galos' answer to that. Instead, the man only sighed.

"But no, instead you resort to this." Now it was Lukas' words that dropped like stones.

"What?" Galos leapt to his feet.

"You must think me a fool," Lukas growled, suddenly at bay, edging out from the narrowing gap between Galos and Tom and squatting down to be at Gareth's side. "You must think my son a fool too."

"No one thinks that—" Ebba began, moving round to stand between the men.

"Be quiet; this is your doing, woman," Lukas snapped, getting back to his feet.

"Mind how you speak to my wife, Lukas," Galos retorted.

"If you kept her under control, I wouldn't need to."

Galos' fingers drummed on the table. Tom took a step back, slumped down on Galos' chair and set Maya on his knee. Elsa risked a glance in Fran's direction, and he saw she was pale.

"Perhaps you should think of your own wife now. She'll be worried about her son," Galos said, his voice even again.

"The night's fine, and we can make a stretcher to carry him," said Willett, stepping forwards.

Gareth edged himself up, leaning on one elbow and coughing. "Father?"

"Right, I'm taking him out of this rat hole now. You" – he pointed at Willett – "help me."

Galos gave Willett a nod, and he and Jake took a loop of twine from a hook on the wall and left, presumably to fashion some sort of stretcher.

"I'll go and help my father," said Frey, slipping away from Fran and Cader.

Cader turned to Fran. "Sorry I didn't stay with them. It was just so ..."

"It's all right. You're best out of it, anyway."

"Do you know what happened?"

"Not really, but he has got a head injury, and a lot of cuts and scrapes."

For a split second, Cader's face was unreadable. "Who found him?"

"My mother."

"Oh." Cader turned back to the opening.

Fran sighed, remembering his mother's words. *No one will believe us.*

Presently, Willett, Jake and Frey returned with a stretcher, helped Lukas transfer Gareth to it, and carried him out.

"This isn't over, Galos," Lukas said from the doorstep.

"Lukas, wait, please—"

"Ebba, be quiet," Galos snapped, his eyes fixed on Lukas. "Let's see what Gareth has to say, shall we."

Lukas bared his teeth in a snarl, then he turned to follow the stretcher party, smashing the door back on its hinges as he went.

Silence descended on the stone house. Fran looked for his mother by the silver birch, but she was nowhere to be seen.

"Mother, come," he called out softly in the direction of the wood, then he slipped back into the house behind Cader. He set his sword out of the way, in the far corner behind a crooked stack of baskets, and sat down with Cader on the bench, while Galos and Tom huddled together near the door.

His mother appeared and slipped over to the chair by the fire. Elsa ladled out five drinks then went to the table to cut a loaf, presumably brought by Ebba. Maya, meanwhile, yawned and curled up on the chest below the opening where they had recently been eavesdropping.

"Annerin, it's good to see you." Ebba went over to Fran's mother and hugged her briefly, and she nodded to Fran without quite looking at him. "Fran."

"Thank you for bringing the bread, Ebba," said his mother.

Fran didn't trust himself to speak.

"Well, we must decide what to do before morning." Ebba sat down on the far side of the table, opposite his mother. "If you can tell us any more about what happened ..."

"Well, it's exactly as Fran and I've already said, Ebba; we found him unconscious. Some might say we're owed a debt of gratitude, but it sounded as if Lukas didn't see it that way."

"You heard what went on then, Annerin." Tom took the chair next to Ebba. "I don't blame you for not coming in. I ..."

"Your restraint was the stuff of legends, Tom." Fran's mother smiled faintly. "The man hasn't improved with age. He's a man without honour."

Fran moved to his mother's side.

"Nevertheless," Ebba broke in, "he is the chief of March, Annerin. You must see there will be consequences for what happened today."

"What do you mean?" Fran shot at Ebba.

"Fran, sit." Galos appeared next to Fran, pulled out two stools and waited. "What she means is, we ... I may not be able to keep the peace now ... to protect you and your mother in the way I have tried to do these many summers and winters."

Fran made to speak, but Galos held up his hand.

"I know you don't think it, but I have always looked out for you. You know only those who answer to me hunt on this side of March."

"Yes." Fran stared at the tabletop.

"Until today," said his mother.

Galos threw back his head and groaned.

"Gareth did wake shortly after I found him," she added. "We spoke a little. He knows full well neither Fran nor I hurt him. He seems very different from his father. He's Luwain's grandson, after all."

"Oh, what did you speak of?" Ebba asked, her chin rising.

"The past, and the forest, but not the future."

Galos gave a humourless snort of laughter, half, Fran suspected, due to Ebba's obvious discomfort. "Well, all we have are riddles," he said to the room. "I wish Gareth hadn't come here today."

"But he did. And Ebba, your matchmaking hasn't gone well. What will Hilda say?" his mother asked.

"That depends very much on Gareth, doesn't it? And he's happy with the arrangement we've made," Ebba snapped back.

"Happy with the arrangement! Marriage is an arrangement for two, Ebba ..." His mother paused, and Fran saw Elsa's head drop. "In trying to secure the future, Ebba, you've woken the past. And what of my future? What of Fran's?"

"Perhaps Lukas can yet be persuaded he owes you his thanks," said Galos eventually. "As you say, Gareth has much of Luwain in him. Let us pray he recovers enough to speak soon, and that he does speak well of you."

Fran's mother turned her gaze to the fire. Galos and Tom put their heads together, their faces grim. The exchange included so few words that Fran couldn't follow, but then Tom whispered something to his mother and, giving him a grateful smile, she nodded.

A short time later, Fran handed Elsa a lamp to light the way back to March. She and her mother led the way down the path with a full moon casting faint silver light across the night. The tiny lamp bobbed away into the darkness like a golden firefly.

"She's settled there, and safe with her uncle. Best not disturb her. The gods only know what reception we'll find waiting for us in March." Galos spoke half to himself. His gaze crossed the room, resting on Maya where she slept beneath the window, and he nodded to Tom in the nearby chair.

Fran saw the shadow in his face and glanced round. It was hard to know where was safest on such a night. "She can have my bed," he offered. Galos nodded. Their eyes met for a moment, then Galos turned to go, and Fran felt a great stab of sadness cut through him, as if desolation itself had whirled up and enveloped him from the packed, dry earth at his feet.

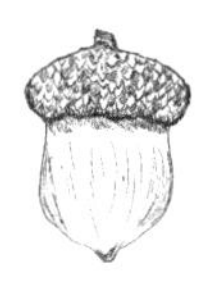

Chapter 7

Witches and Ghosts

Fran closed the door and turned back into the now very quiet house. His mother remained by the fire with Tom next to her at the table, and Maya snuggled tighter under her woollen blanket. Memories of the evening hung in the air – voices echoed in his head. Fran glanced over at the sword hilt, peeping out from where he'd tucked it behind the baskets, and he remembered it balancing at Lukas' throat. His innards ran cold. He took a deep breath. *The man had it coming, but there would be hell to pay.*

"Let's put her in my bed now. It's better than lying on a box," he told his mother and Tom. He lifted Maya carefully and carried her around to the far side of the fireplace, where a partition that was hung with ironware and utensils split the little rectangular house, creating two cabins off the main space. He flicked the door to his cabin open with his foot and placed her down on his own cot. Maya rolled and stretched but her eyes didn't open. Fran gently straightened her blanket and tucked it in at the sides.

The room was dark, lit only by a few stray shafts of light, and when he moved to go, it occurred to him that he'd never seen either Maya or her sister asleep before, but now, in this time of trouble, their father had set a watch on them all, as if they were one family. The emptiness inside him receded a little, and when he recollected Galos' hand raised in defence of his mother, a lump came to his throat. He looked down at Maya; long curls – lighter brown than Elsa's – stuck to her temples in the heat. He brushed one off her little face, stepped back out of the cabin and closed the door.

"Thank you, Fran," said Tom. "I'm almost as tired myself. The night should be quiet – Lukas likes nothing better than to fester a while and stew in his cups – but I can't vouch for tomorrow."

"Thank you for staying," Fran's mother added. "We'd probably all be safer together under the circumstances, but our coming to March won't make life easier for you or for Galos."

Tom gave her a wan smile.

She was right, of course, Fran realised as he took his usual seat across the fire from her. Drinking in the silence, he watched the shadows from the fire play across the familiar, uneven walls and gnarled roof timbers before he stooped down to ladle out three cup of nettle tea.

His mother took one sip, grimaced and spat the drink back into the cup.

Tom snorted.

"Stewed," she said. "Let's get the jug of ale."

"Not for me." Tom waved to decline. "The sooner I sleep, the sooner I wake. Besides, I'll be sleeping with one eye open."

Fran's mother slipped into her room for a pillow and then opened the trunk and handed him blankets. Tom went to the bench where Gareth had been recently lying and made himself up as best a bed as he could.

"Fran." His mother nodded in the direction of the ale then gestured towards the door. "Come on, there's things we need to talk about."

Fran went to get the ale from the cupboard alongside Tom's bench then bid Tom goodnight and followed his mother outside, shutting the door quietly behind him. She unhooked the lamp and moved it round with them to the bench where Fran had recently spied on the others. The air was warm and still and the moon was full. Moths fluttered around the light, and somewhere away towards the mountains, an owl screeched, its cry piercing the night.

"Was it only this morning the little girl got lost," she began. "You said you found her on the far side of the clearing. Did she tell you what happened?"

"She was upset about Ebba arranging for Gareth to go with them."

His mother stiffened.

"She told me she saw the creature too," he continued.

"It's probably fortunate she did." They sat quietly for a while, with the night's sounds around them. "I'm truly sorry about how things have turned out, Fran," she said eventually. "Your grandparents and I had to make a choice, but it was so long ago ... You weren't even born. And now ... well, it breaks my heart." She turned to look at him, her expression one of infinite sadness. "Ebba's always been very determined – good at getting what *she* wants."

Fran turned away, unable to answer.

"Fran, I think Elsa ... she was very upset about being sent out with Gareth today. She told me so. I think she thought her father ... well, he was busy and thought – well, I suspect he thought they'd all just give Gareth the slip and it would put him off a bit. He almost said as much."

Fran mulled this over. After all, Cader and Maya had managed to slip away. Just not Elsa.

"That aside, what I wanted to say was, Fran ... that I think Elsa loves you right now."

Right now. The words hit Fran like a dose of ice, and he shivered, suddenly cold in the night air.

"What I mean is ... it's summer; the days are long, and you see her most days." She paused, and Fran guessed she chose her words carefully. "If you want Elsa, you need to tell her ... and tell Galos. Tell her now and make her your wife."

Fran turned to her, trying to comprehend the urgency. "Mother, Elsa's only sixteen summers' old. I don't think ..."

His mother held up her hand. "I agree. She's not ready to be anyone's wife, but Ebba has already promised her to Gareth. After what happened tonight, she'll stop at nothing to marry them off quickly. Once it's arranged you won't even be able to see Elsa without ..."

Fran dropped his head, scuffing his boots in the rubble beneath the bench.

"Fran?"

"I'll ask Tom if I can take Maya home tomorrow, and I'll speak to Elsa then. I'll speak to Galos too." Then he added, with a confidence he didn't feel, "Together, they can withstand Ebba."

"I hope they can. But this is no courtship, Fran. Our lives hang by a thread." She indicated at the house, where Tom slept, ready to defend them. "You mustn't dally. And keep your father's sword to hand, mind. Never set it down. Galos is a good man, and he was a loyal friend to your father. He'll want Elsa to be happy. Fran, promise me you'll speak to him tomorrow, without fail."

Fran's empty ale cup slipped from his hand. He studied his mother, but she wore a mask he couldn't penetrate.

"Yes, Mother, I promise."

The pair fell silent. Fran wiped blades of grass from his cup and stared into the trees behind the silver birch.

"Your father would have been proud of you today," she began.

"Edwyn." Fran relished the word like no other, and it needed to be said out loud sometimes. At least by them.

"Yes. Edwyn. What happened today brought back memories ..." Her voice faltered then gained warmth as she spoke of the young knight from Glendorrig and how like Fran he had looked, reiterating how proud he would have been. Fran drank in the words like wine, forgetting for a while their troubles. His father's family had been ... were wealthy, hence the sword, and this had put Edwyn in line for some quest, the details of which were hazy. The upshot was that he'd spent a summer lost in the mountains, then he'd followed the pass down from Elden Deas, crossed the old stone bridge spanning the Everlode, followed the rangers' path, waded the Cloudwater below Deas Howe and arrived in March one late summer afternoon. March had been intrigued, and having heard the story so many times, Fran's mental picture of it was indistinguishable from memory – the heat of the sun and the faded shirt; the worn leather jerkin and the shining sword that still continued to shine while everything else decayed. It was a thing that defied time ... and death – a treasure defining them as they lived, and which would outlast them in the end. His mother always said they were alike, aside from his father having blue eyes, and whenever Fran caught a glimpse of his own reflection, the story came to mind. For comfort, he sometimes allowed a habitual daydream about Glendorrig to flicker into life behind his eyes, a dream about a house where he would find welcome – be recognised. A place beyond the mountains that he could call home. Perhaps, if it turned out they did need to, they could flee – try and find the place ...

His mother took a swig of the ale, pulling her shawl tighter around her shoulders. "When I see you with Cader and Frey, it reminds me of how your father made friends here – at least with most of the young men. He, Galos and the others would go on hunting trips together – the same route Galos follows now – then spend hours by the copse outside the stockade, fencing, drinking and laughing."

Fran wished the scene was familiar. Yes, he, Cader and Frey laughed, but there was no larger group, and the lack of fellowship ached like some great canker lodged beneath his ribs.

When she mentioned Lukas – although never by name, instead calling him a wretch and a bully – the darkness around them seemed to deepen, and the night's noises closed in. A savage rivalry had erupted back then between his father and Lukas – one that had resulted in Lukas secretly being ridiculed. Knowing that his poor father never took the man seriously until it was too late sent a chill through Fran. At the time of his father's arrival, Lukas' father, Luwain, had been chief. Although he was remembered as a good man, he seemed to have been unable to moderate his son – or perhaps he had just been blind to his true nature, like many a parent might be.

His mother's voice brightened when she mentioned Gareth, and she went on to say how he had only been a small boy back then, the apple of his grandfather's eye, apparently. Listening to her, an image of the clearing in the wood flashed through Fran's mind, complete with Gareth and his mother sleeping, their backs against the oak. He glanced round at his mother, shifting uncomfortably on the cold bench.

"We married at harvest, of course," she continued, "and when winter came, we were all indoors, so it all stopped. There could no more fighting about who was the best hunter or swordsman. We all but forgot about it, huddled by our fires; the joke died, but not the danger."

She paused, and Fran's head spun. The reminder of winter was real. There were days when he had done nothing but watch for Cader and Frey or searched for their prints in the snow in the clearing, afraid of missing them, and missing news of Elsa. Short, bleak days and long, cold nights. As if in answer to his thoughts, the solitary owl hooted again.

When she spoke again, her voice sounded high and strange. "That winter brought much snow and hail," she began, "but there was something more – the mountain itself appeared angry. We knew Elden Deas wasn't a fire mountain, but there were always storm clouds round its peak and thunder and lightning to the south. It bothered everyone, especially your father. He seemed haunted, sometimes not eating or drinking. Your grandfather tried to rouse him with jokes."

Fran held his breath as he listened. This tale was a horror story the young shared in whispers. His mother had alluded to it occasionally, but no one who had actually been there tended to speak of it.

"Then the elders began talking about Arete, the woman you all call the witch. You know the old tales, but they told stories I'd not heard before, stories from hundreds of winters past, from the time of Vaden. Some said she was his friend, others said that she breathed fire like a dragon. But it was all too long ago, and the storm horribly real. It raged on, and the nights were cold and dark. Fear won out. By midwinter, it had turned to terror. Luwain ordered spikes be set in the stockade, and at night we locked and guarded the gate, burning lanterns to mark the edge of the defences. It felt as though we were trying to keep the darkness out.

"On the night before midwinter's day a storm blew up from the south, and a blizzard of hail and sleet funnelled into the valley. The drifts were vast. When night fell, Arete came. Perhaps she'd come down the mountain pass, the same way your father came. Or perhaps, well ... We couldn't see her, but she called out – a willowy reed of a voice, almost lost on the wind – for us to open the gate. I can still remember the sound of it – like the distant howl of a lone wolf, carrying for leagues and playing over and over in the mind, never quite letting go.

"She sounded utterly desolate – part of me wanted to open the gate for her – but the fear felt very real. We no longer knew her, I suppose." His mother shook her head sadly. "The men had dug out all their old weapons – rusty old swords and battered shields handed down from their grandfathers. They just stared at the south gate. Despite the cold, and the wind spinning the sleet, the place stank of sweat and urine. Children sobbed and hid behind their poor cowering mothers.

"After a time, she started to beat on the gate." She paused, seeming lost in the past.

Fran sensed she felt pity for Arete. This was a far different story to the "witch at the gate" legend the young told one another. That was a second-hand story with a borrowed ghoul. This version reeked of pain.

"She kept on beating." His mother banged on the table – drumm, drumm, drumm, drumm. "On it went, into the night, amid the howling wind and swirling sleet. Sometimes it stopped, only to begin again, then Luwain raised his arm and signalled for two volunteers. Two boys, not much older than me, stepped forwards. Their names were Elin and Roe. I was standing a little way from Luwain, but it seemed to me a shadow passed across his face, and your grandfather noticed it too. Shame at his own son letting others of his kin – boys next to him – stand forwards.

"And so, they went, but your father wouldn't stand by. He ran for the postern, and Galos followed him, but Luwain and the other elders held Galos back. They left your father – he wasn't kin." She fell quiet, anger hardening her jaw.

"Mother?"

"The banging stopped. We waited. Thunder cracked overhead, loud over the wind, and lightning struck beyond the stockade. I remember your grandmother's hand on my arm – perhaps she thought I'd follow your father, perhaps I'd moved because I remember thinking it. The lightning hit, and then the smell of burning flesh reached us on the wind, and we watched two columns of flames dance against the night sky."

She stopped again, this time to take a long draught of ale. The anger had gone from her, replaced by sadness. Fran knew the fate of Elin and Roe all too well. They were heroes killed by the witch; heroes of a story that didn't mention his father. He hung his head.

"This is why those who were there never speak of what happened. Not because of your father. Not because of a fight, or because of a sword, but because of reality. Somehow, I felt he was safe, that it wasn't him ... I don't remember the next few hours well. I must have been afraid for him, even so, because he didn't come back straight away. I stayed with your grandmother and grandfather until the storm passed and first light came from over the moors.

"Elin and Roe were burnt to nothing, but your father returned. He was unharmed physically, but, well, there was blood on him, and I have never seen a man so changed ... When the men ventured beyond the defences at daybreak, there was no sign of Arete."

Like many a true story, Fran noticed, the ending was where this one always differed, depending on the teller.

"There was blood in the snow too, outside the stockade, a great puddle of it, dirty against the wet sleet still covering the ground; so much blood – more than a life's worth, it looked, so perhaps Elin and Roe were injured before they died. There were also tracks through the snow, leading away towards the forest and clearing." His mother shook her head. "We didn't understand what had happened. Elin and Roe were dead, and your father was frozen – he'd lost his cloak, I think – and he seemed distraught. He was in no state to explain. They kept asking him, but he just kept saying she'd gone."

They sat for a long time with moths fluttering under the eaves and the light of the tallow lamp fading. Fran's thoughts turned yet again to Galos – and to what happened next. *We spoke of it once.* That's what she'd said.

"I've known what happened next since I was seven summers old, Mother. Cader and Elsa too. The man's eyes have followed me so many times when I've been in March. I see fear in them. Fear and guilt."

His mother nodded, long suppressed tears flooding down her cheeks, and her chest heaved. Bats flickered over their heads, black against the dark sky. "It killed his father, Luwain, in the end," she said, drying her eyes on her apron. "The dishonour."

With night's chill growing around them, Annerin went on to recall how Galos fought Lukas on that midwinter morning, and how the two would have fought to the death if their respective families had not separated them. Both had ended up badly wounded, taking until springtime to mend. "Ebba nursed Galos ... and kept him quiet," she added, speaking half to herself. "I tried to take care of your father afterwards too, but he was grievously wounded. Your grandmother and Galos' mother bandaged him as best they could, but there was so much blood ... We left March that day and brought your father here."

Fran listened to her, but all the while he was shivering and fighting sleep. He realised she wanted to impress on him the importance of their relationship with Galos. He, after all, represented authority in March almost as much as its chief. Theirs was a truce as delicate and strong as spider silk. It bound March in its web. His mother was scared about what would happen tomorrow, but in the end, Lukas would have to listen to Elsa and Maya, wouldn't he? They were Galos' daughters. And Gareth, what would he say? A lot depended on that. He tried not to think about holding the sword at Lukas' throat. His mother had reminded him to keep it at his side from now on, at the same time bemoaning the fact that no one had spent much time teaching him to use it. Still, if it came to it, the hand-me-down lessons from Cader and Frey were better than nothing, and he was a keen shot with the bow—

His mother's next words halted his thoughts. "He died that night. The next day, my father and mother carried his bones to Spiral Cove and buried him." Silence wrapped around them, with the tawny glow from the flickering tallow lamp stuttering in the dark. Fran could not see his mother's face. "It's sacred earth. We could have chosen there or Mirrormantle Grove, but I have always been glad they didn't take him to the barrows."

Fran reached for her hand; he was glad too. The barrows were half a day's travel from March, on a stony outcrop leading east, with marshland on either side. Ancient places. Places of bones. Fran preferred the mountain and the forest.

Anger, sadness and exhaustion all mingled, and he felt the need for sleep overwhelming him. Fran put his arm around his mother and they went indoors, where they were greeted with Tom's snores rising heartily from the bench, and where the darkness seemed even thicker, with milky starlight just visible through the vent in the thatch. They bolted the door then went to warm themselves, huddling round the remains of the fire, which flickered beneath the cauldron, sending shadows dancing. Fran stared down at it until only the last flecks of orange glowed beneath the whitened logs.

The first pale shafts of morning light picked their way between gaps in the shutters and stretched out long tentative fingers, feeling their way through the darkness of the cabin. Annerin opened her eyes and lay still for a few moments, brushing aside the loose threads of a clutch of ragtag dreams.

A click of the door told her someone was up. *Tom or Fran?* Probably Tom. Hearing shuffling outside, she peeped through the shutter and saw Tom dip his hands in the pail, splash his face, dry his hands on his trousers, and then make off towards the trees behind the silver birch. *Hopefully, he would take some time.*

Dressing quickly, she packed a few spare items of linen into a bundle and tied a headscarf around her head. When she inched open the door of the cabin, she heard deep, even breaths coming from the makeshift cot made up by the fire. *Poor Fran, but he had been exhausted.*

With her eyes growing accustomed to the dark, she carefully avoided treading too near him, and she placed the bundle on the table before going to the chest below the wall opening. She lifted the lid, leaning it carefully against the wall so it didn't make a noise. She took out her cloak and placed this on the floor beside the chest, then she picked up a sword belt and fastened it around her waist. Reaching down to the bottom of the chest, she pulled out a parcel wrapped in cloth. The cloth fell aside to reveal a short scabbard and a small iron sword. Even in the faint light Annerin could see the kinks in the blade and the speckles of rust dotting the surface – her father's sword. She glanced towards where Fran had half-hidden Edwyn's sword and smiled. She remembered more than saw its elegance compared to the dark stumpy weapon in her hand. But this sword was a good size and would suit her well.

She hooked the scabbard to the belt, noting with satisfaction how it stopped just past her knee. Then she picked out her father's shield – a rough circle of wood covered with hide – lifted it over her head and rested the strap across one shoulder.

Next, she rolled her cloak up and placed it in the bundle, along with the remains of the loaf from the previous night, then she unhooked a waterskin from its place on the wall, filled it from the bucket by her cabin door, and attached it to her belt.

Lastly, Annerin moved round the table to the cupboard, eased open the top door, lifted out a small package wrapped in cloth, and placed it in the pocket of her dress. *Edwyn's.* He'd always kept it so well hidden. She pressed it down to where the fabric constricted, making sure it was safe.

With the creak of the cupboard door, Fran rolled over and mumbled in his sleep. Annerin tiptoed with her bundle to the door and slipped outside, checking for Tom, but there was no sign of him, so presumably he was still in the trees.

The morning was still, and the sky was clear. She lifted the bundle onto her shoulder and turned to take a last look at the stone house, her heart heavy at the thought of Fran waking to find her gone. But at least he was not alone. Tom was there – and Maya; the child's presence was strangely reassuring. Maya had a quiet, knowing way that often made her seem beyond her ten summers.

Fran must leave and go to March now, she told herself. The events of the night before made staying here impossible – at least for the present. They had nothing – nothing aside from the friendship and trust she shared with Galos, and now with his two daughters. The only safe place in the world for Fran was with Galos and Tom ... and now they would have one less person to defend.

Chapter 8

Wise Council

The day was set to be hot, but first light held a coldness that chilled Ebba's bones. On their return the night before, March had been unnaturally still and quiet, with only pale arrow slits of light between shutters giving the watchers away. Hilda, meanwhile, waited on her doorstep, and she received the stretcher bearing her son without uttering a single word.

What was more, they had been halfway home before she discovered Maya was not with her husband. She had been furious, but suddenly realising their home might not be safe either left her sleepless. Now, Galos lay fitful on the cot beside her, and little creaks and snuffles told her that Elsa was awake at the opposite end of their tiny house.

Ebba knew this morning would bring questions – questions no one wanted to answer. Her frustration at Galos for not waking mingled with fear about what would ensue when he did. She peeked out of the door at the silent square then went to Elsa.

"Elsa, are you awake?" She stood over her daughter's cot impatiently, but Elsa only frowned and rolled over. "Elsa." Ebba shook her daughter by the shoulder.

Elsa snapped awake and surveyed Ebba, her forehead wrinkling. "What is it, Mother?"

"What do you think it is?" hissed Ebba. "You were there last night, were you not?"

Elsa sat up and tousled at her hair, eyes wide and sleepy. Ebba waited as she rubbed her nose and scratched at her ear but failed to reply.

"How did a simple walk to collect firewood end like this, Elsa?" she asked eventually. "I mean ... how in the name of the good green earth could you turn things into such a disaster? You and your father both. And what were you and Gareth doing that you completely lost sight of Maya?" Ebba paused, letting her words sink in, and with grim satisfaction she watched Elsa's mouth fall open. "Do you have any idea what you've done?" she continued. "It's all very well speaking up for Fran and Annerin, but Gareth's mother and father won't rest until they have answers."

She stopped for breath. Elsa mumbled something unintelligible, her eyes brimming with tears, and she hung her head. Ebba fought back against an impulse to grab a handful of Elsa's curls, wrench the girl's head back and make her answer. But it wouldn't work; there'd just be more tears. And why was it even necessary to spell out the hideous range of possible explanations likely to be weighed, measured and, no doubt, believed by their neighbours?

"Gareth will tell his parents and the rest of March what happened to him," Elsa answered, her usual note of defiance returning. "Everyone will just have to wait until he's able to speak."

"But what if he doesn't know what happened to him, Elsa?" Ebba plumped down beside Elsa. "It sounds like he was attacked from behind, so he may well have no idea. What then?" Ebba, fought to keep her tone even. She would be having the same conversation shortly with Galos, she knew, and she would have to spell out the consequences for him in just the same way.

Elsa turned away from her, and Ebba stepped back, shaking her head.

"You need to get up now and bring your sister back. Right now, do you hear? I want to speak to her straight away." Ebba waited but got no response other than to see Elsa reach for her day shift.

"Go across the fields. Hurry back and speak to no one. We will see what your sister has to say."

Ebba knew there would be little point trying to get Maya to say anything but the truth, so she aimed, if necessary, to frighten her younger daughter into saying as little as possible. Sometimes she did worry that Maya was a little simple; at other times the child made her feel like she herself had the wrong end of things. Ebba tutted to herself while she chivvied Elsa along, her brain scrambling to keep them all one step ahead.

With Elsa ready to leave, Ebba returned to Galos. *Still sleeping*. Unable to stop herself, she nudged him. Galos opened his eyes. As he focused on her, his expression turned sour.

"What is it, woman? Why do you wake me in the night?"

Ebba, determined to remain calm, looked back at him but said nothing.

"Well?" Galos spat.

Feigning bewilderment, she cooed, "Galos, it's me. Ebba. Don't you know your own wife?" She waited for a thawing, but none came.

"I thought you'd want to be woken early; besides, I have your breakfast cooking."

Galos sat up, took a slug of stale water from the cup on the floor beside the low wooden bed and rubbed at the stubble on his chin. He glanced around the room, and a troubled look clouded his face.

Ebba sat down beside him, as she had done with Elsa. "Once you've eaten, we'll need to work out what to say to Lukas and Hilda. We'll need to speak with them soon – to ask after Gareth at least. He's most likely awake and mending by now, but if not, there may be trouble ..."

"Trouble resting, which you've woken, Ebba," Galos snapped.

Ebba took a step back.

"What does it matter what time I wake? There'll be no hunting today; no tending the horses and pigs; no patrol of the land. Instead, blood will likely be spilt. The gods only know, I have enough memories of it – and scars." He gestured at his chest and arms, which were knotted with welts. "Foul work. Your memory's short, Ebba – short."

Galos got up, dragged on a pair of trousers, tied the waist and strode to the front of the house, where he splashed his face with water from the bucket at the door. With his arm resting on the doorpost, he looked out across the square.

Ebba untied the bedroom shutter. The square was still empty. The shadow of the longhouse stretched out towards her across the dirt, almost touching their home, but a cloudless purple sky lightened behind the dark bulk of March Hill and the promise of heat sparked in the air. Time was critical.

Galos returned, and Ebba proffered him his shirt.

He snatched it from her. "Get me my armour, shield and sword. Get them now. I'll speak with you in the copse." He didn't wait for an answer, only turning his back to her while he dressed.

After a moment's hesitation, she went away. In the main room of the house, she picked up one of the four stools set around the central fireplace and carried it to where, after dragging clear the table, she could stand on it to lift down Galos' sword and shield from their places high on the back wall. Next, she opened a large wooden chest set against the right-hand partition and took out Galos' heavy leather tunic.

When Galos came in, she handed them to him without a word. He put on the tunic, slung the shield across his back, and slipped the sword through his belt. Once done, he turned to her, his face softening slightly. "Is Elsa going for Maya?"

"Yes, she should have left by now; I told her to hurry."

"Good. I asked Tom to stay down there until we signal him. I've got people watching both gates too, but I'd like them back before all the coming and going starts."

So, Galos did understand the danger they were in; somehow, that wasn't reassuring. "I still think she'd have been better here." Ebba sat down heavily in the corner chair. Galos sighed and turned away. "If anything had happened ..."

"Nothing was going to happen last night. You know Lukas. Full of bluster and wind. He'll puff and blow half the day. Besides, Tom's there."

"But you worried enough to leave him there. If something had happened, she might have got in the way, and she would have seen ..."

"Seen what, Ebba?"

Ebba shut her eyes tight, forcing unwanted images back.

"Like I said, foul work. Now, the copse – wait a short while before you follow me. We don't know who's watching."

Galos left, ignoring the fresh porridge set out on the table but snatching a chunk of stale bread from the top of the food cupboard as he went through the door. Ebba tried to organise her thoughts, but her heart raced, and order would not come. Yet it seemed her husband had a plan.

She reached for her shawl, drew it about her shoulders against the early morning chill and left the stockade via the main gate, which was often left open overnight in mid-summer. Once outside, she turned right and followed the stockade round a quarter circle to a copse of trees just behind the settlement and on the edge of the grazing land at the head of the valley.

Ebba found Galos waiting under cover of oak and beech and out of earshot of anyone lurking behind the stockade. He rubbed at his armour.

"Husband?" She approached him and kept her voice low. "You speak of foul work, yet you take up arms with so little thought," she chided, coming level with him as he unsheathed his sword and held it to the light.

"And what would you have me do, Ebba, when so many summers and winters of silence come back to choke us all?"

"We would do better speaking with our neighbours."

"More wedding plans."

"Gareth's a good man; Elsa will come to terms with it before long."

"We might all *come to terms*, as you say, but what happens when we can no longer abide those terms?"

Ebba took a minute to digest this. She was still breathing hard from the walk, but Galos wasn't even looking at her, he only had eyes for the sword.

"But, Galos, what has been forgotten for so long can fall out of memory again easily enough."

"But what if it can't? Can Annerin forget again now? Or Fran?"

Annerin. Annerin. "Annerin wouldn't be fool enough to set Fran's mind to revenge. He can come to March; the young will accept him. It's his choice whether he comes, but he judges without appreciating our position, and at the same time tries to steal our beautiful daughter away ... just to make his own life a bit less lonely." Ebba paused for breath.

The sword's tip rested on dry moss, next to a spent drift of celandine.

Now she had Galos' attention. *Good.* "It's no life for Elsa out there," she continued. "A raid from the south will bring death, or worse, to everyone at that house. Can't you think ahead? Can't you see?"

Galos raised the sword again, this time scrutinising more closely the marks and notches on the blade. "Are you expecting a raid, Ebba? Why, we were not even wed the last time March was attacked. What do you suppose a raider would ride off with? Cabbages? Barley? A fattened pig? The reason no one travels here, from Eruthin or from anywhere else, is because there's nothing to come here for, not because of any witch stopping them. The mountains have myriad ways through them – the Nethermore Pass is just the easiest. March is a backwater; those who leave never come back, and it isn't because they can't find the way. Why, Edwyn had more spirit than any man here."

Ebba eyed her husband carefully; her man of few words. She held her tongue.

"You broker peace – at any price – but I see only shame and disgrace," he continued when she didn't answer. "Can't *you* see? Fran couldn't live in March. He'd have to sit in the longhouse with Lukas, and ... and what would he do with his father's sword? Even if he were to come, I couldn't look him in the eye. Why, only last night Lukas could so little bear the sight of Annerin he raised his hand to strike her. If she'd been alone, he'd have beaten her bloody and named her a witch. He didn't wait to hear what happened to Gareth; he didn't ask, and he barely acknowledged when I told him Annerin was with Elsa ... the girl who's supposedly marrying his son."

Galos stopped, red in the face. He jabbed the sword into the packed grey earth, and they both watched it reverberate. Ebba mulled this speech.

"Do you think me a fool – one who fashions little bonnets for a grandson – sending Elsa out with Gareth?" she spat back. "Forget your shame, and your pride. You rule March unhappily alongside Lukas, but Gareth is unlike his father, and that's our gift from the gods. You've a beautiful daughter, one who can hand you more power than any son. Someday your grandsons will rule March."

"You run a little ahead of yourself, woman. I rule March unhappily with Lukas because I listened to such words as yours in the past – honeyed words of peace and tolerance, but they're the poison and lies of those too old or weak to fight for what's right. It's simple, Ebba, simpler than you think. Lukas killed Edwyn in cold blood then named him a traitor and a thief, and yet you reason his crime away to nothing. Before the sun sets today, I will make him answer for it."

Ebba snatched his wrist and dropped her voice to a hiss. "Make him answer for what, Galos. Remember, he struck in the heat of the moment, on the night Elin and Roe died ... You'll get no thanks for dragging all this back up now. Too many summers have gone by. Too many, Galos. You must move on – and so must your friend and her son."

Galos sat down on a tree stump and began to flick at the sword edge with the sharpening stone he carried in his pocket. "My guilt and my wife mock me." He met Ebba's eyes. "I intend to chasten both."

Ebba took a deep breath and pulled her shawl more tightly around herself as he frowned over the blade. She had not seen him this way in many moons. "Galos—" Then his fingers were over her mouth.

"You won't peck me into silence twice, woman." He glared at her for a couple of beats.

She wanted to turn away, escape the accusation in those brown eyes. When his hand dropped, she spun to follow his gaze and saw Tom, Jake, Willett, Cader, Frey and several others crossing the field towards them.

Ebba stepped aside, picking up the sharpening stone and sword and putting the first in Galos' pocket and offering him the second.

"Yours, I believe."

Galos took the sword, looking down at her questioningly.

Ebba smiled. Another opportunity presented itself here, and a far better one than Elsa wedding Gareth and everyone tolerating each other through gritted teeth for the rest of their days. Galos was still solid and strong with a full head of dark hair, but Lukas grew bald and had run to fat. *Galos could outmatch Lukas now.*

"If you're set on this path, there's only one way – kill Lukas and have done. Kill him as you should've done that morning and put an end to this restless peace."

Galos' mouth dropped open, anger replaced by surprise. "What? That's not justice, Ebba – it's revenge." His eyes narrowed and his expression grew unreadable. "Go, woman, your counsel's done."

Ebba hesitated, but the seed was sown. She could do no more for now. She slipped away as Tom drew nearer, but she had no intention of leaving the wood just yet. She hid behind a beech tree a short distance away, tucking in her skirts and listening.

"All's quiet at the stone house, but I've left a new watch just nearby." *Tom's voice.*

"Thank the gods. I hope you got some sleep." Galos' tone was entirely different, Ebba noted, among his men.

"March is awake, and men are arming themselves." *Willett.*

Ebba's heart skipped a beat. *What happened last night?* She had anticipated a visit from Hilda and possibly Lukas, but not this taking up of arms. Maybe others smelt opportunity too. Her thoughts turned to Elsa and Maya; perhaps they were safest at the stone house for now.

Willett continued, "Only Lukas' home stays shuttered and silent. There's no news of Gareth."

"Then he spoke to Ileth and Wyntr last night." *Galos.*

"He must've done, and now they'll come to their own conclusions." *Jake.*

"Even if Gareth wakes, perhaps it's already too late." Her husband sounded weary, and she felt sick.

Leaning back against the tree, she ran her fingertips over its smooth bark.

He continued, "I won't stand by and watch Annerin and Fran butchered like Edwyn. I don't know what today will bring, but I'd rather die than let history repeat itself."

The group fell quiet; a blackbird sang out over Ebba's head.

"We stand together, Galos, as always." *Tom.*

Sounds of agreement followed.

Ebba closed her eyes. The tree towered solid behind her, but she shook uncontrollably. Bodies would be piled high by sunset. Better the compromise. If only Gareth would wake before it was too late.

"Fran took his father's sword last night and almost drew Lukas' blood," Tom continued. "Unless he comes to March to try and sort this out, Lukas will seek him at the stone house or make war on you, brother. We must watch closely. No party has left March yet. We can see the road clearly from here. No one has passed."

Ebba's head spun. *The sword. Fran turned Edwyn's sword on Lukas.* Small wonder Galos behaved in the way he did, and presumably Lukas would confide this to Ileth and Wyntr, despite the humiliation of it. Fran was so reckless, just like his father.

"You're right." A stab of pity shot through Ebba at the hollowness in Galos' voice. "Frey or Cader, can one of you go back to March and find out what's going on? We'll wait here for now. It would be easiest for us if Lukas came out this way, then we could confront him."

Ebba didn't need to hear any more. *The sword. The wretched sword.* Why on earth hadn't someone taken it from Annerin long ago? It could be hanging safely on the longhouse wall now.

Ebba busied herself sweeping the floor and rotating the quern until her arms ached, but the swishing broom felt like a shield, and she could not sit idle. Women continually gravitated to her door, asking whether all was well, or venturing other such pleasantries designed to entice information from her. She remained taciturn, and resolutely unsmiling, and eventually the steady stream of visitors dried to a trickle of the more persistent and the rude.

"Where's your husband, then? And where were you all yesterday?" demanded Vanna, an ancient and stooped matriarch from the far end of the settlement.

Ebba fought to conceal her disgust as she caught sight of the old woman's whiskery chin and the glint of malice dancing beneath the heavy brow. Vanna wasn't someone with whom she normally exchanged more than a cursory nod, but somehow this old woman now felt at liberty to make herself at home on the bench outside their house and interrogate at will. What was more, a small audience was surreptitiously gathering to watch what would unfold.

Ebba lifted a basket of vegetables and brusquely motioned at Vanna to move, swinging it deliberately close to the old woman's head. Vanna didn't flinch. Instead, she turned to Ebba again, a smile playing on her pinched little mouth.

"I haven't seen Elsa for a bit. Has she been staying with Annerin?" Vanna let the question hang. "Oh, I'm sorry, my dear. Did you want to put the basket down?" Moving with surprising nimbleness, Vanna left the bench and sidled across into the threshold, thereby cutting off Ebba's retreat.

Ebba glanced at those coyly milling around the square with one eye on herself and Vanna, and then she looked at the ragged old woman who blocked her door.

"My husband and daughters have gone out early and are about their business. I thank you for your kind concern, but I wouldn't wish to keep you from your ... from your home and all the chores you must have there. It is, after all, some little distance away." Ebba set her hands on her hips and waited for Vanna to move from the doorway.

The old woman shuffled her feet. *Hit a nerve. Good*. Not all houses in March were equal, and those facing onto the square and adjacent to the longhouse were the largest and most prestigious. Increasingly, makeshift huts webbed out to the north, and Vanna's home was the humblest of dwellings, set right by the stockade that wound its way around the settlement.

People began to move away, and Vanna drew herself up to her full height, which was still a head shorter than Ebba's, before replying. "Well, my dear, it's clear you're busy, so I'll not keep you any longer. It's good of you to let an old woman sit by you on such a hot day." Vanna spoke loudly enough for the passers-by to hear, and then she shuffled off back towards her hut. Ebba watched her go with a tinge of regret. *Nasty old witch. Wanted a fight then changed her mind.*

Ebba looked out across the square, watching Vanna until she disappeared around the side of the longhouse, her thoughts whirling like dry leaves caught by the wind. *Where was Hilda, damn it?* Perhaps she should go to the house. But no, Galos was already angry with her. Best to wait until Lukas was not there ... *And where were Elsa and Maya?* Ebba gritted her teeth as she, like everyone else, waited and watched for fate to reveal its hand. She knew only one thing – they would not wait long. Galos must return soon, but still no word of Gareth had reached her, and his father lurked behind closed shutters like a spider crouching at the heart of its web, malice brewing as the sun climbed higher and the heat grew.

Chapter 9

Lightning Rod

Fran woke shortly after dawn, disorientated and stiff from being curled up on the hard floor. Looking around the room, he saw Tom's bed empty, his mother's door closed and Maya across the hearth from him, her head down as she tried to relight the fire. He closed his eyes again, sifting memories of the night before. His dreams had been dark and strange – images of blood and fire – Lukas' pasty skin ripped apart by the claws of an unknown beast, blood pouring from his neck ... being hunted by pillars of fire which erupted beneath him, so he was running, always running ... and Elsa, always just out of reach, behind the next tree, the next bend in the path ...

He pushed aside the fading dreams – although they left a heavy feeling – and remembered bidding Galos farewell, Tom snoring on the bench and the promise given to his mother to speak with Galos about Elsa. Pushing aside his blanket, he rose and went to open the shutter by the wooden chest, which let in the best of the morning light.

"Morning, Maya," he whispered. "Did you sleep well? I hope my bed was comfortable."

"Yes, it's very comfortable. Thanks for letting me sleep in it." Maya smiled up at him before turning her attention back to the fire.

"Leave the fire, Maya. I'll light it in a bit." He leant over and ruffled the mop of light brown curls as he went to fill two cups from the water bucket set against the partition. "Has Tom gone?"

"He's somewhere outside."

Fran nodded. His sleep had been restless, and he seemed to remember the click of the door. He sat down, resting his head on the table and wishing the day would go away.

Maya turned to him. "Gareth saw the dragon too," she ventured.

"So my mother said. It just sounds strange when you say it out loud."

"It won't to the elders."

This gave Fran pause for thought. The old people of March were generally kind to him, particularly Arthen the healer, and others who had been friends of his grandparents. They always asked after him and his mother.

"No, perhaps not." *But would Gareth be brave enough to tell them the truth?*

"I like listening to their stories."

"You like tall tales." Fran smiled despite himself as he imagined Maya agog, with the old folk endlessly embellished their favourite stories for her.

"It's better than talking about farming. A lot better." Maya rolled her eyes and Fran laughed.

"Yes, I think we prefer tall tales here too."

"I know you do. That's one of the reasons we like it here," said Maya. "Me and Elsa, I mean. I love the stone house, and the wood, and your mother's stories about Eruthin and the magic water and the swords. I've always wanted to stay over. I wish we could stay more often."

The morning light picked out the wood and straw of the roof, and dust motes sparkled in the air above their heads. Fran nodded. Normally, he loved this hour of beginnings – the only time when the sun really entered the house.

"It would be nice," he replied, realising, for the first time perhaps, how pleasant it would be to stay here, surrounded by those he cared for the most, rather than always hankering after a life in March. He sat down at the table and looked, as he always did in the mornings, for stray sparks in the ash. There were none.

Maya's words, however, gave him pause for thought. His agreement with her was a platitude, easy to say when the thing itself remained distant or unlikely, but his mother's words the night before gave an immediacy to the idea of Elsa coming to live with them that set him on edge. *Too soon. Far, far too soon*. It would be a delight if they were to visit as friends, but with Elsa as his wife ... He found the scene difficult to imagine, reserved for some sunny future day when he was older and their troubles were behind them. He shifted the scene to a new home he might build adjacent to the stone house. Still the disquiet.

"We should light the fire to make tea for my uncle and your mother," said Maya.

"Very well. I'll do it. You go outside to wash if you want to. It's quite light now."

Maya opened the shutters by the door, then the door itself, and went outside.

Fran looked around the room, waiting for the fire to catch. His father's sword – now his sword, he remembered – was standing where he'd left it in the corner farthest from the door, and the lamp borrowed by Elsa last night was missing from its usual place on top of the cupboard ...

The cupboard door was ajar. Fran sprang to his feet and around the table. He opened the top door of the cupboard – the packet had gone. He strode to his mother's door, snatching at the handle. *Gone! Taken the packet and left.* Flat-footed, he stared at the empty cot, heart cold in his chest. As a child, he'd secretly opened the packet more than once. The contents were a puzzle, and an intriguing one at that. His mother always told him to leave it alone, and he learnt never to ask about it, but her taking it now told him all too well where she had gone.

Fran's stomach knotted and his legs threatened to give way. He opened the shutter covering the narrow window in his mother's room, letting in light and cool drafts of morning air. Grasping the sill, he steadied himself. Dew glistened on the grass and a blackbird ruffled its tail feathers as it perched in a hawthorn bush – one of those set around the house, demarcating their land from the adjacent fields of wheat. He did not know what to do. There was no sign of Tom out there either. Outside, water splashed as Maya washed at the pail under the eaves then stepped into view, shaking her hands before drying them on the pinafore she wore over her dress. Taking a thick wooden comb from her pocket, she moved into the patch of sunlight and began brushing through her hair. These were all actions his mother had performed a thousand times on a thousand mornings and Fran would have given anything to see her green dress flickering in and out of view now. But it was Maya outside; Annerin wasn't here.

Fran slumped down at the table, fighting the impulse to cry. He had promised his mother he would go to Galos, but how could he do that now? He wasn't a child to be sent to Galos for protection while she braved the forest and mountain alone. And what of the witch – the spider at the heart of this web – Arete? No, he would not let his mother face that terror alone – not even ... no, not even for Elsa.

Maya came back in, still tying her hair. She froze when she saw Fran.

"Mother's not here, Maya. She's gone. Her room's empty. All this time, she wasn't there." He bit his lip, remembering she was ten summers old.

Maya looked at the open door behind Fran, then she ran over to check for herself. "Where is she?"

Fran hesitated. "I'm not sure. But where's your uncle? Could you see him?"

Maya shook her head. "He'll be somewhere." She slipped back out to shout for Tom, but there was no response. "He's out there somewhere," she repeated.

"We'll find him before I go and look for my mother," said Fran.

"I wonder why she's gone out without telling you. She'll probably come back soon."

"Maybe."

"Did your mother say anything to you last night?" Maya searched his face, and Fran found himself avoiding her eyes. "Did she ask you to do anything?"

"What do you mean?" Fran went to his mother's window again. Maya had an uncanny knack – she was like a lightning rod for the truth. Perhaps it would be best to tell her. After all, his friends were few and he needed them – and Cader wasn't here. He turned back to Maya. But how could he burden her with the truth? She was just a little girl. Reluctantly, Fran decided he could not – he must bite his tongue, hand her over to Tom, and then follow his mother – but at that moment there was a knock on the door, which Maya had left slightly ajar, and Elsa's voice called out to ask if anyone was awake yet.

Maya ran to the door to let her sister in.

"Oh, you're all awake ... but what's the matter? Where's my uncle? Where's Annerin?"

"My mother's left because of yesterday," Fran blurted out.

"Yesterday." The one word held in it a world of despair. Elsa closed the door, then she sat down heavily at the table. "What do you mean, she's left?"

Fran took the seat beside her, and Maya retreated to the bench where Tom had slept the night before. "I think my mother's gone to look for Arete – the witch. Whatever happened, that night she came here – the night my father was killed – well, we can't ever get away from it, can we?" Fran recounted what had happened at the ford the night before.

Elsa's eyes widened and her gaze flashed to the sword. By the time he'd finished, although her face was drained of colour, the tilt of her head told him she was proud.

"I don't know how we can stay here," he added, looking around the tiny house as if seeing it for the first time. "I suppose she's hoping Arete might help us, find a way to restore the peace ..." *Or let us cross the mountains to Glendorrig to find my father's family.*

Elsa reached out tentatively for his hand. "Your mother may find peace for herself, but I don't think she can bring it back to March. My father dresses for battle already ..."

She looked like she would say more but for Maya. He felt the pressure of her fingers and saw her fear. Cold sweat pricked his skin. What had he done?

"He flew at us in a rage. It all happened so fast."

"My father's been tired of Lukas' rages for a long time. Don't blame yourself, Fran. He remembers your father. This would have happened sooner or later. I just wish ..." She pulled her hand away, but their eyes met, saying the unspoken things.

"I wish your mother had let things alone." The words escaped Fran before he could stop them. "I'm sorry."

"It's no one's fault. And I won't marry Gareth. She can't make me."

Fran realised Maya had slipped outside and took Elsa's hand again. "I'm glad to hear you say that." *And it's a pity you didn't say it to your mother yesterday.*

Elsa sighed, as if reading the thought. "It's true. Besides, everyone knows Lukas can't keep his temper these days. Whatever he says, half the village will take it with a pinch of salt."

"And the other half?"

Elsa shrugged, her head dropping.

"We're strangers to so many people. A lot might just believe whatever their chief tells them."

Fran tasted the edge of bitterness creeping into his voice, but as he looked at Elsa a great flood of anguish replaced it. Soon he would have to leave her to whatever the day brought.

A short time later, all three stood in the lane outside the stone house, Fran with his pack, shield and bow slung across his back, and the silver sword at his hip.

"So, you're going to find your mother." As usual with Maya, it wasn't a question.

"Yes. I'll bring her back."

"But maybe she went on her own because she thought it best."

"She went alone because she's brave, and her journey's dangerous."

"Perhaps it's better to see Arete alone, without a sword or bow. Your mother's not going to fight her."

Maya's words gave Fran pause for thought. He exchanged glances with Elsa then bent down to be level with Maya. "Maya, you've spent a great deal of time with my mother and listened to her more than anyone else. You're probably right; she doesn't want me to follow her, but tell me this, do you always do as you're told?"

Maya looked at Fran and shook her head, a small smile playing on her lips.

"I thought not, but I think you always do what you think is right." Fran straightened and turned to Elsa. "She makes me see I have no choice."

Elsa searched his face, and her forlorn look struck Fran to the core. The forest must seem like an escape when their father might have to fight that very day. Indeed, it was the only escape in this lonely place, with no other settlement for leagues in each direction and impenetrable mountains separating them from Eruthin. Fran hesitated, and Maya went to sit a short distance away at the foot of the silver birch, where his mother had sat the night before.

"Part of me thinks I should go to your father, to be at his side," he began, "but the bigger part of me can't leave my mother to do this alone. She's not strong, and it's not good to spend nights alone outside. I wish I could be in two places at once. I don't know which path is the right one."

Elsa glanced away. Around them, birdsong filled the dappled air, but Fran knew she heard only the clash of swords. When she turned back, her smile was watery and brave. "There's no right or wrong here, only choice. My father's following his path. You must do what your heart tells you."

"I'll come back as quickly as I can." Fran tried to keep the desperation from his voice. He remembered his mother's instructions, but he had no right to ask for promises before leaving. Besides, her refusal to wed Gareth must count for something, and Ebba's plan lay in a million pieces now. Or did it? With him and his mother gone, a truce made sense – or would to Ebba – but any wedding must wait for the harvest to be gathered, so time was on his side. "I promise I'll return before harvest," he heard himself say.

"Very well." Elsa nodded, her tone bleak. She took a step back. "We'll look out for each other then. May the gods protect you. Your mother can't be far ahead. Do you know what route she's taken?"

"She didn't tell me she was going, so ..." Fran shrugged. *Was there more than one way?*

"She'll probably follow the Cloudwater to the bridge near Deas Howe. If you cross at the shallows and cut through the forest on the old rangers' path, you may get to the foot of the Nethermore Pass before her even now."

Yes, of course. That was the shortcut his father had taken, but his mother would probably choose to follow the main route and keep dry. "Thanks. That's what I'll do. You should go back to March now. To your mother."

Maya, who had slipped back to Elsa's side, took her sister's hand. "And to Father."

Chapter 10

The Worm at the Heart of the Apple

Galos sat alone in the wood, perched on a tree stump amid thickets of nettle and bracken. He did not hear the bird-song either. A short distance away, Tom, Jake, Willett and the rest of his men waited, casting anxious glances in his direction. Galos kicked at a grey knot in a tree root, Ebba's parting words ringing back and forth in his head. *Kill Lukas and have done. Kill him as you should have done that morning ...*

But what did either of them even remember of that morning? It was so very long ago now. It might as well be part of a legend because he could not recall the witch beating at the gate, the lightning bolts or the screams, only blackness, thick and complete, the orange of the fires and the besieging terror of the storm. And his own shame – Luwain calling for volunteers and Edwyn's eyes boring into him as he stared down at the sodden earth of the square. His hesitation only lasted a moment, but that moment was the nexus of his life.

He remembered running after Edwyn and fighting against his father and uncles when they held him back. Then came the colourless dawn.

Then the blood.

Sleet, sludge and blood. His stomach churned at the recollection – Edwyn bleeding out and Annerin's mother unable to stop the flow. And now Ebba wanted more. But no, that wasn't what she said ... Galos glanced towards Tom, wanting his advice but knowing – on this one – he stood alone. The quarrel, as it had been all those winters ago, was between him and Lukas.

Closing his eyes and listening to the scurry and chirp of life in the sun-dappled canopy above him, he recoiled at the thought of going back to March, with its stockade and its truce. For the millionth time he wished he and Edwyn had replaced Elin and Roe; hot-headed perhaps, but both had been better men than him. *Neither hesitated.* Both died, and in the pale morning light, all that remained on the blood-soaked turf were two sorry little piles of ash and brittle bone beneath their blackened swords.

For so long he'd tried to forget everything, but the sight of Fran holding the sword forced him to remember Edwyn – dearest of friends – who'd followed Elin and Roe, encountered the witch and somehow lived. And the irony was that afterwards, Edwyn kept his sword drawn, staring at it often, as if the world sat squarely on its crossguard.

And now, perhaps it did. Seeking strength, Galos forced himself to remember what unfolded on that winter's day, and how, shivering, he watched men creep out of the stockade, while he and Annerin perched on a damp bench facing the longhouse and waited for Edwyn to explain to them what happened outside the gate – how it was that he alone came back unscathed. Edwyn wouldn't answer, but the change in his friend had been stark. On his return, Edwyn had blood on his shirt and carried the look of someone broken.

The women and children, meanwhile, had retired to their homes, leaving the square dank and empty, the mud churned to a quagmire, with wails of keening from beyond the stockade filling the clammy air.

Galos, shivering in the morning's heat, ran a frond of bracken through his hand, peeling its leaves to a clump. Some things were best forgotten. That sound was one of them.

Elin had been Lukas' nephew, and when Lukas approached them and stood in front of the bench, rage choking him, it formed the template for their every subsequent confrontation – hurt writ large, and there was incomprehension at the man Galos chose as a friend. And through it all, Edwyn just kept saying she was gone but wouldn't explain what happened outside. Eventually, Lukas' rage gave way to suspicion. Suspicion that Edwyn knew the witch, had drawn her to March in the first place, perhaps, then he'd helped her escape. Someone had cleared a path through the snow leading away towards the forest, after all ... This, Galos knew only later, but at the time, Lukas' rage only gave way to a waiting silence, the memory of which now filled Galos again. His skin crawled, and he pulled the leaves clean away, staining his fingers green and making his thumb sting and burn.

The sword. It was always the sword – as if the thing worked its own will, slumbering all these seasons. Yet it had been a burden to Edwyn too. Once, they had swapped, but the sight of that rose shining on the hilt made Galos uneasy, as if it mocked March – poor little backwater clinging to a legend because it had nothing else. *Better rusting iron and an ordinary life. Better the empty longhouse wall.*

What happened next brought an end to a story that began one late summer's day, when Lukas, wielding a great heavy iron sword, demanded a match with Edwyn. He had lunged like an angry boar, but Edwyn's silver sword moved with a light and grace all its own. It finished with Lukas lying in the dirt at Edwyn's feet, blond hair soaked with sweat, angry beads dotting his brow. The word "thief" formed on his lips, and winded as he was, it carried on the summer breeze and fluttered on through the bright green leaves and into the hearts and mouths of the villagers; it was a thing of endless life, spontaneously brought into being by hate.

That fight started a feud that led to Edwyn's death, four moons later, on that midwinter morning. Edwyn was standing beside the old roundhouse, looking heartbroken, and the blow came from behind. He turned but did not raise his sword in time to parry the strike. It cleaved through leather armour and collar bone, the weight of the blow forcing him to his knees.

For Galos, the next few moments moved with the slowness of forest nightmares. Everything slowed, every detail hung in the air – the glint of gold in Annerin's hair as she rushed out of the shadows, the anguished howl that ripped out of his own throat and startled the beasts, the weight his own sword raising and smashing down, the crack of Lukas' shield ...

During the time Galos lay wounded, Annerin and her parents quietly left for the stone house, and as the shadow of the witch withdrew, the will to bring Lukas to justice ebbed. Eventually, Annerin's kin, tired of fighting the battles of an empty hearth, shared what became an uneasy truce with the majority, who, given the silence from Luwain, did not question Lukas' version of events. Not everyone saw the scant piles of bones, but all had seen the blood-soaked earth outside the gate, and more lurid explanations of Elin and Roe's fate found a receptive audience. Edwyn, having returned unharmed, had quickly became a shadowy figure, a stranger who had not been what he seemed, a thief and a traitor, inviting darkness and death into their peaceful world. In contrast, Lukas, steadfast, and burying his nephew with a great show of grief, became a hero.

Galos spat on the ground, as though to purge the memory. He wiped his hand on his leg and reached for the sharpening stone again. Those were bitter times, and their aftermath brought painful choices – forgetting the past and accepting the future. Annerin, meanwhile, grew ever more distant. He missed her, and surely, she missed him. Once, they were a group – he and Ebba, Annerin and Edwyn – and when Edwyn came, their young lives finally fell into place. Annerin loved Edwyn so wholeheartedly that no one dared question his right to be in March, or his right to claim her for his wife, but it also opened a gulf between Annerin and the rest, a gulf now much wider than the few little squares of field he looked out across now, separating the stone house at the ford from March.

At last, his thoughts returned to Fran, and the point of the silver sword balancing at Lukas' throat, and he knew beyond any shadow of doubt he was glad. Eighteen summers and winters of peace like a choking vine, and he was as proud of Fran as a father would be proud of his son. Ebba did not understand; only Tom understood – and Annerin, alone at the stone house.

Galos beckoned to his brother, and Tom came over, his brow furrowed.

"The morning wears on." Tom cast a quick glance at the sun, rising above the distant moors.

"I was remembering that other morning," Galos began. "And Edwyn. I've been a stranger to Fran. Things haven't turned out as I intended."

"A stranger and a friend." Tom's smile was unusually gentle as he flattened down a patch of bracken opposite to make a place to sit. "You've been their shield these many seasons. You've controlled everything – except Ebba."

Galos pulled back, startled, but Tom's gentle smile remained.

"You're right, Tom. I should've stopped Ebba's matchmaking; I thought it only talk." But the talk made sense, that's what he'd missed. Ebba was right – Gareth's reserve could be wearing, but he did lack his father's narrow-mindedness and arrogance. What's more, he was Luwain's grandson, and Galos' own father had been close friends with the old chief. A union would likely have healed the rift, but Gareth, despite constantly watching Elsa, had made no advances, and Elsa clearly favoured Fran, lanky stripling that he was – an inconvenience Ebba steadfastly ignored.

"It was just talk, but Ebba saw Gareth needed a push, and then the girls came home late ..."

Galos, catching the sudden mischievous twinkle in Tom's eye, finished his brother's thought. "Looks like someone – or something – else thought Gareth needed a push too."

Tom's face, an easy map of his moods, relaxed for a moment before darkening again.

"So, if Maya saw the thing," he mused, "we've a fair idea what happened. Even so, it's unfortunate. Lukas still feels guilty, so he wants to believe the worst. Besides, he doesn't know Fran. The lad doesn't want revenge, he just wants to belong."

"True, and I suppose Fran thought I'd agreed to this marriage thing."

Tom nodded. "He's got a bit of a temper though. It surprised me a bit."

"The thing is," said Galos, "what Lukas said last night drags us into it. Cader and Frey particularly."

Tom scowled. "They got back really early with their kill, so they were well out of it."

"I know, but it all does look a bit convenient, doesn't it?"

"I suppose."

The pair fell quiet for a while and Galos was aware of Jake and Willett's anxious glances.

"The thing is, too," said Galos, "Fran was the only one who raised a sword. Lukas didn't. It was just the usual load of bluster ... then threatening to hit Annerin. He knew we'd stop him, but I guess Fran didn't."

"Perhaps it isn't Lukas we need to worry about – it's Wyntr."

Galos shivered; Lukas' nephew had everything of the usurper about him. Wyntr was Elin's younger brother, deformed by grief, bitterness and anger at his brother's death, and Gareth was no match for him. Witnessing this day after day disturbed Galos, and although Gareth offered neither friendship nor challenge, there were times when he pitied this young man, born to be a farmer, not a chief. Gareth was calm and practical, Wyntr domineering and oppressive. Occasionally he even challenged Lukas, who Galos suspected grew tired of his responsibilities and yet more tired of the underlying tension in March. Perhaps Ebba sensed this too – Lukas and Hilda's need for unity, at last.

"I dread the sight of him," he said at last. *The worm at the heart of the apple.*

"He's a fine swordsman ... and utterly ruthless. Lukas won't be allowed to let this go – even if deep down he wants to."

"Lukas left Annerin alone all this time. He could've pushed to take that sword, but he didn't. He knew it would have brought things ... well, it would have brought things to this, wouldn't it?"

"It would, but like I said, if Lukas tells Wyntr about Fran, he won't be allowed to let the matter rest. Wyntr's influence is growing. Don't you see it, Galos? Ebba does." Tom flushed red under the thatch of blond and looked away.

"Perhaps." Galos' heart hammered. *First Ebba, and now Tom.*

"No perhaps, Galos. Think of this, in two days' time our wives and your daughters will be weeping over the charred remains of our old friend Annerin and her son – whatever he may or may not have done – and before many more harvests your Elsa will be balancing Gareth's child on her hip." Tom's voice grew shrill. "And we'll carry on, just like we did before. We'll sit with Lukas and Wyntr in the longhouse, and summer, winter, we'll carry on, because it's too late. And we'll cross the ford each day until one day we'll not remember where their tiny house once stood. And each of us will walk on – until the day a stray arrow finds its way into our backs. But today, only today, it's not too late."

Galos found himself staring at his boots. *Sometimes we do not want advice because we know what it will be.* Eventually, he heard himself answer.

"Then today we act." As he spoke, Galos thought of Fran again. He rose, his fingers gripping the hilt of his sword, and Jake, Willett and the others – whose silence and furtive looks betrayed their eavesdropping – scrambled to their feet and jogged over to join him and Tom.

"Well, the morning wears on. Let's go to March," said Galos.

Tom, still sitting amid the bracken, nodded. "The past is restless. We must put it to bed at last."

Galos offered his hand to pull Tom up. *Restless.* Or do evil deeds just lie dormant until touched by even a single shaft of daylight?

Chapter 11

A Morning's Work

The gates of the stockade looked like huge jaws, ready to snap shut. Galos must have walked through them a thousand times in the past and he took care not to break his stride now. He told himself this was just like any other day, any other return from hunting or patrol. But it wasn't. Instead of bows, spears and knives, he, Tom, Jake, Willett and the rest carried shields across their backs and swords at their hips. Women, children and the elderly melted from view, while men perched on stools or upturned buckets outside doors, hunched over their carving and mending. Others hung back in doorways, hands deep in their pockets, eyes averted.

The hush was only broken by a distant drum, a threat sounding in its solitary beats.

He passed his own doorway, nodding imperceptibly to Ebba, who was a step back in the shadow of the eaves, her face carved stone, and he continued around the side of the longhouse in the direction of Lukas' home. Alone among the many dwellings, it remained shuttered and still. Galos was about to raise his voice and shout for Lukas when the sound of unbolting came from within, and Hilda appeared, blinking in the glare of the morning light, dark circles under red-rimmed eyes. She stepped out and walked towards Galos.

"Galos, you come to my door with a newly sharpened sword. Are you armed to go out and find whoever injured my son?"

"I've come to speak to your husband, but we also look for news of Gareth. Gratitude is owed, Hilda, to those who found him and carried him back to March."

Hilda's brow furrowed. She opened her mouth to reply, but before she could speak her eyes widened as she looked past him. Galos turned and found himself facing Lukas. A short distance away, his kinsmen Wyntr, Gyll and Seth, Hilda's cousin Ileth, and several others waited. Their own swords clanked at their hips, some more worn and tarnished than others. Tom, Willett and Jake retreated a few paces, mirroring the other group, until he and Lukas stood alone, face-to-face again, just as they had so many winters before.

Time slowed. *Today the sun shone.* Galos exhaled, and icy clarity took hold.

They were both older and heavier now, but he stood half a head taller, and Lukas had run to fat, his leather armour stretched across his great belly, the stitching loose at the sides. Galos took in the red eyes and greying beard that hid several chins. *The man hadn't slept.* As they faced one another, the story of the intervening seasons unfolded – what was once an even match was now skewed in his favour. The mismatch wasn't lost on Lukas either. The habitual sneer might still be there, but Galos saw fear flicker too.

"Stand aside. My quarrel isn't with you. Our dispute's a thing long dead, but someone attacked my son." Lukas raised his voice so those around could hear his story. "Someone ambushed Gareth yesterday –

as well you know – not a league from here, practically in the Starling Wood. He's still unconscious."

From somewhere away behind the houses there came the hack of a cough. Feet scudded in the dirt, and fingers drummed, slow and quiet. Galos registered the two long shadows on his right, and while Lukas paused for breath, Hilda stepped level, making them merge.

"We doubtless owe Galos, Tom, Jake and Willett our thanks, husband, for bringing Gareth home last night."

Lukas grunted. "Indeed. Then we're lucky to have such friends. Perhaps they'll join us to hunt down the enemy."

"As I said yesterday, Lukas, if Gareth's still unconscious, you've no idea what happened. Likely it was an accident."

Lukas sneered and spat at Galos' shadow. "It's perfectly clear what happened. Open your eyes."

Galos followed the trajectory of the spittle and raised his eyebrows. "It's not clear," he answered, keeping his voice low and steady.

The two weighed each other, everything unsaid broiling like a river surge in spring. Corvids wheeled overhead, their prescient cries breaking the stillness.

Lukas glanced up and adjusted his weight. "But Galos, surely it must be clear to you of all people." Now he was the honeyed voice of chief and protector, palms raised in appeal. "Your beautiful daughter is bewitched by the boy from the woods. She's slipping out of your control, and it was my son you turned to. *My son.* Gareth looked after both your daughters, and for his trouble he lies injured."

Mutterings of agreement came from several directions.

"Where's Elsa now, Galos?" shouted a voice from behind him.

Lukas smirked.

Galos fought the impulse to, just once, publicly call out Lukas for the murderer he was. He scanned the watching faces. None of them cared anymore. Who gave Annerin a second thought? Or even remembered Edwyn? No one ever mentioned Edwyn by name. Not to him. Not ever. And what of Fran? *What of Fran?*

"You're a man of short memory and tall tales," Galos whispered. "Remind me, Lukas, what are Gareth's injuries exactly?"

"He's got a head injury, as you know, Galos – on the back of his head. He's still unconscious and he's covered in cuts and bruises. It's clear as day, someone attacked him from behind."

Galos caught the intake of breath from the women behind, then the cooing of support for Hilda.

Lukas scanned the perimeter of the square, where Galos sensed most of his neighbours lurked. Ebba, a small group behind her, stood to the right, her face turning from white to grey.

"You guess without knowing the truth. As I said, he likely fell and banged his head. He'd ventured well beyond the fringes of the clearing, and we all know the forest is treacherous, don't we? Who hasn't slipped and fallen down the banks of a stream? Why must you accuse when you owe Annerin thanks for raising the alarm? Gareth was treated with great kindness in her home, and Tom and Fran carried him a long way. We've good neighbours at the ford, and their presence there makes us all safer."

"So, you'll be happy to see your own daughter go there, Galos."

"Fran's a good man, one of honour and courage."

"You don't know him to be any of these things."

"He is his father's son."

Galos spoke these last words quietly, but each dropped like granite at Lukas' feet.

March held its breath. Sweat beaded on Lukas' brow, and his right hand reached for the hilt of his sword.

Galos caught the flash of triumph on Ebba's face, accompanied by Hilda's gasp. He lifted the shield from across his shoulders and slipped his left arm through its leather strappings. Then he drew his own sword and took a step towards Lukas.

"Fran is his father's son, and so, when he asks, I *will* give him my daughter."

The words were for Lukas alone; they found their target, and with barely a scuffle, the crowd receded, surrounding the two men in the square, and filling the shadows.

Leaving the empty house at the ford behind them, Elsa and Maya walked hand in hand along the path back to March. Elsa hesitated at the start of the incline leading to the gate and shielded her eyes as she squinted at a crow banking overhead. *All's not well.* She knew it even before looking down at Maya.

Unable to let go of the little hand in hers, she shivered. Sweat clung in her palm, and she cried out and recoiled when, from within the settlement, a clash of swords rang out. Like the first clap of thunder in a storm, it was swiftly followed by crash after crash of iron against iron, reverberating, heavy and ugly against the freshness of the morning. The reality of it too much to bear, she ran with her sister to the edge of the stockade and huddled in the ditch beneath the great wooden stakes.

The storm raged on. Maya covered her ears, but Elsa strained to recognise her father from the grunts and gasps. *It must be him. Who else could it be? Father and Lukas. Again.* Unbidden, she recalled Gareth's gentleness – his shyness at the stone house – and wondered if he still lay unconscious, or if, like her, he was witnessing this unfolding horror – this shattered truce.

And what of Mother? She would be with Nell, and Frey's mother, Finola, but— Elsa kept tight hold of the hand in hers to stop Maya breaking free and running to their mother.

"Hold still, we will go soon enough."

"No. Now."

Both girls jumped when Frey, having appeared from the direction of the gate, sidled down the grass bank and landed beside them.

"How did you know we were here?" Elsa whispered.

Frey pointed at a small slit in the stockade, his smile tight. "It's all right. Come." He put out a hand to Elsa, avoiding her eyes as he did so, and pulled both girls up the side of the ditch, then they set off at a run back towards the gate.

Once through the gates, a stretch of open ground led them behind the cattle pens and stables to a storage house, beyond which the dwellings began. Frey slipped along the backs of the last row of huts until he reached the one directly behind her parents' hut. He led the girls through the ginnel to where their mother stood, her back to her home.

Wordless, the girls went to their mother, and she put an arm round each. The ring of iron against iron melded with shock in the still air, and Elsa, numb, met the bitter reality of watching her father fight for his life, blood trickling from a gash on his thigh. She watched him drive Lukas back towards the gate, around the longhouse and down the length of the open square in front of their home. Her fear became crystalline; she was surprised her heart continued to beat.

Galos gasped for breath, sand and grit scratching his eyes as he forced his shield arm up. Lukas' sword swung down like a hammer against the wooden shield, the reverberations running through his arm while the sword continued its trajectory and hit the floor.

Lunging forwards, Galos swung at Lukas' head, narrowly missing his shoulder as the shield raised awkwardly, deflecting the blow and making him stumble. He advanced again, thrusting the sword in below Lukas' shield this time, making contact with the thick leather vest. Lukas leapt back with surprising agility, striking upwards towards Galos' exposed thigh and narrowly missing where he had already sliced.

Both paused, raising their shields and watching each other through narrowed eyes. Galos blinked away stinging sweat then darted forwards again, throwing his bodyweight behind his sword when it locked with Lukas'. He forced it down and Lukas fell back, momentarily unbalanced. Galos moved again, hacking at Lukas' left-hand side and landing a blow which sliced skin from his shoulder.

Lukas gasped as blood sprang from the wound and trickled down his shield arm. Raising his sword, he roared and swung again with his full weigh down on Galos' shield. This time a crash of splitting wood mixed with the scream of metal as the tension in the frame of Galos' shield gave way and it fell in on itself, slack.

Blind panic melded with utter clarity. Running forwards, Galos swung at Lukas' shield, cutting in sideways and twisting Lukas, making him lose balance and stagger away to the side. This time his sword struck home. With sickening ease, it found the exposed flesh below Lukas' vest – jagged iron rasping against hip bone.

Lukas fell, his arm shaking as he fought to shield his wounded side. In Galos' head, the drumbeat rolled on, iron singing its victory song. A finger of blood rolled out from the pool gathering under Lukas, wavering through the dirt towards Galos.

With both hands gripping the hilt of his sword, he raised the point over Lukas' heart.

Then a shadow passed overhead – a crow landed on the roof of the longhouse – and for a moment, less than a heartbeat, Galos heard the silence all around him. In it he sensed Ebba holding her breath, he imagined Tom's heart thumping hard against his ribcage, and he felt the tears massing in Hilda's eyes and begin rolling, unchecked, down the flats of her cheeks. In that tiniest of pauses, Galos made a choice. It may not have been a wise choice, but he made it, nevertheless. Lowering his sword, he stepped back.

While he and Lukas fought, the people had stood rigid – petrified beings, reminding themselves to breathe – but when Galos lowered his sword, the spell broke. Lukas' kinsmen, watching from the foot of the path leading to the hilltop, ran to him, wary faces not quite looking at Galos, or at Tom, who stepped up beside Galos and towered over them.

No one spoke. The only sounds were the horrible little twisted cries of pain coming from Lukas. Hilda ran to him, a small clay bottle – doubtless Arthen's henbell mead – in her hand. She twisted out the rag stopper and put it to his lips. Lukas dropped his sword, instead snatching the bottle and emptying the entire bitter contents down his throat. Hilda, kneeling over him, recoiled, and the bottle rolled away across the dirt.

Galos and Tom stepped back a couple of paces, and Galos sheathed his sword. Ebba and Elsa ran to them, and Jake, Willett, Cader and several others gathered around.

Breath hoarse, he took the damp cloth Ebba proffered and wiped the sweat and dirt from his face. Someone else passed him a skin of mead, which he took and emptied.

With the warmth of the mead flooding him, Galos allowed his gaze to pan round. Eyes flashed in the shadows, gone before he could register who they belonged to. *Hiding.* But it was finished; Lukas was badly wounded but would probably live. Arthen's skills had only improved since the healer treated them both, all those winters ago. Yes, there would be hell to pay, but not right now. And he could have finished it, but then Wyntr ...

Galos, weary in body and unready to face these lurking questions, turned to Tom, who caught him in a rough embrace, conveying more than words. Then he turned to Ebba. Her usually rosy cheeks were the colour of cold ash. She stared at him as if she were searching for the place where reality had gone.

Those blue eyes held Galos, nevertheless. With the mead and the heat, everything else spun. He focused on them, waiting for her to speak, but instead she recoiled, face twisting in horror, and he spun to find Lukas back on his feet, staggering forwards and swinging a great iron hammer in both hands. His eyes, which were locked onto Galos, shone unnaturally, and his grey face was so mottled with rage that Galos cried out in fear, cursing his lack of shield and fumbling blindly at his hip for his sword. He saw Lukas' three kinsman, taken by surprise too by their looks, seeming to move in slow motion as they raised their shields and edged forwards, wanting to stop him. To his right, he caught the metallic swish of swords being drawn. Wyntr's shield met the raised hammer first, but Lukas pushed back, growling and sending his nephew stumbling backwards. Lukas lurched sideways, and without thought, question or hesitation, Galos swung his sword. The blade met Lukas' neck, momentum taking it through skin, muscle and sinew, and on, slicing bone until it stopped just short. Lukas' head lifted from his neck like the lid of a box resting open on its hinges.

Galos staggered, falling backwards into Tom's arms. A grey pile of cloth crumpled to the floor where moments before Hilda had stood, and bright spurts of blood shot into the air as Lukas' body slumped forwards onto the dirt, the hammer following, its thud deadening March.

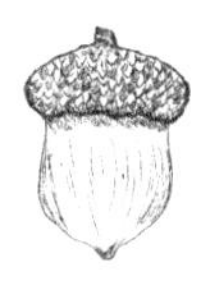

Chapter 12

A Fool's Errand

March was numb for the rest of that day. Women went to the well to draw water; men sharpened tools and mended thatch. The mundane, for a little while, felt precious and sweet. Sunlight warmed faces, and a soft, warm wind ruffled hair and caressed skin. People spoke in whispers.

Beyond the gates, a pyre was being built.

Maya lay on her cot, alongside Elsa, watching the patterns the sunlight made as it pierced through holes and chinks in the shutters and cast dim shapes across the walls. From these she conjured cloud-topped mountains with tall sail boats from Annerin's stories resting between them on a sea of amber light. Both she and Elsa were beyond talk or sleep, shivering in the cool of the house but not yet knowing how to walk back outside into the open day. Maya itched to run to the stone house by the ford, bury her head in Annerin's floury apron, and sob. She wished for the golden-eyed dragon in the forest as if it were the hearthside cat, and she thought of Fran – igniting the daydream in which he became her own big brother – and how he would most likely have caught up with his mother by now.

Presently, she turned to Elsa. "Elsa, we should tell Mother about Annerin and Fran."

Elsa buried her head in her hands.

"Elsa?" Still no answer. Maya peeped round the corner of the partition at her mother, who poked and prodded the fire distractedly then snatched up a piece of mending and slipped away to her bed area behind the opposite partition.

"Elsa, we need to tell Mother and Father they've gone looking for Arete."

Elsa's eyes were red from crying. "Maya, Father can't go after them. Not now. He won't leave us alone here."

Maya stifled a sob. She tried not to think about the crying and the women's screams. Then there was the thing she'd seen from behind Frey ... and later, through a tiny gap in the shutter, she'd watched the men carry the chief away on a bier, which meant he must be dead. And on the spot where he'd fought with her father, crows had gathered over a dark stain soaking into the dry dirt, and the men threw stones then emptied buckets of dry earth from outside nearby doors to cover the mark. She climbed again to look outside and could still see where it had been – not far from Gareth's door, which had been closed since they'd carried Hilda inside. Longing to escape from the silence and memory of blood, she slipped past Elsa into the main area of the house and then around the end of the partition to where her mother sat sewing on her bed.

Putting her arm around Ebba's waist, she leant against her and watched the fine, slightly curved bone needle moving back and forth along the seam of a skirt. Her mother kissed her head and for a while the two huddled quietly together until a clatter of buckets came from the ginnel outside and her mother put down her work and let out a sigh.

"Were you all right last night, sweetheart?"

"Yes, Mother," Maya answered. "But Mother ..."

"What, Maya?"

"Annerin left the stone house before we woke up. Fran says she's gone to see Arete."

Her mother's eyes widened, and she stared at Maya, her mouth working as if she were chewing mutton. "What?" she asked eventually.

"She's gone to see Arete. Fran wanted to help Father, but he had to go after Annerin first."

"Did Fran say why she'd gone looking for the ... for Arete?"

"No." Maya shook her head. "Fran didn't know she'd gone. He was upset. We were going to make breakfast for her; he thought she was in her room."

"But he said she'd gone looking for the witch."

"For Arete, yes."

"How did he know?"

"I don't know."

"Go and bring your sister ... no, wait. Come with me." Her mother took her hand and they slipped across to Elsa's cot.

Ebba sat down on the edge of the cot and waited for Elsa to realise she was there. The girl lay prostrate, face down, but was no longer sobbing.

"Elsa?"

Elsa rolled over and frowned. Ebba brushed away wet strands of hair from Elsa's cheek then put her arms round her eldest child, kissing the hot, red face as the girl shook with renewed sobs. *Something to hold on to at least.* The relief was intense but transient. When Lukas first fell, Ebba felt a sense of elation difficult to hide with pretence of shock, but what followed truly shocked her, and now, alongside relief, she felt sorry for Hilda – and for Gareth – and ashamed for having wished it.

As for Galos, her heart went out to him as he sat out there under the longhouse eaves with Tom, Jake and Willett, his head hung low. That final sword swing had been a reflex, self-defence even, but it was also an unforgiveable act. No one went near him or darkened their door, and now the shattered pieces of their lives lay around them, strewn in the silence. Yet they lived – they all lived, but their fates hung by a thread, and something told her Maya's information would be of use.

Pulling away at last, Ebba gave Elsa her most reassuring smile, along with a linen square.

"Come, so many tears help no one. Will you tell me what happened at the ford this morning?"

Elsa pulled away, seeking out Maya, who only stared back, impassive.

"What do you mean?" Elsa reddened, refusing to meet Ebba's eyes – a sure sign something was afoot.

"What do you think I mean?" Ebba jumped up and went to the opening to check on Galos again. The sun beat down on the square, the long shadows of early morning gone, replaced with those growing out from under the eaves. She spun back round. "Maya told me Annerin's gone looking for the witch."

"That's what Fran said." Elsa looked up, blue eyes red-rimmed and wide. "He wanted to come and help Father, but he had to go after Annerin first, so now the house is empty."

"Do you know why they went?" Ebba threw up her arms, narrowly missing Maya. Stepping back, she took a deep breath, pushing away the brewing hysteria she knew would cow both girls into sullen, single word responses.

Elsa fidgeted with the edge of the grey woollen blanket covering her bed. "Fran said she'd gone to get help, because this … this quarrel started the night Arete came."

"What?"

"She told Fran to come to Father, but he went after her instead. What else could he do when she's alone?"

Ebba wasn't sure how much the background to Edwyn's murder mattered anymore, but it meant Annerin and Fran were out of the way, at least for now.

"Perhaps it's for the best, Elsa. They'll come to no harm, and your father has enough to worry about without always thinking of Annerin and Fran."

Elsa looked ready to disagree – after all, who could say what Annerin and Fran would find if they made it as far into the mountains as Lake Everlis? – so Ebba gave both girls a quick hug before ducking back through to the main house space, grabbing a light shawl from the hook and slipping out through the door. As she emerged, she sensed movement opposite and Galos glanced up briefly before his head dropped again. She stepped out into the square, pulling the door gently to behind her.

Fresh air felt good after the time indoors. Ebba caught up an empty jug from the stool beside the door and, with a nod to Tom, strode out across the square towards the well, which was on the far side of March hill, set on a path that followed the loop of the stockade, away from the dwellings and longhouse. When the well came into view, she saw Lukas' kinsmen Wyntr, Seth and Gyll standing by it. They were deep in conversation and still carried their weapons. Doubling back, she instead took a narrow path to the summit, winding back and forth across a hillside alive with the hum of bees on clover. She stopped near the top, at a point where several paths intersected, by a low seat edged on three sides by steep grass banks tight with bramble and foxgloves.

From here, Ebba could see her own front door beyond the roof of the longhouse. She set down the empty jug and forced herself to look south, to where, outside the main gates, men added more wood to an already huge pyre. Ebba's heart faltered at the sight, cold pain in her chest running through her until she no longer felt the sun's heat on her bare head. Unable to watch, she turned to look across the tops of the packed mass of dwellings north of the square. Here, people moved quietly, like so many ants navigating the ginnels between the houses to avoid the square, or stood in gaggles, heads down. Lost in thought, she didn't notice Arthen – March's healer, and an old friend of her father's – until he plumped down heavily beside her.

It took Arthen a while to catch his breath. He looked at her for a moment before tracing a circle in the dust between their two sets of feet. "It seems, my dear, we're back at the beginning again."

"Or the end." Ebba shrugged.

The old man pondered, the light wind catching his thin, white hair and blowing it askew. "No. Galos has finished what he started, but that doesn't make it the end. It makes him a little slow, perhaps." Arthen frowned and clicked his tongue as they watched the men leave the pyre and return through the gate.

"Annerin's gone to look for the witch," said Ebba.

Arthen looked up sharply. "Annerin's gone to see Arete."

"Apparently." Ebba shrugged. *Perhaps Annerin hoped they might be able to flee to Eruthin.*

"A brave thing to do. And what of Fran?"

"He's gone too."

"Ah."

"I don't know what will happen now, Arthen." Ebba fought to keep her voice level.

Arthen scuffed over the circle. "March will eat, then it will light a fire. In the morning a set of bones will be taken to the barrow. After that ..."

One day at a time. "Yes, the ceremony." As she spoke, Ebba realised she was, indeed, hungry.

Arthen patted her on the cheek and, with difficulty, rose and began retracing his steps down the path to the square.

She watched him go, as he shuffled slowly until his stooped figure was lost amid seed heads and tall grass. A cloud of pale butterflies danced across her path, settling beside her on the orchids, then they scattered when a shadow loomed. Cold seized her heart. She turned to find Wyntr and Gyll standing on the hillside behind her, with Seth a little distance behind them. They were looking, not at her but out over March, towards Elden Deas.

Ebba sprang to her feet, snatching up the jug, ready to take flight after Arthen.

"Sit down, woman. If I'd wanted to kill you, your head would've rolled to the bottom of the hill already." Wyntr's smile stopped well short of his eyes.

Ebba fell back down, cold sweat soaking through her dress.

Wyntr and Gyll sprang down from the slope and sat one either side of her.

"Do you want to know what will happen now, Ebba?" Wyntr's voice was impossible to ignore. She turned to meet Lukas' familiar sneer but set on a face young and handsome, with brown eyes glittering cold as ice.

"It's not like you to be short of words, Ebba, but I think you do want to know, so I'll tell you." He paused and, heart hammering, she followed his gaze as it settled on the mountain again. "March will eat. You'll go back to Galos, send Tom, Jake and Willett back to their wives, and then you'll make dinner."

"Then" – Gyll's voice made Ebba spin round – "March will light a fire. Galos, Tom, Jake and Willett will stand side by side with us, and we will light that fire together."

"Elin was my brother," said Wyntr. His stare cut out the sun's heat.

Elin. She knew the name ... Her head spun.

"Roe was our kinsman," said Gyll.

Elin. Roe. The boys killed by the witch. Elin and Roe had been kind and brave. She'd wept for them, long ago.

"I remember them," she said to Gyll. Then she turned back to Wyntr. "I remember them."

"There were no bones to take to the barrow," said Wyntr, turning from Ebba as he spoke. "Only ash. We took ash to the barrow for my brother."

"Annerin's gone looking for the witch." Pure, blind instinct drew the words from Ebba. In the stillness that followed, the hum of the insects seemed a deafening roar.

"My uncle never hated Annerin," Wyntr began, his eyes raking over her now, "but he hated the stranger. I was only a boy, but I remember."

Ebba waited. Despite her fear, she found Wyntr compelling.

"March has lived in peace and plenty for so long, but now we wake from our slumbers and start killing one another in the square. And in the end, it takes a woman to make us want to climb that mountain." Wyntr laughed – a dry, humourless rattle.

Climb the mountain. Ebba's thoughts flashed to Galos. "Why should anyone want to climb the mountain?"

Wyntr looked her over again, this time smiling a little. "Indeed, Ebba, you at least, I didn't take for a fool. Men will follow her ... each with his own reason. I always thought you remarkable for your curiosity. Does the witch hold no interest for you?"

Ebba eyed the path taken by Arthen. The hillside was steep. If she ran, she would fall.

"You're very quiet today, Ebba." Wyntr's hand landed on her sleeve. "Annerin, if she gets that far, will find a still, cold lake and an empty cave. Or maybe the witch sleeps, like March, or perhaps she travels through the mountains and valleys, dining with trolls and goblins."

Ebba recoiled but the hand still gripped her arm. This type of talk wasn't common in March, except among the very old, who generally kept such tales to themselves. The witch's visit was now mentioned with cynicism, the young talking glibly of a lightning strike, while the rest grew to doubt the veracity of their own memories.

"I went up the mountain once, Ebba, when I was young and foolish. There's no cooking pot steaming with the haunches of dead villagers. No mound of skulls and bones. Annerin's son – who is with her, no doubt – will bring her back, and that will be an end to the matter."

The hand let go and a smile flickered. She shivered, the unpinned arm still rigid. Lukas she'd had the weight of, but not this man. She clutched the thin shawl tight about her.

"So, Ebba, now you know what will happen next." Wyntr jumped up, and without so much as a backwards glance led Gyll and Seth back down the path to the well.

Ebba remained, replaying the exchange. Her blind gambit missed the mark, that much she knew, but at least she would be prepared if Galos began any talk about following Annerin, so perhaps she'd had the better of it after all ...

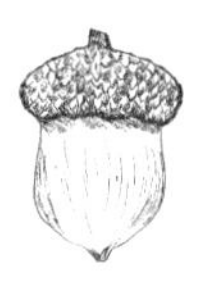

Chapter 13

Ghosts and Dragons

Annerin climbed through thinning woodland, stumbling continually over exposed rock. Ahead, the roar of the waterfall at the Rumbling Crags filled the air as streams from Lake Everlis tumbled down the mountainside. The air itself felt moist, as if it held the mist of the falls, but perhaps this was simply a trick of the growing heat and her nagging thirst.

She weighed the almost empty waterskin and sighed. Having eaten and drunk as she walked, only a hardening crust remained, along with a handful of wild strawberries picked along the way. *What to do now? And why even come this way?* In her haste to disappear before Fran woke, after crossing the river at the ford she had turned south into the forest, making for Spiral Cove, but this route was longer and now meant following the escarpment to the foot of the pass. The old rangers' trail leading straight to the pass would have made better sense but meant travelling in the open along the forest's edge or going via the rise then heading east.

Annerin slumped down between the spreading roots of an ash, amid brittle, grey seed pods and cushions of moss. The earth beneath was dry, the clinging dampness of early morning long gone as midday approached. Beside her, a ladybird crawled on one of last summer's curling leaves. She surveyed the scratches crisscrossing her forearms. Along with the strawberries, miserable tangles of briars grew all about, often covering the meagre patches of fruit.

She finished those berries now and rested her head against the rough bark, closing her eyes for a few moments – as long as she dared this deep in the forest. Having slept fitfully the night before, her mind drifted after the small patches of cloud shifting above the canopy and her eyelids grew heavy, letting shapes float behind closed lids. First, the face of a woman imperceptibly became one of a pig, then the fur of a speckled doe slowly deepened into golden scales and watching animal eyes melded into the more knowing stare of a dragon. A grunt came from close by, and Annerin realised she had fallen asleep. Too tired to fight the stupor, she knew the height of the day was, perhaps, the safest time of any to sleep alone in the forest, so she held her father's sword between her knees, draped her cloak across the top, and let go, just for a little while …

Annerin snapped awake. The crashing water seemed louder, and the sun was directly overhead. She rose, her head spinning as she saw bursts of light. Leaning back against the ash to steady herself, she finished the last few sips of lukewarm water and the bread, put her cloak away, fixed the sword to her belt and set off in the direction of the waterfall.

She had not gone far, climbing through tangles of briar and coarse grass, when the trees fell away abruptly, and Annerin found herself staring up at sheer cliffs towering away in each direction as far as she could see. High up, green ledges met blue sky and falcons wheeled, wings spread to catch the wind. To her right, water tumbled, seeming like a living thing as it fell headlong down the rock face, bounding from rocky ledges and outcrops into the pool below before fanning out into forest streams.

Annerin filled her waterskin at the first stream, drained it, and then refilled it again. When she drew nearer, she craned her neck to see the head of the waterfall, imagining Lake Everlis lapping at the edge of the cliffs, and the woman she sought, if woman she was, looking out, forest stretching away beneath her feet. Unbidden tears came, stinging and flooding unchecked down her cheeks. With their salt on her lips, she turned away, making for Spiral Cove to the east, feeling utterly lost, but for the first time that day, she acknowledged to herself exactly where she was going and why.

Often stumbling and sometimes falling, Annerin walked away from the Rumbling Crags, over boulders and strewn rock beneath the sheer walls of Elden Deas. The forest grew thick on her left, its shade almost black in the brightness of the day, and the ground rolled and buckled beneath her, stunted blackthorn tangling in the grikes. The unyielding grey of the mountainside radiated the sun's heat. Weary from the day's walking, lack of food and her earlier tears, when she entered the rocky amphitheatre of Spiral Cove, she wanted nothing more than to sleep. The place was a cauldron of heat, dry as the bones buried there, and the air was still and thick so that even the silence seemed to echo back, magnifying itself off the walls.

Annerin sat down with her back against an angle of smooth rock and took a long swig of water. The scarf tied around her head was baking hot, and her head with it. Seeking out shade, she looked about her. It was just the way she'd imagined – a vast, empty space strewn with endless shapeless heaps of broken rock. Boulders and fragments rested against one another at impossible angles, and twisted, tortured hawthorns tried to find their way into a space which could only truly be owned by the ancient dead who rested there. To her left, the abrupt lushness of the forest curved away, as if cowed by the sheer might of the cliff face.

Above, the sun slid west, offering a little shade beneath the cliff behind her, but Annerin no longer had the strength to stand. Instead, she moistened the headscarf and retied it, giving a little relief to her aching head. Again, she tried to move towards the cliff base, but her clothes were damp with sweat and even the small pool of shade growing in the lee of the rocks where she sat made her shiver. Her eyelids could not bear their own weight, and with the scabbard pressed against her thigh and the shield and cloak slung protectively across her chest, she sank down and down into a sleep which did not ask or care which little cairn, of the many dotted around and about the cove, belonged to Edwyn.

When Annerin woke, refreshed from her sleep, the afternoon heat of Spiral Cove had mellowed into the gentler warmth of evening. Looking around, she noticed a tiny stream tracing its way from the foot of the cliff out towards the forest. She followed it back to the cliff face, where it sprang from the entrance of a small cave at the base.

Stooping to drink, she splashed her face with the clear, cold water before ducking into the cave. Beyond the low arch at its mouth, the cave went straight on, tunnel-like, for the short distance the light penetrated. Annerin took a few careful steps forwards until the floor fell away quite suddenly and she half skidded downwards, towards a passage twisting away into complete darkness.

Inching forwards, her toes traced at the smooth rock floor, but without warning she slipped and lost her footing, sliding again, this time into water – deep, cold water. Still water. It wrapped around her, and she plunged downwards, water covering her head before she had time to do anything other than gulp clammy air. Arms flailing, Annerin sank further, taken by a spinning current as if she were being swallowed by the earth.

She registered the numbing cold and the sickness from being spun, but she didn't register fear. A notion of purpose and direction took hold until she felt herself rising, moving towards light. Soon, blackness gave way to orange sun, mauve sky and green forest. When she reached the surface, she floated, her mind bobbing anchorless, the puppetry of clouds playing overhead.

Annerin lay in the water, full of morning drowsiness despite the setting sun, her thoughts slowly shuffling. Then she snapped awake. She recalled the cliffs in Spiral Cove, the stream and cave, but she was in a different place now. Tall mountain pines towered above her, and the water was shallow enough to stand, with smooth pebbles shifting beneath the soles of her feet – the edge of a lake with a narrow shoreline quickly giving way to sparse, straight trees. Recognising the peak of Elden Deas rising behind the opposite shore, she guessed she must be standing in Lake Everlis. Annerin walked out of the water, an unformed question nagging as she noticed a small sunlit clearing with a boulder on which she could sit and dry out.

Yellow moss dappled the boulder's surface, and she perched on a flat section with the sun warming her back, although the shade of the trees loomed not far behind. She shivered, pulling free her headscarf and wringing her dripping hair. Water spattered the carpet of browning pine needles. There were dry clothes in her pack, but where was her pack? Stashed in the lee of a different boulder ... no matter now. Nothing was clear, and her mind felt like a basket of tangled fleece as she scanned the plateau stretching around her.

The lake was framed on three sides by tall pines, creating a pleasant mountain glade. To the north and south, the belt of trees was thin before the ground dropped away, affording views for many leagues. Ahead, to the east, the peak rose steeply above the water. Behind, the mountain chain framing Eruthin dominated. Annerin took off her boots, and she wrung out her socks, the hem of her dress and her apron. Pine needles lay thick and warm beneath her feet, and rolling her skirt to her knees, she moved onto the ground, leaning back and stretching out her legs in the sun, but in the instant before closing her eyes, a movement caught her attention from across the lake, some little distance away, on the opposite shore. A tall auburn-haired woman, wearing a long dress, mauve like the sky, stood with her back to Annerin and the water, facing the entrance of a cave.

As Annerin watched, a man emerged from the cave. He was tall and slim with dark hair, but he was too far away for her to see his features clearly. With her heart beating hard against her ribs, she remembered the blue eyes and once familiar smile. He looked remarkably like Fran, but how could it be Fran with ... well, an auburn-haired woman who surely must be Arete? Although she had expected an ancient to look older, and this woman only looked some thirty summers, perhaps a little more. She recalled her grandmother's tales of Arete; there were many stories but few descriptions, and after that terrible midwinter night people began calling her a witch, so now everyone pictured a hag.

Thought after thought flashed through Annerin's head like sparks igniting a forest fire – questions never framed before. Arete who dwelt on the mountain was a constant in March. She was also an idea, a myth, thunder and lightning, ogre and scapegoat, almost lost beyond memory, scarcely believed, a fairy tale to frighten children but one the grown-ups secretly feared too ... and it wasn't Fran across the water. Annerin choked back bile, her throat burning and a sting in her eyes. Her wet clothes clung to her shivering body and pain pierced her heart like a ragged blade of ice.

The man opposite was Edwyn.

She recognised his red tunic from that long-ago day he arrived in March. Staggering, and with her vision blurring, she slumped down on the boulder. *But Edwyn died.* Then her parents carried his body the long, weary way to Spiral Cove – didn't they? It seemed implausible, and now she realised it had always seemed implausible, the doubt always kept at bay, in the depths of her mind, away from the light. And the packet Edwyn secretly carried – something had made her bring it today, as if it were a lucky amulet. She took it out and opened it. It contained a little lock of auburn hair, tied neatly with fine leather cord. She stared at it, trying to fathom what it all meant, having clung to this little packet for so many summers and winters, remembering only that Edwyn came to March – chose her. She had always known the lock of hair belonged to Arete, and because of it she'd known Arete was solid and real – not just a willowy voice calling out in the night – but not this real, not this unbearably, vividly whole and real.

Numbly, Annerin watched the two figures sit down to eat in the evening sun, the light of a small fire flickering between them. Perhaps she could hear laughter carrying across Lake Everlis; perhaps it was the wind. They were far away, but it was as if Annerin could see the tiny wrinkles at the corners of their eyes when they smiled at one another. It was as if she could smell the grease covering their fingers and lips. She saw Edwyn's red shirt and black hair, and the mauve dress, in her mind's eye trimmed with silver, bright against the red hair.

Sunlight lit the colours, and from the shade where she stood, her wet grey dress and apron sagging around her ankles, she could not watch anymore. She turned away and moved between the pines, drifting through carpets of needles, sick and hollow inside, just a wraith, everything real ripped from her and discarded in the water.

But then Annerin thought again, and this thought sparked the tinder. She turned back and, looking to the eastern sky, saw a crescent moon, when that morning she had left with a near full moon setting behind her. Squinting across the water, she focused on the red of Edwyn's shirt. Edwyn looked like Fran because when she knew him, he had been little older than Fran, and it was a young man she now saw, arms pillowing his head as he lay on a bed of pine needles outside the cave in the last of the evening sun.

Annerin stared until her eyes grew dry and a warm breeze blew across the water, making the surface ripple. The ripples spread, while overhead, the branches rustled as they swayed, their shadows playing on the water. Annerin's head swam. Edwyn slipped out of focus ...

Annerin blinked, then she blinked again, but now the opposite shore was empty, and the crescent moon had been replaced by one near full. She returned to her seat by the log, and her eyelids grew unbearably heavy.

Edwyn sat up, peering out across the lake. Arete stirred, and a frown flitted across her face when she noticed the lowering water, but she only smiled before drifting back to sleep as he idly twisted a lock of her hair about his fingers.

Careful not to pull, he ran the lock across the sharpened blade of the sword lying at his side and tucked it into a tattered pouch on his belt. Clarity came, a wind blowing through the fog of his mind. Memory followed, flickers of hearth and home, and the pain of a summer dream ending. Grabbing his sword, he stole away east towards where the Nethermore Pass led downhill, breaking into a run as the surface of the water settled back to a flat polished grey.

With the last rays of the setting sun picking out the top of the cliffs at Spiral Cove, the dragon Ladon, emerged from an already dark forest, mounted the first rise of rock and stretched out his wings. Had there been anyone to see him, they might have thought he grew in stature. Equally, they might have rubbed their eyes, attempting to focus on an image never quite fully solid or real, and in the growing darkness they would have told themselves that perhaps no dragon existed, only tricks and patterns in the fading light. They would, however, have found it harder to ignore the snort echoing around the cove, or the acrid smell of smoke emitted when Ladon's nostrils flared as he caught an unfamiliar scent.

It was not long before Annerin's sword, shield, cloak and pack also caught his attention, and he flicked them out into the open with one movement of a heavy claw. Eyes narrowing, he surveyed the worn and snagged grey wool of the cloak and the dull, pitted blade. Then he crouched to look around the cove before folding his wings and lumbering towards the mouth of the cave discovered by Annerin a short time before.

When Ladon approached the narrow entrance, it was as if his wings folded until he became small enough to fit through, and then he too followed the tunnel to where it descended into darkness, with water on one side and a passage rising on the other. He followed the passage, climbing for some little time until, eventually, weak light from above told him he drew near, and he emerged from a low entrance, partially concealed by bracken, into the forest beside Lake Everlis. Dusk had fallen, and the trees towered black all around him. He moved through them, towards the lake. Orange embers in his nostrils gave enough light for reptilian eyes, accustomed to dwelling underground, to make out something lying prone on the shore. Bending down to sniff, Ladon encountered an inert pile of wet skin and clothing.

Carefully probing the bundle with the flat of his snout, Ladon flicked Annerin over onto her front, opened his jaws around her, and then gently lifted her clear of the floor before stretching, spreading his wings and lifting off. It was a short flight back to Spiral Cove, where he set her down. Towering over her, he tilted his head to one side in the manner of a child who, having discovered an injured bird, wonders how best to help.

His sharp eyes picked out the ripped cloth, torn against his sharp teeth when he carried her. Stretching his neck towards the darkened sky, he beat his wings and vented steam before stooping again to hook a tooth through the ties at the back of her dress and dragging her towards the sheltered point at the edge of the cove where her possessions lay.

Annerin's head bounced against the rocky slabs as Ladon set her down. Her eyes flickered, but either this second view of Ladon, or the smoke billowing from his nostrils, perilously near her face and making a small cloud in the cleft of the rock, caused her to lose consciousness again.

Ladon went to the forest's edge and tore down a swathe of branches from the nearest tree, then he returned and dropped them some little way from where Annerin lay. One large claw stamped them down and swept them together in a heap before the dragon let out a breath of fire to set the pile alight. He returned to the forest for more broken branches until a small bonfire spat and crackled in front of Annerin. It shed an eerie orange light over the sleeping woman and dragon, flitting off the high walls of the cove and dancing with rock shadows.

Chapter 14

Night Sky and Firelight

The sun fell away, leaving the sky rosy in the west, but the eastern horizon held the pallor of sour milk. Ebba watched Arthen, Vanna and the other elders lead every man, woman and child out through the southern gate of March, making a slow, silent chain that encircled the pyre.

Only Gareth, who still lay insensible – unaware of his father's death – remained inside the stockade. Hilda made a sorry sight, falling behind, and she was now almost at the back, supported by her sister and cousin, blind to the words of those turning to commiserate.

Ebba held her head high and kept her distance, a daughter on each arm, the air around her charged as if with thunder. Part of her wanted to scream that Galos stayed his hand – walked away. Their own kin acknowledged this. Perhaps the rest would remember in the morning. But not tonight. Not now. Now they must stand behind Wyntr, and alongside Hilda and her sister, and bow their heads while the pyre burnt.

Galos, meanwhile, already stood watch with a small group of his men, a little way back from the main circle. He remained silent, and she could not tell whether his baleful looks spelt remorse or recrimination. It was tiresome, this refusal to talk, and tomorrow would be harder than today. Yet unfinished business had stalked March for as long as she could remember. It took a strong spark to make things flare. Like Arthen said, who could know what would happen next?

In any case, the harvest loomed, and it took all hands to bring in the grain. Fight now and by late winter they would starve. And then there was the daily necessity of tending to the cattle, hunting, spinning, mending the thatch ... The list went on; today was an aberration – the pyre a beacon marking an end.

Arthen droned prayers and Ebba's mind churned. Wyntr lit the hay at the foot of the pyre and spirals of smoke twisted in the still air, followed by a roar and rush as dry wood caught. Before long, Lukas' body disappeared behind a wall of hungry flames, orange against the growing night.

Wind gusted, eddying pungent smoke. People retreated – mothers snatching up little children and making haste towards home, older children running ahead. The rest pulled cloaks around their noses and mouths and turned their backs on this lively fire, wanting instead their own supper and steady hearth. Lastly, the gaggles of elders retreated, congregating in the square to say again all those things each knew by heart but needed to hear repeated in the cadence of another's voice.

At last, only Wyntr, Seth and Gyll remained, seated some little way from the pyre, watching bright flames flicker against a darkening sky. A large funeral urn rested on the ground between them, along with waterskins and bundles of food for the morning's journey to the barrows. These were several leagues away, on an outcrop rising from the marshy wasteland to the east. Three horses were hobbled beside the palisade, out of sight of the gate because it was usual for a pilgrimage to the barrows to be made on foot, and Wyntr did not wish to court the disapproval of the elders.

As night fell the three men set themselves down to rest, huddling under their cloaks for warmth, their bundles makeshift pillows. The nearby animals huddled, ears pricking at the hoot of owls swooping at the field's edges, and alert to the scent of badgers and foxes moving across banks and through ditches, where the lower slopes of March hill flattened off into scrubland and marsh.

From her seat high on the mountainside, Arete looked out towards March and saw three fires. One flickered several leagues away to the north, outside the stockade; another burnt large and bright below her in Spiral Cove. The third was faint – a line of smoke rising from the forest away to the east, near the foot of the Nethermore Pass.

While sleeping in the evening sun at the mouth of her cave, she had dreamt strange dreams and now a discord of voices echoed in her mind, leading her up onto the grassy slope and vantage point above the cave mouth. She tapped the red rose in the centre of the sword clasped between her knees. *So much time gone since that awful night.* Enough time for her once bright dress to turn ragged and grey, its silver trim frayed to nothing. *Not enough time for them to forget, though.* But now they needed her again. Turning away, she stared ahead into the blackness of the night, towards the hidden valley where Eruthin lay.

After a time, the sound of great wings cutting the air filled the glade, and Ladon appeared above the pines surrounding the lake, his vast, jagged outline set against the night sky as he circled high above the water before dropping the sacks he carried in his claws, then he landed beside her.

"Dear one, remind me, how long has it been since that night?" Arete asked the dragon when he came to rest.

Ladon slowly turned his head and looked down at her, his amber eyes narrowing. The cavernous mouth, with its sharp yellow teeth, was not made to form words, but the gentlest cloud of smoke drifted over Arete, and she heard his thoughts in answer.

"Enough seasons for time to rot the dress you wear." Ladon's tone carried a sigh – small gesture, but sky and earth from a dragon.

"Suddenly, I recall that evening as if it were yesterday."

"Enough seasons have passed for a child to be born and grow into a man," answered the smoke. "But now I sense the time has come for me to fly west and steal a new gown for you."

She laughed, hollowness filling her. "Yes, and still we must steal. Even when our beloved Krataia hoards gold enough to buy me a hundred dresses in the markets of the west but still prefers to use it as a cushion."

Ladon blew another haze of smoke – both shrug and smile – and Arete scrambled down to the cave mouth and ferried the sacks inside.

"And so, what now?" she asked, emerging from the cave to where Ladon rested, his tail flicking the dark surface of the lake, cascading water in silvery arcs.

"Fly."

Arete climbed up onto Ladon's leg, across the wing and swung her leg over his back, folding her arms around the great neck and leaning her cheek against his scales. They felt cold and clean, and the weariness of ages seemed to fall away as Ladon's wings beat and the dragon soared into the night sky.

Beneath them, the lake shrank away in the moonlight, and as the land got further away, the sky grew. The east of the vault was indigo, shot with blue and lilac and peppered with stars that spun out like streaming ribbons, some as tiny as the finest grain, and others like far off discs of gold, silver and red. Ladon circled the lake again and swept out over the cliff.

"Where shall we fly?" he asked as he crossed the dark bulk of the forest, heading towards the Starling Wood.

"A new gown can wait a little longer. Let's go to the house where my sword is kept."

Ladon did not answer immediately but followed the line of the forest clearing and lighted down at the ford. "The sword isn't here. Its young master carries it, and he sleeps in the forest."

Ladon's words repeated in Arete's head. *A slip of the tongue from a dragon.* The location of the sword was a moot point between them; Ladon thought it safer where it was. She remembered the smallest of the three fires, then she looked towards the stone house, a short distance away, black and silent in the moonlight.

"A fire burnt tonight in March," she said, changing the subject. "We shall visit them. Let's go and see the little dwellings and the longhouse my dear Vaden built when he was king, so very long ago now."

Ladon slowly lifted into the air again, circling low over the wood before turning back to fly high over the ford, and higher still to pass over March.

"Look, Ladon, the pyre burns low, and there are three men outside, guarding it."

"I see them, Arete. They bear us great ill will."

"I feel it too, but I don't want to see these people hurt again. They're Vaden's kin, but they no longer know me."

"You've wandered in the mountains for too long and passed out of time and mind."

"Set me down a little way from them."

Ladon landed out on the plain behind March, on grassland dotted with brakes of hawthorn, briar and fading yellow gorse. Arete climbed down and took her bearings. The grass was course beneath her feet, dotting in clumps, and she picked her way towards where the three were sleeping, avoiding the trails of bramble reaching out from the shadows of crouching thickets. Two older men lay side by side with one much younger set a little apart, a small iron cauldron by his side. Their fire was dying, only embers flickering, its last heat catching on the eddying breeze. She stood between them, frowning down at the two older men and reached for the hilt of her sword. Her fingers drummed on the crossguard; something unseen shuffled in the undergrowth nearby and the silhouette of a bat shot low overhead. She shivered, turning to the younger one and bending down to look more closely at a pale, narrow face beneath a mop of sandy hair, with barely the beginnings of a beard. Relaxing her grip on the hilt, she rose, watching a patch of cloud track over the moon before turning to look for the reassuring glow of Ladon's nostrils. *Fire that never dies. Hearth and home.* How she loved him.

Moving towards the open gate of the stockade, Arete caught a movement some distance away on the perimeter. She crept closer, sensing fear, then she smelt the grassy tang of manure. There were three horses – the poor beasts left hobbled on open ground and now with a dragon nearby. She untied their ropes, whispering nonsense words of reassurance before setting them free to roam.

After this, she returned to Ladon and climbed onto his back. The wind from his wings unnerved the animals again and she heard them canter away, their hooves thudding softly then fading as Ladon turned and flew back towards the mountain.

"These men have long nursed dreams of vengeance, Arete. They climbed the mountain not many summers ago, and found nothing but an empty cave, and our pet to frighten their horses."

"They bear me great ill will, as you say. They still seek revenge for their kinsmen, but they'll seek it more slowly on foot."

"I sense their thoughts drifting beyond revenge now. They show grief, but their hearts hunger for power."

"But they're not responsible for this pyre. There's something else – the silver sword. It wakes and troubles them from their peace."

"Their own nature troubles them from their peace, Arete."

Ladon landed on the sparce grass above the cave, and Arete slipped down from his back, giving the scaled neck a last embrace before striding down the mountainside and scrambling down the final slope and round to the mouth of the cave. A pair of eyes glittered from the recesses, locating the wildcat adopted by Arete several winters ago, now temporarily woken from her sleep. Thumps from overhead reverberated through the hillside, then the interior of the cave turned from grey to impenetrable black as Ladon lay down across its entrance. Fumbling in the gloom, Arete reached towards the embers of the fire near the cave's entrance, poking them and adding fresh tinder. Soon, orange flames flickered below the pot, and a pool of amber light grew, pushing back the shadows.

Arete looked around, glad to be home, and glad of the reassuring presence of Ladon at the door. The flickering light revealed so many comforting things – myriad ledges and holes set in the walls contained bottles and boxes, or such things as knives, ladles, spoons, bowls and beakers. Where the cave widened, a vast pair of antlers ornamented the wall, casting crooked shadows in the firelight onto a great rug made from the skins of many deer and set beneath a narrow ledge seat running around the cave's edge. Above it, an ancient tangle of lines that made maps and symbols filled the wall – circles connected to one another by lines. Problems so old they fell almost from memory, hers at least. On the far side, a wide ledge, covered in skins ranging from white through to fawn and then to black, made a sleeping platform, and a canopy of ancient and faded crimson silk spanned the ceiling, its corners held fast by lumps of clay moulded to the roof.

Beyond this living area, the cave continued some way, narrowing before it reached a side chamber hewn out to form a pantry. The haunch of a deer and several bundles of herbs hung from iron pins in the roof. Arete went there now, intent on finding supper. Beneath the hooks, a high wooden table held several ceramic jars of various sizes that were filled with wine, dried fruits and grain. One of the new sacks lay out on top, covering a dry loaf, a block of cheese flecked with green at its edges and a fist of ham that emitted a strong, smoky odour. Arete set some bread, cheese, ham and fruit on a plate, half-filled a pitcher with wine, and returned to the fire.

"You say the boy with the silver sword – Edwyn's son – is in the forest," she asked Ladon, stroking the sleeping cat as she spoke.

"He's on his way here."

"Why so?"

"There was an accident in the wood. I surprised a young man – one not accustomed to seeing me – and he fell unconscious. I thought to return him home once darkness fell, but someone ... one of the villagers, claimed him. Now they accuse Edwyn's son of hurting this young man, and by and by their chief is dead." Ladon turned away, smoke enough to fill the cave billowing from his nostrils.

"You're angry. Why?"

"No matter."

"You're fond of the boy – Edwyn's son."

"I hear him speak. And perhaps he hears me."

"Oh." Arete put down the poker and sat back, her food and wine forgotten. Those with the ability to speak with dragons were rare. Her own father had been one such man, gifting a dragon egg to each of his three children. Krataia hatched from Arete's egg, but now they were estranged and barely spoke. Krataia's anger was a slow, smouldering thing, and Arete remained unforgiven for the loss of the dragon, Thalia, along with her rider, Dalred, who was Arete's own brother, and also for the death of their poor sister, Everlis, who had been Ladon's rider, and after whom the lake was named. Such was the price of helping Vaden when, two hundred summers ago, he marched to Eruthin to confront ... well, to face *him*.

"Do not think of him. If he moves again, I will know."

She took a deep breath and pushed the memory back. "Someone claimed the young man, you say. Do you mean the woman Annerin?"

Smoke billowed again before Ladon answered. "Yes."

"And so, that was my dream. She came and rescued Edwyn from me." Arete sighed.

"Yes."

"You're talkative tonight, Ladon, but it wasn't the silver sword that woke the people of March from their peace – it was you."

"Indeed."

Arete smelt heat in the smoke and remained silent. *Ladon didn't have Krataia's temper, but still ...*

"But I must watch over the silver sword," he continued. "Besides, they don't normally believe what they see. Dragons aren't in fashion in March, but then neither are witches."

"Witches!" Arete snatched up the poker and the cat slunk away. *Misunderstood creatures, always, witches.* But since that night, that was how they thought of her. She recalled the boy in the red tunic who had been her friend. He'd carried her away through the snow ... *Oh, why had the other two acted so ... swords drawn ... why not listen? But when did humans ever listen?* It had all been over so quickly, but she hated the snow and long nights even now.

At first Edwyn thought she'd come to reclaim her sword, but no ... *If it had only been that simple.* Besides, he'd have given it up ten times over rather than hear the news she brought from Eruthin ... *Poor Edwyn.* Maybe he picked up the wrong sword in his haste to leave, but he might as well have taken a grinding stone and hung it about his neck—

She stopped, suddenly realising that moonlight flooded the cave. Looking up, she saw Ladon watching her.

"Why are you smiling?" she challenged him.

"Because the world is turning, and now the silver sword is coming back."

Chapter 15

Stew and Suspicion

Sunlight filtered through thatch where pillars met roof. Gareth twisted, freeing his shoulder, then he let the criss-crossed patterns drift to a smudge behind closed eyelids. He lay like this for a while, but when the effort of waking became too much, he slid down into a parched dreamscape, turning corners, following voices that were always just out of reach. He checked the longhouse, but the voices were outside, and when he went outside again, peering down the narrow alleys between the dwellings, each was empty. This torture repeated until nearby sobbing pulled him free, and Gareth spied his mother seated beside him, head bent, her greying hair parted unevenly. He remained quiet, focusing again on the familiar morning tracery winking above him as pieces tumbled into place ... *Annerin ... the wood ...*

Before long, Aunt Reya came in, easing the door shut behind her and greeting Hilda in a whisper. Gareth's eyelids shut and he breathed long slow breathes until the silent weight of scrutiny receded and his mother sniffed, scraped her chair, and then shuffled away towards table and fire. This gave him some privacy because although his cot was in the main room (his parent's cabin being set behind a partition, beyond the hearth), two adjacent timber pillars surrounded by suspended clothing and baskets partially shielded his bed from view.

He opened his eyes and glanced around. The way the light pierced the straw at the eaves meant it was mid-morning, but the slight movement of craning to see it tweaked his side and back. He winced at the sharp rawness trapping the linen of his shirt. An accident in the wood ... somehow, but he would mend. Surely his mother could see that, and yet among the sniffs he still caught an occasional sob.

His stomach growled and his thoughts turned to food. He sniffed the air for cooking smells, but only the stale memory of yesterday's stew hung in the stuffy air. *Why were the shutters closed?* Dust motes wheeled in the shafts of sunlight permeating at the eaves, and the door and shutters stood black in bright frames. Gloom held sway – hushed gloom, filled with whispers, the scrape of flint and the snap of kindling. *What on the good green earth engrossed them so much?*

Silence fell at the other end of the room, followed by more shuffling around the hearth before the whispering started again. Straining to hear, he caught only odd words. Gareth leant up on one elbow, wincing when the linen of his shirt pulled free. *Annerin ... the wood ...*

The whispering stopped abruptly. Raya peered round at him, while his mother's chair jolted backwards and she appeared too, mouth agog, as if he were a phantom. Her haggard look made Gareth recoil. She flinched, but then she darted to his side, taking her seat again, wordless, searching him, as if for something lost, brushing at her tear-stained face, breath ragged.

"Mother. Mother, dear. What's the matter?" Gingerly, he sat up, reaching for her hand.

There was no reply, only the wide, lost, red-ringed eyes searching at him, a note of recrimination amid the sorrow.

Raya carried a stool across and wedged it between him and his mother. "Gareth, we're glad to see you awake at last. How are you feeling?"

"Well, I'm all right, but clearly, you're not. What's happened here? I can't remember properly."

"You've been unconscious for two nights. You were injured in the forest. Your ... your father brought you back, and yesterday we couldn't wake you. Your mother's been frantic, haven't you, Hilda?"

His mother's head sank, and she cried into her apron. Great ragged sobs.

Gareth's chest tightened. *Where was Father with all this grief?* He lowered his feet to the floor and put his arms around her. After a moment she drew back, wiping away tears.

"It has been difficult." Fighting back sobs, she straightened her back and blew her nose.

Raya turned from one to the other before standing up. "The fire's lit, so I'll make tea. Gareth, you must be hungry. Will you eat something?"

"Yes, thanks, Raya. That would be good," said Gareth before turning back to his mother. "My head hurts, and I'm cut and bruised in many places, but otherwise ..." He shrugged, unsure what else to add and needing time to remember; what was it? Fear ... and then wild hope. Wild hope – a cloudburst in the chest. The dizzying childhood joy of spinning in his grandfather's arms. *Annerin ... the wood ...*

His mother's sigh drew him back to the close, darkened room. "We were hoping you could remember what happened. It was ... it was that ... it was the widow from the stone house by the ford who found you, I think."

Again, the spark caught tinder ...

Gareth looked past his mother and at the light ready to burst through the shutter opposite – radiant light trapped behind the meanest scraps of timber. His thoughts reached out for it as he fought to remember, but all he could see was Annerin. Annerin in the wood.

"I remember Fran blowing a hunting horn ... and I remember Annerin."

His mother's expression grew cold. Her forehead creased and her gaze flashed towards the door.

Gareth quailed, fearing his father returning, but somehow he was unable to resist the urge to say that name – to break the spell, slay the dragon, breathe the clean air ...

"Annerin looked after me." Gareth focused on the brightness, but just then the sun slipped behind a cloud. "There was something in the forest ..."

His mother waited, unblinking.

"Something attacked me. It seized me, but Annerin was there. She was carrying a sword. She stood by me. I think she saved my life."

Hilda gasped, her eyes narrowing and mouth curling. The change happened almost imperceptibly, but it had all the power of a ragged blade in his chest.

She turned, searching out Raya, who moved in a flash from the hearth, her face – a rounder and softer version of his mother's – tight, gaze darting between them.

"He has no sword wound."

His mother spun in the chair. "So, what does that prove, exactly?"

Raya took a step back. "He has a nasty head wound, though." Raya flew towards Gareth, hand reaching for the back of his head, checking while she spoke. "And some nasty bruises and scratches on his back." She pulled at his shirt, fanning cool air over the wounds. Pushing back the stool, his mother loomed over him too, peering down at his exposed back.

Gareth snatched his shirt from them and jumped to his feet, making the two retreat a step.

"You say the woman from the stone house stood over you with a sword." His mother drew herself up as she spoke, voice quivering.

"No, I said she saved my life. She was carrying a sword and she tried to protect me."

"Protect you against what exactly?"

"I ... I don't know. I remember seeing yellow eyes." Gareth slumped back onto his bed, hugging his knees to his chest. "You say Father brought me back. Where is he?"

"Hilda, your son needs to eat. The stew's hot and the water's near boiling."

His mother threw up her hands and returned to the fire.

"I'm sorry, Gareth, I just wanted to check your injuries." Raya reached over to take his hand, but Gareth turned away, resting his head on his knees.

"What's going on, Raya?" he asked, turning back to her when the silence stretched thin, and he looked properly at her for the first time. Despite the poor light, her face looked haggard too.

"So much happened yesterday, Gareth. People thought Fran attacked you in the wood because you went there with Elsa."

"Elsa?" *Elsa and Annerin*. Faces merged and Gareth's head swam. Pretty Elsa, who he could not talk to because ... because she loved Fran ... because she was bright and funny, and he dull as rock ... because she was young, and he was not ... because the joy was long gone from him ... because, because, because ...

"Gareth?"

"We lost Maya in the wood. I went to look for her."

Raya just stared, her mouth falling open slightly and her gaze raked him as he curled tighter.

"Did Elsa find Maya?" he asked.

"Yes – well she's back at home anyway, so someone must have found her."

"Good. We were so worried, although I don't know why the child wandered off in the first place."

"Wasn't she with you and Elsa?"

"Yes, but she wouldn't keep up, and when we looked back, she'd disappeared."

Raya acknowledged this with a nod and waited for him to continue.

"We thought she'd gone to the stone house, so we went there first. Annerin was there, but she didn't want to speak to me, so I went to look for Maya."

"I see."

Behind Raya, his mother sidled into view, ladle in hand, then she disappeared again as the water cauldron bubbled, its splashes making the fire hiss.

"Was Fran at the house?" Raya asked eventually.

"No. I don't think so. I didn't see him if he was."

"And when you looked for the girl?"

Gareth let his mind wander back. He caught a whiff of mint from the water pot where the tea brewed and it took him back to the small garden at the stone house, with its herbs tangling and the branches of the silver birch swaying, making shadows that reached for the sunny herb patch, grasping but never quite reaching. The memory was sharp, like a turn in the road or a change in the weather.

"I couldn't find Maya," he said at last. *Not the answer to the question asked, but then ...* "It's no wonder they get back late if she wanders off like that all the time. I walked quite far into the forest, I suppose

– I kept thinking I saw movement – and then ... and then, well, a hunting horn sounded, and something reared up. I remember falling then being grabbed and lifted up. I couldn't rightly say what it was."

Enough said. More than enough. Food beckoned, so he swung his legs down, stretching as much as he dared without pulling at his cuts, and went to the table.

Raya and his mother sat down, one on either side of him, to drink their tea.

Several portions of stew later, Gareth finished chewing his last mouthful, set down his spoon, met Aunt Raya's steady gaze then turned to his mother, who set down a half-empty cup of cold tea, and waited.

"If you had to guess, Gareth, what would you say attacked you?" Raya asked.

Gareth cleared his throat and took a swig of tepid tea. "I thought at first it was a really big stag, but I wasn't sure ... Had it been a bear, I don't think I'd be sitting here now, but ..."

Raya shivered. "True enough."

"Surely you'd recognise a stag – however big." His mother's eyes gleamed dangerously.

"Well ..."

"Oh, for goodness' sake, Gareth. Isn't it obvious Fran attacked you?" The curl of the lip grew.

Gareth stifled a belch, the stew suddenly a dead weight in his stomach. "Why would Fran attack me?"

"Because you were with Elsa."

His mother radiated accusation, but how could she think this? That Fran and Annerin would attack him – try to kill him – all because he walked to the wood with Elsa. It sounded ridiculous. Gareth remembered Annerin – the time spent in the wood – and he knew, without a shadow of doubt, it *was* ridiculous.

Raya reached over and touched his arm. "Gareth, that's what your father thought. He believed Annerin and Fran planned to kill you rather than let you take Elsa away."

"But Father's always disliked Annerin and Fran, anyway. He can't bear to see Fran in the settlement, but isn't that just because he hated his father so much?"

His mother straightened, turning to her sister for support, but Raya looked away.

"The quarrel between your father and Fran's father took place a very long time ago. Much has happened since," said his mother.

Nothing has happened since, and that is not an answer.

"It just seems obvious they did something to you," said Raya. "They ... they knocked you senseless somehow, and you thought you saw some ... some creature."

"Father can say what he wants, but I'll have no part in it. Annerin saved my life. I'll tell that to anyone who asks."

The squeal of his mother's chair leg against the hearthstone made Gareth jump. She stalked away to her bed, behind the partition.

"Gareth."

Raya waited.

"Yesterday your father and Galos ... it happened in the square. They fought."

"Where is Father?"

"They fought."

"Raya. No."

"Gareth, your father died yesterday."

The floor lurched. The room swam.

Raya caught him by the wrists.

"It was an accident. All of March went to your father's funeral last night." Raya's grip tightened. "Wyntr, Gyll and Seth have taken his bones to the barrows. We didn't know when you would be well again. We couldn't wake you."

Gareth pulled away, his chair clattering over.

"I don't understand." *What were these lies? What game? A deception – and Mother couldn't bear it. Wyntr ... Wyntr perhaps. And wretched Gyll.* A sob caught him unaware, and he sat back down, ready to force his aunt to tell him the truth.

"Why would he fight Galos again? What's Elsa's father got to do with any of this?"

"Your father was very angry when he brought you back. He was angry with Fran and Annerin. And with Galos, Tom and everyone else. Your mother and I didn't know what happened, but your father talked with Wyntr. Perhaps he can tell you more when he comes back."

So, Wyntr was at the root of this!

"I would as soon speak to Galos as Wyntr, Aunt."

Raya flushed.

From outside came a flurry and squawk of fowl being herded past the door, then hushed voices.

"Look, there's still blood."

"Shush."

The footsteps shuffled faster and the flapping and clucking receded.

Raya, with her elbows on the table, set her face in her hands.

The fire sputtered, sparks launching onto the hearthstone at Gareth's feet.

"Father isn't here."

"Dead." Muffled. Raya was still hiding.

Orange flames licked the cracked hearthstone. Gareth scraped at ash with his foot, letting the warmth reach him through the wool. "I've slept too long, haven't I, Aunt Raya."

Raya raised her head, briefly meeting his gaze. This time there were no words.

"I'll take care of Mother. But, Raya ..."

His aunt nodded slowly then left, closing the door quietly behind her.

Gareth sat silently with his mother, watching bright slivers of light shift slowly across the floor. Lukas, father and husband, head of their household and chief of March, was dead – and all but interred – and he had played no part in it. The emptiness of it swamped him, and neither he nor his mother had anything to say.

Eventually he roused himself and, having stoked the fire, he boiled fresh water, filled two large beakers, scattered a few camomile flowers in them and stirred. A grassy tang filled the darkened room. It made Gareth realise that, with nothing more to be said or done, what they needed most was daylight, air and company.

He went to the front of the house, unfastened the shutter and tied it back. The fierce brightness of the day reminded him of the troubles he had woken with, which now seemed small. People walking nearby grew furtive when he peered through the opening. Leaning out, for the first time in his life Gareth did not feel the need to call out in greeting or be concerned about who he might soon meet in the square. The emptiness inside him was unruffled. *Perhaps Wyntr would not hurry back from the barrows. Perhaps ...* Shameful thoughts slipped into his mind. Unbidden thoughts.

He stepped back from the window and turned to her. "Mother, take off your apron and tidy your hair. We'll take these drinks up onto the hill."

Gareth spoke without any real expectation his mother would agree, but after studying him for a moment or two she untied her apron and took a comb to her hair.

Gareth watched her, then he realised his clothes were blood-stained and torn. He took a bowl, filled it with water from a jug set down by the partition, topped it up with hot water from the cauldron and set it on the table to wash. His mother came through, and she dipped a cloth in the water and bathed her own face before helping him wash the cuts he couldn't reach.

"Your father was defending you too," she said, breaking the beats of silence. "Something must have happened to you in the wood to knock you unconscious, after all."

"Mother, I can't tell you anything more. I understand how it appears to you. I know the truth of what happened, but I can't say exactly how it happened." He shrugged "I'll go and speak to Annerin today—"

His mother stopped abruptly and set the flannel down.

Damn.

"I only meant—"

"You can't go running to that woman now."

"I intended to walk."

"You don't know what you intend. Go nowhere today except the hill. Speak only with the elders and kin."

"I must speak with her."

"And your father?"

Gareth spun to face her. "I'll deal with Galos in my own time."

"No, stay away from the man. Our kin will work out what's to be done. I can't ..." His mother, stifling a sob, picked up the flannel again. "See, we're nearly done. Let me finish."

"Very well, but I'll go tomorrow. I must see what the woman ... what Annerin remembers. I talked with her for some time. She's not at the heart of this. I'm sure she's not."

His mother waited for him to put on a clean shirt. "You'd do well to keep your council and bide your time. Perhaps your father should have done the same." She licked her lips. They were dry and cracked, thinner than ever, and the lines on her face deep, relieved only by the slight colour the rub of the flannel had brought to her cheeks.

"It's too late now." *Too late. Too late. Too late.*

"Yes, well, we'll talk to Arthen and the elders before we do anything else. Then my cousin Ileth must have his say; we'll speak with him before Wyntr returns." She took a step towards the door. "Come before these drinks go cold."

Chapter 16

Witches and Dragons

Gareth let the warmth from the cup seep into his hands. It gave some small comfort as he led his mother from the house to a path winding around the base of the hill, leading to the well. Soon, a small path branched off and tracked up the side of the hill to a level area part way up. They took this path, ascending slowly, careful not to spill the tea, and sat down on a bench set in the northern side of the hill, overlooking the square and longhouse below. To their right, March sprawled out over the flat ground to the north. Beyond it, the plain stretched away, faint tracks snaking back and forth, worn by generations of patrols scouting the land, fearing raiders where once caravans of travellers moved. In the west, the mountains towered, the line of peaks making Vaden's Crown, with the sloping shoulder of the Hart's Horn tapering down until it levelled out into pastureland. Here, their cattle grazed, and green wheat moved softly in the wind. The sun climbed behind them, and the air sparkled, a relief after the confines of the house. Gareth set down the cup on bare earth, leant back and took a deep breath.

Before long, however, they were noticed, and one of their kin, the old woman, Vanna, began her slow climb to reach them.

"Thank the gods, Gareth. Vanna's coming." His mother went to help as Vanna drew near.

Vanna sat down heavily between them, grabbing Gareth's hand while she got her breath back.

"It's good to see 'im up and about," she said to Hilda before turning to Gareth, her smile exposing a row of worn, brown teeth.

Gareth returned the smile, slipping his hand free as he did so.

"It is. And good to see you too, Vanna," his mother replied.

The three stared out over March, over myriad bugs and bees darting between the flowers cloaking the hillside. The sun warmed Gareth's back, making him loosen the shirt where it stuck to his wounds. A butterfly settled on the path by their feet, and even the old lady seemed lost for words until she leant towards his mother with a whisper louder than her usual voice.

"Ebba's worried away the morning. She doesn't know where to put herself. Her floor'll be a deal lower for all 'er sweeping." Vanna nodded and leant back.

Gareth stared down at the house. Elsa's house. Ebba's house. And Galos' house ...

"An' Galos. He sits outside with his men, wishing someone would speak to 'im. But no one's going to. No. Even Arthen hasn't. Watch 'im run off the moment 'e gets the chance. Any fool's errand will do. And now I hear Annerin's gone looking for Arete."

The mention of Annerin pulled Gareth back sharp. He turned to Vanna.

The old woman chuckled. "Yes, he'll be off after Annerin if Ebba lets him. Anything to get away from here for a bit."

Gareth glanced at his mother, whose eyes widened. She shook her head as if to clear it.

"Yes, well," Vanna continued, "I remember a time when he was quite fond of Annerin, but I think Ebba will have something to say if he wants to run after 'er now. Yes, she's not too popular with Ebba, isn't Annerin, what with 'er son turning Elsa's head."

Gareth stared at his boots.

"An' after all the trouble Gareth went to taking those girls collecting wood for Ebba. Still, I don't know why she kept letting 'em go alone. No control, if you ask me. Letting 'em run wild wherever they please. Too busy poking her nose into other people's business, Ebba is. She'd be better worrying about 'er own family. And now look at the mess—"

His mother let out a cry.

Gareth jumped up, hardly able to resist putting his hands over his ears. "You say Annerin's gone to see the ... to see Arete."

"Er ... yes."

"Do you know why?"

"Well ... I don't ... I suppose ... I suppose it's to do with what happened outside the gate all those winters ago."

"Or what happened the day before yesterday."

No answer.

Below, in March, Galos' home was in his sights.

"It would make more sense, wouldn't it?" Gareth spun and Vanna gazed into the middle distance. "Why would she go now about what happened eighteen winters ago?"

"Well, I don't know," said his mother. "Maybe after what happened when your father found you ..."

Gareth turned away again, willing Vanna gone, but instead the old woman fixed on his mother, forcing her to continue.

"Well, whatever happened, it ... it brought back the hard feelings between him and Galos."

Vanna eyed Hilda greedily. "He said his quarrel wasn't with Galos though, didn't he? Don't you remember?"

"So, he felt convinced Annerin or Fran hurt me, I suppose," said Gareth. "And presumably Galos didn't think they had." Catching his mother's eye, Gareth snatched up the cup, ready to return home, but then he noticed Arthen making his way up towards them. Unclenching his hands, he set the empty cup back down and perched on the edge of the bench. The earth beneath was dusty grey and a beetle scurried, carapace shining in the sun.

"Gareth. I'm glad to find you well," said Arthen. "Hilda, my thoughts are with you." With an effort he stretched out his hand to take his mother's. "Vanna, I didn't think you climbed so high these days; Hilda and Gareth are honoured."

"Really, Arthen? My legs are as strong as they ever were, but I know you can't say the same. That stick gives you a new lease of life."

"Our friends' misfortune gives your tongue a new lease of life." Arthen watched Vanna, looking for all the world as if he had been privy to the recent conversation. Eventually, he sat down on the far side of Gareth.

Below, wheat swayed in the fields running down to the old bothy and river, and sheep and cattle dotted the patchwork. Clouds gathered around the sharp peak of the Hart's Horn, higher than Elden Deas to the south. And Gareth realised, while he'd slept, Annerin had climbed, perhaps was still climbing ... Getting away from this place ...

"Still catching your breath, are you?" Vanna leant round Gareth to address Arthen, her tone arched.

"No. I'm waiting for you to go."

"Well, you might be waiting a while. I'm still resting *my* legs."

"I thought you said your legs were as strong as ever."

"It's always wise to rest when you can at our age, Arthen."

"Indeed, but Galos obviously doesn't need rest. He's getting ready to leave."

"Where's he going?" Vanna demanded.

"I don't know. I thought *you* might be able to tell me that."

Gareth took a few strides along the path. People moved in the square below, but there was no sign of Galos.

"I'm trying to get rid of you, Vanna. Go and find out what's going before it's all over and Ebba's gone back in and bolted the door behind her."

"I've no interest in what Ebba does, but your manners are failing, so I'll leave you to come to your senses." Vanna stood up. "Hilda, dear, I'll call on you soon."

"Is ... are they going after Annerin?" Gareth asked Arthen, once Vanna moved out of earshot.

"Oh, no. Not as far as I know, anyway. One of the boys came in from the fields saying some of the horses have strayed loose near the marshes, so Tom, Willett and Elsa's father have gone to bring them back. I imagine they're glad of something to do."

"You have a lot to think about," Arthen added. "I take it you're well again."

"The accident ... whatever happened ... doesn't matter now." Gareth paused and Arthen remained silent, a silence quite unlike Vanna's. Gareth recalled his grandfather, Luwain. *What would he do?* "I should've been the one to take my father's bones to the barrows. It was my job, not Wyntr's."

"Yes ... I suppose no one knew when you'd wake, so your cousins took on your duties for you. It's a shame, but perhaps you and your mother can visit the barrows together soon."

"It would be something."

His mother cleared her throat. "Yes, Gareth, and it would be better than running off to see Annerin at the ford."

"Well, I can hardly go to see her if she isn't there, can I?"

Arthen glanced from one to the other. "If I understand rightly, Gareth, Annerin found you."

"Yes, she saved my life."

His mother's jaw shot out and she looked away.

"Something attacked me in the wood. I can't remember what happened, but I opened my eyes and saw Annerin standing by me with a sword."

She cleared her throat, but Arthen's gaze remained fixed on Gareth.

"Later, I woke up again. She was still there. She brought me water. She tried to get me to walk, but I couldn't. Then Fran came. The last thing I remember is him blowing the hunting horn. In fact ... yes ... I remember. I heard the hunting horn just before I met Annerin too."

The horn sounded twice. That was it, twice ... but different ...

"Was the horn loud?" Arthen asked.

"Yes, very loud. Horrible. But no, it sounded faint – in the distance. I heard it twice. The first time from far away, and the second time close by."

"So, the second time was when Fran found you."

"Yes, it must've been."

"Perhaps the first call you heard was Fran signalling he'd found Maya. I believe this all started with the little girl getting lost."

"Yes, perhaps."

"And Annerin, who was looking for Maya too, ended up finding you."

"Yes, that must be it."

"But it seems something else found you first, no?" Arthen's face, suddenly sharp, studied him.

Gareth fixed his gaze on the Hart's Horn. *Not now. Not with Mother here.*

"I'm an old man now," Arthen began, "but I've not always spent my time leaning on a stick. When I was young, I too walked in the woods. Sometimes I saw a stag – a stag that seemed too big – one I could never see quite clearly. I'd want to rub my eyes, but if I did, it disappeared. I know we don't talk about magic anymore, or talk of *the witch,* as you young folk sometimes call her, but she's out there, somewhere on the mountain. Her, and others of her kind. Whatever you met, or whatever met you, and made Annerin draw her sword, belongs to Arete." Arthen's voice shook. The past swelled around them like storm clouds descending on a hilltop. Blinding and chilling.

"It did look like a stag, the thing I saw. But I wasn't sure. In my mind ... well, the first thing I saw ... the first thing I remember was a dragon, but then in my head it was the image of a stag, so I don't know. I don't know what I saw and what I imagined. But I think it was still there when Annerin came."

Arthen jabbed his stick around in the dirt as if he were trying to pin something down. A bee disappeared into the purple hood of a foxglove and his mother shooed away a fly from the rim of her cup. A shout from the village below was followed by a laugh. Gareth strained to recognise the voices. His friend, Godwen, perhaps. Later, he would find him, share a jug of ale and find out the truth.

"The old stories said Arete helped us once, hundreds of summers ago. It's said she walked with Vaden, back in the days when March was ... a place ... and travellers passed through on their way to or from Eruthin. The stories say they were great friends, and they would walk through the streets and dine together in the great longhouse. When March was attacked, and the longhouse burnt to the ground, the stories tell of Arete riding on the back of a dragon and driving away Vaden's enemies. Hilda, you must remember the stories from when you were a little girl."

"Yes ... I do remember them. My mother told those stories too, but after Elin and Roe were killed ... well, no one wanted to hear them anymore."

"I know. Everything changed that night. Everything. Perhaps Vanna's right, Gareth, and I'm just a rude old man who doesn't know what he's talking about. Perhaps you startled a stag or boar, then slipped and fell. You could hurt yourself if you fell through one of those fallen trees, and you could knock yourself out too."

Arthen's eyes flashed to his mother, who nodded in agreement.

She stood, rearranging and batting down her dress.

Arthen turned back to Gareth. "Forget about witches and dragons, Gareth. Someone just needs to bring Annerin and Fran back, and to settle this mess once and for all."

Gareth nodded. *Settle this mess once and for all.*

Arthen struggled back to his feet and Gareth helped him down the hill. His mother followed, carrying the two beakers. In the distance behind them, a single grey horse wandered away across the plain, grazing steadily as it went.

Chapter 17

The View from the Hill

Maya pulled at the straw peeping through the doll's belly, then she pushed it back, dragging the faded fabric straight and plumping the little toy. A patch would be needed, but not now. *Not today.* Beside her, Elsa fidgeted and sighed, twisting her mending back and forth, but the needle hadn't moved since the sun cleared March hill. In the adjacent room, their mother's broom scraped and scratched relentlessly; Maya feared the angry glint in her mother's eyes might set it ablaze, making it breathe fire.

Outside, the silent square was springing to life. Whispers, whistles and scuffling feet skirted the longhouse, some lingering, others heading for the south gate, their words maddeningly out of reach, broken by the odd dry cackle or the bray of a goat. Her poor daddy, meanwhile, had left his seat beneath the shutters and gone with her uncle and Willett to find the straying horses. Without him outside, the house felt like a trap, and Maya longed to climb out through the tiny window and climb the hill so she could watch for his return.

She would be the first to see him, and he would pick her up like he always did and swing her round and round until she grew dizzy. Her running away from Elsa and Gareth would be forgotten, all forgotten, like the sword being cleaned and put away again because it was no shining thing to hang on the wall, like Annerin's; it was dull and grey, but sharp ... ever so sharp ... The familiar sound of the stone against its edge replayed, and Maya shook her head and covered her ears, making Elsa drop the mending, but the scene wouldn't go away. *Horrible. Bad dream. Nightmare. No.*

"Come on, let's go for a walk on the hill," said Elsa, tossing aside the mending and moving to a vantage point by the shutter from where the narrow window opening gave a view across the square.

Maya ran to her.

"Come on, then." Elsa perched on the edge of the opening, swung her legs over, jumped down and put out her arms to catch Maya as she followed.

"Mother, we're going for a walk." Elsa leant back through the opening, but before their mother could answer, she grabbed Maya's hand and ran across the square towards the path leading up the hill.

Elsa was glad to be free. Clutching Maya's hand, she ran part way then sat down on the hillside, in the spot overlooking the square, where their mother often sat. The peaks of Vaden's Crown towered in the distance, forest at its flanks, while closer by, an eagle hovered at the edge of the starling wood, its great white-tipped wings set against blue sky. A predator scouring for prey.

"I wonder if Annerin's found Arete yet," asked Maya.

Or Arete's found Annerin. Elsa shook her head, watching the eagle and pulling Maya close. Fran's story had at first seemed nonsense, with Annerin simply fleeing and the witch a bogeyman from fireside tales. But now a full day and night had passed, and he was still out there somewhere. Annerin too. Dread gripped her. *Where were they now? Could they be back?* Her heart leapt at the idea. Then it froze.

She forced herself to look properly; just visible over the stockade, black ash smoked, whitening in the breeze. The funeral urn, a lidded pot designed to hold Lukas' remains, and destined for the barrows, lay askew on the bier. Below it, the pyre – as befitted his rank of chief – rose high, too high for those moving in and out through the gate to see the bier resting on top. Next to the urn, clear as day, she could see the rounded outline of a skull. Bile burnt Elsa's throat. Her eyes watered.

She jumped to her feet. Where was Father? *Oh, where is he?* She ran to the top of the hill from where she could see out across the plain.

"Elsa, what is it? What's the matter?"

"They're still moving away."

"Father and Willett are. Tom's waiting with the two brown horses," said Maya.

"The grey's so far away. Oh, Tom must come back."

"Elsa, what? ... Why?"

"Wyntr hasn't taken the funeral urn. He's left it. It's just lying there. How could he? Even Wyntr ..."

Maya turned to look at the pyre.

"They haven't come back here," Elsa whispered.

"Are you sure?"

"How can I be, but they can't have gone to the barrows without ..."

"They've gone after Fran." Maya's eyes brimmed with tears.

Elsa looked over towards the stone house by the ford. No smoke came from the chimney, but on such a hot day that meant nothing.

"Come." Grabbing Maya's hand again, she ran back down the hill and round to Tom's house, hoping to find Cader. But no, he was out somewhere with Jake and Frey, watching Ileth and the rest, and their aunt was nowhere to be seen. Next, she went to Jake's house to double check he had not ducked back there or whether Finola might know something. No one was there either. Elsa took a deep breath. Part of her wanted to go to the ford. But no, that would not help.

"Wyntr hates Annerin and Fran. He hates us too," said Maya, as if reading her thoughts.

"He'll kill them if he finds them. I know he will." Elsa spun, first this way, then that. *Jake must be quite near, but where?*

"Elsa, we must tell Mother. She'll know what to do."

Elsa, looking down at her little sister, saw certainty. "Quick." She grabbed Maya's hand and ran home.

"Mother," said both girls together.

Their mother jumped up, the cup she was cradling clattering down on the hearth. "What is it? What's happened now?"

"Mother, we climbed the hill. From the top we could see the funeral pyre. Wyntr, Gyll and Seth have gone, but the urn and bones are still on the bier."

"And the horses were straying." Their mother's brow furrowed as she glanced from one to the other.

"We could see Father and Uncle Tom. They're still rounding them up. They're leagues away," said Elsa. "I think Wyntr's gone after Annerin and Fran. He'll kill them. He'll kill them in revenge. I know he will."

"We need Jake," said their mother.

"We went there first, but there's no one there. Cader's with them too, and Nell's out."

Their mother stared, her hand over her mouth. "If they're at the stone house, it's already too late."

A sob escaped from Maya.

Their mother snatched at her stool, scraping wood over stone, and slumped down, staring at the sparse embers.

Elsa waited, then grabbing an iron, she prodded the slow fire.

"Leave it," Ebba snapped.

"Then what must we do?" Elsa spat back.

Her mother, white-faced, snatched the iron from Elsa. "You say Fran went after his mother."

"Yes, we saw him go. But that was yesterday morning."

The stool crashed backwards. "We must find Jake, Cader and Frey. Some of the others will come too."

"But we don't know where they are. They might not even be inside the settlement. We looked down all the alleys but we didn't see them. It depends where Ileth is, but Jake's not expecting Wyntr to be here."

Her mother's hands wrung at the iron. "Then close the shutters and bolt the door."

"We can't just hide."

"Elsa, if they've killed Annerin and Fran, there's nothing to stop them coming here. Wyntr, Gyll and Seth are ... they're dangerous. We must delay – feign sickness, perhaps. Have Arthen attend one of us. As you say, your father and Tom are leagues away."

Elsa's skin crawled, ears alert for every outside sound. *But no, Wyntr couldn't just return without doing his duty.*

"Even if your father gets back in time, they may still be outmatched."

"There must be something we can do. Arthen should know, at least. And Gareth ..."

"Arthen, perhaps." Her mother threw her hands in the air. "But close the shutters before—"

The strident blast of a hunting horn shattered the silence of the square, bouncing off the timber walls of the house. Elsa staggered and heard herself scream. Her mother recoiled, covering her ears. Maya, meanwhile, standing outside in the square, raised their father's hunting horn to her lips for a second time.

Again, Maya sounded a short, solitary note on the horn – the distress signal. People stopped and stared. Shutters rattled and faces peered around corners. Vanna hobbled back from the well, and Arthen made his way round the side of the longhouse, followed by Enic and Tomas. Nell and Finola appeared from behind the longhouse and darted towards them, followed by several other women and a couple of men home from the fields for lunch. Behind them were a gaggle of children and Farran, the smith, down from his workshop by the north gate of March.

The three old men reached Maya first.

"What's the matter, child?" asked Arthen, turning from Maya to Elsa, and then towards their open door.

Elsa followed his gaze. Her mother remained frozen on the stool.

"Wyntr hasn't gone to the barrow," said Maya. "The urn and the bones are still on the pyre."

"What?" Arthen frowned and turned to Enic and Tomas, who hung back, lingering in the shade of the longhouse.

"We climbed the hill. You can see the top of the pyre from there," Elsa explained.

Arthen's look was sharp, but he did not answer. Around them, a hush fell. Children ran away past her. Elsa's heart twisted as she caught sight of Gareth. His face was set, eyes fixed on her. He stopped short, a few paces from herself and Arthen. Behind him, a crowd began to gather as people slipped into the square from adjacent alleys and from behind the longhouse.

For a too-long moment, she stared. Blood rushed to her cheeks. Gareth's face told of so much anguish and pain. She needed words, but there were none. The silence stretched, his eyes imploring. As ever, he would have no words, so she must find them. She opened her mouth, little knowing what she would say, aside from his name, but then, from the corner of her eye, she caught movement.

Her mother edged towards them. "Gareth, it's good to see you're well," she called out.

Gareth recoiled and stumbled backwards.

Slipping out from the crowd, Hilda and Raya appeared beside him.

Elsa grew dizzy, her heart thumping. The crowd seemed to melt into the background, leaving her mother facing Hilda. Ebba's cheeks shone red, while Hilda's face was as white as new-spun linen and her chest heaved. The air buzzed. A lone gull cried out as it sailed overhead. In the distance, a baby howled.

Arthen, meanwhile, stood stock-still.

Why didn't he act? Who, if not him? The answer came quick enough.

Hilda took a step towards Ebba. "Get away from my son," she barked.

Elsa jumped.

Arthen's hand found her arm.

Raya moved forwards too, glaring.

Her mother stepping backwards, found Maya, and put her arm round the little girl's shoulders, gently wrestling the horn from her grasp. Her voice sounded unnaturally high as she faced the crowd. "Elsa and Maya have just come down from the hill ... from where they could see ... from where they could see the pyre. The urn is lying on top, with ...

"We are ..." She cleared her throat. "Three horses are loose on the plain, and my husband has gone to round them up. We don't know where Wyntr, Gyll and Seth are."

Elsa scanned the crowd frantically, waiting for someone to understand, but there was only silence and many shadows, all stretching towards her door.

Hilda strode towards Ebba and roughly pushed her back.

Ebba stumbled, her shoes scuffing in the dust. She steadied herself and pushed Maya away.

"My husband's bones aren't your concern. How dare you stand here and speak! How dare you. What do you care where my kinsmen have gone?" Hilda's voice shook. She pushed Elsa's mother again. "Answer me, damn you. Answer me."

Maya ran to Elsa and clutched her tight.

Arthen clamped down harder on Elsa's arm, his nails digging in through the thin cloth.

Hilda's voice rose to a scream. She grasped hold of Ebba's arm, shaking her.

Ebba offered no argument, instead, she pulled away and used the other arm to shield herself.

"Arthen?" Elsa pulled her arm free.

"Wait." He reached for her again, this time gripping her wrist.

Gareth set Raya aside and came to his mother, gently leading her away from Elsa's mother.

Arthen's grip loosened, but then his head sank as Vanna approached Hilda, who was now grouped with Gareth and Raya, her back turned against Elsa's mother.

"She should not answer you, Hilda. She's already said enough and done enough."

Sniggers came from the back of the crowd. Maya hid her face in the folds of Elsa's dress.

"I have said little and done nothing." Her mother, standing utterly alone, spoke quietly, but with a dignity that quietened the square. "We all know the root of the quarrel between your husband and mine, Hilda. That quarrel ended yesterday. Perhaps you should answer *me* now when I ask if a new one has begun."

Hilda spun round and glared at her. Her expression, still angry, now contained a question too.

Arthen motioned Vanna to be silent. "Ebba's question's a just one, Hilda, but not, perhaps, one you can answer."

Hilda stared at Arthen.

"And Ebba, I believe you may be mistaken when you say one quarrel has ended. Do you recall your old friend – the girl who, not so very many summers ago, ran hand in hand with you in this square?"

Now it was her mother's turn to stare at Arthen.

"Well, that friend has gone to end the quarrel the only way she knows. But if I'm not mistaken, Maya believes she's in danger because she's being hunted by Wyntr."

Maya looked up, her pale little face awash with relief.

"It's true. What she says is true." The voice, breathless, came from a boy running full pelt down the path from the hill. "I've seen from the top. He's still there ..."

Voices drowned him out. Hilda stumbled and was caught by Raya. A murmur rippled through the square. *The urn. The barrows.*

Elsa, transfixed, felt the collective gasp.

Only Gareth stood firm – centre to a spinning world. Then, without warning, he ran to her mother, snatched the hunting horn from her hand and blew one long, loud note. Deep bass, it reverberated around the square.

Maya cupped her hands over her ears. Elsa winced.

This time the sound carried beyond the confines of March, across the fields and out onto the plain. The men and women sweating in the fields stopped their work and listened, then, with yesterday's events still fresh in their minds, they set down their tools and hurried home.

The signal just reached Galos, Tom and Willett, who mounted the horses and rode hard, heading for the southern gate.

Gareth lowered the horn and took a step towards Elsa. She waited, reddening again under his gaze.

Around them, the crowd dwindled. Her mother slipped back into the house, and Raya led Hilda away. The elders sought the shade again, breaking into tight little groups beside the longhouse, while Elsa, Maya and Gareth were left alone in the middle of the square.

"We ... I have to go after Annerin ... and Fran. If you and I act together, people will follow." Gareth searched Elsa's face while he spoke, then he handed Maya the hunting horn. "You can have this back now, Maya."

He waited. The sun beat down and Elsa struggled for words. Yesterday, her father killed his, yet here they stood. He was too calm, and it made her sad.

"You're right. Of course, you're right." *You're right, but Wyntr won't listen to you*. "My father will be back soon," she added, then she turned involuntarily towards the gate, unable to look at him any longer.

As if reading her thoughts, Gareth made to go.

"Gareth," Elsa called after him.

He spun, face unreadable, and stepped back towards her.

"I'm sorry for what's happened between our families."

"As am I, Elsa, but I've no quarrel with you, nor with your sister." Gareth glanced towards Maya, who stood nearby watching the gate, wide-eyed and lost. "I'm going to pack some supplies. Godwen, at least, will go with me, so I won't travel alone." Without waiting for Elsa to reply, he turned and ran towards his home.

Elsa watched the gate, dreading Gareth meeting her father on his way back in. *May the gods grant you speed, but may you walk separate paths.*

Chapter 18

New Beginnings

When the sun was at its midday position, Galos, Tom and Willett cantered into the square. Galos slipped from the grey horse and weighed the scene. All seemed peaceful, sleepy, with dust churned by the hooves. Jake, Cader, Frey, Tom's wife Nell, and Jakes' wife Finola were gathered outside his home, waiting with Ebba and Elsa. Beside them, Maya played, her little doll in her lap. He hesitated, hoping she would run to him as she so often did – break this awkwardness newly his – but she would not look up, instead scuffing at the grey dirt with her foot.

Under the eaves of the longhouse, several field workers congregated. Two were friends; even they avoided his eyes. The place hung in limbo. They didn't know who was chief, but neither did he. He didn't want the title, not this way, anyhow. By rights, it should be Gareth's, but he didn't seem the man ... and then there was Wyntr ... So, what were his options? Sit and wait until Wyntr called him out? Or Gareth? And what of Ileth, Hilda's cousin and Lukas' closest friend, who now sat outside his home, hard by Lukas' house, whittling away at an arrow and watching from under those great bushy brows.

"The horn was sounded, but what is wrong?" Galos asked Jake.

Jake stepped forwards between Galos and Tom, a hand on each of their shoulders. "It would seem Wyntr has not gone to the barrows, nor is he here."

"What?" Both men spoke together, stepping back and taking in the scene anew.

"What do you mean? Where is he?" said Galos.

"Err ... it seems Annerin and Fran have left, and ... well, we're wondering if Wyntr, Gyll and Seth have gone after them."

"Left? What do you mean?" said Galos.

"You'll need to speak to your daughters for the full story. They were on the hill ... and ... well, they could see the bier ..."

"Gods help us." Galos gasped. "Gods help me. I cannot think." He moved to the water jug on the stool outside the house and washed the dust from his face and hands. Tom appeared at his side and did the same.

"We should sit and hear this story out," began Tom as Ebba proffered them a cloth.

"Jake, come." Galos moved inside, followed by Tom and Ebba.

The three men sat around the hearth, while Ebba hovered nearby. When Jake had explained what had occurred, a heavy silence fell over them.

"If they came home last night, it's already too late," Ebba ventured, "but there's no smoke coming from the stone house, and no sign of Wyntr, Gyll or Seth, so it's likely they're still in the forest or on their way up the mountain. Elsa says Gareth blew the horn to get a party together to go after them."

Galos felt himself slump even further down on the stool. His eyes were gritty, and his stomach empty. Picking up the iron, he ground at the grey ash and looked around for bread. *What was this? Annerin, why?* No matter; he would go after her. *Now. At all costs, and without fail.* Whatever the reasons, she and Fran – Edwyn's family – were in danger and it was his sworn duty to protect them.

"Someone needs to check the stone house. Gods willing, they've not returned," said Tom.

"Gods willing."

"We're not safe, either ... I cut down one, although I wish ... Now there's three in his place," Galos muttered.

Tom gave him a sharp glance. "I'll go for my armour," he added grimly. "Eat something, brother."

Jake followed him from the house, pulling the door closed behind them.

"You shouldn't have gone so far," Ebba began.

"I heard the horn, didn't I?"

"Thank the gods you hadn't gone further." Ebba cut some bread and a hunk of venison.

Cold food, but no matter. He moved to the box for his armour and sword, snatching a chunk of the bread as he pulled on the cracked leather vest. It smelt of yesterday's sweat. The sword's hilt felt tacky too. It needed air, but he'd wanted it out of sight. He set it at his belt, then he ripped off a chunk of meat. The venison was unsalted but old. Chewy, and carrying its usual warning. Tonight, the last scraps could feed the dogs. But it would do. He washed the final mouthful down with a swig of lukewarm water, then he filled a waterskin.

"But why has Annerin gone, Ebba?" With the food, his head had begun to clear a little.

Ebba shrugged. "Maybe she's just run away, Galos."

"Maybe."

"Whatever once lived up there ... well ..." Ebba mumbled.

Galos reached for another piece of bread. Ebba brushed the floor by the fire. Above, something stirred in the thatch. It was hard to think, but something niggled. A snag in the song, as Arthen would say. "When did you find out Annerin had gone?" he asked, pausing as he adjusted the scabbard.

"Maya told me yesterday," said Ebba, moving away behind the partition.

"So, you knew ... Why didn't you tell me?"

"I ... you were so preoccupied."

True enough, but now there was a moment of clarity and Galos didn't like what he saw. He followed Ebba into their sleeping area.

"How did Wyntr find out?"

Ebba, kneeling to arrange the great knotted woollen blanket covering their bed, didn't look up.

"I suspect he overheard me," she muttered eventually, sniffing. "But it's no secret, Galos. Why, Arthen just told the whole square."

Galos glared down at her, his breath ragged, and disbelief cracking his voice. "Except from me."

"It's like I said, you were preoccupied. I couldn't give you something else to worry about, could I?"

"You suspect he overheard you. You're normally more careful than that." Galos fought to keep his voice low. "Since when do you confide in Wyntr and not in me?"

"It was only ... I think he heard me by accident."

"Accident be damned."

"It can't be helped ... and you know now."

"Can't be helped!"

Ebba stood up, sweat shimmering on her forehead.

"You did this. Tell me it's not true that you did this."

"I didn't mean for it to happen ... You can't leave us again."

"And I can't stay. Damn it, Ebba, how can I be in two places at once?" Unfamiliar tears prickled. He would have to go alone, and leave Elsa and Maya with Tom. He turned away. "This isn't over." His head swam, and he felt sick. "We'll have this out once I'm back. If Annerin and Fran are dead, then you and I ..."

Ebba let out a sob and retreated to the bed.

Galos fought to compose himself as he put his horn, knife and flint in a pack. Outside, the square was quiet. Ileth had vanished, but Tom and Jake were back, filling in Willett, who had dealt with the horses and now ate a hasty lunch as he listened. Several other men who had come in from the fields listened in too. Cader and Frey sat nearby on a bench with Elsa and Maya, their conversation breaking off when they caught sight of him.

"Elsa, come here." He stepped away from the group to meet his daughter. "Tell me exactly what happened yesterday."

Elsa recounted the events, while Galos ticked off the facts, one by one. His head spun. He had left Jake to shadow Ileth, but he had not foreseen this.

"I'll check the ford, then I'll go after them," he told her. "Your Uncle will stay here to take care of you." He kissed the top of her head, his heart twisting as he let her go. *Poor pretty child. Why must she always be at the heart of everything?*

He returned to the waiting men. "You heard what she said. Do we guess correctly about Wyntr?"

The group seemed to agree it the most likely scenario.

"Where else could Wyntr be?" said Jake.

Heads shook and boots scraped gravel.

"It's lucky they left," someone ventured.

"The gods intervene," Tom answered.

"Perhaps so."

"Perhaps this is what he'd have us think, though." Willett this time.

Tom shrugged. "A trap. It's possible. And if we go ..."

"I've no choice but to go," said Galos.

"We split up, as you say. I stay; you go," Tom answered.

"There's no other way. Wyntr wants revenge, and he probably wants that sword," Galos ventured. Around him, eyes widened, realisation dawning.

"I think they're all in the forest," said Tom. "But if it's a trick, Gareth's plan might spoil it for them."

"Perhaps we should check the pyre again too," added Willett. "It's quite a distance from the hill to see clearly, isn't it?"

Galos turned towards the gate. There was nothing he'd less rather do. "Don't go near it, Willett, but send someone with keen eyes up the hill. Elsa, what's Gareth said?"

"He wants to go after Annerin and Fran. You weren't here, Father, so he asked me to help him." Elsa shifted, lowering her eyes. "Perhaps he'll speak to you now."

"I'll have to speak with him, I think. There are things ... but we must leave soon. Elsa, try and talk to Gareth again when he comes back, but be careful. His family will go to the pyre now they know, and I imagine he'll lead them. Wait 'til he's done. Don't get in the way and keep your mother indoors. I'll check the ford with Cader and Willett. Gods willing, we'll find the house empty. Once we've been there, we can all search the forest. Tom, can you Jake and Frey stay here? The rest of you, keep out of the square and wait for when Gareth pulls a search party together."

Tom's face was thoughtful. "I'll shut these gates once they're done. Jake can do the north one. We'll keep lookout on the hill and sound the alarm if Wyntr appears."

"Challenge him if he comes this way. He'll have to answer to Gareth and Hilda for leaving his kinsman's remains out in the open anyway. Remember though, we've no idea why the horses strayed. There may yet be some explanation."

"No one's travelled this way. Who'd take those three but leave the beasts?" Tom's frown deepened.

"I don't know, but even so ..." Galos glanced around. The square remained deathly quiet, and the longhouse empty. Maya sat with Frey, swinging her legs and scraping her toes in the dirt.

"Nothing will happen to them," said Tom at last.

Tears prickled again and he made a silent prayer in thanks for his brother.

"Go," said Tom, "before Gareth comes. May the gods grant speed, and may the forest provide cover to our friends."

Galos nodded, then he remembered Ebba. Slipping back inside, he pushed the door shut. She squatted on the bed, sobbing. He sat down beside her.

"I'm going after Fran and Annerin. The boy put Lukas at sword point for threatening his mother. That's what made Lukas so angry."

Ebba looked up, her eyes red-rimmed.

"Now Wyntr uses our misfortunes to his own ends. His brother died so long ago, but Elin's death ate a hole in his heart. He'd kill us all. I'm a fool for not seeing it. If only Lukas lived. We managed in peace together these eighteen summers and winters."

"It's not your fault."

"It's not yours either. I must go. You'll be safe here but be sure Tom minds Ileth. The man's taken to brooding at his door."

"Yes, he was there earlier."

"Keep quiet in here with Tom and Nell when Gareth and Hilda go to the pyre. Keep Maya inside and the door closed. Someone will be on the hill too."

Ebba said nothing, only pulling him close.

Elsa watched with Maya and Frey as her father rode out with Cader and Willett. Tom and two others manned the gate, while Jake rode across with a small party to close the stockade's northern entrance.

Before long, Gareth reappeared. Elsa moved away from her door and met him under the eaves of the longhouse.

"Elsa, has your father left already?"

"Yes, he's ridden to the ford with Cader and Willett. He's desperate to find Annerin and Fran."

"He expects to find the house empty."

"Yes."

"And he's joining me to search for Annerin."

"He'd make peace with you," said Elsa. She waited, hoping for the earlier warmth. Gareth avoided her gaze. The sun remained high, but the shadows were lengthening. A little breeze whirled here and there, catching a stray leaf and tumbling it across packed earth. Elsa looked towards the mountain, mulling his choice of phrase. *Wasn't the search Father's to lead? Why did Gareth care so much for Annerin and Fran?* "He's left men here to go with you. He'll not rest until they're found."

"Very well. We've business here first, my mother and I, but after I've gone, it would be best to close the gate." With a final glance towards Tom, who was now standing in their doorway, Gareth strode away and beckoned to some men waiting behind the longhouse. The group, led by Gareth's closest friend, Godwen, comprised his small band of followers and around half of Lukas' men. Arthen, Tomas and Enic appeared too, sitting themselves down outside the longhouse.

Elsa returned to the bench outside her home and began peeling turnips for the pot. Glancing up from time to time, she observed many a wary scowl. Ileth, meanwhile, had resumed the vigil outside his house. Elsa tensed, careful not to look his way. He didn't stir when Gareth spoke, although Gareth's voice carried across the square. Its tone caught her attention in a way she little expected.

"You were all my father's friends ... loyal friends, but my father is dead, and I must speak plainly with you now. You've all heard about my being injured in the wood. What you haven't been told is that Annerin saved my life. She could've left me to die, but she risked her own life for mine. My father defended me bravely. You'll also recall how, long ago, it came about that he killed Annerin's husband." Gareth paused.

Elsa sat rigid. Someone gasped. She risked a peek. The younger men were wide-eyed; the older ones stared at the ground. She had never heard it so baldly spoken about. She wanted to see Ileth's reaction but didn't dare look, although his cold disdain radiated across the square. She saw it in the red necks of the men opposite, their stiff stance, the shuffling. She caught the sour smell of sweat from across the square, borne on a tiny gust of wind. Ileth might be Lukas all over again. *Poor Gareth.*

He continued, his voice barely faltering. "My father believed they attacked me in revenge. He was mistaken. Neither Annerin nor Fran was to blame, and I won't allow them to be butchered by Wyntr in revenge for my father's death."

A hush followed, broken only by the tap of Arthen's stick while he rose to his feet and the shuffling of boots as a couple of the older men turned to regard Ileth.

Elsa held her breath. *Speak now or hold the peace.* The moment crystallised. Gareth cleared his throat and Arthen, having shifted to his side, gave a single nod.

"Our first duty, however, is to my father. His good friend ..." Gareth faltered, watching Ileth. The old warrior shifted, his face a mask. "Ileth has attended to the bier. Now I'll bring my father home. His urn will rest in the longhouse for the present."

The surprise made Elsa forget herself. Panning round, she caught the stealthy glances. They knew what she had seen. She quickly dropped her head, neck prickling, and her heart beat out the silence. It was broken when Gareth raised his grandfather's ancient and rusted sword.

"Today, I'm proud to carry this weapon. I trust it above a newer blade. It belonged to my grandfather and sits well in my hand. It needs the smith, but there's no time today."

Forgetting the knife and pot she held, Elsa stared, recoiling at the blade's rust bitten edges. She thought of the silver sword and remembered it lying on the grass outside the stone house, bright amid the clover. This thing looked beyond repair but Gareth didn't see it. He saw only Luwain, and the strength of the past surged in his arm. Perhaps it would be enough, or perhaps if he met Wyntr, the blade would just snap. Who could tell? Gareth lowered the sword and waited. Arthen smiled a slow, triumphant smile. Ileth shuffled inside.

"I depart before the sun leaves Elden Deas. I'd be proud to have my father's men at my side. When we come back, we'll carry the urn to the barrows together."

"You've my answer already," said Godwen, walking to Gareth's side.

"My heart goes with you, Gareth. I'll be here, watching over the urn." Arthen edged back and waited.

One by one, the men stepped forwards, and Gareth, leaving Godwen to organise them, came over to Elsa. "I'm leaving shortly. We'll find Annerin ... and Fran and bring them home. There'll be time enough for peace making when I come back from the barrows."

Elsa nodded. She tried hard not to look at the sword. Something about it was wrong, so very wrong. It cried out to the heavens, and she didn't understand why. Gareth's grandfather had been a good man, better by far than his son. She missed her father already. He would have checked the ford by now, but she knew the house stood empty. Fran's fate was not the source of this dread, but under a clear, blue sky, it filled the square, creeping out from every alley, from every scrubby patch of grass and every loose tuft of thatch.

A short while later, Gareth led a party out along the pathway leading to the rise, a patch of high ground commanding the area to the south of the stockade. Elsa watched him go, her misgivings growing with every beat of her heart. Tom stood nearby. As they receded from view, he dragged the gates shut, banging the bar down into place.

She followed him the short distance back to the square, past the cattle pens and an old roundhouse filled with long grass and nettles opposite the path leading to the well. She glanced down the path, startled to see women going about their daily chores on such a day. It brought to mind the cold hearth and sour venison, reminding her she too must work. Hunger would only add to their woes, but there was enough kindling left for the day and sufficient grain for the pot. She folded her arms tight across her chest, the call of ordinary times sweet and distant like the purple moorland where the sun rose, now bathed in afternoon light, with shadows of clouds brushing the heather.

Tom waited in the square. It began filling with women, children and the elderly, quick to notice the closed gates. He moved to the front of the longhouse, waiting to be noticed and for the chatter to stop. He didn't wait long. He towered head and shoulders above those present, the sun catching his fair hair. A man of few words, he cut to the chase.

"Wyntr, Gyll and Seth are missing. They didn't go to the barrows. We don't know why, so Galos and Gareth have ordered the defences be set. We'll watch from the hill day and night. Those who can, keep weapons to hand."

Tom's words, together with the fall of the bar locking the gate, told Elsa her father needed her. Leaving Maya and her mother in the house, she ran to Tom and asked him to let her out.

"But Elsa, your father left me looking after you. If I let you out—"

"Uncle, whoever's on the hill can watch me. I should've gone with him. Please."

"Let me see where he is." Tom signalled for her to wait while he jogged up the hill to the watchers.

He returned quickly, and Elsa ran to meet him as he slowed. "Very well," Tom said, catching his breath. "They can see Gareth waiting at the rise. Your father must still be checking the river and clearing. I don't see what harm can come to you, but in any case, the lookout has a bow. He'll cover you."

"He won't need the bow."

Tom shook his head then walked with her to the gate and yanked the postern ajar, letting Elsa slip through and onto the path leading to the rise.

Chapter 19

Wordless Prayers

Where there was carnage, there would be birds. The curve of the path at last brought the stone house into view through the trees. Galos exhaled, registering fully the silence overhead – providence indeed, whatever Annerin's motive for leaving. The shutters and door were closed, and a robin hopped back and forth in the vegetable patch. He dismounted, followed by Willett and then Cader, who went to open the door.

"No one's here," said Cader, emerging from the house a moment later. "It looks as they would've left it."

"Thank the gods," said Galos, moving around the side of the house. "Cader, check the field with the hens, and the back between here and the copse. Willett, you do these trees and the river. I'll cross the ford and check the clearing. If either of you find anything, sound the horn."

Cader and Willett tethered their horses and Galos remounted, then the three men moved off in opposite directions. They returned a short while later, having found no sign of either Annerin or Fran.

"They must be in the forest or on the mountain. I hope they're together, but we can't assume Fran's found his mother." Willett spoke for them all.

Tiredness engulfed Galos as he surveyed the forest. It wrapped around the foothills of the mountains to the west and stretched south, unbroken for many leagues. *Vast. Dark, tractless and vast.* Elden Deas itself seemed to taunt him with the enormity of his task, its pinnacle rising in the distance and the outline of its cliffs and crags just visible above the trees.

"Come, we should find out where Gareth plans to search." As he spoke, Galos avoided Willett's eyes. "We'll make two parties at least."

They set off for the rise at a steady canter. Galos fought exhaustion, hunger and dread, little able to separate one sensation from another. His duty took him to the mountain, and his path led him beyond the rise. From here he would cross the shallows in the Cloudwater River and follow the old rangers' trail, which led to a stone bridge at the foot of the mountain pass. It meant leaving Gareth to search the forest, and it meant leaving March. But at least there was Tom; Tom and Jake both. But it all felt wrong. So wrong ...

Drawing nearer the rise, Galos slowed the horse to a walk. On its far side, Gareth was pacing, his head bent. Even after the horror of the day before and with the memory of Lukas' final moments replaying over and over in his head, some crooked imperative drew Galos onwards, resigned to the fact he must face the man.

Gareth seemed oblivious to their approach. He stopped, facing down the path that would be Galos' route onwards, his gaze intent on the slopes of Elden Deas. His men, meanwhile, huddled in the shadow of the rise, shuffling uncomfortably.

Galos stopped a short distance away and waited. Gareth looked up, recoiling and reaching for the hilt of his sword.

"I intend to head that way. I'll climb the mountain to look for Annerin and Fran." Galos' voice sounded strange to his own ears, cutting through the silence as it did. He dismounted and handed his reins to Cader. Behind him, Willett's horse shied.

"Set aside that sword. I want to speak with you," countered Gareth, still motionless.

Galos glanced down at the newly cleaned blade. "As you wish."

He turned to Willett, reading the doubt in his eyes.

"This isn't a good idea," his friend whispered.

Galos heard, but it was in his mind that the sword had done enough yesterday. Besides, he was exhausted and hadn't the stomach for more. He and Gareth just needed to talk, but suddenly he couldn't imagine what either might say. He felt the sword leave his hand and pass to Willett. His heart thundered in his ears, and nothing would take shape. It was as if he were fighting his way through a storm, no longer sure of the way home but too numb to pause for bearings. Willett's face flickered in front of him, and a moment later Galos found himself holding a spear in place of the sword.

"Lean on it, if you must," Willett muttered.

Like an old man. But perhaps that was how he felt. He walked a short distance back along the path, the spear hitting the ground in rhythm with his stride, then through a line of hawthorn and alder and into the long grass of a fallow field.

Once in the field, he turned. Gareth followed him, his sword now unsheathed at his side. Clarity came to Galos at last, and with it, realisation. His guilt was misplaced, and this was a mistake – a terrible, horrible mistake. He sent a silent beat of thanks to Willett for the spear, then he looked at Gareth's sword, registering with horror the ragged blade. *In the name of the gods ...* Ebba flashed into his mind and all his misgivings crystallised with the memory of her voice. *Can't you think ahead? Can't you see?* And who would take care of them now? Tom again. *Oh, Tom, where are you now?*

Starbursts blinded him, and he staggered backwards, levelling the spear in his hand and stumbling in the knotted grass. How had he so misjudged Gareth, dismissing him – perhaps in just the way Lukas always did – judging him as some endlessly malleable thing? A spectator, forgotten and unnoticed, while he, Illeth and Wyntr traded hard words. Well, words must suffice now; his best armour was persuasion.

"Before you think of striking at me, you should know the truth. Perhaps no one's told you yet."

Gareth fingered the sword gingerly, his mouth twisting.

Galos quickly changed tack. "The forest is vast, and Annerin's in danger. So's Fran. I'd give my life to protect them. We'll have time to settle our differences later."

"I'll hear the truth from Wyntr when I find him, and I'll weigh the value of your *truth* with this sword arm." Gareth spun the rusting blade, levelling it towards Galos. His face contorted and the point twisted nearer. Galos leapt back, grasping the spear shaft in both hands and weighing the option to run. His vision swam. Gareth's rage broke. He leapt forwards and the ragged edge of the blade loomed over Galos. It came down, smashing the spear shaft. Then it swung again.

Gareth's head throbbed. Thoughts rained down like fists, and the pounding of his heart filled his ears. The sword was all that seemed real in the world – grey, flat and hard, an answer and an end to the whirlwind in his head.

Galos, the man who killed his father only yesterday, stood in front of him, leaning on some ancient spear as if he were an elder, trying to better the strength of a sword with the cut and thrust of words. And how quickly he laid down his sword. The sneering arrogance of the man bit at Gareth with the sharpness of steel.

And so, he raised his grandfather's old sword in both hands and swung it backwards. It stopped short, hitting something behind him, the sickening drag unbalancing him. Gareth reeled.

In front of him, Galos crumpled to the floor, howling like some stricken beast then lurching towards him on all fours.

From nowhere, a fist landed hard on his jaw. Light burst. Hurting, blinding light. Someone clawed at his hand, pulling his fingers from the hilt of the sword. The voice belonged to Godwen.

He tasted blood.

The light receded for long enough for him to see Edric and Sennen, one either side of him, dragging him away. And then he was falling – falling backwards, down into the grass ...

Cader, having slipped through into the field behind Galos, watched transfixed, his feet leaden and his chest tight. The hawthorn gave scant cover, but neither man noticed him. Galos' miscalculation became horribly clear; the change in Gareth had been swift.

Before he could move, someone flew past him. *Running. Elsa running. In the name of Vaden, no.* Cader heard his own scream. He sprinted to catch her, but Elsa ran fast. *Always so fast.* She lunged at Gareth's arm, but she was out of breath and stumbled. She missed. The flat of the sword hit hard against her upturned forearm, and the edge of the blade carried on, striking her below the ear. The world exploded. Men's shouts and her father's screams melded like screeching metal. Men descended on the field.

Cader was nearest. He ran, then he punched Gareth as hard as he knew how. Gareth fell backwards, his friends surrounding him. Elsa lay still, blood coursing from her arm and neck. He lifted her clear, pushing grass flat with his foot so he could set her down again. A ragged cut ran down the inside of her arm and a smattering of gashes along her jaw. The main cut was in her hair, but he could see only a bloody tangle.

Willett appeared, and Galos staggered to get upright before turning away to vomit at the field's edge. Willett ripped two sections of clean cloth from Elsa's skirt and folded them before applying them to the wounds. Cader held each in place as Willett, hands fumbling, tore another, longer strip and knotted it around Elsa's arm, below her shoulder. Next, he took over pressing down the cloth at Elsa's neck, leaving Cader to hold together the cut on her arm. Fleetingly, their eyes met. Willett's face was pasty, a contrast to the livid red now staining both their hands. Tears prickled as Cader pressed together the skin on Elsa's arm. Both stared down at her limp body, making wordless prayers.

Chapter 20

A Bitter Truce

Insects buzzed and sunlight dazzled. Peering up through stalks of long grass, Gareth shielded his eyes. Starlings spun and danced overhead, dark specks against the glare. He sought time and place, but memory found him, and for the second time that day, he woke to bleak news.

His lip stung and a dull throb filled his jaw. He reached down, hoping to lay his hand on a waterskin, but found none. The cuts on his side pulled as he lifted himself up on one elbow. Edric and Sennen sat one either side of him, their faces stony. Edric stopped chewing a stalk of grass and looked away. Godwen stood a short distance from them, his back turned, staring towards March.

"What's happened here? Edric? Sennen?" Gareth sat up. His head grew light, and his vision blurred. "What hit me?"

Edric spun back round. "You tried to kill Galos, but your sword hit Elsa." His voice dripped ice.

The ground lurched beneath him. *What? Elsa! That could not be.* "No, I left her in March."

"Well, she didn't stay in March."

"What do you mean?"

"You swung that rusted old sword and it caught her. How can you be so ..."

"I ... Where is she? Is she all right?"

"No, it's like Edric said; you wounded her."

Gareth turned to Sennen, and his friend's face softened slightly.

"She'll live. The bleeding eased before they left. It's a cut to the skin, nothing more."

"But Elsa was fortunate," added Godwen, walking back to the group. "And so were you, my friend. Today the gods smiled on you and stayed your arm. It wasn't so for Galos yesterday. He showed your father mercy and was ill repaid for it."

Gareth exhaled. *What? Mercy and ill repaid.* But Elsa ... she had been here, and he'd injured her. He couldn't look at Godwen. His head sank, and he slid his heel back and forth and watched the grass unbend. *Perhaps no one's told you yet.* Galos said this before ... He shut his eyes, forcing back the scene – the memory of the catching sword. *That was Elsa? No, it couldn't be true.* Misery piled on misery. *How much more?*

"Gareth." Godwen waited.

Edric and Sennen shuffled away, cursing quietly and swatting at hoverflies.

Gareth sought the strength to accept the kindness he surely did not deserve. *Godwen, tell me these are lies or let this furrow swallow me up.* He met his friend's gaze at last, but he had no words.

Godwen sat down opposite. "I've not had the chance to explain properly what happened yesterday, Gareth. There wasn't time before we left ... but you need to hear the truth."

Edric and Sennen were out of sight now, beyond the hawthorn at the field's edge. It was just the two of them. Long grass and big sky, with the high branches of the alders swaying in the breeze and a solitary rook pecking.

Godwen cleared his throat, his expression fraught. "Galos stepped away when your father fell ... but your father – he was so strong, and very angry you'd been hurt – without thinking, he got up ... somehow ... and he lunged with his axe. Galos had walked away, then he turned and swung. It was over in an instant. Your father died instantly ... I'm so sorry, Gareth. Your poor mother ... but it's so unfortunate, so very unlucky a thing. Such horrible ill fortune."

All warmth seemed to leave Gareth. A shiver ran through him. Away from his mother and Raya, the reality of this ...

Godwen's hand fell lightly on his arm. "It's hard to hear, I know. So very unreal. I wish it wasn't true. Such ill luck; no one can believe ..."

Again, Gareth sought words, but there were none.

"No one can blame you for being angry, but ... but be thankful you didn't kill Elsa today. If you had, we'd all be lying dead in this field now, with these ravens."

Gareth saw the dark rings under Godwen's eyes. The fear. Edric's anger came from fear too, whereas he himself felt only regret. Elsa might be injured, maimed even, but she had saved her father's life. She would never feel like this.

A part of him wanted to cry, but he came from a house where tears only brought contempt, and now, when perhaps they would serve him better than a sword, they would not come. Then he remembered Annerin, and his promise to Elsa, and the bitterness of guilt reminded him to keep it.

"You're sure Elsa will recover," he asked Godwen.

Godwen shrugged. "I can't promise, but Willett said the bleeding had slowed and he thought the sword missed her veins. She'll be with Arthen by now."

"I'll have to go back and check before I search for Annerin."

"I'll go ahead. Let's hope Galos isn't out to kill you now."

Gareth came through the gate and caught sight of Galos ahead in the square. He hesitated beside the stables and cattle pens, in the lee of the old roundhouse, weighing the scene. A mid-afternoon hush reigned. Crows dotted the longhouse ridge and lazy smoke drifted through breaks in the thatch. Godwen waited opposite, in the alley beside Arthen's home, watching the gate. He gave a single nod. With a final glance towards the resting horses, Gareth approached the square. Galos' whole demeanour seemed changed. The man's shoulders were slumped, his face grey. *What one day could do. One moment. One misjudgement.* For Annerin's sake, they could afford no more of this.

A hush descended when they came face-to-face. Galos' jaw dropped and he took a step back. Too late, Gareth realised his own hand rested on the hilt of his sword. Galos half drew his weapon and Tom appeared at his side. This time Gareth saw no arrogance, only his own hurt and confusion mirrored. He stepped back, bending to set his sword down on the ground between them.

Galos' brow furrowed as he lowered his weapon.

"She's the last person in the world I'd want to hurt. I wish I could undo this ..."

Maya's sobs reached him from the house.

He fought to control his voice. "I didn't know exactly what happened yesterday ... only that you killed him."

Tom melted away, leaving Galos alone.

"Elsa's all that matters now. Good news is worth more to me than my life."

"She'll live ... Elsa will live." Galos slid his sword back into its scabbard. "Go; make your peace with her." He motioned for Gareth to go to the house, then he slumped down under the longhouse eaves next to Tom, his head bowed.

Elsa greeted Gareth with the ghost of a smile; it made him recoil in shame. The gashes along her jawline flared dark and ugly against the white of her skin, and congealed blood glued the waves of her hair into an unsightly knot. Her bandaged arm hung limp at her side, red peeping through the fine, pale linen.

He knelt beside her, lost for words. It was not until she tried to look away that he remembered that they hardly knew each other. They were not friends. Not confidants.

She tried to speak, but as she did so, she winced, her good hand flying to her jaw.

"Don't move. Please. I've only come to say I'm sorry. I would never ..."

Elsa pulled away, her expression sad.

"Godwen's explained exactly how it happened ... yesterday. I didn't understand. No one told me. I shouldn't have ... I should've heard your father out. I got so angry when I saw him. I—"

"Gareth, I knew. That's why I went."

"Then you knew more than me." Emptiness raged inside him, enough to drown him or wash him clear of this place.

Elsa picked at a thread on her blanket. “Please, Gareth, speak to my father then find Annerin and … and find Fran.” Her voice trailed off into a sob, and she turned away.

Gareth got up and left, pushing past Ebba at the door. He emerged to find the square empty aside from Galos, who was still slumped outside the longhouse, Tom at his side.

“She wants us to find Annerin and Fran,” he began, his words sounding shrill and unnatural to his own ears. He moved towards them. Feet scuffed behind him and Godwen appeared at his side. “We saw smoke rising from Spiral Cove.”

“Spiral Cove isn’t on the way to the pass. We need to split up,” Galos replied, taking a step towards him.

There was a moment’s silence. The sun warmed Gareth’s back. A blackbird landed on the thatch and pecked. Away in the distance, probably at the forge, a hammer rang out, breaking the afternoon’s stillness. He would send his grandfather’s sword there before leaving. “I’ll go to the cove,” he volunteered.

“Very well. May the gods grant you speed.” Galos made ready to go. “If you need help, sound the horn and I’ll come.”

“Likewise.” Their eyes met fleetingly. This was not friendship – everything felt too raw – but it was a truce for Elsa’s sake, and for Annerin’s.

Tom left to fetch Cader and Willett, while Galos described the quickest route through the forest to Spiral Cove.

“When you’re in among the trees, you’re following the sound of the crags. But you know this; the forest grows just as dense to the north.”

Gareth nodded. *But nothing lurked in the northern woods.* Only wolf and boar, and his father had been a thorough teacher.

Soon the two parties were making their way back towards the rise together. Galos, Willett and Cader kept their horses at a walking pace and led two other animals laden with supplies for their trip up the mountain. Gareth, Godwen, Edric and Sennen, meanwhile, travelled light, their packs on their backs, and Gareth now carried his father's sword.

Ebba, with Nell and Tom beside her, watched them leave. Galos' dejected aspect haunted her. Few words had passed between them, even when they helped Arthen tend Elsa. Only Willett's account and her daughter's ruined face stood as explanation, and to cap it all, the man responsible then walked through her house without so much as a word, sweeping her aside like so much loose straw beneath his feet. Words failed her, so when Tom closed the gate, she turned to her cousin, Nell.

"Come." Nell took her hand. "Elsa needs rest. Finola's with her, and Tom's in the square. Arthen's tonic will do its work. We should check on Maya. I haven't seen her for a bit."

"She's with Liselle and Frey on the hill. Frey took them up earlier."

Nell led the way to her home, several doors away, on the edge of the square. Ebba sat at the table while Nell lit a fire beneath the water cauldron.

There were times when Ebba found Nell's silence irksome, but it soothed her now – when words meant so little. The scrape of the flint soothed, and when the flame lit, although its warmth was unwelcome, it brought comfort. She looked down at her hands and noticed they still shook. The rest of her was numb. The fear of violence, she now realised, had always been there, lurking in every quiet moment, in the sun, rain and snow, waiting like a dormant seed in the ground. *But Elsa. Why did she run? And if she hadn't run ...*

The fire flickered into life, crackling as it caught. The smith's hammer rang on, marking time. Nell drowsed, occasionally checking the cauldron and fire. Eventually, a tendril of steam crept over the rim.

"Wyntr, Gyll and Seth can't be a match against so many, do you think?" said Ebba.

"They must take heed of Gareth now, mustn't they?"

Ebba shook her head. *If only.* Gareth's anger, terrifying as it must have been, was an aberration, lightning from a clear sky. His mild good nature could not withstand Wyntr's malice. What did Galos say? *Elin's death ate a hole in his heart.* The image of the red rip along Elsa's arm, and the blood in her hair, danced before Ebba's eyes. Annerin was out there alone, with this man hunting her down, and she— Ebba pushed the thought away. It left her cold inside.

Nell jumped and Ebba turned to see Vanna standing in the doorway, leaning heavily on a stick.

"I'm so sorry for your trouble." Vanna waited. The stick appeared new, and the old woman clutched it with both hands.

Nell hesitated then motioned her in. "Come, have a seat."

"Thank you, Nell. You're always so kind." Vanna lowered herself carefully onto the stool between them. "I'm sorry to see your Elsa hurt." She patted Ebba's hand.

"Thank you." Ebba resisted the urge to rub Vanna's touch away. The feel of it lingered like a stain. She fought back a sob at the memory of Elsa's wounds. *That this should reconcile them.*

"Gareth's a good boy," continued Vanna. "It wouldn't be natural not be angry about his father's death."

Nell ladled out three beakers of tea.

Vanna took the cup from Nell, but her eyes never left Ebba.

Ebba held herself still. "Gareth's done what he's done, but what happens when Wyntr returns?"

"You fear the same again."

"Obviously."

Vanna set down the cup untouched. "Our kin tires of Wyntr's anger."

"What does that mean?"

"Hard to say. But it's why I came."

Ebba nodded, only half understanding.

Vanna grabbed the cup again, swirling the dark liquid and frowning. "Nettle?"

"Yes."

"How many leaves did you put in?"

Nell's cheeks reddened. "I didn't count."

"Just drink it," snapped a voice from the doorway.

All three women jumped.

Raya took a couple of steps forwards before addressing Nell and Ebba in a gentler tone. "I hope I may pay you a brief visit."

Nell proffered a fourth stool at the table.

"Vanna's right," Raya continued. "Not about the tea, I mean."

Ebba looked away.

"Of course, please sit." Nell, regaining her composure, stooped to dredge the leaves from the cauldron and top it up with fresh water.

Raya cleared her throat, casting a sharp glance at Vanna as she sat down.

"Everything so dreadful, isn't it?" Ebba sipped her tea gingerly.

"It is," said Raya. "My kin feel sorely tried, Ebba. Heartbroken it should come to this ..."

A young mother shuffled past the open door, averting her gaze. *A pestering child and a sloshing water bucket. Life went on.*

Raya continued. "Now the sun falls away. Gareth won't reach Spiral Cove tonight, and when he does get there, we don't know what he'll find."

Ebba waited, sensing more was to come.

"But we do grow weary, as Vanna says. Our men will look to Gareth, but Wyntr adored Lukas. He became more father than uncle. You see" – Raya took a cup from Nell – "for Wyntr, Lukas was the one who fought for Elin and Roe; the only one who cared enough to take up arms when they died."

The debate was wearisome, rehashed a million times. "It's all so long ago," Ebba answered.

"He's not alone in thinking this way," continued Raya. "The gates are shut against Wyntr because Gareth let Tom and Jake shut them, but there are those who'll open them for Wyntr if he returns first."

Ebba met Raya's unflinching gaze. *So, power – safety even – rested in influencing Gareth, and here sat his aunt.* "What does Hilda think?" Ebba asked.

"My sister does not love Wyntr, nor does she love you."

"If Gareth marries Elsa, as Ebba wants, all this will be resolved." Vanna flicked the dregs of her tea onto the fire as she spoke, making it spit and hiss. "We all know that's what you wanted. The boy and his mother may be dead by now anyway. Wyntr won't spare them, and he left before dawn. He'll find them before anyone else." The old woman leant back, folding her arms and waiting for a response as if she were haggling over linen in the square.

Ebba froze.

Nell got up and went outside.

When no answer came from either Ebba or Raya, Vanna persisted. "We need the likes of Wyntr to defend us, anyway. He's a fine swordsman – takes after his brother. He could teach the rest a thing or two."

With still no response forthcoming, Vanna struggled to her feet. "I speak true, mind. Someone must say these things. It falls to me with age. Good day to you both."

Ebba moved her stool to let the old woman past, trying not to recoil at the sight of the twisted hump and grey hair, yellowed with grease.

"She's not the voice of our kin," said Raya once Vanna was out of earshot. "The old have long memories, that's all."

Ebba thought on Vanna's words, then she remembered Willett and Cader carrying Elsa in ... *Such a union might not so easily have brought peace.*

"We've long days of waiting ahead," she said at last. "May the gods grant speed to Galos and Gareth."

Chapter 21

Seeing Red

With midday past and the sun moving west, Fran spotted a flat section of rock on which to sit and plumped down. From so high on the mountainside, he could see March and the horseshoe of the valley spread out before him. Beyond it, the plain stretched away to the horizon, featureless and flat, scrub and marsh fringed by the moors in the east. The sight of it brought a lump to his throat – a world so big, and all the places he had ever known so tiny in it.

The newness of it made him dizzy. For the first time in his life, he could not look up at Elden Deas; it was beneath his feet. He took a long swig of water then unwrapped some bread, meat and a wedge of sweating cheese. Below, March resembled an anthill. He could make out the stockade, the longhouse and the dwellings, together with a heap of wood piled beside the gate, presumably for repairs to the stockade, an endless job by all accounts, and something Cader often complained about. His own home was hidden by trees, but he could see the outline of the clearing. All seemed insignificant, though, compared to the vastness of the mountains. Elden Deas towered behind him, guarding the pass, while stretching away to his left, the twin peaks of the Hart's Horn and Berry Drum rose, shadows draping their flanks.

Was it only yesterday he had left Elsa?

He had come so far since their parting, first finding the old rangers' trail where it cut through the forest, and then making a beeline for the foot of the Nethermore Pass. This way, he had hoped to make up time and catch his mother, who would certainly take an easier and more winding route. Undergrowth had choked the trail in several places, affirming his suspicion. Beating it down had slowed him, but dusk had found him within earshot of tumbling water. Then the ground had risen, and the trees had thinned. He'd seen the river Everlode tumbling to the forest floor before flowing to meet the Cloudwater at Deas Howe, where an old stone bridge crossed. Fran, remembering his grandfather's wistful and detailed descriptions of the forest, had known this bridge marked the foot of the pass. Little more than an arch of crumbling grey slabs remained, the stones from the parapets strewn in the water. It told the story of March's long isolation from Eruthin all too well. Fran, standing on it in the fading light, with the water rushing beneath him, had tried to picture his father crossing it all those summers before.

From this juncture he had been able to see the pass as it climbed away into the sunset. Reassured there was no one on it, he'd made camp for the night, all the while expecting to see smoke rise from a nearby fire lit by his mother. He'd chosen a spot where the trunks of two fallen trees crossed, creating a bower of branches that was easily accessed by snapping away a few twigs, which he'd rearranged around the opening. The smaller twigs he'd piled for a fire before searching for animal tracks leading down to a nearby stream and laying snares. He'd kept checking for smoke but saw none, and in the last of the day's light he'd cooked a grouse and a rabbit then slept fitfully.

He had woken at first light, stiff and cold in his bed in the crook of the fallen branches, the world around him earthy and black. When he'd reached out, his hand had brushed last season's leaves, still clinging on, their crispness tempered by a transient coating of dew. Shivering in his blanket, he'd waited for daylight to reach down through the trees. Eventually, the first note of birdsong came, sharp and clear. It had brought him back to himself, and he'd crawled out of the shelter and set twigs over the spent ash. Impatient for heat, he'd crouched, warming his hands. The worries of the night had receded as the warmth grew, and once the fire fully caught, he'd gone to the steam to wash and refill his waterskin. The cold, clean water had felt good; it spoke of reality and of practicality, if not certainty. Before long, a breakfast of meat and bread had sizzled over the fire, sending a lone tendril of smoke curling out above the trees.

A short while later, Fran had traversed the bridge, and fearing he might somehow have missed his mother, he'd set off up the pass. He'd moved swiftly, soon leaving the forest behind and following the well-worn, ancient path as it cut through sparse, rocky soil swathed in bracken and tangling briar. The day had worn on and there was no sign of her. Eventually, he'd slowed, having little choice but to go on, yet he'd been uncertain whether waiting at the bridge might have been a better choice.

Now, with the prospect of a second night alone weighing on him, Fran noticed a faint trail of white smoke rising from a point in the forest directly to the west. Spiral Cove. Spiral Cove, with its haunting little cairns; the place where his father was buried. He had travelled there last summer – once alone and once with Cader – drawn by sadness and the knowledge that his mother never went, but standing among those stones brought no revelations, and without even knowing which cairn covered his father, it felt like the loneliest place in the world.

He left his seat on the rock and moved on, his heart heavy. His mother could not have travelled so far already. Something was awry. Fearing she was ahead of him, he had moved too fast. What if she were behind him, needing help? Should he go back? Perhaps he had miscalculated. The missing packet had made him jump to this conclusion, but now it seemed crazy. Chances were, she was at last making the pilgrimage to Spiral Cove to be out of the way, and that was all. With no way of knowing, he trudged onwards, intent on finding a suitable place to spend the night.

The state of the path only reinforced his misgivings. Pristine bracken continually blocked the way. Eventually, it levelled out and skirted behind the high point above Spiral Cove before winding its way parallel to the edge of high cliffs.

Fran stopped where a small path began snaking its way steeply up the side of the mountain. Unsure how close to the lake he might be, he scrambled a short way up, hoping to catch a glimpse. Before long the path levelled out, tracking around the side of the mountain. Lake Everlis appeared below him, ripples twinkling on dark water in the afternoon sun and tall sparce pines ringing the far shore.

He flopped down on a patch of scree, longing to take off his boots. The water beckoned, but there was still no sign of his mother. The section of shore below him remained hidden, so he inched forwards until he could see all of the lake. Several boulders sat by the water's edge directly below, on ground thick with pine needles.

He wriggled free of his boots, took a swig from the waterskin and lay back, shielding his eyes from the sun. A gentle breeze eddied back and forth, and his eyelids grew heavy.

Fran woke with the sun still high but further west. He blinked and stretched. Nearby grasses prickled his fingertips, and the stones and gravel were warm beneath the soles of his feet. He sat up, and a figure caught his eye, moving towards him around the edge of the lake.

Red hair hid her face and her bare feet made stepping stones of the rocks littering the shore where the source of the Everlode left the lake. *Who was she?* A beggar in a greying, ragged dress; her torn sleeves hung limp, and her skirt was ripped past the knee, the hem a ring of tatters. As if in answer, she stopped and stared up at him, blinking in the sunshine. Fran stared back.

Time passed – an age, and yet no time at all. He slipped back into his boots and scrambled down the slope to the shore, searching for footings, slipping and sliding. He jumped the final section, and they came face to face.

Green eyes twinkled with the faintest hint of a smile.

Fran brushed himself down, glimpsing the mouth of a cave directly behind him; it was the action of a moment, but he found himself at sword point. A sword exactly like his own.

Her chin tilted and the ghost of a smile played again when she flashed a glance towards his sword. She took a step back and waited.

"I don't mean you any harm," said Fran. "I'm looking for someone. That's why I climbed the mountain."

"Well, you've found someone, have you not?"

Fran wobbled, suddenly feeling as if he were falling through water. He pulled his sword free of its scabbard.

At the sight of it, she froze. "Tell me, where did one as young as you come by so old a sword?"

Theirs eyes locked. A sense of déjà vu overwhelmed Fran. "Do I know you?"

"Well, that's a question I ask myself daily." As she spoke the woman's expression grew cold. "Because none of you visit me, do you?"

Fran realised he was speaking to Arete.

"I know who you are. I won't fall under your spell."

Arete laughed, letting the point of the sword fall to the ground. "Who do you think I am to cast such spells? The mountains hold many secrets, but there are few left who can weave charms to bewitch a passing traveller and steal their wares. Come." Arete went to the opposite edge of the cave mouth and leant her sword against the wall.

Fran hesitated, his hand still on the hilt.

"You at least have found my home. You must be weary. Sit." Arete motioned towards one of the boulders, which he now noticed made two seats outside the cave. "If I were a caster, I'd conjure myself a new dress, perhaps." This time the smile was real. "Come."

Unsure what else to do, Fran perched on the nearest boulder, keeping his eyes on Arete. He found something about her familiar – disarming even – but what was it? She sat across from him, studying him intently.

"You look familiar too. I'll make something to eat, and you can tell me who you are, although I can guess already."

Fran, remembering the packet, thought of his father again.

With Arete muttering softly and striking flint, Fran relaxed sufficiently to take in his surroundings – still lake and sparse, tall pines, their tops framed against a blue sky, a shoreline of pine needles, strewn with rocks at the water's edge. *A good spot to rest for the night. Too good, perhaps.* A huge brown and black mountain cat slunk out from the cave and slowly circled his boulder. Sweat prickled as it slid behind him.

"Begone." Arete sprang up, startling Fran as she clapped her hands at the cat. "When I found her, she was a rag of fur shivering in the snow. She's haunted this cave for many a season now; my kindness is repaid by the scratches and tears in this dress."

Fran watched the cat skulk away along the shore while Arete disappeared inside the cave. Beyond the trees, something in the distance made him catch his breath. *The west. Eruthin.* His heart jerked. And Glendorrig; his father's old home. Somewhere beneath those mountains stretching away as far as the eye could see, there was a house, and the people inside it were his. *Family – uncles, aunts and cousins. Grandparents, perhaps.* A sob came from nowhere, taking him unawares. Eruthin had always been a land from the realm of fireside tales, its myths precious and transient as the warmth from embers on a chilly night, and then lost on the morning breeze.

Further away still lay the ocean; endless water, told of in stories. Arete would know about it all, would tell him new things. But where was she? He stepped towards the cave mouth, skirting to the side of the cauldron, which hung on chains over the fire, still rocking slightly, steam gathered within. Fran's stomach growled.

Dusty bottles lined ledges cut in the wall. At this time of day, when the sun dipped in the west, light travelled down into the cave, and he could make out a bed canopy hung over a raised slab and plush skins on the floor. Then there was darkness, indicating the cave continued.

Arete emerged from it carrying a platter of bread and two fine silver cups.

"Come." She knelt beside the fire.

Fran sat down on a tattered rug opposite, the sword, now in its scabbard, stretched out behind him. The aroma of stewing venison filled the air.

"You'd be more comfortable if you set aside your sword, my young friend." Arete handed one of the silver cups to him.

Fran took a sip of wine. It tasted strong, sweet and a great deal different to his mother's ale or the village mead.

Arete leant forwards, gesturing for him to unclip the scabbard from his belt. He recoiled, hesitating over where to put the cup down. She took it from him and stepped away, the unsheathed sword in her other hand.

"Give it back. It's my father's." Fran inched round the fire, edging towards where the other sword leant against the wall.

Arete, clutching the sword, seemed to grow taller. The glow of the fire reflected orange on the upturned blade. "Perhaps you're mistaken." She looked at the sword as if it were an old friend returned unexpectedly.

Fran grabbed Arete's sword. He raised it and steel met steel, but he was unpractised, having only sparred with Cader and Frey.

Arete pushed him back, dancing across the pine needles. He retreated, stumbling blindly backwards along the water's edge in terror of the fatal blow.

Arete pressed forwards, deftly avoiding the water, until they were among the pines on the western shore. The cat's tail brushing the pine needles alerted him to the creature's presence; it was behind him – closing in.

The swords clashed and Fran threw his weight forwards, forcing Arete to take a step back. For the first time the sword became a part of him, some subconscious fragment of his mind registering the red rose. This was a brother to his father's sword, equal in strength and balance. He flowed with it, metal screaming and his heart hammering, the trees and water a dreamscape backed by blue. Instinct told him push for the water, and as she neared it, Arete's hesitation grew until moving backwards, she stumbled and fell. An image of Lukas flashed into Fran's mind. The sword point rested at Arete's throat, but her eyes were on him, and he hesitated, finding that familiarity again – the disarming smile. It did its work and Fran's anger melted away.

A lesson. He drew up the sword, relaxing his hand and admiring the decoration on the rose; fine workmanship, like hard, painted clay.

"That sword is but a toy. Put it away." Arete sprang back to her feet, the movement so quick it startled him.

He stood alert again, ready for another attack.

"Begone."

Fran spun round and saw the cat. It lurked behind a tree trunk, the fur down its back bristling.

"Now, please put your sword down." Arete set hers down gently on the moss and needles at the foot of one of the pines. "It's of no use against me."

Fran scoffed. The blade was deadly sharp and she was overconfident. He had chosen to step back. He could reclaim his father's sword at any point.

"It's a dragon blade, yes. It will slice a man in two – skin, muscle, sinew, bone. It will be your strong left arm in battle."

What? Yes, he was holding the sword in his left hand.

"But I know you won't hurt me with it, so please put it down."

"I'll take my own sword back now."

"And then you'll leave."

Fran started, remembering his mother. He was here to find her, not be caught by these bamboozlements. "Where's my mother? What have you done with her?" Again, he levelled the sword at Arete.

"I've done nothing with her," Arete spat back, her face suddenly twisting. Then, instead of retreating, her hand grabbed the blade, and she grimaced as she forced it downwards. Blood from her palm trickled down her wrist.

Fran dropped the sword. Retching, he grasped a nearby trunk for support.

"See, I've kept it sharp for you all these summers and winters," she said, turning sickly white.

"Why would you do that?" Fran dropped down beside her. *Those green eyes. Who did she resemble?* "What's wrong with you?"

He grasped around for something to staunch the wound, eventually hacking free a lump of moss.

Arete, meanwhile, held her hand clear, turning the palm in on itself to close the wound. "What must I do to make anyone listen?" she asked.

"I have been listening, but you don't make any sense."

"I told you to put the sword down."

"I only wanted my own sword back. I told you; it belonged to my father. My mother only gave it to me two days ago. You stole it and attacked me with it."

"As I explained, you're mistaken. Your father may have carried it to March, but another owned it before him." She turned away, cradling her hand.

Fran moved away, down to the shoreline. On his left, the pines cast long shadows across the water. His stomach growled and tears welled. What a miserable day this was. And where was his mother? Exhausted from the climb and tired of riddles, he exhaled, letting the tears roll down his cheeks. *Two fights. First Lukas, now Arete.* He recalled the same choking anger and his mother's hand, pushing gently down on his arm. *Best to be rid of the damn thing. It brought only trouble in its wake.*

Chapter 22

Suspicion and Stew

"Why are you crying?"

The voice made Fran jump.

Arete still clutched her hand, but she now sat straight, her legs curled beneath her.

"I'm not." Fran scooped water from the lake to splash his face. Drying it on his shirt, he strode back towards her.

Drops of blood marked the tattered skirt, but her palm seemed unblemished. The swords lay nearby; traces of blood smeared the red one and stained the adjacent moss.

"You were hurt. You pushed down the blade." The flood of relief brought him to his knees.

Arete wiped her hands together as if she were batting off damp grass. "I told you; that sword is but a toy; it can't hurt me. So, yes, there's a little blood, but it will wash off."

Fran stared from sword to sword, noting the torn patch of moss used to staunch the wound and wondering if this were a dream from which he would shortly wake.

Eventually, Arete stood up, picking pine needles from the torn and bloodstained dress.

"You're not hurt at all, then," he asked.

She spread her palm in front of him. A glance told him she was fine, although the sickly pallor remained. "I told you" – Arete spoke more gently this time – "it's a dragon blade but not one that can hurt me. You've seen my companion in the forest many times, I think, yet you still don't understand."

Shade gathered around them, the sun descending fast. Fran shivered, his damp shirt clinging. Somewhere away behind him he caught the swish of the cat's tail again. Arete waited for his answer, her gaze searching. *Again, the familiarity.* Shades of oak and beech, recollections of the forest – rustles and bird calls, leaf mould, earth and sap. Those eyes held it all, but what was more, they evoked the safety of the forest. He exhaled then let the scent of pine fill his lungs.

"I know the forest well, but not your ... companion."

"Indeed, he also knows the forest well. He's most likely there now. But there's time enough for you to meet him. Come, we interrupted our meal, didn't we?" Arete extended the healed hand to Fran.

When he accepted it, she hauled him up in a flash. It took him a moment to regain his balance, long enough to realise he presented as sorry a picture as she, less bloodstained, but with stale clothes clinging and dirt beneath his nails. He turned to the lake, a patch of which remained in the sun.

"You can bathe if you want," Arete said, as if in reply to his thoughts, then she picked up the silver sword and walked back to the cave.

Summer held sway in the mountains. The margins of the lake were warm, and only the odd ribbon of snow decorated the highest peaks. Fran's clothes hung on a pine branch, with the sword beneath them at the water's edge. Now he floated on his back, watching corvids spin and thin whorls of cloud drift. The water sang in his ears; the world of March seemed a faraway thing and the mountain a fairy kingdom. Sculling round, he saw Arete bathing in the headwaters of the stream at the opposite end of the lake. The water there would be warmer still, trapped in the clear, shallow pools he had seen from the hillside.

When he finished bathing, he was not sure what else to do, so he walked to the cave with his shirt that he had rinsed in lake water and, still wet, draped it over his shoulder.

Arete knelt by the fire, stirring the cauldron. She glanced up and tossed him a blanket. "Here, it's getting cold. Now we can finish our meal, and perhaps you'll tell me your name." She motioned Fran to set his shirt to dry over a frame by the fire then pointed him to one of the rocks outside the cave.

Fran remained standing, fingering the blanket. The wool was finer than his own at home, smooth to the touch. Behind him, a ruddy glow in the west signalled the end of day – food, firelight and rest. He shivered, recoiling from the wet shirt.

"Put it here to dry."

Again, he hesitated. She wore the same dress, the bloodstains washed out, but seemed unperturbed by wet or cold.

"I don't feel cold in the way you do." Again, his thought was answered.

"You said you already knew my name." He moved round the fire and hung the shirt to dry.

"I said I can guess who you are."

Ah. "My name's Fran and yours is Arete."

No answer came. She bent over the cauldron, her face hidden by her hair.

Fran moved away. "Well, are you going to deny it?"

"Fran, my sharp young friend, of course I'm not." Arete smiled and, leaving the cauldron, walked out onto the shore, sitting down a little way from him. With the setting sun at her back, she slipped into silhouette, and he, perching on the boulder, shielded his eyes.

"My name *is* Arete, and I'm sorry our evening began so badly."

Fran hugged the folds of blanket round his shoulders. "Well, I'm a stranger in your home."

"A guest who's hungry and impatient with the fire." Arete shuffled pine needles with her toes.

Fran realised he was smiling too. "Perhaps. My day's been long."

Arete went to the hearth for a basket of bread, offering it to him and motioning him again towards the rug by the fire. "Understand I mean you no harm. You handled the sword well. Believing I would kill you made a thousand lessons from one, and there's not time for a thousand lessons; March is awake and at war."

At war! "How could you know that?"

"I can see March from here, remember. And I hear its voices on the wind. Joy and sorrow, birth and death, peace and strife."

More riddles. Riddles and guesses. "If you mean me no harm, give me back my sword. If there's war, as you say, I should return to my friends."

"But you left March. Where were you going?"

"I told you; I'm searching for my mother."

"Ah ... your mother."

"Yes. She ... I thought she wanted to find you, so I followed her."

"Yet you didn't travel together."

"No."

"I've not seen any other travellers this summer, and before that, I can't recall."

"I may be mistaken. I must leave to find her."

"But if she's coming to find me, why not wait for her here?"

"She left before me. She may be elsewhere, lost or hurt."

"She left without you, and you followed her. Maybe she doesn't want to be found."

"I thought she was coming to see you. She ..."

"What?"

"I thought she was coming to see you. There's a problem in March; a matter that needs to be settled."

Arete fell silent, watching both Fran and the pot. Away in the distance, crows were cawing. She stirred it, nodding as she tasted the stew.

"It's been a long time since anyone from March came to me with a problem. They're strangers to me, and I to them. Strangers who won't open their gates when I knock. Strangers who attacked me with swords and spears while I stood unarmed and shivering in the snow." Her face darkened like a storm cloud, and she turned towards the lake, where the trees grew black in the twilight, their shadows reaching across the water.

He hugged the blanket closer, glad of the fire's heat. His mother's tale again – he guessed its ending and glanced around, looking for the silver sword. It was nowhere to be seen. The red one rested against the cave wall behind him. Fran held his tongue. The silence stretched and the sun faded, leaving only the fire, crackling as it caught the wood. Flames licked the pot, and the stew bubbled, hissing when it overboiled, the rich aroma filling the cave.

Arete woke from her recollection, prodding the piled logs out from under the cauldron. They fell, the flames ebbing, and she again stirred the stew. "I've lived by this lake for many lifetimes. If she wants me, she'll find me – we can be sure of it."

"But, what if—"

"She'll find me. You're a good son, but she didn't want you to follow her."

Fran stared at the cauldron, recalling Maya's words from the day before. "But *I* wanted to follow her."

"No, Fran, you wanted to be useful. Following her won't help. First, you must learn not to lose a sword so easily. Then you must learn to fight ... with the sword that's rightfully yours." As she spoke, Arete produced the silver sword from under a fur and pointed it at the red sword resting behind him against the wall.

Fran flashed a glance from one to the other. *You must learn not to lose a sword so easily.* "Just give the thing back to me." He knew he should be on his feet, but they throbbed, and his belly growled and ached. *Just keep it in sight and wait for a chance ...*

Arete avoided his eyes but swapped the sword for a ladle and spooned out the broth.

The bowl she handed him was hot, so he balanced it on folds of blanket and skimmed the surface with a spoon, holding a chunk of venison clear to cool. He sank gratefully into the rest; the tender meat and strong rich gravy were studded with wheat and another grain he did not recognise.

Arete proffered a chunk of hard bread that had been slathered in grease and toasted over the fire.

He broke it into pieces and dropped them into the stew.

They ate. The fire flickered between them, clear of the pot and lively again, pine logs spitting when flames met sap. When he had finished a second bowlful, she swapped the empty crock for the sweet wine.

Fran slipped on his dry shirt, wrapped the blanket round himself again and leant back against the cave wall, cradling the silver cup. His eyelids were heavy, and he soon slipped into a fitful doze. When his head jarred for the third or fourth time, Arete spoke from nearby, taking the cup and handing him some extra furs. He set one down on the old wool rug and, still clinging to the blanket, pulled the other over his chest. Across the fire, red hair fanned out across fur, reminding him of a small cloth packet he had seen somewhere, once. Then the memory bobbed away again, a little reed boat on the water.

Meanwhile, below in Spiral Cove, huddled beside the remnants of Ladon's fire, Annerin sobbed, the little packet still crushed between her fingers and faintly damp.

Her hair clung about her face, and she sweated and shivered, too tired to open her eyes. The setting sun picked her out, a little spot of darkness in the crevice of the rocks, and high above, a raven circled before landing on the clifftop.

Somewhere in Annerin's head, amid the fitful ebb and flow, a word tried to form. Its sounds fell randomly again and again as she imagined her fingertips gripping the rough pouch and lifting it to her lips. The effort proved too much and eventually she slid back into a torpor that offered neither refreshment nor rest.

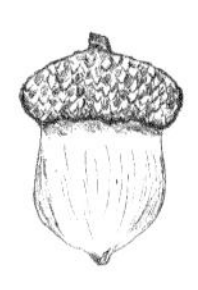

Chapter 23

Safe Harbour

Gareth, Godwen, Edric and Sennen had hurried towards Spiral Cove. Their journey took them to the same fording point on the Cloudwater used by Fran the morning before. From here, they followed an ancient track, intent on arriving by nightfall. They too found their way overgrown, and the dwindling tower of smoke rising from Spiral Cove, while allaying some misgivings, also stoked their worst fears. Someone had been at the ancient burial ground and, on the hottest of days, found need of a vast fire.

Gareth, with one eye on the sun and intent on clearing the path, said little. Each flurry of feathers and cracking branch made his heart jolt. Godwen's concern for him was obvious from the little furrow of his brow whenever they stopped to catch breath. Meanwhile, Sennen and Edric baulked at every obstacle blocking the way, their constant cursing enough to make a man scream. But they feared different monsters. Small wonder Annerin fled and that her son followed.

When they reached the River Everlode, they removed their boots and waded across, thankful for the icy water. After this point, the terrain became rockier, and the undergrowth thinned. Gareth's head ached. He signalled for the group to stop in a small clearing.

"We'll stop here. It'll make a good place to camp."

"But you do intend to travel on to Spiral Cove tonight, don't you?" Godwen asked. "We must be very near."

"Yes, there's still light enough, and we need to know why there's been such a huge fire."

Godwen turned away, watching the smoke still twisting up.

What other reason could there be? Gareth set down his pack and reached for his waterskin. He needed a brief rest before facing it ... "We still might need to search between here and the foot of the pass," he ventured.

"That'll take days, and it depends on what we're looking for." Edric watched the drifting smoke. "Those paths will be worse than the main route. Who's used them this summer or last? No one. They're long gone, and the forest's well-nigh impenetrable."

Sennen turned away to watch the smoke too.

They were expecting only bones. For a beat, he wished Galos were here. At least the man would have the courage to hope. Gareth's temples throbbed, the headache stabbing. "Well, whoever's gone to Spiral Cove today took a different route to ours."

"Yes, that is curious," Sennen conceded. "Cutting through the forest from the ford isn't the quickest way. It speaks of hasty thinking."

"Indeed," said Godwen. "Or the fear of being seen skirting the forest."

Sennen shook his head and the group fell silent.

Gareth dragged himself to his feet. "Let's go while we still have light."

With the sun's glow fading in the west, eventually the trees gave way to rising ground backed by towering grey cliffs. Gareth quickened his pace to a run, with the others close at his heels. Out of breath, he scanned the cove – a wilderness of tumbledown cairns with a raven circling overhead. It was smaller than he remembered, more haphazard, with rockfall barely distinguishable from the farthest cairns at the cliff foot. He let out a gasp then broke into a sprint. The fire smouldered right of centre, tiny sparks still escaping from between blackened logs. Nearby, a crumpled figure lay in the narrow slot between two enormous boulders. *Annerin.*

He reached her first and dropped to his knees, grasping her shoulders. *Alive, at least. No sign of wounds. No sign of Fran.* He peeled away the hair sticking to her forehead and cheeks and saw she was unconscious, her skin as pale as mutton fat and her lips colourless and cracked. *That face – so familiar, so ...* Something twisted inside, hitting him sidelong. Tears prickled. He prayed he wasn't too late. He fumbled for his waterskin, then he put the spout to her mouth. Water trickled over her lips, and she murmured something he could not catch. He tipped the waterskin again, but Annerin had a spasm of coughing. Gareth set it aside, holding her as she choked and spluttered.

"Give her more." Godwen pushed the skin to Annerin's lips. "Drink."

Annerin blinked and her hand came up to grasp the skin and pull it away. Eventually the spasms subsided, and Gareth lowered her back down. She sat forwards, tears running down her cheeks. After a few moments, she lifted the skin, swilling the water gingerly.

"Are you hurt?" Gareth asked.

Annerin stared at him, wordless.

"Annerin, are you hurt?"

"No. No, I don't think so. But I've slept far too long. I don't know how."

"She's travelled too long in the heat," said Gareth, spinning round and catching the bemused looks. "We'll take her back to March."

"NO." Annerin edged away, scowling when she caught sight of Edric and Sennen behind Godwen. "I don't live in March anymore."

Gareth felt the blood rush to his face. Why, she behaved as if he were Wyntr. Or perhaps she just distrusted his friends. Either way, he could not drag her back.

"Go and set up camp where we stopped. I'll follow you," he snapped at his friends.

Godwen shrugged and turned away, leading the other two back towards the forest.

"Annerin, please, talk to me." Gareth sat back as far from the fire as he could, pulling his knees to his chest. His time in the forest with Annerin eluded memory. After it, nothing else seemed quite real – his father's death, his mother's coldness, poor, sweet Elsa – all a waking dream. If the sun had got to Annerin, then surely the darkness had got to him.

"You've come from March ..." she began. "Fran. Is he ...?"

The question hung in the air like fire smoke.

"He's not there," Gareth began. "Elsa said he followed you ... but he thought you'd gone up the mountain for some reason, so ..."

Nudging a loose stone with her foot, Annerin almost smiled. Then she glanced down at something clutched in her hand before slipping it into the pocket of her dress.

Nearby, a white butterfly landed on a stone, its wings gently flexing. The place was not so lifeless after all. Tiny flowers grew in seams on the rocks and insects flickered by. *Could the news about Wyntr wait? Annerin wasn't even fit to walk.* He weighed the matter and decided not. "The thing is, Annerin, we came after you … after you both … because we were worried."

Annerin frowned. "When you say we …"

"Galos is also searching for you. He's gone up the mountain."

"So, he'll likely find Fran and bring him back." Annerin sat back and signalled for the waterskin.

"Err … yes, but the difficulty is …"

She froze, waterskin forgotten in her hand, her eyes burning into him.

He took a deep breath. "We … Galos and I … believe Wyntr followed you both. Something else happened, you see … my father … he's dead …" Unable to go on, Gareth looked away, out towards the forest, after Godwen, who was now lost from sight.

"But I only left yesterday. How …? And he's not here so he's gone after Fran." Annerin's voice rose, and she tried to get to her feet but slumped back down, holding the rock to steady herself.

"It is better that you left. Had you stayed …"

"I sent him to Galos."

"Well, Galos can't fight everyone." Gareth thought of Elsa and stopped himself. "What I mean to say is he is only one man. Wyntr, Gyll and Seth tricked everyone. Fran is most likely safer in the open. Your house is watched, but one burning arrow …"

"And so it has come to that." Annerin spat the words, but then she looked at him, her eyes widening. When she spoke, her voice was unexpectedly gentle. "But your father … How …? What has happened?"

Gareth recounted as much as he knew and could bear to repeat, leaving out the incident with Elsa. That could wait. She listened, but her eyes began to glaze, and he saw she fought to stay awake. The light was fading fast, and she needed food. They must get away from this place. Roles were reversed, and now *he* was rescuing *her*. She seemed ill, and he would have to take her to Ebba until Fran reappeared. He kissed the top of her head, registering the salt of her sweat on his lips, then he lifted her and made his way slowly back to the camp, where Godwen, Edric and Sennen waited with a fire and food.

Gareth reached the camp at dusk with Annerin slung over his shoulder. As he approached, his friends smirked and rolled their eyes. The lightened mood was a tonic, but his cuts and bruises hurt, and his head still ached, leaving little appetite for banter.

"What've you done to her?" asked Edric.

"Didn't she want to come?" chirped Sennen.

"She fainted." A sharp stab in the temple made him wince.

"Was that after you asked her to come back with you again?" ventured Godwen.

"Make yourself useful, will you." Gareth gestured at Annerin's pack, which hung over his left shoulder.

Godwen took it and spread Annerin's cloak out on the forest floor near the fire. Gareth put her down on it and sat nearby. The other three joined him, launching into the first batch of hot breads with gusto. After a short while, Annerin woke and turned towards the fire, where Sennen was roasting a haunch of venison and heating the second lot of flat breads on a stone.

Gareth gestured for her to move forwards and tore her a chunk of bread. "Come. Eat."

She moved towards the fire, but her hesitation and the ensuing silence made Gareth wince.

Opposite, Edric picked at his bread, head down, while Sennen focused on the meat.

Well, soon it would be dark.

"We're relieved to have found you so quickly, Annerin," said Godwen at last. He was sat on the far side of Annerin, so Gareth turned towards them, making a smaller group on one side of the fire. No one spoke much more, and his mind wandered. The smell of venison filled the air and fat made the fire spit. He recalled the feelings of distrust he too once harboured about Annerin – and which now seemed so bizarre – only a few days earlier, when he waited in the garden of the stone house.

With the meat shared out, each of them stared into the fire. Around them, rooks and starlings gathered in their roosts, huddling against the gathering dark. Gareth groped for something to say, but as usual nothing came to mind. At last, the silence felt comforting; the world faded to black and white and tree trunks towered like guardians, circling their little group. His earlier terrors were gone, inexplicably gone. Furtively, he glanced towards Annerin. The firelight lit her features.

"We carried you home," she began, turning to him. "Fran and Tom carried you home. You'd fallen and hit your head. But you're better, it seems. I'm glad." She dropped her head, her hair falling forwards and hiding her face.

Godwen cleared his throat and shuffled towards Sennen, leaving Gareth and Annerin together on one side of the fire. Sennen pulled a small wooden flute from his pack and began to play.

"I am better, thanks to you. You saved my life. But how is it you're here, and what happened to you?"

"I ... it's a long story." She threw a rind onto the logs. "I missed my way and got to the cove, then something strange happened, or so it seemed." She gave a weary shrug. "Or perhaps I'd just spent too long in the sun."

"Oh."

"Whatever found you that day, I'm no longer convinced it meant to hurt you. That creature could have killed us both, but it didn't."

What did Arthen say? When I was young, I too walked in the woods.

"I'm sorry, you didn't see it, of course," Annerin added.

"I did see it," he said, meeting her eyes.

"I wondered. You bumped into it ... that's why you fell."

"Yes."

Annerin's voice dropped to a whisper. "I didn't tell Galos ... or your ... but Fran's seen it too; he admitted it. Perhaps I should have come to March instead of ... well, instead of going looking for ..."

"For the witch."

"How d'you know that?"

"The whole of March knows it. Mainly thanks to Ebba. I don't think it would have changed anything. The problem was no one wanted to believe you ... or Galos."

"Galos has been such a good friend to me, but I'm more afraid of March than I am of the forest."

It was Gareth's turn to stare at the fire. Flames still flickered. Sennen was a shadow, but his notes floated around them, long and slow, making the sparks dance and weaving a protective spell around the glade. He yawned. In the distance an owl hooted.

"You have more friends in March than you think, Annerin."

"Yes ... I'm sure that's true. Absence leads to forgetfulness."

"I would count among those friends ... if you'd count me ..."

She flashed him a glance, but just then the music paused and she turned towards Sennen. *Answer enough.* Sennen struck up another tune and Gareth craned his neck to see the moon, full and bright in the sky above them.

Annerin woke, stiff and cold in the growing half-light. Lukas had haunted her dreams; violent man that he was, his death shocked her. *Poor Galos – and typical, wretched Ebba with her wretched plans.* Picking a dry leaf from the forest floor, she crumbled it between grimy fingers. A new day, still shapeless, beckoned and loomed. Gareth lay to one side of her, shifting fitfully under his cloak, Godwen sprawled on the other.

She rose and began gathering wood for the fire. As she tiptoed round the four sleeping men, yesterday's misgivings returned. What would be made of Gareth leading out a search party? What would Hilda say? Annerin shuddered at the thought. Bad as Ebba could be, she was not without good cheer, whereas Hilda had ever been grim and superior, trading on position as if it were gold. *What did Mother call Hilda's mother? A long, tall, slit-lipped witch.* Horrible family, but not Gareth; always he was ... well, just Gareth – a subdued boy who grew into a reserved man, one who now visibly brightened at the sight of young Elsa.

She stole a glimpse at him, recalling his words the night before ... his look. He seemed to have taken to her a little – not surprising given the incident in the wood – but her doubt still lingered. And worry. *Where was Fran now?* One thing was clear though – she could no longer climb Elden Deas and find Arete as originally planned. Fran must have guessed the sword's origins troubled her. Did he also suspect, like she did, that the dragon was patrolling the forest to guard the sword? Perhaps so. If he'd set out to follow her, he should have reached the lake by now. What would he find? Hard to know, but he would probably be safer there than in March.

She, however, needed to return to March for Galos' sake. Ebba's meddling had sparked the trouble, but his defence of herself and Fran would have shocking ramifications. Besides, she was fond him, so she could not simply run and hide. What she could do to help him, though, was unclear.

The remnant of a log remained on the fire, so she flicked the ash aside and, careful not to snuff out the embers, she added a handful of twigs. Several caught and started to smoke. It was touch and go, but she blew gently, and a tiny flame licked upwards. She fed the fire with more kindling, adding a few larger pieces around the side and fanning the growing flames.

Now she gauged there would be a short window of opportunity before anyone else stirred. Grabbing her bundle, she walked a short distance downhill to one of the many streams cutting through the forest. The brook was surprisingly wide and its water chilly, but she wanted to change the miserably dirty shift she wore, so she took off her outer clothing, hooked her apron and dress over a branch and slipped into the water.

It ran shallow but fast. The cold took her breath away, but it felt refreshing too, and the day promised to be hot. She lay in the current, letting it flow around her. Cocooned between the steep banks, she listened for sounds from the camp. There were none, but eventually a solitary blackbird's song became a chorus, and feeling the press of time, she clambered back onto the bank, dried herself hastily with her apron, swapped the sodden shift for a clean one from her bundle and wrung the water from her hair.

All the time listening out, she slipped her dress back on and pulled the apron over the top. As she tied the cord at her waist, she caught the crunch of footfall. Gareth appeared, striding towards her through the trees.

"Found you." His wide smile warmed her like the sun. "Did you sleep much?" Without waiting for a reply, he leant round and gave her dripping hair an additional wring.

"Yes, I feel much better," she answered, surprised both by Gareth's easy and familiar manner and by how little she resented it.

"Good. We'll leave straight after breakfast. We should be at the ford by mid-afternoon."

Annerin, thinking of both the stone house and flaming arrows, said nothing for a while. She would be forced to go to March – at least until Galos and Fran returned. And if Wyntr ... her heart lurched, and she pushed the fear away. No. Fran would hide. Mountain and forest were much alike. Fran could get within spitting distance of Wyntr and the man would never know ...

"I meant to ask, how did you find me at the cove?" she said eventually.

"We saw smoke rising from the forest at midday. You built such a fire." Gareth smiled, motioning for her to sit down on dry ground by a patch of bracken.

"A fire?" Annerin sat down, confounded. "Yes, there was a fire, wasn't there, but gods help me, I don't remember building it."

"It's strange," replied Gareth, still smiling. "*You* brought *me* back from the forest and I remember so little, although ... perhaps there's no more to remember. I saw the creature, fell, and then you found me.

We found a vast pile of ash by you. You built a great bonfire and slept in the heat."

Annerin's head swam. She hardly knew Gareth – he was Lukas' son – and yet here they sat like old friends. Something in his look spoke far more than words. And he had come after her. No doubt he too wanted answers about what happened in the forest. She, after all, had ventured out with only a half-formed idea about seeking Arete, but she'd found her, if only in a dream. But was it a dream? What else could it be? Or had she lost her mind, somewhere, somehow, in the forest, in the dark, alone? Whatever it was, it remained vivid. The image of the crescent moon nagged at her, but last night she and Gareth talked beneath a full moon. Now that alone seemed real, together with her fear for Fran.

"I remember the heat," she answered, recoiling at the memory. "And how my head ached."

"Then we're even. My head still aches too."

Annerin laughed, startling herself with the unfamiliar sound. She stood up. "I must have slept a long time, but Fran's a day ahead of Wyntr. He likely reached the lake yesterday."

"We need to get back to March. If fortune's good, Fran and Galos will be back shortly too. As for Wyntr, I'll make issue with my kinsmen when he shows his face. No harm will come to you."

The five made a hasty breakfast of cold meat, tea and bread before retracing their steps. Godwen led, and Gareth followed at a steady pace, talking quietly with Annerin. Edric and Sennen remained at a distance, their manner strained.

Chapter 24

Comings and Goings

For Frey, the watch started at first light, with black fading to grey and the first notes of birdsong breaking the night's stillness. As he neared the top of March hill, he caught sight of his father squatting by a tiny fire set behind a low semicircle of stones on the summit. Jake's haggard face told its own story; it had been a long and weary watch. Torches made bright dots around the settlement and hill, giving sight to the watcher, but there were too few men on hand to keep them lit, and with the moors now silhouetted in the east, several guttered.

Leaden limbed and drowsy, Frey shivered under his cloak. His sleep had been short and fitful, his worries tormenting him. The question hung heavy in the air – *who would return first?* The day before, following the departure of Galos, Cader and Willett, a subtle and disquieting change had overtaken March. An undercurrent of distrust began snaking its way through the settlement; men watched and calculated, leaving the fields unattended and gathering in small groups, their tools idle.

He stopped and set his torch in the holder behind the wall.

"Thank the gods, Frey. I thought daybreak would never come."

"Father, you look dreadful. Go home to bed."

"Ah, I'd sleep better if Galos were on the horizon."

"Indeed. They fear Wyntr as if he were ten men. We'll want friends if he's back before Galos."

"True." His father's rugged features settled somewhere between smile and grimace. He gave Frey a rough embrace before picking up the torch and turning to go.

"Father."

"Yes, Frey?" He spun back round.

"Eat and sleep, please. We'll need you if Galos doesn't get back soon."

His father's expression became grave. "Ay, he was hasty. He was furious with ... anger clouded his judgement. He should've gone to the cove and sent Gareth up Elden Deas."

Frey said nothing. His thoughts were the same, ever since seeing smoke rising from Spiral Cove.

"Now there's too few swords and too many women and children." His father squinted in the torchlight. "But I say too much. Look to your post. I'll be ready when I'm needed."

When morning came, Elsa slept on and Maya waited beside her, playing quietly with her doll. Meanwhile, their mother and Nell tiptoed back and forth, acknowledging her with an occasional pat on the head. Time dragged, so when a face appeared at the window opening, Maya threw down the doll and darted over.

"Lift me through, Liselle," she whispered.

"Where's your mother?"

"She's just in there with Nell," Maya replied. "They've been talking for ages."

"Finola's taking breakfast to Frey. We could go after her and see if there's any sign of your father."

Liselle hoisted Maya up and over the sill, and the two girls ran across the square and around the longhouse, towards the hill path. They climbed it, Maya lagging behind a little, while Liselle bounded ahead, her skirt growing dusty and her hands drifting through the long grass as she ran. Maya too flicked absently at the stems. Butterflies still flitted, but everything held the heaviness of dread. Elsa's bloody arm haunted her, and nothing could be well until Father got back. She had slept poorly, her dream an endless chase, with the dragon always just out of reach behind the next tree or around the next corner. She did not, however, want to tell Liselle about either her encounter or the dream, and so while Liselle chattered on, she remained quiet.

Near the top of the hill, she stopped and turned towards the mountain, conjuring in her mind's eye the image of Fran on the dragon's back, returning home. All would then be well. *How could it be otherwise?* Father would banish Wyntr, and Gareth would listen to him, laugh with Cader and Frey and get a house away from his horrible old mother.

Liselle ran back to her. "What're you smiling about?"

"I didn't mean to be smiling. I was just thinking about Father coming home, and how glad I'll be."

"I will too. My eyes are tired from staring at the forest. I wish we could send the birds to spy for us. Just think, they must know where each person is ... your father with Willett and Cader, Fran, Annerin,

Gareth, and even Wyntr. Why, they must even be able to see Arete in her cave."

Delightful thought. With the idea of it, the sun's warmth made it through. Maya hugged Liselle. "I wish we could ride a bird – a bird as big as a dragon – and go to find them all. And breathe fire at Wyntr. I'd kill Wyntr, but I might not kill Gyll or Seth. Well, maybe Gyll."

"I'd not kill Seth," said Liselle, her broad, freckled face suddenly serious. "His father and mother are both dead and he's frightened of Wyntr, that's all."

"And Wyntr was frightened of Lukas. And Lukas was frightened of Father," mused Maya.

"And now I don't think Wyntr's frightened of anyone," said Liselle. She stretched out her hand to Maya as they climbed the final section of hill.

They found Frey sitting cross-legged on the ground, eating his breakfast hungrily, while his mother scanned the horizon.

"Maya, Liselle," called Finola, waving them towards the large basket of bread and dripping in front of Frey. "Have you had breakfast?"

"No," replied the girls simultaneously.

Frey smiled through a mouthful of bread and waved for them to sit. "It's half a day's travel to Spiral Cove," he began, washing down the bread with a beaker of water. "I pray to the gods of that rocky place to guide Gareth to our friends. It was too far away to be sure, but I thought I saw smoke above the forest again at dawn."

Finola and the girls turned to look. In the far distance, Maya could just pick out the grey arch of cliffs marking the position of Spiral Cove.

The morning passed slowly for Frey, the relief of daylight quickly giving way to the despondency of waiting. Although his gaze remained on the southern horizon, his thoughts continually drifted back to the village below, and to Elsa in particular and whether he should visit her at the end of his watch. Throughout the morning, Maya and Liselle made their way up and down the hill, alternating between keeping him and Elsa company. Apparently, she was now awake, slowly recovering from the effects of Arthen's tonic. As the time for changeover approached, he decided it best to make do with the girls' reports, although in his heart of hearts he very much wished to call on her himself.

At noon, Tom climbed the hill to relieve him. Frey's eyes were dry and sore, but as he readied himself to go, he rubbed them and took one last look out towards the wood. A flicker of movement beyond the rise caught his attention. Tom saw it too. Both watched. After a short time, they could make out five figures approaching.

"Gods be praised, I think it's Annerin," said Tom when the group became clearer.

They watched together until the figures grew distinct – four men and a woman – and turned at the rise, heading towards the ford.

"It's Gareth, Godwen, Edric and Sennen, with Annerin, I'm certain of it," said Frey. "They're going to the stone house."

"They must be checking for Fran. But Gareth needs to make her come back here. He'll understand that." Tom's expression belied his words.

"She'll come here. She must," replied Frey.

"She's not slept a night here in eighteen summers." Tom's fingers drummed the hilt of his sword. "I'll come down to see she's all right. She can stay with me and Nell. Go down and wake your father and get him to send someone to swap with me ... then make sure Arthen knows; he'll do the rest."

"I'll slip through the postern and go to meet them," Jake said to Tom when the latter reached the bottom of the hill. "Frey's told no one but Arthen and Ebba, but everyone'll soon be drifting back in from the fields. We must take care. Annerin's a stranger here, as much as Edwyn once was, and blood's been spilt."

"I've decided she'll stay with me and Nell, at least until Galos gets back," said Tom. "It's not only Wyntr. Lukas may be dead, but his words still hang like poison in the air."

"Very well." Jake left via the postern to meet Annerin.

As Annerin approached March, her feet and nerves both faltered. The place had been her childhood home, and now friends waited, but after so long – eighteen long winters of exile – far from expecting welcome, she felt all the misery of a kin-wrecked soul dragged through a jeering mob to the gate.

Jake met them at the rise and explained there was no news – no word of Fran, or of the growing spectre of Wyntr, which loomed large in Annerin's mind. When Jake told her Tom's plan, a wave of relief swept through her. *No Ebba*. Nell would leave her to her thoughts, although their house sat in the centre of the settlement, far from either gate. Besides, she would still be able to see Elsa and Maya. They would not be far away, and Maya's dear little face was always such a welcome sight.

Annerin eyed the closed gate and surrounding stockade, willing herself to feel something more than she did at the sight of those rough timbers, still full of the same gaps and holes she remembered. Then she caught the smell of the place, and the faint buzz of voices, a baby's cry, the shout of a boy, harsh for a moment, then it was gone. A volley of memories followed, some sharp-edged and painful, other softer, cutting deeper. She took a slow breath and fought back the tears.

At the postern, Tom's enormous frame blocked the way, but his smile held warmth and he extended open arms. "It means something to see you safe, Annerin. And thanks to our good friends." Tom spoke to Gareth, nodding to his three companions.

"I'm forever in their debt." Annerin fought back the urge to say more. Under Tom's gaze, she felt awkward. There would be time later, and although he tended not to quiz, she sensed his curiosity.

She turned to Gareth as Godwen, Edric and Sennen followed Tom and Jake through the gate. "I'll stay here until Fran's back. After that, you'll always find welcome at my home." Then without waiting for a reply, she slipped through the gate.

Gareth watched her go, the pyre towering behind him, taunting him, it seemed. He was exhausted, and the sun, now high, scorched his head. His headache returned with a sharp stab, reminding him of his duty, his pride and his mother, all in one fell swoop.

When he ducked through the postern, Godwen, Edric and Sennen had already disappeared, and Tom and Jake were escorting Annerin to the house at a pace. Spotting Arthen sitting quietly in his favourite place under the eaves, he went to greet him.

"So, young man. What did you find in the forest this time?" Arthen waited while Gareth took a swig of water from a nearby urn.

"I found what I was looking for; I found Annerin. She lay unconscious by the remains of a great fire."

"And ..."

"There's nothing else to tell. No trace of Wyntr or Fran. It's lucky I saw the smoke."

"So, what will you do now?"

"Do?" Gareth shrugged. He felt too weary for this, but he badly needed the old man's guidance. "I haven't time to visit the barrows, I've wounded Elsa, my friends grow distant and ... and I've no stomach to go back home. Worst of all, the approach of my cousin overshadows the death of my father. Arthen, if ever a man needed advice ..."

Arthen said nothing.

The sun encroached on the shade, warming their knees. By the corner of the wall, a beetle baked in the sun. Opposite, Ebba slammed a shutter closed.

"I'd advise you first of all to steer your kinswoman away from Nell's door."

At these words, Gareth lurched as if from a blow. Exasperation met exhaustion head on. His headache stabbed and hunger made him queasy. He hauled himself up and put on his brightest smile to greet Vanna.

Sometime later, after Vanna, at Gareth's suggestion, had taken tea with his mother and Raya, and Nell had developed a defensive strategy largely involving tying the shutters closed, Gareth sat back down with Arthen. This time each held a bowl of Raya's stew.

"Your cousin does indeed cast a long shadow," began Arthen. "I can't know the future, but I've seen what's gone before. There's no easy path for you. If you support Galos, your friends will be faced with a choice, and it may be happiest for them to stay loyal to their kin. If you support Wyntr ... well, I fear you'll spend each day fighting your ground until one day when you look down, you'll have nothing under your feet and no one at your back."

Gareth mulled this over. "I thought to do neither, actually. March is one settlement, is it not? Blood will be spilt whatever I decide, so I think I'll look to my friends before I side with either Galos or Wyntr."

Arthen smiled. "You're in far less need of counsel than you think, Gareth. You can't leave for the barrows just now, and Elsa will forgive you in time. Your friends followed you once and they'll do so again. Remember, many fear Wyntr, but few love him."

Gareth turned to the old man, his smile faltering. "Then you have no remedy for Mother."

Arthen chuckled. "Perhaps you should give up your bed and let Vanna keep your mother company more permanently." As he spoke, he nodded towards the dilapidated round house away to their left. The thatch was missing in places and a rickety bench stood outside.

At the sight of the forgotten little dwelling, a fire lit in Gareth. The house was set a little back, and it was smaller than the ones edging the square – a relic from earlier times. Its position, in full view of the square, made it all the more invisible, as eyes were drawn to the handsome rectangular structures facing the longhouse, boasting partitioned off rooms and shuttered slits for windows.

Without waiting to thank Arthen, Gareth strode across to inspect it more closely. His discovery did not escape Ebba, who loitered behind her own threshold, sweeping minute particles of dust out into the square.

Chapter 25

The Water

Fran woke late, shivering in the cool of the cave and hugging a fur round his shoulders. Outside, a breeze ruffled the water and sunlight lit the far shore, dappling the water's edge with silver and promising a warm afternoon. He watched a kite swoop over the distant treetops then he shuffled towards the fire, which had been rebuilt and relit since last night and was now heating a cauldron of water.

A moment later, Arete appeared from the back of the cave with a platter of bread and cheese and a heap of the tiny, wrinkled fruits he had tasted in the previous night's stew. She sat down opposite, smiling.

"Eat," she said. "You've slept the morning away." She set the platter down between them and went to retrieve two fine pottery beakers from a ledge in the cave wall then took a sprig of mint from a small willow basket. She dipped the cups into the steaming cauldron to fill them before scraping leaves off the stem and scattering some in each.

Fran ate, with one eye always on Arete. She wore the same clothes, but now he noticed not only the tears in her dress but also how faded and worn the fabric was, with myriad tiny rents.

What need for this? Dressed like a queen, but in rags. Why, even the poorest in March had more than one set of clothes and cloth for patches to boot. The price of isolation, no doubt. Memories came unbidden; those many bartering trips to March, with goodwill often scarce and its absence reflected in the price. *An arm's-length boy who made the laughter stop.*

Setting aside the fur, he stretched out his feet to warm them, putting them as near to the fire as he dared. Arete ate slowly, and the silence between them was easy, broken only by the crackle of twigs on the fire, and the chatter of a flock of tiny birds bathing by the far shore.

With the meal finished, she took away the platter and cups. Fran, close to the fire and still drowsy from his long night's sleep, closed his eyes for what seemed only a moment. Perhaps it was longer, but something brought him back sharp. He had not caught the sound of her footfall across the furs, but now she stood close by, the rags and loose threads from her hem falling untidily around her ankles.

"Come, the day wears on, and we've a great deal to do. Pick up your sword."

His silver sword rested in her hand, and the sword with the red rose lay just a little way down the cave.

The corner of her mouth twitched as she dragged its hilt towards him with her toe. "Let's not go through this again," she said, pre-empting his complaint.

"I'm not leaving without my father's sword."

"Pick it up." She nodded towards the sword by her foot. Fran hesitated, having no wish for a repeat of yesterday's events.

When he did not move, Arete squatted down, balancing on the balls of her feet, the sword resting carelessly on her fingertips. She eyed him steadily and he tried to look away.

"Fran, neither sword's any use to you if you don't know how to use it. No one's taught you, despite March having several fine swordsmen. It's more than an afternoon's work, but let's at least make a start."

She was smaller than him. The sword dangled under his nose. But none of that mattered; like a dog defending a bone, she would be quicker.

He remained still.

She rose and walked outside.

Fran slipped his boots back on and picked up the red sword. *What difference, after all?* All the difference in the world, but what she said was true – he could use neither.

He walked out to where she waited on the shore.

Arete proved a good teacher, and the afternoon unaccountably long. The sun seemed to pause in the sky. Several times they stopped for food, drink and rest. Once or twice, he felt sure he slept, but still the afternoon sun beat down, and still they parried back and forth around Lake Everlis. After a while, he forgot to fear the cat, hissing at it when it slunk behind him. He learnt to block her assaults, and then to hold his ground. Lastly, she taught him to attack, and the silver blades danced together in the sunlight and flashed in the shade of the tall pines. Fran was tireless, and eventually, when they set to after a break, he managed to push her back until her feet slid into the water.

"Enough." She gasped. "Enough for one day."

He lowered his sword, suddenly realising how his arm ached. "You're only saying that because you've got your feet wet," he countered, fighting the urge to laugh.

"Perhaps." She smiled, taking the hand he proffered to pull her out.

"And do you intend to give me back my sword?"

"Very well, but if you want this sword back, you must win it from me."

Fran swung.

Arete sprang away from the lake, making space between them. He pursued her, and knowing he could not hurt her made him bold. He backed her along the shore, always pushing her towards the water. She would not go, but as they fought, they reached the point on the lakeside where the shoreline folded and water overflowed into a stream that fell to meet the river Everlode.

She had her back to the water now. Her face grew still.

"Enough!" she shouted, when again she stepped backwards into the lake.

Fran ignored her, intent on reclaiming the sword. Raising his left arm, he brought his sword down over hers, forcing her arm down. He leant in, intent on taking her feet from under her and plunging her into the water.

Arete pushed back, her voice deadly level and her face a breath away from his. "Don't do this."

"How else can I get my sword back?"

"Not the water."

He caught the panic in her eyes ... then glanced at the lake behind her. Where earlier the sunlight had flashed on ripples and dark water echoed blue sky, now the surface lay unnaturally still. The sun shone, but Everlis sucked in the light.

Fran slipped his arm around Arete's waist and swung her clear of the water's edge. At once, the gloom dispersed. Opposite, bright sunlight bathed the far shore, hitting the tall, sparse trunks, shafts cutting into the woodland space. He set her down and stepped back, confounded. She looked back at him, and Fran realised he held both swords. He turned, scanning water and sky. There was not so much as a cloud.

"The water – it changed."

"You made the right choice. Come." She crossed the stream and walked back towards the cave.

Fran moved further from the water's edge and compared the two swords. They were identical aside from the colour of the rose on the hilt. One was silver, in harmony with the bright steel, and the other was a dark, almost translucent red, done in a manner he had seen only once before, on an old brooch his mother treasured. If only March could see what he saw. This confusion had cost his father his life. With a sword in each hand, he almost understood it. And yet neither was black. Question after question sprang into his mind. His father, the sword, the lock of hair, Arete at the gate ... Arete herself. All pieces of the same puzzle, waiting to fall into place. And now he could discover the truth. He followed her back to the cave.

Fran and Arete sat facing one another on the boulders outside the cave. Geese swooped across the water, landing near the spot where he bathed the day before. Their haunting cries soothed, speaking of a day near complete and tasks all done.

"Many summers ago, your father took that sword from here," she began, pointing to the silver sword held in Fran's right hand.

"Are you saying he stole it?"

"I don't think so." Arete shrugged. "But they're very similar in appearance."

An unfortunate truth, entirely lost on so many in March.

"I think he only made a mistake. Despite their appearance, they're not the same, as I explained yesterday."

"The silver one's more powerful."

"Yes, the red sword's only a replica. The red rose is the symbol of Glendorrig, the kingdom you would soon reach if you continued along the Nethermore Pass. There are many red swords. You'd see that if you visited King Redwin's court."

"But I'm not likely to go there, am I? No one traverses the pass anymore."

"No, because the great dragon, Krataia, doesn't allow it, and that's one of the reasons why." She pointed at the silver sword again.

"Oh." Fran's grip loosened on the thing, and he proffered it to her as if the hilt were red hot.

Arete ignored it, shaking her head. "I decided it was safer with you in your little house – hiding in plain view."

"With a dragon to guard it."

She nodded. "And you'll need it before long."

"I don't understand."

"You will soon enough." She looked beyond him, towards the slopes of Elden Deas rising above the cave and lake.

They ate by the fireside, with the sun setting over the water and the two swords leaning side by side against the cave wall. Arete took the silver goblet from him and refilled it with sweet wine.

Fran's head swam. Hugging a blanket round his shoulders, he turned towards the vast set of antlers mounted on the cave wall opposite. "I've never seen an animal so big in the forest."

"An old friend of mine hunted that stag. He shot it with the bow I gave him." She smiled, her expression growing distant. "It was long ago, but my old friend had the same black hair and green eyes as you."

"What was your friend's name," asked Fran, although he thought he already knew what the answer would be.

"His name was Vaden." Arete glanced away, prodding the fire and sipping her wine. "He came up the mountain, just as you have. Even then, he was the only one not afraid of me. A worthy and good king."

"I know his name, but he lived hundreds of summers and winters ago."

"Yes."

"Then you've lived for hundreds of summers and winters, and ... and you can't die."

She met his eyes, face impassive. Waiting.

"And on that winter night, before I was born, you came to March to see my father."

Arete's head dropped. She stared down into the dregs of her wine until Fran turned away. He opened his mouth to say sorry, but before he could speak, she looked up –yesterday's pallor had returned.

"I've lived for many long seasons, Fran, but that was one of the worst nights of my life. Your father crossed the pass, but his journey bore consequences. Eruthin burnt. Krataia is quick to anger and slow to cool."

Outside, the sun glowed red, and the shadows lengthened, draining colour from the tall pines and marking them in silhouette.

"My father would not have known," said Fran.

"He was a reckless man to defy a dragon. Brave, but reckless ... and I loved him. Had I loved him better, I would have turned him back round the way he came."

Silence echoed round the glade, reverberating off the cave walls and thundering in his ears. He had waited so long for the truth. Now he pulled the blanket over his ears.

"So, yes, Fran, on that night I came to see your father ... to bring him news, but in the end, I only brought death. A storm is an unpredictable thing, more so even than a dragon." Arete looked up, her watery smile one of the saddest things he had ever seen. "A hazard of being ancient, you see."

Chapter 26

Elden Deas

In a small cleft in the hillside, near where the Nethermore Pass skirted above Spiral Cove, Galos set up camp for the night. Willett and Cader made busy lighting a fire and cleaning two grouse caught in the forest the night before, while he tethered the horses and left them to graze. Their climb had revealed snapped branches and trampled bramble on the path – clear signs of a recent traveller. *But who?*

"I'll go ahead to the lake. There's still time," Galos told Willett. "It can't be more than a league from here, and there's plenty of daylight left."

Willett only stared.

Galos held his friend's eyes, squatting down to pick at the sparse grass, waiting for the inevitable words of caution. Yes, they'd climbed in the heat of the day – even Cader was tired – but there was daylight still and their friends were in mortal danger.

Cader tore the final feathers from the grouse then added more wood to the fire.

"It's not wise," said Willett eventually, with little conviction.

"I'll go with you," said Cader.

"No. You're needed here. There may be wounded to carry home. I'll scout ahead and sound the horn if there's need."

"You've not eaten," added Willett, ramming the spit through the second grouse and balancing it over the fire.

Galos retrieved a small pack from the supplies and slung it over his shoulder. "Food must wait."

Willett turned back to the fire, adjusting the spit.

Galos jogged away, following the path round the side of the peak.

The evening air grew chilly on the eastern slopes of Elden Deas. Seth, who had finally been allowed to build a small fire, sat across it from Gyll. Emptiness stretched out below them – the forest appeared foreshortened, then a wasteland of marsh extended in the twilight to meet the eastern moors. It felt like the loneliest place in the world, and their meal, the meanest – watery stew made from a brace of skinny mountain rabbits. An eagle soared in the distance, seeking scant prey, and Wyntr paced, his bowl tipping as he gazed northward. After only a couple of spoonfuls, he strode towards the fire, looming over them, his feet inches from Seth.

"They've camped well below the crag. They can't see us. Wyntr, sit," Gyll snapped.

"I can't just sit and sup. The boy's with the witch. Have you forgotten? He near cut our uncle's throat, and now he lies with her, the same as his father did."

"And what's it to us now?" Seth's legs ached almost as much as his back. Wyntr's bowl slopped over, drips landing near him. *Just eat the wretched meal, why don't you? There's little enough for three.* He shrugged up at Wyntr.

Wyntr sneered.

Seth's food lost its savour.

"That sword's valuable. I told Uncle to reclaim it these ten summers. It was his by right. It hung in Vaden's longhouse then disappeared when Vaden died. He wanted it. Our uncle always wanted the sword, and it was his by right."

"But Wyntr, we've talked about this so many times; he didn't take it." A weary note crept into Gyll's voice. "He cut Edwyn down in anger after ... after your brother was killed, but he chose not to take the sword."

"Chose not to!" Wyntr retorted. "Pecked into leaving it for the sake of peace, more like. Don't you listen to Mother Vanna's gossip?" At the mention of the old woman, the usual contemptuous smile appeared.

Seth opened his mouth to defend Vanna, but Gyll was watching him, that all too familiar mixture of pity and disdain souring his face. Unable to bear it, Seth looked away. Vanna always stopped when she saw him and always found a kind word to say. He could never think of her without remembering his own poor mother and the kindness Vanna had shown to her.

"So, you're going to claim the sword," asked Gyll. "And then ..." He paused, avoiding Seth's eyes.

"I just wish our uncle had taken it back. He chose to share power with Galos these many summers and winters, but if he'd wielded Vaden's sword it would have been different. He ended with it at his throat when it should have been in his hand."

"Perhaps this isn't the best time to take it back," began Seth. "If Fran's with the witch ..."

Gyll cleared his throat.

Wyntr squatted down on his haunches, fixing Seth with a baleful glare, his stale breath hanging in the air between them.

"Do you understand nothing? That's why we're watching."

Seth didn't reply, and Wyntr rose, snatching a chunk of bread from Seth's hand, tearing a piece from it, and tossing it back. It missed and fell against a tussock. Seth glanced from the bread to Wyntr and back.

"We've still got to take Uncle's bones to the barrows," said Gyll. "This should've waited. Everyone will be angry. It's disrespectful ... but maybe someone took him to the cove instead."

"His place is at the barrows, as everyone knows," Wyntr snarled. He turned away, jaw set in defiance.

So, you're not sure. Seth recalled the great billows of smoke from the cove. *Perhaps someone else had died.*

"There's been enough waiting, anyway," Wyntr continued. "Our uncle waited. He let Annerin alone, and all the while she plotted. Now the son's looking for revenge and he's gone to his father's old ally. We'll burn again unless he's stopped. They'll come round quick enough when it's our swords protecting them."

"And this is what you think Fran wants. Revenge," Seth asked.

Gyll's attention returned to the cold stew.

"The boy wants what his mother tells him to want. She rejected her own people and made the witch an ally long ago. I've told you before; I've seen them consorting with the witch's creature in the wood. That's why she never came home or took another husband. Now she plans to marry her boy to Elsa. She'll use the alliance to avenge her husband's death and we'll be driven out onto those marshes. Ebba's meddling just forced her hand, and her enchantments fell short on Gareth. A surprise, but ... well."

Seth and Gyll both contemplated the fire; Gareth's position in things had become a moot point. Wyntr seemed to calm a little and sat down to eat. Seth took a deep breath. Gyll exhaled and lay back, his empty bowl and spoon wiped clean with bread and discarded by the fire.

Seth mulled Wyntr's words. Did he think they now understood? These rants sounded more ridiculous by the day, and Gyll was right – they should be at the barrows, not here. He called to mind Fran, Cader and Elsa. So many times, he had watched them when Fran came to March, their laughter forgetful of the many baleful stares. Feeling invisible, and setting his own worth at less than nothing, Seth had stored these memories to be wrapped and unwrapped like treasures. Small vignettes, full of sunshine and laughter, they felt worlds away from life in the shadows of Lukas and Wyntr. He watched, not in envy, but rather the sound of their laughter gave him hope; with Fran always seeming free, bright and happy, not a creature gnawed by anger or seeking revenge.

And then there was Elsa. He felt certain she did not know he existed. At any rate, he generally hid if he saw her coming, but had anyone asked, he could not have explained why. One thing he did understand, though, Wyntr's plan was wrong. He would rather die than be part of it.

"What're we going to do next?" Gyll asked Wyntr.

"We'll camp here tonight and watch again in the morning. I want to see how Galos fares with this witch. We need to know what hand he plays in this." Wyntr spat a chunk of gristle into the fire, making it hiss, then he tossed his dirty bowl and spoon down beside Seth. He stood and stretched.

Seth stopped eating and contemplated the fire.

Galos slowed as the path widened and the lake came into view. To his left the ground rose, climbing steeply to the summit of Elden Deas. He took a few more strides and the lakeshore spread out in front of him, the water dark in the fading light. When he saw the edge of the cave mouth, his stomach gave a queer twist. Outside it, a small black cauldron and two beakers sat atop a boulder.

He stopped and ducked back flat against the rock face, checking the shore and peering across the water to where the darkness gathered among the tall pines. His heart pounded so hard it threatened to break free of his chest. He forced himself to take deep breaths. Checking the sword in his belt, he thought of Elin and Roe. He could still picture those two miserable little piles of ash. Galos exhaled, fighting to control the rising tide of fear. Annerin's plan to go alone, mad though it was, made more sense than approaching the witch with sword raised. Even so, he was reluctant to leave his arms unattended. There were two cups, and he had no idea who else might be here, or whether Wyntr could be nearby.

Keeping his back to the wall, he edged along slowly towards the mouth of the cave. When close, he stopped to listen. Nothing. Very slowly he inched his head around to look inside the cave. One eye first.

Surprise and relief hit simultaneously. He saw Fran, a little way down the cave, sleeping snugly beside a mound of spare furs strewn over one side of the floor beyond the fire. He took in the great stag's head, the rock shelves strewn with bottles, cups, flasks, and strangely carved boxes, and the collections of pinecones, pebbles, stones and wood. Beyond these, there was a canopied sleeping platform, and a twig torch at the mouth of a dark passageway. At last, his eyes came to rest on a bundle of red hair, almost lost among the amber and tawny of the furs. He gaped in wonder, forgetting himself in his delight at finding Fran, and in marvelling at the cave.

Then he sensed, or perhaps he smelt, something behind him, over his right shoulder. Little hairs on the back of his neck prickled and his hand found the hilt of his sword. Galos turned. Only a few strides away, on the opposite side of the cave mouth, a great brown and black wildcat arched its back and spat, tail erect.

He had encountered many such beasts in his journeys around plain, forest and mountain, but usually such animals slunk away from a party of men, content with easier prey. This one showed no such reticence. Aside from the cave, there was no place to hide, and a split-second decision told him the creature was guarding it. He began to inch backwards, away from the entrance, his back to the rock face. Heart in his mouth, and fingers twitching at his scabbard, he continued stepping away.

The cat advanced, fangs bared.

Chapter 27

Lost and Found

Galos came to, with a sore head and lying on furs on a hard, stone bed. The morning light brought with it a great stab of pain. He winced, trying to recall time and place. An attempt to move revealed a bandaged forearm. His heart raced. Above him, suspended from the roof, hung a great canopy – rich cloth of faded crimson traced through with yellow and gold – and to his right, a cauldron on its tripod, then daylight. Its brightness hurt his eyes. Questions bounced through his head and memories fell into place. The cave. Arete and Fran. A cat leaping, all claws and fangs. Then pitching backwards, clutching his sword ... But where was his sword? He recalled raising it a fraction too late, the weight of the cat hitting him ... then nothing.

He sat up, peering round to check for the animal. The cave behind him was empty as far as he could see. His heart hammered and he realised he was sweating. *How many near misses?* His luck must be running out, but maybe it already had. Shielding his eyes, he turned towards the cave mouth, where the daylight seemed blinding. The absence of his sword did nothing to allay his fears, but Fran was asleep on the floor nearby and looked unscathed.

"Fran, wake up," he hissed.

Nothing.

Galos swung his legs off the stone platform, making the world spin. He took a deep breath, gingerly checking his head with his good arm. There was a small bump on the back that was painful to the touch. "Fran. Wake up." He leant forwards, grabbing Fran by the shoulder.

Fran stirred, coming to and focusing on him.

"What's going on here? Where is ... where is she?" Galos asked.

"What?" Fran leant up on his elbows, eyeing the bandaged arm. "Who are you?"

Gods help us. Galos regarded his young friend. *Perhaps he received the same reception and it's turned his mind.* He looked Fran over again, but there was definitely no sign of any injuries. "It's me. Galos," he replied.

Fran's head tilted to one side as he looked Galos over.

"Oh, for the sake of the good green earth, it's me. Elsa's father. What's wrong with you? There's not a scratch on you."

At the mention of Elsa, Fran's face lit up, but then he hesitated, his eyes darting round the cave. "You mean Arete. I think she's gone for firewood."

A dart of fear shot through Galos, then he reminded himself that she must have saved his life, although to what end? He took a deep breath, glancing out of the cave and scanning what little he could see of the far shore for movement. He saw none, meaning she could reappear any moment. He turned back to look at Fran again. "What's wrong with you? How long have you been here?"

"Nothing's wrong with me. I'm perfectly happy."

"Are you really." With a pang, Galos recalled his poor daughter. *There would be a scar ...*

Fran studied him, his expression thoughtful. "You're not. I assume you met the cat. That was unlucky."

"I met the cat, among other things ..."

"Oh, what else happened to you?"

Where to start. "Well, first of all, I'm worried about you. I think you've maybe hit your head. Does it hurt anywhere?"

Fran sat up and felt his head, a look of puzzlement on his face. It grew as he took in Galos afresh, as if memories were igniting like hilltop beacons. "No, but ... now you say it, I ... I can't think straight." He looked around, as if noticing the cave for the first time, then back at Galos.

Galos followed his gaze. He noted the cooking pot, and a queer feeling ran through him; it called to mind the old stories. Suddenly the cave felt very cold, and larder smells drifted out from the darkness ... He peered down the cave and his movement disturbed the furs behind him. Something heavy scraped. Pulling back a dark pelt, he gasped at the sight of the hilt of his own sword, with Fran's gleaming beside it and then another one identical to Fran's beside that but with a red rose.

"There's another sword here. One from Glendorrig."

Fran craned his head to look at them. "Yes ... yes, you're right. It's my father's ... was my father's."

Galos grappled with what the boy had just said. *Of course it was. Of course. How simple. How obvious.* The story made sense. *Swords swapped.* Everyone knew the stories of the swords being forged, but the absence of any trace of colour had been so confusing, lending weight to any conspiracy ... So the silver sword must have belonged to Arete. Galos stared at the thing. He had always guessed its red colour had simply rubbed off over time, as had most people. Now he wondered what manner of weapon had been among them all these seasons ... and if it was as powerful as the black sword. Had Lukas seen the two together, what would he have said?

"I came to find you, Fran," Galos said at last. "You and your mother – you both disappeared the day after you found Gareth injured."

"Yes, my mother found him." Sadness filled Fran's face. "Then she left, and I went looking for her. And you. She made me promise to speak to you."

"You remember me now."

"Yes, she made me promise to speak to you. To speak to you ... to ask you ..."

"What?"

"To ask you about Elsa." Fran shook his head as if to dispel a fog. "What's happened to me? I scarcely remember ... I seem to have been here for several moons."

"You haven't. It's been, what, two days. No more."

"But my mother. Do you know where she is?"

"I suspect she went to the cove. Someone lit a fire there the night before last. We saw the smoke and another search party went to look. She'll be ... well, I've quite a few things to tell you. She's in March now, with Tom."

"You're sure?"

"As sure as I can be, Fran. Jake signalled me from the hill. She's alive, at least."

Fran scuffed his boot back and forth on the floor. "I did see some smoke," he mused.

"As I said," Galos continued, "too many things happened. Lukas and I fought, and ... well, he's dead."

"Dead! That must have been the day I left." The colour drained from Fran's face. "Was anyone else ...?"

Galos shook his head quickly. "No, it was single combat. I was tired of the endless ... well, you know how it was. But we think that Wyntr took Gyll and Seth and went after you and your mother. He thought your mother was coming up here, so it means he's here somewhere on the mountain."

Fran's jaw dropped. "We've seen nothing of him," he said eventually, staring wide-eyed at Galos.

"No, but that might not last. Besides, we need to get away from here. Go home," said Galos.

A shadow filled the cave mouth. "If only it were so easy to return home and find the door open, and welcome within."

Galos froze, registering only that Arete had bare feet and her dress had a ragged hem.

"But now it seems I have two guests. Welcome Galos."

Wyntr had woken early, and with the sun breaking over the moors, he left Gyll and Seth sleeping and tracked round the upper slopes of Elden Deas and down towards the cave. Having glimpsed Fran with the witch the previous day, he hoped to spy them lying together.

Edging his way along, keeping to the grass and careful not to dislodge any gravel, he skirted Galos' camp and eventually reached a point almost directly above the cave. Below him, morning's shade stretched over the water, while opposite, the sunlight caught high branches and the air sparkled with the promise of another hot day. With heart hammering, he caught sight of a woman on the far shore of the lake. Dark red hair hung down her back and she appeared to be barefoot. A great cat with dark fur followed her, tail swishing like a tame dog. Confounded, Wyntr stared. In his mind's eye, this witch was a monster, raining fire, not this slight figure of a woman, dressed in rags. *Was it her?* Instinct told him it was, and for a moment he longed to catch sight of her face. But no, her absence was better ...

At his feet, a well-worn path led down to the mouth of the cave. He held his breath to listen for movement and caught only what might have been a snore. *Perfect.* He slipped down the final stretch and onto the shore. Every scrape of his boot seemed to echo horribly. Gripping the hilt of his sword, he took a deep breath and peeped inside the cave.

After a few moments, his eyes became accustomed to the dark, and then ... vindication. Sweet, sweet vindication. Fran lay sleeping by the fireside, almost hidden by rugs, and behind him – Wyntr could hardly believe his eyes – Galos lay atop a rock ledge, yet more furs arranged about him and a great rich canopy above. Both slept like babes. Wyntr almost danced with glee.

He checked the far shore, then he moved to the far side of the cave, away from where Fran lay, and stepped in. He slipped past the fire and lifted a small, dark, dusty bottle from its place on the ledge. The bottle felt smooth and cool, and it was made from a thick, highly polished, bluish substance the like of which Wyntr had never seen. He tilted it, starting as he caught the movement of liquid inside. *What wonder was this? No one in March would ever have seen such a thing.* No one could doubt he had been to the witch's cave now. Scanning the place once more, he noticed something lying on the ground at his feet. *Fran's cloak and brooch. Oh, this was more good fortune indeed!* He stooped down and hastily unpinned the brooch. He slipped it into his pouch, and he clambered back up the hillside and retraced his steps to where Gyll and Seth were camped.

Later that morning, Seth struggled to keep pace with Wyntr and Gyll on the descent. Streams cut through boggy ground strewn with boulders, and his ankles twisted repeatedly as he sought sure footing amid the rough grass. Wyntr had kicked over their fire on his return, waving a strange little bottle at them and snatching at the food like a starving man. Without so much as standing still, he ordered them to pack and be ready to leave. The bottle came from the cave, and apparently both Fran and Galos were there. *Well, maybe the witch gave them breakfast.* Seth forced the bowls into a pack, lending only one ear to Wyntr's chatter. *Much good would this do anyone. Why not leave well alone?* But apparently the bottle was significant, although the gods alone knew why.

Wyntr led, closely followed by Gyll. A light running pace would bring them to March by nightfall, and although Seth remained eager to avoid a fourth night camping, the bouncing of the heavy iron cauldron against his back became so painful and wearisome it eventually forced him to stop. He squatted down to rearrange the packs. While he did so, he mulled over, yet again, the late-night talk on the way up the mountain. Its direction had unsettled and confused him greatly. Now, as Wyntr stomped towards him, he sat back on his haunches and waited. Their pace was unsustainable. They ran as if a hoard of the trolls and goblins so much derided by Wyntr bore down the mountainside behind them.

Wyntr came to a halt in front of Seth, his breath ragged and cheeks red. "What ails you? You've seen them signalling to each other. Things are happening in March. We have to get back before Galos."

"It's the cauldron. It's hitting my back." Seth got to his feet and dragged the bundle from his shoulders. "I've carried it for three days and I'm bruised and sore."

"What would you have me do?" Wyntr stepped closer. "What would you have me do, Seth?"

"Maybe you should try carrying it," said Seth, taking a step back and throwing the cauldron down too. It gave a solid thud against the grass before rolling a little way and coming to rest in a divot.

"You ungrateful little cur. How long have I taken care of you? Without me you're nothing." Wyntr's hand shot out and he pushed Seth hard, making his teeth snap together and knocking him off balance. "Now, pick it up and move."

Seth stumbled and fell, slicing his hand on a sharp rock as he landed.

Gyll, who had followed Wyntr back, saw the blood but only shook his head before turning to follow Wyntr down the hill.

Seth cradled his hand. Dirt and grit filled the cut already. He looked around but saw nowhere to bathe it. Tears prickled. He was indeed alone, and more so for remaining near Wyntr. This fact he understood better each day.

Gingerly, he poured a trickle from the waterskin onto the heel of his hand. It stung, but it washed away the muck. He sucked the cut clean, then he spat out the grit and wrapped his scarf around it. It was grimy, but it was better than leaving the cut open. When the pain subsided, he got up and took stock. They had come down the eastern side of the mountain and would meet the Nethermore Pass where it climbed from the valley imminently. Perhaps, if he took his time, he would meet Galos. He could make his peace ... or even warn the man. But it was probably too late for that. Wyntr and Gyll were running onwards without even a glance backwards. No, he counted his debt to Wyntr discharged. He would go to Gareth now. Gareth and Godwen.

The cauldron lay a little distance away, so he went to retrieve it, then he stood still and looked around. Swallows swept low across the hillside and Wyntr and Gyll were fading from sight. Peace descended, only broken by the chatter of bird call. What need did he have to run? Or worry? After all, if Annerin could disappear into the forest just because she felt like it, so could he. And disappear he would – at least for a little while. The pass was the main route up the mountain, but not the only one. Forest covered the lower slopes east of the pass, and no one would be hunting there now, certainly not at this height.

Seth climbed back to a point where he could discern a way across before heading east and down towards the forest. His sole intention was to hunt and to catch himself some breakfast. Should Wyntr and Gyll decide to come back for him, he would be out of sight, sound and smell.

Chapter 28

Old Spells and New Friends

The look on Galos' face was one Fran had never seen before – one of pure, naked fear. The colour drained from his cheeks, and he went to speak, but no words came out and he shrank back onto the ledge, as if wanting to blend lizardlike with the cave wall.

"I have taken the cat away. It guards the cave while I sleep, but your reception was unfortunate. Now, before you go home, we will eat." As she spoke, Arete's eyes never left Galos. "Come, put aside your fear. I mean you no harm and your arm will soon heal."

Perched on the rug, with his knees drawn up to his chest, Fran felt invisible.

At last, Galos spoke, raising his bandaged arm in a gesture of acknowledgement. "Thank you. Your beast took me by surprise. I meant no harm. I only came looking for Fran."

"Well, you have found him safe, and a better hand with a sword than when he left you."

The words were spoken pleasantly enough, but they clearly stung Galos, who looked away before replying. "I've been remiss in that, I grant. I'm sorry, Fran. Tom and I should have taken you better in hand."

"You were always there."

Galos nodded. It was no less than the truth, but Galos was not forever at their door, although Elsa and Maya had, perhaps, made up for that.

"He was not the only one." Arete smiled, unhooking the cauldron and slipping it down onto the ash as she did so.

A tentative smile lit Galos' face. "We always wondered, Tom and I ..." He got to his feet and strode forwards. "Here, I will see to that in the lake. I have one good arm still."

"Very well, but keep the bandage dry a while."

Galos strode away with the cauldron, leaving Fran with Arete.

"You must gather your things and get ready to go. You've made yourself quite at home." Arete smiled, her eyes taking in the bow and shield leaning against the cave wall then straying to the cloak, which lay pooled near her feet. With that, and a backwards glance towards Galos, who was cleaning the cauldron at the water's edge, she strode down towards the larder.

Fran got to his feet and set about gathering his few possessions into his pack. When he went to the cloak, he noticed the brooch was missing. *Strange.* It was his habit to keep it firmly pinned on one side, but the metal was old, and perhaps it had bent and worked free. He looked around, expecting to see it, but there was no sign of it, so he sifted the pine needles with his foot but found nothing.

He walked round the fire, then he saw it had been placed on the shelf. The pin was a little more damaged than before, as if it had been stood on, but there would be time to straighten it at home. He slipped the brooch into his pocket and stepped outside, where the sun's heat was growing. The day would yet again be hot, but there was time to bathe before setting out on the long two-day journey home, so he went round to the far end of the lake again, to a patch where the sun was on the water.

Fran took off his shirt and boots and slipped into the water, pushing off into a swim before there was time to register the shock of the cold. Overhead, the rooks took fright and flew away squawking. Flipping onto his back, he sculled out, watching them go until a wave caught him, washing into his mouth and up his nose, making him splutter. Straightening, he reached a toe for the lake bed, finding it momentarily, but something dragged at him, making him flounder, and he became aware of voices ... Galos and Arete, shouting. They were telling him to get out of the lake, but it took a moment to register them, then something pulled him under. Heart pounding, Fran kicked his legs to propel himself back up. He broke the surface momentarily, reaching out for the shore, remembering how the water's surface had changed the day before. Dragged back under again, panic took hold of him, and he took in a mouthful of water. It was as if some great sink hole at the lake's centre were whirling and pulling ... Fran could not work out what direction to push for. His legs fought, but he sank further down. He registered the light above, blurry through a depth of water, and then that too became dark ...

Numb with terror, Fran made one last attempt to reach the surface, and as he did so, he heard something – a voice speaking in his head. It called to him, not in words but in an arc of the deepest shades of orange and red, spelling dread and the need to keep fighting and reaching upwards for the light. Every fibre of Fran's being heard the voice, and he fought afresh until he felt something powerful pulling him up – a great claw wrapped around his middle – and he rose from the lake into sparkling daylight like a fish in an eagle's claw, water spinning from him as he gulped in great drafts of air.

The dragon set him down by the cave mouth, and he saw that it was in disarray, rocks dislodged from above and chaos inside, as if a great wind had spun through the place. Arete, meanwhile, was lying prone a little way down the shore, her dress and hair soaked, Galos beside her, his hair awry and with the look of a one whose mind is displaced. He stared uncomprehendingly at Fran, then up at Fran's rescuer – a magnificent golden-brown dragon, no longer camouflaged by the forest but in full view with the sun glinting off its scales. From the hillside above the cave, it looked down balefully at the scene below.

Fran drank in the sight, sending a silent *thank you* to the creature. Then he staggered to his feet, dripping like a wet dog over the sand and pine needles, and ran to Galos and Arete.

"Is she all right?" he asked.

"I think so ... she's breathing, and she isn't injured. I think the water threw her back and the landing's knocked the wind from her."

Arete groaned, as if to prove Galos right.

"I don't understand what's just happened," Galos added, "and I don't want to look up."

Fran didn't need to look up; a message came into his head again, telling him to leave Arete and get back inside the cave. He told Galos to come, but the older man moved not one muscle, only staring him out of countenance.

"Do you mean carry her in?" Galos asked at length.

"No. He's telling us to move."

"Oh, and you know that, how?"

"I just know ..." Fran faltered.

"I have been absent too much, haven't I?"

Fran and Galos sheltered in the cave while the dragon swooped and picked up Arete, flying away with her in the direction of Eruthin. She hung limp in his claw while the beat of wings filled the glade. When they had disappeared, silence descended. The lake sparkled innocently in the sun but there was not a bird to be seen in the sky.

"I don't understand what's just happened," Galos repeated, his gaze sweeping Fran head to toe.

"Nor do I, Galos. I only went to refresh myself in the water, and something tried to pull me under."

"Something?"

"Like I said. I don't know. It seemed like the water was doing it. Something similar happened yesterday, but it didn't cause ..." Fran stared around the cave. *Whatever happened, it almost brought the mountain down.*

Galos clapped him on the back, his face relaxing slightly. "Seems like those old tales about the water might have some truth in them, then. Let's get back to camp while the gods are still with us." Galos lifted the fallen canopy from the bed platform and picked up his own sword, which still lay beside the other two, a clumsy and dull thing by comparison. "Don't forget your sword – whichever one's yours, that is."

Fran glanced at the red sword, but then remembering what Arete had told him, he picked up the silver one. He weighed it in his hand, a new confidence flowing through him. Next, he stuffed his cloak into his pack, then he went to retrieve his shirt and boots, skirting very clear of the shoreline.

With everything gathered together, and his shield and bow on his back, he and Galos set off down the mountainside at a jog, pitching through waist high bracken. They were a league or so from the lake when Fran spotted Willett, along with several horses.

"Thank the gods, we heard such rumblings we thought the path might be blocked." Willett ran to them, acknowledging Fran then handing a waterskin to Galos. "You found him, I see."

A heartbeat later, Cader appeared, his broad face breaking into a grin. Fran's throat tightened, tears threatening. High on the mountain they might be, but the sight of Cader was the sight of home.

Chapter 29

Shadows and Spider Silk

Annerin prodded the fire and stirred the pot. The porridge grew thick. She ladled in water and yawned. *What price for a safe bed and home?* Outside Tom and Nell's home, March began to stir, with voices muttering in the alley behind and a goat braying in the square.

Out there, somewhere, Fran was alive; she knew it. He was probably at the lake. Alive and free – not caged and half a league from the safety of the forest. A woman's voice outside caught her attention and she recoiled. *Hilda or Raya.* They passed, leaving her alone. *Thank the gods Nell was no chatterbox with neighbours forever at her door.*

After breakfast she left Nell to visit Ebba. News of Elsa's accident had not taken long to reach her. It explained Gareth's silences, at least. She pondered the man; he was kind and awkward in equal measure, but he was not a good match for Elsa. *Too sad and too old*. Besides, this incident must surely put paid to any such ideas.

As it happened, Ebba and Maya were out when she approached the house, so she edged open the door. "Elsa, it's me. Are you there?"

Elsa came running through, her smile radiant despite her poor neck and arm.

Annerin gave the girl a hug, weighing the livid marks. *A mercy he missed her face. He mentioned nothing of this. Nothing. And always that guileless look …* She brushed away the memory of what passed between them. Care of her no doubt assuaged his guilt. *The girl would have been safer at the ford with Fran. And poor Galos … he must be heartbroken.*

"Annerin, I'm so glad to see you. Come in. We were so worried."

Annerin took in the bandaged arm, and then the long cut, running deeper as it disappeared into her tangled hair. She fought to maintain a smile. "Dear Elsa. I hope Arthen's looking after you. Too much has happened. I'm not sure where to begin." *Hard to explain bolting, abandoning Fran.* It made sense at the time, after Lukas. The sight of the man always plunged her backwards – but now he was gone, and the world felt no cleaner or better for it …

"Fran'll be back soon. I know he will," said Elsa.

"The forest's a safe place, especially if you're Fran."

Elsa's smile wavered. She took Annerin by the hand and led her to one of the fireside stools.

Annerin squatted down, glad for the distraction of the whitening logs, whole yet ready to crumble into dust at the prod of an iron. Elsa and Maya knew about the dragon, she was sure, but to speak of it in March felt bizarre. The people here did not relish such talk, except from the elders at a winter fireside. In the cold light of day, they did not encourage any discussion of magic potions, or tales of swords, battles long past or heroic deeds. It generally worked best, in fact, to stick to the topic of farming.

"I know why you went," Elsa ventured. "The dragon."

Annerin hesitated before she spoke. "It's there because of the sword. That damned sword." The words came from her mouth as if they were not her own. *Edwyn's sword. Damn the wretched thing.* He died, and one day, many summers later, the truth dawned. This precious thing rested safe at the stone house because they – she and Fran – were so utterly insignificant. Presumably, someone in Eruthin wanted this sword as well as the black one Edwyn had been sent to find, and the pass had been blocked to prevent them coming for it. That must be the dragon's doing too. Or the woman Arete's. She and Fran were just pawns in a bigger game, a game being played out on the other side of the mountains. So was Edwyn. But how did he alone make it over the forbidden pass? And why couldn't his sword have been red to match the coat of arms of Glendorrig?

If she was right, the silver sword was important – more so than a red, blue or green sword – but were the black sword and the silver sword one and the same? She didn't think so, and the idea never seemed to have occurred to Edwyn, yet perhaps it was an obvious assumption if, like Lukas, you believed you had lost such a sword – one with a legend attached to it – and then a very similar one appeared, being flaunted under your nose.

"I think you're right," Elsa said at last. "Father makes strange remarks sometimes about the forest too, and Maya says she actually saw the dragon."

"Yes, Fran told me. She told the truth, but ... well ..." Annerin shrugged.

"No one's interested in the truth."

"No one ever is."

"Everyone's waiting for Wyntr to come back," began Elsa, after a pause. "He looms like a storm cloud. He went after you."

"Gareth told me." Annerin turned her attention back to the fire. The silence stretched until, looking up, she met Elsa's eyes. "But Wyntr won't find Fran. He knows the forest too well. Less so the mountain, but still ... he understands how to hide."

Elsa hung on her every word, those cornflower eyes pleading.

"And the dragon's still there. It's never hurt Fran, although he's forever wandering, and he goes far and wide, so ..."

"Ah." The shadow lifted from Elsa's face. "And my father's on the mountain. Wyntr wouldn't dare ... I just wish we knew what was happening."

"We'll find out soon enough. Someone'll be back today or tomorrow. The lake's two day's travel at the most," said Annerin.

"It's good you both went. You were safer ... I mean ... well, Wyntr should have gone to the barrows. He'll have to answer to Hilda and Ileth ... and to Gareth. He neglected his sacred duty; he defied the gods. Arthen will banish him."

Elsa's words carried more defiance than conviction, but they struck a chill note, their tone echoing Gareth's reassurances. There would be no escape from further bloodshed. She knew that now, and so presumably did Elsa, better than anyone, despite her brave words.

"It's a long time since I've seen Arthen, but ... well, can he give such orders?"

"Probably not, at least not without support." Elsa's expression grew thoughtful. "And this place has changed since Lukas' death. When he returns, Wyntr will find many a friend he didn't know he had."

Elsa spoke the truth. March brooded. A storm would come soon enough, just like last time, and again there would be bloodshed. Sitting in March again, after all these summers and winters, brought back so many awful memories ...

"Did you speak to Fran before he left?" she asked Elsa.

"Yes, he said he'd be back for harvest."

Annerin waited, but Elsa said nothing else. No matter – she would not be marrying anyone until she recovered. "Very well. Do you feel well enough to climb the hill with me and set prayers for their safe journey home onto the wind?"

Elsa nodded and led the way to the door.

The day stretched on, bright and brittle, pitch rising with the sun. Annerin jumped at every last sound. In the square outside their door, crying infants were taken home, dogs fought and were doused with water, and Vanna, along with several other elders, nodded sleepily under the eaves of the longhouse. People made a show of going about their business, to and fro from the well, or in and out of the longhouse, but buckets clattered more idly than usual, and tongues wagged – *How goes it?* Which meant *give me an excuse to stop.* Words trailed away as gazes drifted towards Tom and Nell's door. Men carried swords and spears, and the blacksmith's hammer rang out unremittingly. Afternoon gave way to evening, and it was replaced by the rhythmic beat of a lone drum deep in the north quarter. Answer came from the lifeless pulse of bronze and bone hand bells.

Night came. A cloth of myriad stars draped an ebony sky, and March fell silent, although the brooding song of the drums pulsed in Annerin's head until she could not be quite sure they did not still beat, out there, somewhere amid the dark huddle of huts. For a long time, she lay in Cader's narrow cot with no thought of sleep. Through the window slit by the door, she caught flickers from the torches outside. Earlier, Tom had lit them strategically around the edge of the square and around the settlement's perimeter, and one stood in front of their house, just to the right of the door, its light revealing multiple slits in the shutter.

Every creak, flutter or owl hoot made her start, but then there came the lightest knock on the door. An axe splintering the wood could not have brought more terror. Within moments, Tom was there, unbarring the door. Jake, who was supposed to be watching from the hill, slipped inside, easing it closed behind him. His presence sent another bolt of fear through Annerin. *What news? He must have seen someone out on the plain.*

She slipped from her bed and joined the men beside the remains of the fire.

"There was smoke, near the edge of the forest, and then some higher up, on the mountainside – and something faint, off to the south. The higher one was Galos," said Jake.

"So Wyntr will be here first." Tom turned to Annerin as Nell appeared at her side. "Willett's signals. I doubt anyone else could read the smoke, but ... well, there's no doubt."

"I'm not so sure they can't. I think it's what set the drums off. They're waiting," warned Jake.

Tom slipped to the shutter, setting an eye to one of the gaps.

Pulling free from Nell, Annerin followed. Testing which slit gave the best view, she peeped out until she could make out the longhouse and most of the square. All seemed still. Beyond the longhouse, there was only blackness, but the torches cast wavering pools of light down the alleys between the houses. No one could walk through the square and not risk being seen. *A blessing and a curse.* Annerin returned with Tom to the hearth, and the four sat in silence for a while until Nell reached for a water jug to top up the brew in the small cauldron.

"Leave that, Nell. It's late. Just pass me the ale." Tom sat cross-legged on the hearthstone, idly prodding the coals.

The night's silence deepened. Torches crackled. Away in the woods, an owl hooted. Annerin sensed the wakefulness around her; or perhaps she heard it, somewhere on the boundary of hearing – the scrape of a foot catching stone in the dark, the clatter of a falling iron or the subtle tweak of a shutter closed too tight. With it was something visceral, its creeping tendrils touching all but the youngest, dreaming their rainbow dreams, and the oldest sunk deep in ancient cots. Shadows flickered. Outside, the square waited, a stage set with an audience of wraiths.

A velvet sky melted to lilac, then pink, and once again Annerin hoisted her small bundle onto her back and prepared to leave. Heart wavering, she slung her father's shield across her shoulders and slid his sword into its worn scabbard before stepping outside. In the hush of first light, she skirted the square with its guttering torches, unbolted the postern and set off in the direction of the ford.

No lookout manned the hill now, an exhausted Jake having decided the watch could resume at dawn, so her departure went unnoticed. Scanning ahead, she saw the plain was empty, and in the fields and meadows, sheep and cattle huddled. The whole valley was deserted aside from herself.

She reached her home with the eastern sky shifting from pink to gold, and the finest coating of dew already lifting from the grass. Pausing at the gate, she imagined Fran emerging from the threshold. She closed her eyes, picturing his tousled black hair falling about his face and the ready smile calling her in and away from her endless foolishness. In, to the familiar fire, cauldron, humming spindle and clicking loom, to the smell of fresh bread and the warmth of venison stew, caught, chopped and smoking until the house stank.

Tears choked her, but she did not move beyond the gateway. The smell of the empty house met her there, and what was more, she knew it offered no safety. *May as well sit in the centre of a spider's web wishing not to be eaten.* Better the forest than that.

Chapter 30

The Long Road Home

Fran and Galos sat down with Cader and Willett to eat a hasty meal before beginning the journey home. Joy at the reunion was transient, being quickly dampened by the awkwardness of exchanging news and everyone's anxiety to get moving. Fran found Galos keen to let him speak, but Fran hated the silence that fell whenever he opened his mouth. Cader, meanwhile, caught his eye several times, and his gaze held many questions.

Willett's and Cader's brows lowered at the mention of Arete, and they stared wide-eyed at Galos' bandaged arm.

"A wild cat, you say," mused Willett. "And she saved you from it."

"Not before I cracked my head." Galos reached round gingerly to check the bump.

Willett watched him, a frown forming. "I can hardly credit all this." He shook his head as if to clear it.

Galos caught Fran's eye, his look holding a measure of warning. *Don't share too much.* Neither had mentioned the dragon, instead focusing on the rockfall heard by the others.

With the food almost done, Cader turned to Galos. "Does Fran know everything that's happened?"

"I've told him about Lukas ... and about Wyntr."

The fire crackled and an eagle swooped low overhead, making the horses whinny. *But there was more.* Fran set aside his measure of ale and turned to Galos, waiting.

Galos stared into the fire, the expanse of pale blue sky behind him endless. "Gareth wanted to help look for your mother," he began eventually.

"He's recovered, then."

"Yes. He says your mother saved his life. He seemed determined to go after her. Most determined." Galos glanced up and caught Fran's eye. Fran rearranged his feet, recalling his presentiment on seeing his mother and Gareth together in the forest.

"And ... and he's on speaking terms with you."

"Sort of."

"But we have made peace with Gareth, haven't we?" Cader asked, his expression anxious as he looked from Galos to Willett and back.

"Who knows. The man's a law unto himself, blowing hot and cold with no warning. At least we knew where we were with his father," said Galos, seeming to speak half to himself.

"He's a better man than his father ... just not a stronger one," added Willett.

"Ay, that might be so, but I near lost my own head, and my—" Galos stopped abruptly. He moved to refold the blanket under him.

Fran turned back to Cader, but his friend's arms were folded over his head. Willett, meanwhile, began rooting in a saddle bag. The atmosphere around the fire tightened like a bow string ready to snap. Fran's chest hurt, and the conversation replayed in his head. *What would they want to conceal like this? And yet they talked of Lukas and his mother openly ...*

"What else did you nearly lose?" Fran asked, suddenly ready to shake the truth from Galos if necessary.

Galos got up and walked away.

"What happened?" Fran asked Cader.

Cader's mouth opened to speak, but Willett interrupted.

"We left all well in March."

"It was an accident. Gareth went for Galos, but Elsa ran to stop him ..." Cader blurted out, his voice catching. "His sword caught her on the backswing. It was awful. I ... we didn't see it coming. She saved Galos' life. Now Arthen ..." Cader's head dropped between his knees.

Hearing his friend sob, Fran spun to Willett.

"She's not in danger," Willett interjected.

Fran sprang to his feet and stumbled back from the fire, his head in his hands. *She was so brave. So very brave ...* All he wanted to do was to run down the mountain to her, but March was so very far away. "I shouldn't have left her." He spoke only to Cader now, his voice choked. "I'll not leave her again."

After a long trek down the mountain, Fran, Cader, Galos and Willett crossed the old stone bridge and reached the rangers' path leading to the river shallows and the rise. The cool of the forest soothed Fran at first. Birdsong rang out among sunlit branches, and the sweet tang of last autumn's crumbling leaves filled his lungs. Soon, however, and with the horse plodding wearily beneath him, exhaustion set in, and with it a growing disquiet regarding both Elsa and his mother.

His mother might be alive, but Wyntr could have seen the smoke and changed course to investigate. She could be gravely injured. There was no way of knowing. And as for Gareth going after her, well ... When he thought about it, he realised his mother might well have gone to Spiral Cove. His father was buried there, after all. Perhaps she'd gone there first, intending to follow the River Everlode and climb the mountain afterwards. Or maybe he'd guessed wrong in the first place about her seeking out Arete.

Unease had followed him down the mountain. Cader rode beside him, but after his friend had explained the extent of Elsa's injuries, they spoke little. Galos and Willett, meanwhile, lagged a few paces behind, Willett also leading the spare horse. They kept up a steady exchange, their voices low. Fran's thoughts kept circling back to Arete. The dragon must be taking her somewhere for help, probably to the great dragon who guarded the pass. But she must be well again soon; she was an ancient, after all. She could not be hurt easily, and now, with Lukas dead, March only a short journey away and Wyntr looming large, he wanted to picture her there, at the lake, watching over him.

They stopped to camp for the night where a small outcrop of rock made a shelf over the forest floor. A stream ran below it, and after letting the horses drink, he, Willett and Cader fed them and rubbed them down then hobbled them close by. Fran drank gratefully while he worked, the water bubbling clear, cooling his parched throat and sun-baked head.

When refreshed, they set to, building a fire and preparing a meal, which they devoured all too quickly. As dusk rapidly approached, they were still scraping at the bowls with crusts of bread while the fire crackled, throwing out a meagre but welcome heat.

Fran shivered. The bare rock, warm from the sun when they arrived, now felt cold to the touch, so he doubled a blanket under him and drew up his knees, pulling his brooch from his pocket and pinning his cloak more tightly about himself before reaching out to warm his hands.

"What really happened up there?" asked Willett at last. "Aside from the witch and her unfriendly cat ... and the sudden, random rockfall ... oh, and Fran finding himself in the middle of the lake and forgetting how to swim."

The tone was unexpectedly genial. Galos, who sat opposite Fran, smiled then leant forwards and prodded at the fire, spoiling it by dislodging the bottom log.

Fran sensed it was a ploy to make him talk. Willett had heard it from Galos, but now he wanted to hear it again. "We met Arete," said Fran. "And then we saw a dragon."

Willett's jaw dropped and he put down his cup.

"I thought I'd let him tell you that bit," Galos told Willett, his smile wry. "He might have been out in the sun for a few days, but he's not had a bump on the head."

Willett snorted. "I'm beginning to think everyone's seen this dragon except me, and even I've heard it a few times."

"Something happened to make it come," added Galos. "You remember the old stories about people disappearing in the water ... well, something happened, and the dragon pulled Fran clear, but the ... Arete – she was thrown clear too and knocked unconscious."

Reassured by Willett's comment, Fran added, "Gareth stumbled across the dragon in the forest that day. We knew, but we didn't say anything because ... well, would you have believed us?"

"Maya told me she'd seen it," said Galos. "So, we guessed."

Willett nodded. "Yes, we guessed, but you're right – it does sound like a bit of a tall tale. Lukas wouldn't have accepted it, that's for sure. He chose what to believe and stuck with it, despite what anyone said."

True enough. Remembering that horrible time, Fran dropped his head and stared at the fire. Orange tongues of flame licked around broken logs, crackling when they met sap – making ash; measuring time.

Suddenly Cader threw back his head and laughed.

"But Fran," he said, glancing at Galos and back. "We heard the rockfall then saw the thing flying away. Either that or we saw the biggest eagle there ever was – and it had a tail."

"So, we did." Willett grinned mischievously at Cader. "I almost forgot that."

Fran let out a snort of laughter. "No wonder you looked so frightened when we appeared. Did you think it had eaten us?"

"Something like that." Cader's broad face relaxed into the grin Fran knew so well.

Forgetting the cold, Fran gave him a playful nudge, but then Galos spoke and broke the spell.

"But what ill fortune brought the creature down into the forest that day, just at the wrong time? Even a wild boar's a rarity so close to March these days. I tell you, it's small wonder your mother kept quiet, Fran. I've no intention of walking into March and telling everyone we met Arete, got attacked by the lake water and then rescued by a dragon."

"No," echoed Willett. "The least said, the better. And if Gareth speaks up for Fran's mother, well, the problem's solved."

"Ay, but peace is broken quicker than it's mended," mused Galos. "I can't put Lukas' head back on his shoulders, can I?"

"Would you, if you could?"

Galos only shook his head sadly. "Probably. I hated the man when he was alive, but ... well ..."

Everyone grew quiet, and Fran's thoughts returned to Elsa. Willett fetched a skin of ale and handed it round. Fran took a huge swig.

Galos' gaze rested on him from across the flames. "Back in the cave, you said you wanted to ask me something, Fran. So ask."

"Very well. I want to ask you for Elsa." With those words finally out, a great weight lifted.

"If it's what she wants, I'll see it done at harvest." Galos got up and came towards Fran, drawing him to one side. "You've my blessing too. I'll be glad to call you son. It's how ... but I've not been ... I'm sorry ..."

Cader and Willett shuffled off to collect more branches for the fire.

Fran saw exhaustion in the older man's face, along with – What was it? – shame, guilt or simply resignation. He recalled standing on the threshold of the stone house on that fateful night, watching Galos leave and suddenly knowing the man felt like a father.

Fran woke before first light, and his teeth chattered as he crouched over the embers left from the fire. After the day's madness, his sleep had been fitful, broken by shivers, and now he groped for the threads of reality to weave a familiar picture again.

Somehow, his thoughts turned to Maya, who had long been from his mind. She stood on a hill, watching the horizon. He pictured her in her blue check dress and brown apron. She was alone and the image filled him with disquiet.

Chapter 31

The Storm Breaks

Elsa woke to hear Nell arrive with confirmation that the smoke from the mountainside included a message from Willett. Although she and her mother had been almost sure, Jake's reassurance was welcome.

Nell was also searching for Annerin. "Her bed's empty, and her bundle gone," she hissed at Ebba. "It makes no sense for her to go back to the stone house, though."

Elsa pulled her shawl around her shoulders and came into the main room.

Her mother took her in with a glance before turning back to Nell and dropping down onto the box beside the fire. "That would be madness," she answered, throwing up her hands. "She's not with Jake and Finola."

"No." Nell shook her head. "I went there first."

Elsa proffered the stool to Nell and sat down on the hearthstone at her mother's feet. She ladled out a cup of water and gave it to Nell.

“I imagine she slipped away first thing,” said her mother. “She’s probably hiding in the forest.”

“I don’t blame her,” said Elsa. “She’s safer out there than she is in here.” Both women regarded her, their brows wrinkling.

“But she’s alone,” Nell countered.

Elsa shrugged. *Alone, but not trapped*. Wyntr’s arrival was imminent, both gates were shut and almost every man carried a sword at his hip. March, with its strong palisade, deep ditch and towering gates, had, in the unforgiving morning light, taken on the guise of a trap. The north quarter, radiating a sullen tribal menace, loomed at their back, while the empty square awaited drama unknown.

“Perhaps it’s for the best,” her mother remarked. “Wyntr will be here before the day’s out. Who knows what will happen then.”

Nell sniffed and blew her nose. “Indeed. Arthen’s pacing already.”

They caught the sound of voices across the square, so her mother slipped over to the door and eased it ajar.

Elsa craned her head round to see out but stopped herself when the cut on her jaw pulled. Tentatively, she checked it for bleeding.

“Are you all right?” her mother asked.

“Yeah, I just moved too fast.”

“Be careful,” Nell muttered.

“Why don’t you go back to bed,” said her mother before peeping round the door.

“I can’t sleep. Not until ...”

“They’ll all be back soon,” said Nell. “Your father’s half a day behind at most.”

Her mother sighed, returning to her seat on the box and rubbing her temples.

Their wait was not long. Sunbeams still poured through Elsa and Maya's window when Tom and Jake's lookout abandoned the hilltop and her father's men converged on Tom's house. Shortly afterwards, the cry went up that Wyntr had been sighted. Footfall behind their home told her that others were making discreetly for the gate. Tom, meanwhile, remained at his door, looking out across the square, which was empty aside for the elders.

"You will not hold the gate," she heard Arthen ask.

"Let them show their hand," her uncle replied.

Grim faced, her mother opened their door and her uncle signalled for them to come over, so the three of them moved across to wait inside with Nell and Finola, while Tom, Jake and Frey crowded the doorway and the other men melted away. They waited, Elsa continually reminding herself to breathe. Maya's hand slipped into hers. Above, a bird fluttered in the thatch, making her jump.

The quiet was unnatural. Only the pound of boots on dirt carried to them. Eventually, a lone figure approached the square. His gait seemed unsteady, but through a gap in the men, Elsa recognised Wyntr. Something in how he held himself gave him away – chin a little proud, challenging the empty space, hand restless, ever moving to the sword hilt, and then a sly glance behind, checking the backup. Behind him, others crept forwards.

Elsa's heart hammered in her chest. Men slid forwards from the alleys, gathering under the eaves of the longhouse until the scene grew horribly reminiscent ... Wyntr's head cocked backwards to hear something she could not catch. A snigger came from under the eaves but was quickly muffled.

Tom braced himself in the doorway, arms folded. But what could her uncle do, or say? Gareth must be here somewhere too. Would he not come forwards and challenge Wyntr? In the end, it was Arthen who shuffled from the longhouse and met Wyntr head on.

"Wyntr. You've been missed."

"Arthen, your greeting's icy, and the gate stood shut."

"Perhaps it was shut against the spirit whose bones you left behind."

"But the living are welcome, or I would still be outside."

"That remains to be seen."

The two men faced off – Arthen frail but standing tall; Wyntr sneering down at him. Behind Arthen, Ileth crept forwards, but there was still no sign of Gareth.

"Perhaps you should all come out" – Wyntr taunted those lingering in the shadows – "and hear what I have to say."

Feet shuffled, but only Gyll stepped into the open.

Wyntr scanned the square, his eyes not quite landing on Tom. Seeing their empty door, a knowing expression crept over his face. He was looking for them. And maybe for Annerin.

"Thanks to everyone who opened the gate for us. I'll not forget it, but I've run down the mountain to get here, scarcely stopping, so I'll take a swig of ale before I ... enlighten you all."

He made to go, but Arthen's voice stopped him in his tracks. "Not so fast, Wyntr. Where have you been while your uncle's bones lie neglected?"

All shuffling and whispering halted.

"I had a fugitive to catch."

"Oh, and did you catch ... him?"

"Oh, yes. I caught the two traitors together, Arthen."

"What do you mean?"

"Don't worry, old man. They live. Whether March will want them back's another matter."

"You reached Lake Everlis."

"Oh, yes. I've seen her with my own eyes – this witch of yours."

"What are you saying?"

Wyntr stepped closer to Arthen. "I'm saying I've seen her – the witch. She's very real – young, and with flaming hair."

Arthen recoiled. "She has a name, and it's not *witch*."

"Be careful, Arthen." Wyntr's voice rose triumphantly. "You leap to her defence so readily. Perhaps her spells reach far." His attention drifted, his gaze shifting again to Elsa's door. But then, quick as a cat, he whipped back round. "Perhaps they always have."

The old man faltered, taking a step back.

"Where's Seth?"

It was Wyntr's turn to jump.

Gareth appeared directly opposite. Elsa realised he must have come from the little round house he had been repairing the day before.

Gyll's boot scraped back and forth across the grit.

Wyntr spun round. "Cousin, you're up."

"I'm recovered, Wyntr. Now, where's my cousin Seth?"

Wyntr's head dropped a fraction and he fidgeted at his belt. "He'll be with us by nightfall."

Gareth said nothing. Gyll's boot continued its scraping.

"Don't worry. He's fine. He insisted we go on ahead. As I said, he'll be here by nightfall."

"It's to be hoped so, Wyntr. He's ... what, sixteen or seventeen summers old. Very young to leave alone," Arthen remarked.

"He knew our errand was urgent. Lukas was his uncle too."

Arthen, arms folded, stared at the floor, and Wyntr followed Ileth towards Ileth's house, dropping out of Elsa's line of sight.

Arthen waited a moment, then he called after him again. This time his voice stayed low, and Elsa strained to catch what he said. "Wyntr, who cut loose the horses?"

The footsteps stopped dead.

"We've been wondering that too," Nell whispered to Elsa's mother. "I doubt he knows."

No answer came, but Arthen's face registered satisfaction before he turned and made his way back into the longhouse.

Outside, a low chatter began while Gyll went for a cup of water and slumped down under the longhouse eaves, head down, inviting no questions.

A lull followed, like a collective exhale. Elsa's mother and the others whispered about what might be meant by *two traitors,* while Maya played near the hearth, heaping cold ash into miniature mountains. Elsa shuffled closer to the door so she could see outside better. Little by little, the square began to fill.

"My friends, gather round." *Wyntr's voice, refreshed by a jug of ale.*

He was still out of view – by Ileth's door from the sound of things – but Elsa's heart clenched as if he had reached into her chest with his fist.

"I will tell you what errand kept me from the barrows." The voice drew nearer.

Elsa noticed that many of the men looked sullen, their tools thumping down impatiently on the packed earth. *They were keen to get this over with and be back at their work in the fields. A good sign.* She reminded herself to breathe. The cut on her jaw itched. Outside, one of the dogs, now tethered by the longhouse, let out a howl.

Arthen's voice rang out, his tone crisp. "The crops don't tend themselves, Wyntr. Get on with it."

"Don't forget, I've covered the distance from the summit at a run," snapped Wyntr, striding into view. He regarded the seated line of elders, most of whom were stony-faced. "The news is grave. I made haste back here so we could ready our defences, but that's obviously in hand. You must all hear me out, I beg you. Arthen, please set aside your doubts."

Several of the men mumbled agreement, but Arthen remained silent. Tom and Jake moved clear of the door, and Elsa's mother and Nell stepped forwards. Elsa followed with Maya and Frey. She was curious, despite herself, but immediately wished that, like Maya, she could slip behind Tom and not be seen.

Now outside, she saw that most of March were bunched in the alleys leading to the square. The scene was horribly familiar. The square had seen too many dramas of late ... She shuddered, noticing a crow atop the longhouse, nipping at the thatch, then two others on the roof of Ileth's house. *Again, they wait.* Gareth remained near the old roundhouse, now with Godwen at his side. He frowned, scanning the crowd and squinting. Elsa realised he must be looking for Annerin. She tried to catch his eye, but to no avail.

"Very well, we'll hear you out." Arthen spoke so softly Elsa could barely catch his words, then he stepped back, whispering something to Enic, who sat with the other elders outside the longhouse.

Wyntr opened the pouch at his waist and took out a small bottle made from some darker material than clay. Next, he pulled out something too small to see. He weighed the two objects in his hands. Those nearer craned forwards to see, and a buzz went round the crowd. With a sudden flick of his wrist, he tossed the bottle at Arthen.

Arthen stumbled but caught it, his eyes lighting at the sight of it.

"I found this when I reached the lake. I've never seen the like, but perhaps it's more familiar to you, Arthen."

People moved to see better what Arthen now held. Elsa, curious herself, saw the old man turn pale and grasp around for his stick, which Enic passed to him. "It's not familiar to me – not in the least. Why should you think it would be?"

"The liquid moves inside for all to see." Wyntr snatched it back from Arthen's reluctant hands. "I found it with this." Wyntr spun round towards them, eyes raking the crowd. Elsa slid towards Tom, shrinking back in horror when his gaze lighted on her. He strode forwards. Tom stepped out to meet him, covering them, but his confusion was palpable.

"You might as well come out." Wyntr waited.

Little trusting her legs, Elsa took a step forwards, remaining close to Tom. Wyntr still gripped something in a closed hand. Her heart – thundering in her ears – misgave her. Opposite, the crow on the longhouse cawed, its cry a mockery, for she must be a pitiful sight indeed. The cut – with every eye in March devouring it – smarted and stung.

From somewhere behind her, a small hand slipped into hers.

Wyntr stopped in front of her. When she looked up, she met not the expected sneer but a question as he registered the wound on her jaw and her bandaged arm. "I see you've been in the wars too. I hope you're mending."

No one spoke. Elsa's throat felt too dry to form an answer.

"She is," her mother whispered, amid the silence.

Wyntr remained focused on Elsa. "This is the second thing I found on the mountain." He stretched out his hand and opened it. Fran's brooch lay in his palm.

With knees ready to buckle, she let go of Maya, put out her hand and took it. Turning it in her hands, she recognised the poor, bent thing, then the view was lost, blinded by tears. The swish of Tom unsheathing his sword brought her back to herself. Blinking away the tears, she met Wyntr's eyes.

He stepped back, half watching Tom, the ghost of a smile playing on his lips. "I've not hurt him."

The hilt clicked back down.

"Where did you find this?" demanded Elsa's mother.

Wyntr ignored her again. "I found it in the witch's cave, by the side of Lake Everlis, high on Elden Deas. Before dawn yesterday morning." At last, Wyntr turned half away, now addressing Arthen again. "I also found the boy, Fran, to whom that brooch belongs." He strode clear of Tom before spinning on his heel to face those massed in the alleys. "I know it belongs to him because he lay sleeping in the cave where I found it, on a bed of furs, the witch beside him."

Gasp followed gasp, whispers jumping from person to person like fire on the heath. All warmth left Elsa. Her arm throbbed. Maya clutched her skirt. Someone's hand went to the small of her back.

Wyntr waited for quiet before continuing. "Perhaps you remember the story my poor uncle told you all not so very long ago. The very last thing he tried to tell us."

Her mother and Nell appeared either side of her and slipped their arms round her waist. She sensed their tension, breath held as Wyntr paused, but she could no longer bear to look at the man. Instead, she cradled the poor little brooch. *Lying beast. And Father missing too ...*

"The last thing he tried to tell us all before he was killed was that there's still an enemy in our midst."

Elsa remembered Annerin. *Oh, wise choice to go.*

She looked towards Gareth. All around him, men stared at their boots, but he remained immobile, arms folded, glaring out across the square. She followed his gaze and found Ileth. The man exchanged a knowing smile with Wyntr.

"We all know what happened long ago. My uncle – despairing over my brother's murder – killed the stranger." Voice momentarily strangled, he paused, but when he looked up his face was stony. "He too came from the witch, and she followed him here. And now the same thing will happen again. And it wasn't just the boy—" Wyntr stopped abruptly; his mouth fell open, face contorting. He staggered backwards, staring out above the heads of the crowd towards Elden Deas.

The sky above March remained a pale lilac blue, morning's pink fading at the edges, but over the mountain, steely clouds gathered, incongruous against the clear day.

Wyntr turned to Arthen. "See, it happens again. This is what I'm telling you."

Cries went up, scaring the crows on the roof, who flapped and cawed, audience in this strange theatre too.

"What he says is true. This is how it started last time," said one of the field workers.

"Ay, ay," echoed several others. Accusing looks followed, directed towards Arthen.

"*You* took the bottle from the cave," said Arthen at last, "perhaps it's *you* who's angered Arete."

His words rippled around the square.

"It was just one of many – from a great jumble all the same. It couldn't possibly be missed." Wyntr twitched, his fingers drumming on the hilt of his sword, still preoccupied by the mountain. "I brought it to prove I've been there, otherwise there are those who wouldn't believe me."

"You can't know whether it's been missed, and we don't know what's in it," said Arthen.

"Very well. Take it and find out." Wyntr thrust the bottle at Arthen, who snatched it up, again drinking in the wonder of it, then he called to one of the boys to bring a mortar. Slowly, he eased out the tiny wooden stopper and held the bottle gingerly under his nose. He frowned, setting the mortar down on a small table dragged clear of the longhouse by the boys. He tipped a little of the liquid into it. Elsa, craning her neck as much as she dared, saw it ran clear. Arthen swilled it round briefly before setting the mortar down on the floor and clicking his fingers for the unfortunate dog, still damp from an earlier dousing and tethered under the eaves. Set loose, it came forwards eagerly enough, sniffed, and lapped the dregs of liquid. A head cocked at Arthen told the story all too well – *Not enough. Fill the bowl up properly*. Then, with nothing more in the offing and freedom beckoning, he wagged his tail and bounded away towards the hillside.

Elsa watched him go. That dog was clever, had there been anything untoward, he would not have drunk it.

Arthen glanced at the sky again, then back at the bottle. "It would appear to be water."

"It *is* only water – lake water. And she can't be angry about that. Why, it's probably just rinsing water. It was just one from a pile of discarded bottles."

Arthen got a fresh bowl, scooped up some water from the longhouse pail, and added a few drops from the bottle. He frowned and shook his head. Next, he flicked a small quantity onto the wooden seat of one of the stools and moved it out into the sun. Everyone waited, chunnering while the clouds grew heavier still around the mountaintop.

Maya, meanwhile, moved round to clutch their mother's hand. The movement seemed to startle Ebba, and Maya turned to Elsa, her eyes hazed with tears. "He won't still be up there," she whispered.

Perhaps Fran was, but at least he was safe. It counted for something …

"At least we know what Wyntr's about," added Nell. "He could have brought back …"

Tom shot her a warning glance.

The dog reappeared, delighted with the attention, and presumably the stool had dried because Arthen turned to Enic with a shrug of the hands. "It seems to be water, but why anyone would put water into such a tiny vessel, I don't know."

"It's an infusion, maybe," Vanna commented, heaving herself up. "Here, Arthen, let me smell it."

Reluctantly, Arthen removed the stopper again and held the bottle under Vanna's nose.

The old woman sniffed. "A mild herbal infusion, I would say."

"Possibly."

Arthen barely had time to return the stopper before Wyntr snatched the bottle back and slipped it into the pouch on his belt.

"Like I said, just rinsing water. But the bottle doesn't matter. I only brought it so you'd understand, but you can see for yourselves …" Wyntr gestured towards Elden Deas. "The boy's not one of us. His father was a stranger, and he does what his traitor mother bids him. She's the one who went looking for the witch, searching for vengeance when her plot to kill my cousin failed." He panned round, gauging the effect of his words. Feet shuffled and heads dropped, but no one spoke.

Elsa fought to remain standing, although stomach, head and legs cried out for the little wooden stool an arm's reach away at the door. *Wretched lies. Poor Fran. But thank the gods Annerin had gone.*

Opposite, the crows were now massing on the longhouse roof. *Long memories.* And why would Gareth not speak. Elsa peeked over at him. He alone cared nothing for the mountain behind him; his unblinking stare never left Wyntr.

"So, where is the woman? Who hides her?" Wyntr took a step towards Gareth, chin tilted, bravado thin as pond ice in spring. "Cousin, you brought her back yesterday, did you not?"

The strange silence continued. Arthen seemed ready to speak out, but he only bit his lip and bent his head. Tom shuffled, hand resting on his sword hilt.

Wyntr advanced another few steps. "Cousin," he repeated, more quietly this time, "where is she? Where's Annerin?"

"I don't know where she is, Wyntr." Gareth's voice held all the menace of a dog at bay. "But I know you're wrong ... about her and about her son. Wrong. Utterly wrong."

Wyntr's chin shot out further, but he seemed to shrink in stature. *Gareth's a lot bigger than him.* Strange she'd never noticed that before. Wyntr, although lithe and strong, was of only average height.

"I'm only pointing out what we can all see, Gareth." He gestured at the mountain, sword forgotten. "And what your father always warned me about. It's why I followed them. He knew ... but you know that too. And the boy; he's lying with the witch – did you not hear me say? They planned to kill you. Your father realised it, but it went wrong. That's why, when they brought you back wounded, she ran off the next morning to get help from the witch." Wyntr paused for breath, his gestures growing impatient under Gareth's stony glare. He scanned the crowd, his expression becoming strained. "Why it's Ebba herself who told me this."

What?

Forgetting all else, Elsa reached for the stool. It brought her level with Maya. Their eyes met fleetingly, horror echoing horror.

Elsa forced herself to look at her mother, who, ignoring Nell's sharp inquiry, shrank towards Tom.

"Ebba, this is true, is it not? Speak."

All heads turned. The sun paused in its transit across the sky. Even the crows, lined on the roof opposite, faced Ebba as one and waited.

"Well ..."

"He overhead me telling Arthen ..." Her mother's voice held no conviction. It did not carry.

Elsa bit her lip. The question of how the news travelled had troubled her. Around them, the spell broke. A rush of chatter brought the square back to life. It startled the birds, who, rasping resentment, took wing for the Starling Wood.

Arthen, now sitting between Enic and Vanna, hung his head, and the dog bounded back into the square, leading its companions out to circle and hound anyone who would give them attention.

Only Elsa's little group remained frozen, Nell's outrage written on her reddening face, and Tom's in his averted gaze. Maya, meanwhile, slipped back inside the house and Frey slunk away to join his own parents.

Her mother turned to her. "He overheard me telling Arthen. He was behind us on the hill, and I didn't see him until it was too late."

Tom and Nell gave questioning looks. Beyond them, Gareth and Wyntr still faced off. Gareth spoke, but Elsa could not hear him properly.

"We need to stop this." Tom spoke into the air between them, his expression growing hunted as, around them, the square exploded into life.

Without warning, a small group of men broke from the crowd and ran towards Elsa's home. Tom made to go after them, but Nell and her mother grabbed an arm each to stop him.

"You can't fight them all. She's not there anyway and they won't dare search here." Thumping, coming from the back of the house, belied Nell's words. Maya ran out and hid her face in their mother's skirt. Light flooded in where a chunk of thatch had been ripped free.

"Let go ... in the name of the gods ... woman, I won't have them tear down my house!" Tom broke free, only to land in Jake's arms.

"Tom, they've moved on. They're just mad with fear. Look at the mountain. Look." As Jake spoke, he gave an anguished look in the direction of his own house.

In the centre of the square, Arthen, arms raised, appealed for calm, but no one heeded him, and his words were lost in the tumult.

"Tom." Gareth's voice cut through like a knife. "Please, Tom, where is she? Has she gone back to the ford? This mob will kill her."

Elsa knew Annerin would not be at the ford, but Gareth's fear was palpable. He fought to remain still, hand clutching his sword hilt, eyes never leaving Tom. Around them, the square was in ructions. Shouting men, crunching boots, crying children and ashen-faced mothers with their backs pressed to the wall. Elsa swayed, pain gripping her chest. She clutched the stool edge.

Her head was still spinning when the gang of men abandoned their search and left the square. They were bound for the gate but were headed off by some of her father's men. She wanted away – to reclaim her home, shutting the door and bolting the shutters – but she could not have stood up to save her life. She shook, head to toe.

The mob swelled; most were armed, several carrying throwing spears. Dogs pranced at their heels. Godwen appeared, also waiting on Tom and Jake. Shouts went up, coming from the gate.

The grunt and thud of contact followed, then the fateful yawning of the hinge.

Godwen moved to follow, hanging back only for Gareth.

"Please, Tom," Gareth said again. "They're through the gate."

"We have to." Jake's face spoke misery. He pushed Frey back. "No, you stay. Take care of your mam."

"You'll need to help Arthen," Tom called back, but the old man had already gone, presumably back into the longhouse with the others because the benches under the eaves were deserted.

"Wounded already," muttered her mother. Absently, she stroked Elsa's hair.

Stay, Mother. Stay. But Nell, Finola and her mother already grew restless in the emptying square, their gaze following the men, who were so quickly lost from view. Their hesitation was fleeting, then they too – casting hasty promises backwards – hurried in the direction of the gate.

Powerless, Elsa watched them go. She recalled Annerin's confidence of the previous day when speaking of Fran. *He knows how to hide.* Those were her words. Elsa guessed that Annerin also knew how to hide. With any luck, she had already disappeared as completely as a fireside hob in morning light.

"Let's check your house," said Frey. Without waiting for an answer, he and Maya ran over.

"No, they've touched nothing," he called back. "They'd not be so brave with your father on his way back."

Elsa followed them, plumping down again on her own little stool. The section directly under the eaves was now moving into shade, so she leant back, grateful for its coolness. Maya and Frey pulled over stools and sat one either side of her.

"They'll not find her," Elsa reassured Maya.

Maya shook her head. "And the dragon may still be there."

Elsa found herself hoping so. *After all, what's more dangerous than a man?*

Frey looked from one to the other, his face a mask. "Is it definitely Fran's brooch?" he asked eventually.

Elsa winced. The brooch had grown warm in her palm. She uncurled her fingers, revealing the familiar circle and pin. All brooches were alike, but this one was older than most, and slightly warped. "Yes," she answered, "this is Fran's brooch." *And Wyntr could have found it anywhere – taken it as he buried Fran or tossed his body into the lake.* It proved nothing. She set it in her pouch and looked up. The shouts from the gate were receding into the distance. The midday sun beat down and the storm gathered at their back. An eerie stillness pervaded, the strange weather having driven the birds to the safety of their roosts. *And where were Arthen and Enic and the rest?*

The thought was barely formed before they came into view, slowing ascending March hill. From there, she guessed they would watch. They could do little else other than call on the gods.

Maya turned her head in towards Elsa as two stretcher parties moved across the square, carrying wounded men home. Elsa averted her face too, but not before catching sight of blood. Her hand moved to her jaw, checking again whether the cut wept.

"It'll get better soon," Frey whispered.

A flash of heat suffused her cheeks. How must she look, with hair flattened to her head and this lumpy mess on her jaw ... but everyone had been so kind, so very kind.

At length, her mother, Nell and Finola ran back to them. "All of March is headed for the ford," began her mother. "Stay here. We'll not be long." She glanced at the hilltop as she spoke. Arthen stood there now, looking out towards mountain and ford. "Annerin won't be in her house. She's fled into the forest again ... but we can't just wait here ..."

In case Tom or Jake are wounded. Her mother didn't need to finish the sentence; the stretcher parties and Frey's bleeding fingernails told their own tale.

"Galos, Willett and Cader should be here shortly." Finola stroked Frey's sandy hair. "Stay here with the girls. Your dad and Tom will break this up soon enough. We'll be back soon."

And they left, the air around them laden with things unsaid.

Above the mountaintop, purple clouds pulled taut the sky, and March, empty as it was, glistened with an eerie brightness. Far-off rumbles portended a coming storm, and the distant cries of angry men carried across the plain.

Elsa shivered. Her wounded arm throbbed, and her jaw ached.

Frey's arm slipped around her shoulders. "Wyntr's a liar," he hissed. "The brooch proves nothing."

"Fran's alive. I know he is. He may sleep in Arete's cave, but he loves Elsa."

Frey's arm dropped away, and Elsa turned to Maya.

"Thank you, Maya. I am sure you're right."

"Annerin's safe too. She's gone to Mirrormantle Grove, and the men won't go near there," Maya added.

Frey frowned. "Only the most desperate would seek refuge at Mirrormantle Grove," he said at last. "Even if the spirits let her through, she may not find her way back out. The ghosts of those long dead enchant the wood there. It's no longer a good place. The forest's better."

Maya craned her head round Elsa to answer him, that well-known certainty lighting her face. "Don't worry about her. She'll be safe. The grove's protected by Arete."

As she listened, a tiny spark of hope warmed Elsa.

"Maya, how can you be so sure?" asked Frey. "I swear, even Arthen begins to listen to you.

At this, both Maya and Elsa laughed, although, of late, Elsa had noticed the old man casting watchful glances at Maya.

"I can't be sure how I feel so sure," said Maya, leaning round again and this time poking Frey in the ribs. "But I know you believe me."

"Yes, I do, because you're always right," said Frey. "Although it puzzles me how."

Elsa rolled her eyes at Maya. Maya grinned and made to hit her, then she stopped, her gaze moving to the wound. Elsa fingered it again, recoiling at the hard, uneven scabs.

"I'm going to speak to Arthen," said Maya at last, standing up and moving the stool clear of the door. "He's worried about the bottle, and I want to ask him why." She paused, regarding Elsa again, now with a puzzled expression. "But somehow, I hate leaving you. Will you come with me?"

"Yes, we'll follow you soon." Elsa felt no inclination to climb the hill, but her sister seemed reluctant to go.

Maya nodded and walked away – a lonely little figure in her blue check dress and brown apron. "Don't be long," she called back, then she disappeared round the longhouse in the direction of the hill path.

With Maya gone, Elsa and Frey sat in silence. One of the crows returned and took up its perch on the longhouse roof, shifting from leg to leg and fluffing its wings. Away to the east, a falcon soared.

"I wish my father would just come through those gates," said Elsa eventually. The emptiness felt strange – an aberration in such a busy place.

Frey nodded, kicking idly at the pale grey dust that coated both their boots. "Fran's lucky," he said after a while. "I think he's lucky, but I'll help you find him."

Elsa froze, then she looked round at him, but he did not meet her eyes, instead tracing patterns in the dirt with his foot. *What to answer?* Like Cader and Fran, he had been her friend ever since she could remember – *the little sandy-haired boy* – and perhaps she had always known.

He turned and smiled, the expression in his soft grey eyes telling her she need say nothing.

It made her realise how sorely in need of fellowship she was. "You're my good friend now and always," she said at last.

Frey smiled back, but suddenly his face changed, and a little whimper escaped his lips.

Elsa spun round and found herself facing Wyntr and Gyll. Gyll's dagger glinted in the sun.

"And so," began Wyntr, "two little birds remain, but one must fly away."

He motioned to Gyll, who stepped forwards, levelling his dagger at Frey.

Elsa struggled to focus, her vision blurring as the blade balanced and spun on Frey's heaving chest, catching and twisting the light wool of his tunic, before slicing though. A trickle of blood swelled and rolled down the metal.

Frey froze, petrified, the light gone from those grey eyes.

Elsa's mouth opened to cry out, but then Wyntr's hand was on it, trapping her lips shut before she could form even a single word.

"One sound from you and your little friend will pay dearly."

Elsa recoiled from the heat of Wyntr's breath in her face.

Threat made, he let go, and with a quick glance over his shoulder, he motioned them inside the house.

Elsa glanced swiftly past him, trying to see the hilltop, but she could not tell if anyone happened to be looking before Wyntr grabbed her good arm and pulled her to her feet.

Twisting her sharply, he pushed her through the doorway and roughly down on the nearest stool.

Gyll followed with Frey.

"Yes, Elsa, unless you do exactly as I say, you'll not see your little friend here again." Wyntr's eyes dwelt on her, as if he sought something he could not quite find.

Frey lay slumped on the floor beside her.

Gyll tugged him roughly upwards, but Frey stumbled and fell back down, banging into her stool and crying out. Gyll picked him up by the back of his tunic and spun him round. The dagger flashed in Gyll's hand, and then she heard a sound she would never forget as Gyll drove it into Frey's shoulder.

A cry escaped her.

Frey, still held by Gyll, cried out too – a horrid little strangled gasp – dragging the sole of his boot down Gyll's shin to push him away.

Gyll jumped back, leaving the dagger behind. "You little ..."

Wyntr moved in, punching Frey in the stomach.

Frey's mouth opened to scream, but no sound came. His knees buckle and his body slumped to the floor.

"That's for his part in killing my uncle. It's but the start," said Wyntr, face set hard. "Put him on the horse."

The room spun – that familiar room – and her friend lay on the floor beside her, a dagger between his shoulder and neck and a mixture of blood and vomit pooling beside him.

She looked away when Gyll pulled the dagger free, images writhing in her head – the ragged sword and the silver blade, then this vile dagger, all whispering in the dark, waiting their chance.

And today, that chance had come; ill deed, breeding ill deed, breeding ill deed ... She watched mute as Gyll dragged Frey out the door and off in the direction of the north gate, leaving her alone – with Wyntr. Elsa's heart hammered, her only thought now to get back into the open of the square. She sprang to her feet and lunged towards the doorway, but Wyntr blocked it, looming over her, pre-empting her every move.

One of his hands locked around the wrist of her good arm, and the other clamped over her mouth again. This time he pushed her backwards, kicking the stool out of the way and slamming her against the partition. "My kinsman, Gyll, has clear instructions. He'll finish the boy if you make a sound. Do you understand?"

The stink of his breath filled her nostrils. She saw the gritted teeth and felt the heat of his gaze, its intensity more terrible than the pressure on her wrist and mouth. Oddly, the only thought she could bring to mind was how similar to Gareth he looked, and yet so different, so very different, brimming with an anger and hatred that would never, ever thaw.

The hand suddenly dropped from her mouth, but her wrist was still clamped. His eyes raked over her, his brow furrowing.

"I like you," he said at last, "you're brave, defending your father with your life."

Chapter 32

Thunder and Blood

Elden Deas glowered, but the threat of the coming storm meant little to Annerin in her hiding place deep in the forest. Bangs of thunder echoed off the mountain tops, and moisture studded the sparkling air. Sweat soaked her dress, making the linen cling, but all this was nothing compared with the clamour rolling towards her, out from March, past her dear little home and on down the clearing towards the ford. Here it seemed to stop, and she suspected she had the brooding heat to thank because, after searching her house, the men fell to fighting in the Cloudwater. What began with the clang of weapons soon muted into the thud and grunt of fist on flesh. Old scores were being settled, and most, she guessed, were nothing to do with her. Presumably, the men were leaderless. *No Galos or Wyntr, and no Gareth*, she guessed.

And so she found herself in forgotten depths of wood, cowering in the scrub where forest met mountain, beneath the peaks of Vaden's Crown. Briar and bramble grew thick among the oaks, but the trees stood firm, a bulwark against the ugly screeches of battle, abundant moss muffling the sharp edges of sound. Standing amid the tangle of undergrowth, she felt compelled to listen, and horrific as her situation was, after the last few days she no longer felt the terror that, perhaps, she should. Worry replaced it, and hunger, together with a gnawing sadness at her own fate, and the curse brought down on her family.

Numerous cuts and scrapes marked her forearms, and the dress, so painstakingly woven in spring, hung damp and torn, snags marring every panel. The way had not been clear. *What matter, though?* At least she was safe, for the moment, having crawled rather than beaten her way through the thicket, leaving the trail of a wolf or boar, not a woman. *Safe, and utterly alone.*

Having borne her estrangement from March as stoically as she could – sad only for her parents and son, who endured it with her – now she could not even return to her beloved stone house, so there was only mountain and forest left. *And what of Fran?* Hope still lay with Galos, but should he come back alone ... what then? She fingered the small cloth bundle in her pocket and wondered again.

A peal of thunder broke her train of thought, and heavy raindrops pattered on the leaf canopy overhead. Needing shelter, she continued deeper still into the wood, the route growing dark and forbidding in the ways between the foothills. Eventually, the trees became ever more withered, and forest floor gave way to dank, moss-covered rock with tortured branches forcing their way up through narrow seams of soil.

Ahead, Annerin could just make out the mouth of a cave; from here, it was little more than a dark slit in the rock. *Mirrormantle Grove*. Her memory had served her well. She shivered as twisting tree arms with blackened claws for branches crowded over her, hiding the sun. Her heart faltered and she gasped as she caught a fleeting glimpse of a face in the trees. A gust of wind brought it into view again – the worn remains of a skull hanging from one of the tortured branches, and then another and another as her eyes grew accustomed to the sickly ivory of bone.

Her memories of this place were old, but it smelt of long neglect. *Forgotten ancestors. Forgotten bones.* Even Arthen forsook the grove, instead trusting his prayers to the wind from the top of March Hill. Mirrormantle Grove belonged to another time. A time when the river had been sacred, and when men would have feared to fight in its waters; a time when drought or flood marked the anger of the gods. But now the silent river gods were all but forgotten – abandoned by the people, just like the poor little cairns at Spiral Cove. Today, most bones were taken to the barrows, a place once reserved for kings.

Annerin exhaled, tugging the damp dress loose. Taking in the lie of the land, calm descended over her. This was a safe place – forgotten and ancient, perhaps, but its stillness belied power. She did not seek sanctuary lightly, and none would dare venture here nursing anger. Distant birdsong broke the hush, but emptiness pervaded. The skulls were like the broken shells of eggs – fragile hollow things from which life had long since flown. Dragging her gaze from them, Annerin chose her footing carefully. All around her, water dripped onto moss and trickled over stone, making the route up towards the cave slippery. At the cave's mouth, water emerged from an underground stream, a steady pulse, eking down between boulders, towards the point, not far away, where the Cloudwater properly began.

Annerin ducked her hand into a shallow pool forming in the rivulet, letting the coolness wash her fingers. She went to scoop, but she hesitated, recalling the cave and stream at Spiral Cove, and the strange and terrible dream induced by its waters. This, in turn, reminded her of Gareth, and a little ray of hope broke through the darkness and found her. She took a drink, then she filled the waterskin before approaching the mouth of the cave.

The darkness was intense, even coming from the gloomy grove, but eventually her eyes adjusted and in front of her she could just make out the channel cut by the stream and on her right something rounded. Reaching out, she felt the contours of a clay urn – cold and smooth to the touch – the first of several similar vessels stretching away into the dark. She took one more step, and all outside sounds were lost – wind, rustle and birdsong, all washed away by the echo of flowing water. The chill of damp clothing brought a shiver, but standing there, Annerin felt more at home than at any time since leaving the stone house at the ford.

The horses cantered through the gate, kicking up dust and throwing back their heads in recognition of home. Fran slipped gratefully from the saddle then looked back at Elden Deas; the sight of it made his heart stutter. The mountain glowered and thunder loomed, bathing March in the eerie light that precedes a storm.

A shout went up and Maya ran down the hill towards them, alight with joy at the sight of Galos, and it felt as if the sun peeped out from behind a cloud and all was well with the world again. Galos dismounted, almost stumbling, but the perpetual frown vanished when he heard Maya. She ran to him, and he swung her laughing in his arms.

Turning to Cader and Willett, Fran caught the disquiet on the older man's face. They were alone. The place was deserted.

Fran hardly had time to wonder before Maya landed on him too, hugging him before moving on to Cader, who picked her up and sat her on his poor, tired horse.

"Where is everyone? Why is it just you?" Cader spoke for them all.

Maya's face fell. Fran watched her – the blue check dress and brown apron – and he recalled his strange premonition. *Where was Elsa?*

"The place is deserted," said Galos. "I've never seen it so ..."

He stopped when Arthen appeared around the edge of the long-house, and after him was Enic, Vanna and the other elders.

The old man looked flushed, and he fought to catch his breath, leaning heavily on a stick. "Galos, we're glad to see you – very glad, but there's not time to explain ... Tom and Jake, and your others left not long before midday."

Arthen's gaze switched to Fran. From somewhere, a cold wind eddied up. "They've gone to protect your mother – to the ford. She fled before dawn."

Fran's head swam. His stomach lurched. Grasping the sword's hilt, he leant against the mare to steady himself.

Arthen came towards him. "She'll be somewhere in the forest," he said before turning to soothe the horse.

Fran stared at the flank, rising and falling as the mare caught her breath. Around him, he felt the others waiting – holding their breath. Maya's feet scuffing down as Cader slid her from the horse. *Nothing made sense. She'd gone to the forest, come back, and now she'd gone again.* But the forest meant safety ... and it meant the dragon. Somehow, that voice had never left his head, and it told him she was safe yet.

"Then she was right," he said, fighting to keep his voice even. "But Gareth's well, so why ...?"

"She's been accused of plotting with Arete," replied Arthen. His hand remained on the horse, but he met Fran's eyes. "And you're accused of lying with Arete in her cave."

Fran recoiled, turning first to Cader, and then to an equally bemused Galos. *What was this? How could this be?* He and Galos ... but ...

Arthen's attention returned to the horse.

The blood rushed to Fran's face. *Not in front of Maya* ... but where was she?

He looked up and the ground lurched beneath his feet.

She stood in the doorway of her home, clutching the frame. Her expression seared itself onto the forever place in his brain. She stared at her father, trying to speak but no sound came.

"Maya, what's the matter?" asked Galos, impatience edging his voice.

Fran's heart slammed against his ribs, but he could no more walk towards that house than the house could walk to him.

"Elsa." The word escaped mid-sob. "She's been taken. She was here, and now there's blood on the floor. I left her here, but I knew I shouldn't. I knew ..."

Inside Fran, something died.

Helpless, he watched Galos duck inside the house and then spin back out again. "Who else was here, Maya? With Elsa?"

"Only Frey. Everyone else followed Wyntr or Tom. Mother and Finola went."

Willett, who had said little and watched everything, now dropped his horse's reins and ran to the doorway. He stepped away again, his face drained of colour.

Fran's head swam. He could not move his hand from the warmth of the mare; he wanted to bury his head in her mane and hide from the world.

Willett spoke at last. "They can't have got far. You were on the hill. Did you see anyone aside from us?"

Arthen and Enic shook their heads. "It's hard enough to see the ford ... but I don't believe anyone's crossed the plain. The movement would likely have caught our eye."

"They're either lurking somewhere here or they've taken them to the old bothy," said Galos. "I'd guess the latter. There'll likely be folk hidden indoors round and about, and the sound carries." He remounted. "But March isn't safe. Follow us but keep to the trees. Maya, I'll find Elsa. Stay with Arthen and I'll find you again soon."

Fran remounted, then he waited for Galos to turn his horse round. Beside him, Willett followed suit. Dust flicked up from the hooves as Galos spurred the horse, making for the alley which led to the north gate.

Fran locked eyes with Maya for an instant, reading there a mirror of his own despair.

Galloping hard, Fran and Galos reached the river first. Dismounting, they drew their swords and ran towards the old bothy. Galos led the way; Fran was at his back, breathless from the ride, hand sweating against the leather of the hilt, and with only the memory of Arete's lessons emboldening him.

A flock of starlings lifted from a nearby tree, squawking in protest. *A good sign.* Aside from their cries, all seemed tranquil, the river flowing softly over stones and the hum of insects in the long grass around the door. The ground, however, had been trampled.

At the sight of the dark doorway, Fran's heart missed a beat.

Galos' nostrils flared and he glanced impatiently towards Willett and Cader, who were still dismounting.

But the hut was empty. Sunlight peeped through thatch, and fresh boot prints marked the floor. *And blood. Bright blood.* Fran shrank from it, his mind recoiling. Around the stain, shreds of roughly cut cord were scattered, indicating someone had been bound then released.

Willett and Cader stumbled in behind them.

"Could you not wait, man? I'm right behind you." Willett picked up a stretch of cord. "They've left for the ford."

Galos shook his head. "Why come here and not stay? Why cut the bonds?"

"Change of plan?"

All questions for which Fran could think of no answers.

"Hostages," said Galos at last, his expression grim. "They're being held nearer the fight. Tom must need us there too, gods help him."

"Aye, we should go." Willett cast Fran and Cader a wary glance before striding back to his horse. "Stay behind us. You two are easy pickings. You especially, Fran."

"You might be a target, that's all," Galos added, avoiding Fran's eyes. "Best hang back, both of you. Keep an eye on the women and children."

Again, Fran thought of Arete ... and of the dragon. The voice still rang in his head – that and the voice of instinct. Both told him to stay close to Galos.

They rode, hooves pounding dry earth, and only the sword at his hip and the rhythmic drum of the gallop were real. He was going home. Home, and his heart misgave him. The mountain glowered but the thunder came from closer by – iron, and many voices raised in tumult. Was it only days since he said goodbye to Elsa at the ford? His ford. Then Arete came to mind and every fibre of his being called out to her for help – so near, up there on the mountainside, and yet so very far away.

There was only the sword. Fran swung back and forth, clutching the weapon two-handed, shield across his back. The suddenness of it all had numbed him, but after dismounting in the clearing moments before, the first contact of metal on metal brought him back sharp. Time slowed, and perfect clarity took hold. Having decided to follow Galos, all his plans gave way to immediacy.

Around him, bodies churned. Blood stained the river, and the stink of urine, fear and sweat filled the air. Men lashed out, their faces unrecognisable, dumb with terror. These were the most dangerous – the mild, driven wild by fear. *Impinge on their space and be maimed.* Others carried their hatred like a shield, always seeking their target. Few men were familiar – no battle colours here – so he held back near the edge, but Willett had been right; the sword drew aggressors, full-grown men with a gleam in their eyes. Fran fought to hold his ground, a tree at his back, checking blows.

He had learnt much from Arete, and it held them at bay for a time, and eventually he recognised an enemy. The man, squat and heavily bearded, pushed through to reach him, his great ugly sword lashing the way clear. *Ileth.* Fran felt his legs ready to give way under him even before dull iron made contact. The blow carried the man's full weight behind it; it fairly brought Fran down, but he sprang back, hearing himself cry out.

With his sword trapped under Ileth's, Fran's vision blurred. The weight twisted his hands. The other sword flew up, a fraction quicker than he could right himself and move. It swung, ready to fall. Fran sprang back, narrowly avoiding the blow, but he landed too far away to take advantage of the older man's momentary imbalance when the sword crashed down. He steadied himself, but Ileth fell on him again, all the time forcing him back and smashing his sword downwards.

Sparring with Arete had not prepared him for this. Light and lithe, she danced with the sword, but this man came at him like a raging bull. That day by the lake, he won by force rather than skill, so now … Unable to shift his gaze from Ileth, Fran cried out to Galos for help.

His plea was heard, but not by the man he might call Father. Instead, Gareth appeared.

Chapter 33

Blood and Thunder

An unending howl of violence filled the air. Maya could not distinguish one sound from another – broken iron or broken bone ... or the hooves of her father's horse, which faded into the distance so very quickly. With her hands over her ears, she followed Arthen and Enic around the far edge of the copse outside March. She willed them on, their slowness grinding. *Oh, why leave Elsa? Why, when all the time ... dread. And then, why not watch?* But everyone's sole focus had been the ford, trying to discern what went on among the trees.

The sick and miserable feeling in the pit of her stomach would not go away. She should not have left Elsa; Mother should not have left March either. And Mother would not have spoken to Wyntr and told him about Annerin. She would not. But she had been overheard, somehow. *By accident*, she said. It made Father so angry. What was it he said? *Accident be damned.* The words echoed back and forth in Maya's head. She tried to push them aside, but they hunted her thoughts down like wolves after a lamb.

Just then, Vanna, who was walking slightly ahead of the group, pointed silently towards a group of trees to the left.

"Stop, pretty girl. Look," she whispered to Maya.

Maya peered towards the trees but could see nothing. She looked back at Vanna, meeting sharp grey eyes almost on a level with her own.

"There – someone's in the trees, see?" Vanna gestured again and dropped onto her knees. Arthen, Enic and the other elders followed suit, ducking down as best they could.

Maya slid behind the nearest tree, peeping out to watch the spot indicated by Vanna. Low branches made the wood dark, but below the bright leaves she eventually caught sight of a boot.

She crawled over to Arthen. "It's the lonely boy," she whispered. "It's Seth; the boy who follows Wyntr."

"Seth?"

Vanna craned her head up. "The child's right – it's Seth. I'll speak to him. He's my kin."

Maya helped Vanna back up, remembering her conversation with Liselle about Seth days earlier. Vanna shuffled towards the trees, calling out softly.

"Mother Vanna. Thank the gods. I'm in sore need of help."

Maya hung back, transfixed by Seth, who, emerging from the trees, brightened visibly at the sight of Vanna. He spoke to her, pointing behind him, his words making Vanna beckon to them frantically.

Elsa. He'd found Elsa. Maya ran to them, leaving Arthen and Enic behind. "You're the lonely boy," she blurted out before she could stop herself. The blood rushed to her face. She had never spoken to Seth before, only noticing him trailing miserably after Wyntr, and sometimes catching him watching Cader, Elsa and their little group.

"Yes," he replied, also blushing to the roots of his sandy hair. "Your sister's here, and Frey. I found them at the bothy. Frey's wounded. He needs Arthen."

Maya ran into the wood and caught sight of Elsa first. Her heart skipped a beat, and she fell to her knees beside her sister, who knelt on the ground, Frey's head in her lap. It was not until Maya slipped an arm around her shoulder that Elsa even looked up, and in those blue eyes – mirrors of her own – Maya saw desolation. Elsa did not speak, only returning her attention to the unconscious Frey. His face was grey and speckled with blood, its pallor a contrast to the ugly stain covering his shirt. He looked old.

Maya stared, an important piece falling out of the world.

"Maya, take Frey from your sister." Arthen spoke gently, his voice almost a whisper. He bent down opposite them, reaching into the bundle he carried and taking out a small clay bottle which he pressed to Frey's lips.

Maya moved to take Frey and found herself shaking uncontrollably. Elsa shuffled backwards, still staring unblinking at their friend.

After a short while, the tonic brought a flash of colour to his lips.

"You're safe now," Arthen reassured him as he and Enic gently lifted away the fabric from around his shoulder, ripping it where it would give, and examined the wound.

The sound of tearing fabric jolted Frey, and his face twisted in panic.

Stifling a sob, Maya stroked the damp hair and whispered, "Hush."

"Hold still." Arthen sprinkled a few drops from a different bottle onto a clean piece of cloth before applying it to the wound.

The tang of vervain drifted up, and Frey winced, his eyelids flickering.

"Give him another few drops of the tonic," Arthen told Maya.

She took the bottle and gingerly uncorked it, remembering Lukas draining just such a bottle moments before he died. She smelt the contents.

"It's henbell mead. It'll revive him," Arthen added before turning to Seth, who hovered nearby. "How did you come to find them?"

Maya concentrated on getting Frey to take the henbell mead. Above her, tension cut the air.

"I ... I knew what Wyntr was planning," Seth began, his voice plaintive. "On the mountainside, we argued, and I left them. I'm sorry ..." Seth stopped, and Maya, flashing him a glance, saw he was looking at Elsa now, his face more pained even than Frey's. "I'm sorry for my part in this. Truly sorry. I pray ... I pray I came in time, and that he didn't ... he didn't hurt you."

Elsa did not move, her attention still fixed on Frey. The chill of understanding crept over Maya, like black night and a howling winter wind at the door.

"He intended to claim me for his wife, but he did not, I swear." Elsa's icy defiance swept away that wind.

A collective gasp of horror passed through the gaggle of elders standing nearby. Vanna tutted.

Maya wanted to run to Elsa, but she must not leave Frey, whose breath grew more even as pinpricks of colour lighted in his cheeks.

"It would seem his lust to see Annerin die was greater," Elsa added, her lip curling.

Maya stretched out a hand to her sister.

The set of Arthen's jaw grew hard.

Vanna spoke to Seth. "You've done well today, young man. Your parents would be proud."

The gentle tone surprised Maya, who knew to be careful around Vanna. Several others voiced their agreement, but when Seth tried to answer, instead of words, great tears rolled down his dirty cheeks and dripped from his jaw. He squatted down, hiding his face in his hands.

Maya pulled at Elsa to try and draw her closer, but Elsa sat rigid as rock, so Arthen indicated he would hold Frey while she went to her sister. Maya shuffled over on her knees and put her arms round Elsa, being extra careful not to hurt her arm and jaw. She wanted to cry but took a deep breath to stop herself. Her lips grazed Elsa's ear as she whispered, "Father and Fran are back." She leant back to watch her sister's reaction.

It took a moment, but the light returned to Elsa's eyes. "Is it true? Really?"

"Yes, they went straight out again to find you, but we've found you instead."

Elsa's brow furrowed. "So, they've gone to the ford."

"Yes, but we should stay here," said Arthen, loudly enough to catch their attention. "We can't risk going back to March either just yet."

"You must stay here." Seth wiped his nose on the sleeve of his shirt as he spoke. "Much depends on how many men stand with Gareth. If they rally to Wyntr, then ... then the odds are much against your father, Elsa."

"Men never tire of killing each other," said Vanna at last. "It's usually over a woman or a chiefdom." Turning to Maya and Elsa, she displayed a row of ragged teeth and added, "In this case it seems to be both."

"I'm going to help Gareth. My part in this isn't done," said Seth at last.

"I'll come with you," Maya replied. "Mother and Father need to know Elsa's safe. And Jake ..."

Elsa opened her mouth, presumably to argue, then she hesitated.

"Your mother will be at the stone house, I suspect," said Arthen, glancing from Maya to Seth and back. "That's where they'll take the wounded."

"Maya, you should stay here. I'll go," Elsa said. She again knelt by Frey's side with his hand held in her lap.

"I think you should stay here," said Arthen. "Frey needs you."

"Arthen's right," added Maya.

The mention of his own name seemed to rouse Frey. He peered up, his face less drawn now. He was slow to focus but eventually he found Elsa.

"You'd best hurry," said Arthen. "The rain's coming, and we'll need to move him somewhere dry soon. Send someone who can help carry him."

Seth nodded. "I'll send two people. I brought him as far as I could on my own."

Maya got to her feet.

"I'll take her to Ebba," said Seth.

Vanna fixed Seth with a steady gaze. "Don't rush to the fight. You've nothing left to prove."

Maya crossed the fields with Seth until Annerin's house came into view. People moved back and forth around it, and children's cries carried across the fields, mingling with more distant turmoil.

"This is where I leave you," said Seth. "Your mother will be there."

"Gods protect you, Seth." But he had already strode away, and Maya spoke to the back of his sandy-haired head. "And may they guide you if you won't use your own eyes," she added to herself, watching his lonely figure move away.

She took a few steps towards the crowded little house, then she stopped, turning back to watch Seth. What use would she be there? After all, she was just another child underfoot. Her mother knew nothing of what had happened in March, and her father ... His words marched back through her head. *Accident be damned.* But none of that mattered now. Father, Cader, Fran – what if, like Frey, they were hurt? Although, it couldn't be, Arete wouldn't allow it. Still, she must see ...

With a final glance back at the stone house, she followed Seth towards the clearing and the Starling Wood. When she came within sight of the ford, instead of heading towards it, she continued across the fields until she reached the shallow section of river near the bothy. In the distance she could see the bodies of men lying at the water's edge. Shivering, she turned away, crossing the river and walking until she reached the trees.

As she approached the clearing, the furore grew louder – metal on metal, grunts and screams. Her skin crawled and her legs shook. Part of her longed to run to her mother, but another part sought the solitude of the forest – the realm of the dragon, where all this would fade into nightmare and dream.

Maya crept through the trees, glimpsing horses wandering loose as they hungrily stripped great swathes of grass. Nearby were several huddled bodies. A spear shaft stood vertically over one. Maya averted her face and moved deeper into the wood.

She drifted onwards, head down, kicking last season's dry leaves before her and trying to empty her head until the stamping down of twigs, horribly close, made her jump. Two men were nearby, circling each other. Snapping alert again, she clambered up among the lowest branches of an oak to hide. Peering down, she saw the now familiar sandy hair and her heart twisted. *He hadn't listened to Vanna.*

"You can do what you want to me. I don't care if I follow my parents today."

"Damn it, Seth, you'll follow *me* today. I'm your family." Wyntr spat out the words, his arm stretched forwards, dancing the end of his sword at Seth.

"No – you're my kin, but you're not my family!" Seth shouted back.

Hand on her mouth, Maya could barely watch his clumsy attempts to parry Wyntr's near horizontal sword.

"You're a boy, Seth. Stop wasting my time."

Seth redoubled his efforts, forcing Wyntr's sword down towards the ground.

"I promised your father I'd take care of you. Stop this and come back to the clearing with me. Gyll's felled Galos, and the stray's tiring under the weight of his stolen sword. I'll finish him before the day's done."

Father! Maya's fingers numbed against the tree trunk, and the cold of its bark pressed against her cheek. Wyntr's words rung over and over again in her head. *But they were not real. NOT REAL.* The only thing real was the tree, with its jagged bark, and she rubbed her face against it until all she could feel was the stinging of the gash on her cheek.

A scream and a grunt came from below. Maya closed her eyes and held tight to the oak.

Chapter 34

A New Chief

Fran froze. Time froze. Sound receded, leaving only a ringing in his ears. It sounded like fear.

On Gareth's approach, Ileth hesitated for a beat.

So, this is what it came to, Fran thought bitterly. There was a pecking order over who got to kill him.

Ileth's brow grew still more heavily furrowed as he seemed to question whether to stand aside.

It was a point he never got to decide. The fleeting pause proved enough for Gareth's sword to connect between Ileth's neck and shoulder. His face froze in an endless grimace.

Fran staggered, nausea making him see stars. "He was your kin." He gasped, his own voice stupid to his ear.

"He was the man who led half of March out to kill your mother."

Fran saw Cader a way down the clearing, wild-eyed as Gyll drove him backwards, away from the battle. Missing his footing, Cader staggered and fell, his leg trapped beneath him. He raised his shield and swung his sword wildly back and forth to keep Gyll at bay.

Fran sprinted, but there was ground to cover and Gyll bore down on Cader, sword raised.

Time stretched. Cader's face became that of the boy again, helpless, staring up at the falling sword ...

Fran swung in full stride, the silver sword arcing through rib and into gut. Gyll fell onto Cader, his fatal blow blown off course. His weight dragged Fran after him, and the sword stuck for sickening moments before Fran could pull it free.

Then Fran pulled Cader free – his best friend and companion of choice – and both looked down at the fallen man, dying at their feet, a haunting memory only now.

"What kept you?" asked Cader at last, forcing the ghost of a smile.

Fran found himself standing in blood and wanted to be sick.

"Come on." Cader set off at a run. "Back to my father."

Tom held the centre of the clearing, exchanging blows with the last of Lukas' old scouting party. His face lightened at the sight of Cader.

Fran found himself beside Godwen.

"You're Annerin's son." Godwen offered a grimy hand. "Where's Gareth, do you know?"

"I last saw him when ... he was last by Ileth."

Godwen spun round, re-checking the fallen. "He's not here."

"Nor is he standing."

As Fran spoke, Gareth appeared from between some trees lower down the clearing with Wyntr bearing down on him.

Fran, Cader and Godwen ran towards them, sidestepping bodies as they went.

Wyntr hesitated, glancing towards where Gyll lay, then he lunged at Gareth again, a crazed light in his eyes. "Who killed Gyll? Damn you all. Who killed him?" His sword sliced down, cutting the flesh away from Gareth's shoulder.

Gareth screamed and his sword fell. Wyntr's boot smashed down on it, and Fran swung in between the two, forcing Wyntr away from Gareth, who staggered backwards.

"I killed him. Me. Annerin's son," Fran yelled.

"Oh, the witch's boy."

"Her name's Arete."

"You know her well, then." Wyntr pushed Fran back, parrying away Cader and Godwen too, with surprising ease. "I've come to know Elsa a little better today. Sweet girl, she is."

"What?" Mid-swing, Fran's hand slipped on the grip.

"You understand me."

A gasp escaped Godwen.

Fran jumped back.

Edric and Sennen ran from the trees and stood with Wyntr.

If it ended here, it ended for all. Arete's lessons remembered, Fran lifted the silver sword and it hacked back and forth as if it possessed a life of its own, while his heart cried out for Elsa, his mother and Frey – all in danger still. Without conscious thought, he plunged it into Edric's chest. A howl went up from Wyntr, and Cader took advantage, forcing him back.

Edric slumped to his knees, fixing his gaze on Gareth before he toppled. Seeing his friend fall, Sennen faltered. Fran's sword found its way under his collar bone, and he too slid to the floor, face freezing in surprise.

Now Wyntr hesitated, and Godwen's sword slid in underneath Cader's, slicing through the leather tunic and hitting flesh and rib.

The blow unbalanced Wyntr entirely and he slid to his knees before toppling forwards in front of Fran.

Fran raised the silver sword again, little knowing what he did, only afraid Wyntr would somehow spring back to life.

Godwen's hand found Fran's shoulder. "Elsa's safe. Frey too. Seth knew of this plan and freed her before Wyntr could touch her. I saw him not long ago. He wanted to find Gareth, but I don't see him anywhere now."

Fran lowered the sword, reading both honour and fear writ large on Godwen's face. He had no quarrel with this man, who, although of Lukas' kin, had always kept himself apart over the seasons and made no trouble.

"Someone was hurt. We saw blood on the bothy floor."

"Frey. Seth told me what he could. Arthen's with him, so ..."

Fran's heart twisted.

Godwen looked away.

"Then I owe Seth a great debt. But ... but what was this plan?"

"I hardly know. Seth didn't wait for long. Wyntr said he saw Galos lying with the witch. He planned to denounce him and demand Elsa for his wife. With ... with that sword." Godwen inclined his head towards the silver sword. "And with Elsa, he thought he could make his claim to rule. He intended taking Elsa from March ..."

Fran lifted the sword and weighed the blade across his palm. The metal felt cold, steel reflecting sky. Wyntr lay motionless at his feet. And still ...

Fran jumped as a hand slipped in and took the sword from him. He spun round just in time to catch it when Tom tossed it back.

"Leave him for the birds." Tom's face was streaked with dirt and blood, his hair matted, and numerous cuts and slices marked his tunic and hands. "There's others need us."

As he spoke, heavy drops of rain began to fall, harbingers of the storm, come at last, in time to clean the field.

"Come." Tom turned towards where a man lay, a short distance down the clearing, at the foot of an oak.

The rain fell harder – big cool drops, washing away the madness, battering down on leaves, bringing reality back. Fran raised his face to the sky, letting them wash over him.

They reached the oak. At first all he saw were two unripe acorns lying on trampled grass, now becoming mud. He stooped to pick them up. Then he forced himself to look at Galos.

At first, he only saw blood. It soaked Galos' tunic, streaked his arms and matted his beard. His head slumped forwards, but ragged breaths still came and went through the parched lips. Fran's heart almost burst with relief. An ugly wound gaped on Galos' chest, but it looked only a flesh wound – and that meant hope. Only a little, perhaps, but hope at least.

With a struggle, he, Cader and Tom lifted Galos onto the horse brought over by Willett. The gasps of pain cut Fran more sharply than the wounds covering his own hands and arms. Galos swayed and almost toppled, but Willett pushed him forwards, setting his hands into the horse's mane, and Tom led the animal away, his head bowed.

Fran watched them go, sensing Cader, steps away, waiting with him. He could follow – go alone to the teeming stone house – but to what end? To watch the man he now thought of as a father die in his bed? On his mother's bed? Laid out on his hearth? No, better the forest; better the tang of earth with rain overhead and damp moss springing underfoot.

He looked up into the familiar branches of the oak, knowing this place would never be the same again, although the earth would heal, and the grass would regrow. Overhead, great dark banks of cloud churned. His stained shirt clung in the rain, and the two acorns, which he had slipped into his pocket before lifting Galos, poked into his side.

Behind him, in the rain, Godwen, helped by Cader, struggled to load a barely conscious Gareth onto a horse.

"Wait," said Fran, as Godwen started to lead the horse away.

Godwen stopped, turning wearily. "What is it, my friend?"

"I don't know Seth, but it's in my mind we shouldn't leave him here. Help me find him. One of ... one must be him."

"You're right. There's no one else will come looking." Godwen handed the reins to Cader.

"I'll find you," Fran told his friend.

Cader hesitated, eyes saucer-wide in his dirty face, then he trudged away after his father.

The sorry work of checking bodies did not reveal Seth. Fran avoided looking at Gyll, whose body lay farthest down the clearing.

Rain dripped from Godwen's nose. He shrugged and shook his head. "All so pointless. So very pointless. Maybe we'll find him at the house."

"Maybe." The rain hammered down, and Fran found himself shouting. Even so, he felt loath to give up – and loath to return to the stone house. But maybe Galos would stay there a while, recovery bound, with his family around him. Hopefully, his mother was nearby too, keeping dry.

He scanned the trees, every rustle of weighted leaves catching at his hopes. *Nothing. But wait.* Something lay near the edge of the Starling Wood. A log he did not recognise ...

He ran, soon making out a prone form with sandy hair. A boy – a little like Frey. "Godwen. Here."

"Gods be praised, it's him." Godwen brushed back his rain-soaked hair and bent down.

Together they gently turned the body over, jumping when the eyelids flickered.

"Gods be praised," Godwen repeated. "Seth."

"Father?" Seth's voice wavered, but he attempted to focus on Fran.

"Seth, it's Godwen. We've got you. We'll take you back home. Arthen'll help you."

Seth's focus shifted to Godwen, and tears sprang up, mingling with the rain.

They lifted his shivering body as carefully as they could.

He must make it. We found him and he must make it.

No horses were about, so Godwen took the first turn carrying him, and Fran followed them, squelching over sodden grass with water soaking through his boots.

Fran took over when they reached the ford, and moments later the stone house came into view. *Home. The same as it ever was, except for one thing – visitors.* Watching the women mill around the garden and door made his heart hurt. Never mind, they'd scatter sure enough when he arrived, Seth or no Seth. Even now, his mother probably watched, feeling just the same. But no, if she could, she would help. She always had before.

Trudging on, Fran's thoughts darkened like the afternoon, but when he glanced up, the anger melted. Women edged down the clearing, wary faces set against the misery waiting for them – endless care and endless woe. *All so very pointless*, as Godwen had said.

And in the trees, the ravens slowly gathered.

But Seth breathed, and for that at least he was glad.

The sight of Jake and Finola stopped all of Fran's thoughts in their tracks. A mother, oblivious to the rain, Finola clasped a bundle of cloth beneath the folds of her shawl. Jake, empty-eyed, did not register Fran. Behind them, Ebba stood on the doorstep, white as a winter field and clutching the frame.

Fran glanced down at Seth's face, hollow beneath a mass of freckles. It already felt so familiar, but its owner was a dead weight in his arms. His eyes met Ebba's fleetingly, but he read nothing, neither comfort nor reproach. Only pain.

Jake and Finola made to leave, telling Cader to stay behind.

Cader bit his lip. "How did it even happen?" His words were mumbled, and he almost bumped into Fran as he spoke.

Fran followed Ebba inside, registering Galos in his mother's chair and several other wounded men leaning against the walls. On the hearth, the fire crackled and spat, reminding him of his wet feet and clothes. Surprisingly, his own cabin remained empty, so he carried Seth there and laid him on the cot. During the walk down the clearing, he had stirred several times, but he remained dull and confused. Now his head slumped, and he shivered in his wet and muddy clothes.

Fran's head swam, and a pang of regret registered at the loss of his bed. Mechanically, he checked the wound. It was high in the abdomen and deep enough to send cold darts of fear through Fran, but mercifully it seemed as if the sword had caught the bottom rib and deflected outwards.

Returning to the main room, Fran went across to the cupboard and took out a small clay bottle given to him long ago by Arthen. When he turned, he caught Ebba watching him, but her gaze darted quickly away, back to Galos, whose wounds she was bathing. Behind her, a man groaned. *The bottle would have to be shared. Pray Arthen would bring more. Pray he would come – but there must be wounded in March too.*

He pressed the bottle to Seth's lips until they parted, allowing a little of the henbell mead to trickle in. Seth spluttered and then raised a hand to indicate more. Fran tipped the bottle again. Seth's eyelids flickered, then his face relaxed a little.

Sensing a shadow behind him, he spun round. Ebba blocked the doorway.

"Fran, what are you giving him? What tonic do you have?" The sharpness in her voice cooled as she took in his appearance.

"It's Arthen's mead. Take it." He pushed the bottle at her.

Leaning on the door frame, he looked around his little home. Hilda and Raya tended Gareth, who lay on the same cot he had occupied only days earlier. Godwen, meanwhile, sat slumped on the floor below the window, lost in thought. Tom, Willett, Nell and Cader, having followed him in, huddled together around the table with Ebba at their feet on a tiny stool beside Galos; lost in concentration, she pressed the clay bottle to his lips.

He and Cader exchanged a glance, but there was no room at the table, and nothing to be said. Just then, a small group stopped in on their journey back to March with the walking wounded. Some were people he knew, but after scanning the tiny room and not quite looking at Fran, they exchanged the briefest of news with Raya and Tom before going on their way.

"I'll go to the copse and see how Frey's doing ... and Elsa."

At the mention of her daughter's name, Ebba spun, her eyebrow raised.

Recalling his conversation with Galos last night in the forest, Fran locked eyes with her.

"I don't understand," replied Ebba. "Elsa and Maya are in March."

So, she's only got half a tale. God's help us. He flashed Cader a look. The moment lengthened. Hilda and Raya froze.

Willett cleared his throat. "Ileth led the men out of the gate heading for the ford, but it seems ... it seems Wyntr and Gyll hung back. They might have returned through the north gate. They took Frey and Elsa hostage; that's how Frey got hurt – he wasn't in the fight. When we got back, there was just Maya with Arthen and they were only then coming down the hill."

"That's right," mumbled Cader.

Itching to be away, Fran stared at his boots.

Ebba's lips went white.

Gareth forgotten, Hilda and Raya gawped open-mouthed from Willett to Godwen and back.

Eventually, Godwen struggled to his feet and spoke. "We know Wyntr wanted to take your sword from you, Fran. It seems he also wanted Elsa for his wife. This way he thought he could claim his place as chief after Lukas. He knew no one would agree, least of all Elsa, so he took her from March by force."

Still, Ebba found no words.

Godwen continued. "Elsa wasn't harmed, thanks to Seth, but it seems that Frey's badly hurt, and it happened at your fireside, Ebba." He turned to Hilda and Raya. "Seth told me about this a short time ago. We've all been deceived, and now so many have died."

"People need to hear this tonight," said Tom, standing up. "There's no time to delay. Godwen, will you come back to March with me?"

"Yes."

"I'll go too." Hilda spoke for the first time. "Ileth's widow should hear the truth first, and it should come from me."

Perhaps not, seeing Gareth killed him. Fran caught Godwen's eye but held his tongue.

Raya caught the movement, but Hilda continued. "Until Lukas' bones are set to rest, and Gareth's recovered, I am chief." Hilda paused for a beat. Pretending not to notice the astounded looks, she continued. "It's right March hears what's happened from me."

Crystalline silence fell. Fran looked at Galos while Ebba studied the floor.

"Well – is it not so?"

Still, no one spoke. Then Nell, reddening a little, shuffled her chair and addressed Tom. "What say you to this?"

Tom turned fleetingly towards the unconscious Galos before answering Hilda. "I don't know what to say, but we should go to March straight away, and once we're there, someone needs to speak."

"Good. That's settled. Raya, please take care of Seth as well as Gareth. We've neglected the poor boy overlong."

When they had gone, Fran slipped on a dry shirt, getting ready to leave, and Cader retrieved his sword and came to join him.

"You'll send the girls back here," said Ebba.

It was not a question, but Fran nodded. Wild horses wouldn't keep them from their father, anyway.

With a heavy heart, he picked up the silver sword and stepped outside. The rain had stopped, but water still pattered down from the trees.

"I pray Jake's found Frey recovering," he began, once he and Cader were clear of the gate.

"It was Gyll. He did it." Anger gave Cader's voice an unfamiliar edge. "I saw it in his eyes ... in the clearing. Fran, I owe you my life."

"Don't think about it." Fran forced the memory away. "The gods saved you. Let's never speak of it." *Never. Never think of it. Never speak of it.*

"Pray they save him too."

Fran nodded grimly and stopped to catch his breath. "I need to find my mother, too. She's out here somewhere."

Dirt still streaked Cader's face and blood oozed from a cut near his hairline. Only his eyes – so like Elsa's – shone bright and clear as he studied Fran. "You don't need to do it alone, Fran. You're my brother. Don't you know this?"

They were face-to-face now, but still a familiar voice nagged at Fran, reminding him how alone he really was. Salty tears stung his eyes, but, suddenly, out here, cold and soaked to the skin, he remembered the cave and the fire, and somehow the memory of it drove away the tears, replacing them with the warmth of friendship.

"We've lived alone too long if you have to tell me. I know my mother's safe, but she's hiding out there somewhere, and it's getting late. She'll be wet and cold."

Something made Fran glance down. His hunting horn hung forgotten at his hip. He raised it to his lips and gave three short blasts, each note slicing through the sparkling air and rising like a shooting star into the clouded sky.

Cader smiled. "That sound makes my heart glad. Come, let's see Frey and Elsa first. My mother will set lanterns to light Annerin home."

Chapter 35

The Girl in the Wood

The rain fell hard, and droplets of water joined together to form rivulets that slid down rock, through green moss and over blackened roots. Behind Annerin, the darkness of the cave encircled her like a great cold stone womb, full of darkness and silence set against the cracks of thunder, amber light and beating rain.

Clutching her father's sword, she forced herself forwards. She had no place in the grove, it belonged to the dead. She lifted the grey hood of her cloak over her head, wrapped the torn folds of wool around herself and stepped out. The skulls in the trees nodded as rain lashed them, water dripping down through slack jaws.

Annerin nodded back, acknowledging their gift of strength. They were no longer fearful to look upon, their emptiness a reminder of the life they once held rather than a parody to scare – swaying tokens set against the primal force of the water.

She moved out among the stunted trees, and a sheet of lightning lit the sky, giving a glimpse of the path she made earlier through the thorns. Annerin took the old iron sword in both hands and swung it to clear a better way back out. She hit hard, keeping foremost her anger over the ruined cloak and dress. *The thorns were enough. Other things could keep.* In front of her, winding briars with their bitter unripe fruit snapped and fell, making snares for her feet.

With sweat soaking into her already spoilt clothes and beading her brow, Annerin eventually reached clear forest. Setting aside the sword, she took several deep breaths then reached for the waterskin. *Well, what now?* She listened. The rain had stopped, leaving only the patter from dripping leaves and, high above, the flap of wings stretching. *A world washed clean, but no place to spend the night.* With no fixed intention other than reconnaissance, she set out towards the clearing.

The light was fading, the air sodden and the sky a heavy lilac, full of rolling clouds. Annerin shivered, longing for her own fireside, dry clothes, a meal and a bed. Too late, she realised she should have stayed in the cave where at least it was somewhat dry. She could not risk the house. She slowed, her steps faltering, but then a clear, sweet note rang out, one she knew so well ... and another ... and another, lighting the dusk, calling her home.

The same sound echoed through Mirrormantle Grove, reverberating from rock to bone, but Maya, running full pelt towards the cave mouth, barely heard. With curls plastered to her head, she made the entrance, squatting down, her breath ragged and her dress and apron torn by brambles.

Here, she had expected to find Annerin, but both cave and grove were empty. Tears welled. *Oh, Mother, why am I here? Annerin, where are you?* With her whole heart, she longed for the stone house, for her parents, and for Elsa, Cader and Fran .... Arthen and Vanna, even. But she was alone, or at least she prayed she was.

She glanced down, registering the multitude of scratches on her arms and legs, and her ruined dress. Her cheek stung too. She touched it and found blood.

Poor Seth. Coming down from the tree, she had tried so hard to help him, but his wound was deep and he needed Arthen. Eventually, she had helped him crawl to the edge of the clearing, hoping they could find help. And then ... and then Wyntr found them. Putting her head in her hands, she tried to push away the memory; it sent her cold. *A bloody mess with white showing through.* But the wound on his chest had been nothing to his face – glittering eyes and demonic smile –and in his hand he clasped the little bottle stolen from Arete.

Arthen had not wanted to talk about that bottle, and now she knew why. Water it might be, but it was also medicine with powers way beyond henbell mead. Wyntr's wound knitted itself together before her eyes. Fleetingly, it gave her hope – a bottle would mend her father too – until Wyntr's eyes shifted from Seth to her, still with their demonic gleam, and he lurched forwards.

She had run.

He'd followed – a blood-soaked monster pounding after her through the Starling Wood, and on towards the grove, failing to stop at the guardian wall of briar. She homed in on a channel though, recently cut, hopefully by Annerin, while he smashed through on a parallel track, as if cuts and scratches no longer mattered.

So, where had he gone? The mouth of the cave sat at a right angle to the grove, so Maya could not see if he was approaching. Hidden at the side of the cave mouth, she scarcely breathed. Tears stung her cheeks, and water plopped down in a curtain from the arch. He would find her soon. No shadow would warn her, only boot on rock.

With her back to the rock, she inched round to get a better view.

She screamed as she came face-to-face with Wyntr again. Rain-washed blood stained the front of his tunic. He jumped too, a flicker of triumph mingling with animal hatred. Maya froze. Only the gods could help her now.

He lunged forwards with startling speed. Somehow, she side-stepped, running back into the darkness, splashing through water and sliding into a line of pots.

One cracked open to reveal a set of bones. The long thigh bone toppled at her feet. Maya snatched it up, turned and swung. Bone made contact with skin. Wyntr grunted, grabbing her by the hair. She fought, and they spun; she faced yawning darkness leading down and away. A push unbalanced him, but he grabbed her again, and together they tumbled backwards. Maya hit the floor of the cave, cold water soaking through her clothes.

It was deeper than she expected – much deeper – a pool gathering before escaping through the entrance in a channel. She felt its pull; it wanted to haul her down into the depths of the earth. Wyntr grabbed her hair again and her head was yanked backwards, into icy cold water. She flipped over – an impossible feeling, like summersaulting back-wards down a slope. *Or being swallowed.* Wyntr's grip released, and she whorled away amid utter blackness and icy water.

Surprise gave way to momentary relief at escaping Wyntr, then numbness succeeded fear. Soon, the tumbling stopped, and dank air replaced water. Ahead, a torch flickered high on a wall. Its light told her she was alone – no Wyntr, but no cave entrance either, only the faintest flicker of daylight coming from somewhere away round a corner. She sat down on wet rock and shivered, holding her still spinning head.

Looking around properly, she saw she was in a different cave. And she was not alone. Her heart quailed at the scene before her, with the torch threatening to go out, its flame writhing. Below it lay a man, tall and strong, straight and still, lying on a stone bench, his final bed. A shield covered his chest and at his side rested a helmet and a great silver sword. Maya moved forwards, needing to see more clearly what semblance lay beneath the pallor and gauntness of death. Nobility remained, and he was not old. Brown hair fell back from his forehead, and his beard was neatly trimmed. A narrow band of cloth held his jaw closed and kept a small gold crown on his head.

Something in the face ... She raised her hand, but everything jarred. She still clutched the thigh bone. *This is no dream.* But it felt horribly wrong. She hesitated, stepping back, the fear of Wyntr again on her. Darkness crept in, ready to claim the cave for its own, while the flame danced wildly, its light reflecting off the sword at the man's side. Maya's eyes moved down to the hilt. The shape of a rose sucked in the light. *It's real. It's here and it's real, just like Father said ... and Annerin ... and this meant ... This changed everything.*

She set down the bone at the foot of the stone dais, wiping away the feel of it on her sodden apron, and she carefully placed both hands around the hilt of the sword. The blade grated against the stone, and above them the torch spluttered and spat. *There couldn't be much more time. But how was it even lit?* Glancing back at the man, she suddenly understood; these were his first hours alone, and the entrance to the cave remained slightly ajar. Then she knew she must be dreaming, because March had no king, and this man wore a crown. She took the sword and held it aloft, admiring it in the way Annerin always admired Edwyn's sword until the scraping of stone on stone made her jump, and a shaft of daylight appeared, coming from the cave entrance, and lighting the passage to her right. Gently, Maya set the sword down.

Footsteps came, and she retreated to the shadows by the pool. Its black waters still rippled, now beckoning, promising safety. Drops fell from the cave roof, the drips echoing, marking time while the shadows shifted, and the table slipped out of focus ...

Maya blinked, then she blinked again, but around her there was only blackness, accompanied by a deeper chill. *The way out. Ahead and to the right.* She inched forwards, testing each footstep, arms outstretched, aiming away from the dais and towards where she gauged the passageway ran.

Through her boots, she felt the uneven floor, and after only a few steps, her toe knocked against something that moved – something light that chinked against the cave floor. She bent her knees and stretched out her arm, hand groping. It closed around a bone, but it felt smaller than before. Sweeping with her hand, she found another, and another, then her finger encountered something sharper – an edge of broken pot. At her touch, something slipped. Feeling around more, she discovered a number of pots massed at the foot of the stone table, several having fallen and cracked open, making jumbles of bones.

Thinking of the man, her heart twisted. The sense of wrongness she experienced moments earlier had gone entirely. Now there was only emptiness – loss that left no room for fear. She reached out and found him gone, the tabletop now strewn with pots, her left hand brushing them, while her right, as if moving of its own volition, slipped beneath shards and closed around that same hilt, its iron so cold it made her hand throb.

Hardly knowing why, she drew the sword from beneath the pile, fighting its weight as the heap clattered. Her left hand itched to reach out and support the blade, but she stopped herself, shivering at the thought of that slicing edge, and set both hands round the hilt. She gripped harder, but the blade grew heavy, so very heavy. She might only be ten summers old, but Annerin's sword wasn't this heavy. It pulled her arms down, dragging her towards the water. She tried to pull it up but tripped and fell.

This time the dream felt like falling, and being bumped and pulled along, as though the water fell through caves and crevices of rock with an urgency beyond nature. At last, air prickled her skin again, and she half-stumbled, half-fell forwards, her knees hitting hard rock.

On that rock stood Wyntr, framed in the fading light at the cave mouth. Maya heard herself cry out. But perhaps he was the dream – or a nightmare; his skin shone grey, almost translucent, as if he were a spectre risen from his forest grave. Maya swung, and this time the sword felt not quite so heavy ... but it was almost as tall as her, and again she staggered. Wyntr lunged. He clutched her round the waist, and they both fell backwards, again into the water, spiralling away, down and down ...

Chapter 36

Homecoming

In the copse behind March, Elsa leant against a damp tree trunk, hope seeping from her as Jake fell to his knees beside his unconscious son.

"He's slipping away." Arthen breathed the words into her ear, but their weight buckled her knees. "Even if we get back to March, it's beyond my power …"

Behind him, the other elders huddled in the damp, their faces averted.

Elsa watched Frey, recalling their conversation on the bench. *Oh, this could not be … Please gods, make the sun come out and reality return.* But Frey lay peaceful and would not wake. Then everyone jumped at the clear sound of a horn cutting through the dank, half-lit gloom. He stirred as Finola stroked his hair.

"It's Fran." Elsa clutched the rough cloth of Arthen's sleeve, and despite the dripping trees, the world seemed to lighten. "I'd know that sound anywhere. My father must have found him."

"He'll be looking for you and Annerin," said Jake. "Galos found him at Lake Everlis."

"Lake Everlis?"

"Yes. The tale's a strange one, according to Willett."

Jake's attention returned to Frey, whose eyes were open now and fixed on his mother.

Arthen shrugged and turned away.

Elsa put her hand in her pocket, where Fran's brooch rested. *Lake Everlis. But that was just a lie concocted by Wyntr. Why would Jake even say it?* She wanted someone to tell her the stories were all lies. Her gaze returned to Frey; he would tell her – he of all people would not hesitate to tell her – and now Arthen said he would die. Searching the brooding sky, she felt numb, with every shred of happiness trampled into the endless mud by Wyntr and Gyll. The being described by Wyntr sounded very real – very human – but now, because of Frey, none of that mattered anymore.

"Who else is at the ford?" asked Arthen, his voice cutting across her thoughts.

"Galos and Tom ... Willett, Nell, Cader and Ebba ... Hilda, Raya, Gareth, Godwen and ... and Seth," Jake answered. "There might be others. We didn't go inside. Godwen said you were here."

"Then Fran knows I'm here." The words were out before Elsa could stop them.

"I believe so," answered Jake.

Elsa pressed her lips together and hung her head.

"Arthen, will you help me lift him?" Jake asked, gesturing at the cart.

Together, they manoeuvred Frey onto the cart and hooked it to the harness of an old chestnut mare.

"Go slowly," began Arthen. "Enic and the others will go with you. I'll drop in at the ford first."

Jake gasped. "But Frey needs you. No one at the ford's as badly wounded."

"You can't know that. Enic's here. He'll see to Frey."

Elsa noted the careful words and glances with a beat of misgiving. *The ford. Father.*

"Very well, but we'll be waiting for you in March," said Jake. "I'll send the horse back for you."

Elsa and Arthen moved out from among the trees, and a ray of evening sunshine broke through the clouds. In the distance they could see Fran and Cader.

Elsa stopped abruptly, heart thumping, then she ducked back under the umbrella of a large oak.

Arthen smiled softly at her. "You'll be fine," he said. "I'll walk on. I want to get there ... I'll send Maya with news ... with any news as soon as I can."

"Thank you, Arthen. I ... I'll be there shortly."

The rattle of Frey's cart receded and Arthen shuffled away, leaving Elsa alone. She stared up into the oak, watching banks of drifting cloud through the branches, asking herself why she did not run to meet Fran. The sky spun, cloud funnelling stray shafts of sunlight, and she sank down onto damp earth, leaning back against the tree.

Elsa. Elsa.

"Elsa. Elsa."

She jerked awake, groggy and weak, to find Fran on one side of her and Cader on the other, their faces streaked with dirt and rain.

Back for the harvest. The sight of Fran chased the demons away. "You're back," she heard herself say.

"As promised." His expression darkened as he took in her bandaged arm and the cut on her jaw. "Can you stand?"

"Yes, of course. I just felt tired ... and wet." Elsa squirmed, registering the damp seeping through the seat of her dress. "I need to sit by a fire."

"Then that's what we'll do." Fran helped her to her feet.

Cader, silent throughout, leant over and roughly kissed the top of her head. "Wyntr and Gyll are dead," he said, "and I need to see Frey."

Coldness swept through her again and the cut on her jaw pulled and itched. *Oh, Frey. Please gods ... Please be wrong, Arthen.* "You'll catch them; they're heading back through the copse. They only left a short while ago." Raising her head, she saw Cader's eyes fixed on her, eyes full of defiance and hope. *Gods help us all.*

"At least you're safe." He reached out to her again, mouthed *tomorrow* at Fran, then he turned abruptly and ran off into the trees.

"I'm sorry I left you." Fran touched her cheek, frowning as he traced the cut to where it disappeared in her hair.

"It'll heal, and it saved Father's life."

Fran's head dropped. Overhead, a kite took off, shaking the branches and dripping water down on them.

"Gareth saved my life today," he said at last.

Gareth. Elsa looked away, picturing that bright-eyed, guileless face. *Thunder from a clear sky.* The man was an enigma – hard to know and difficult to hate.

"Hey, did you hear me?"

She nodded, watching a rabbit break cover in the field opposite. *Life returning after the rain.*

"Elsa, we need to go to the ford. Your father's wounded. I'm guessing Jake never told you."

Elsa fought the urge to put her fingers in her ears. A sob escaped, along with the conscious thought. *I know. I never gave Jake the chance to say, but I know.*

Fran approached the stone house at the ford with Elsa at his side.

Arthen waited for them at the gate, his expression haunted. "Your father's not in danger," he called out to Elsa, "but Seth's unconscious and Maya's not here."

Maya? The sight of her on Cader's horse flashed back to him. *But she was with you. She can't be far.*

Elsa staggered, and Fran caught her as she grabbed the gate for support.

"He's definitely not in danger?" Fran asked.

Arthen gave the tiniest shake of the head. "There's many worse today."

Elsa pushed past them both and ran into the house.

Fran watched her go. "Gods help us."

"I think we're on our own today."

"She probably doubled back, and you missed her," Fran ventured, barely convincing himself.

"I shouldn't have let her go. That child ..."

"It's what happened that day ... I found her alone in the forest."

"I know. She was convinced your mother had gone to the grove." Arthen bit his lip.

So, you're sending me to the grove.

"Ebba's beside herself," Arthen added. "Someone needs to check, maybe head that way and sound the all-clear again." The old man twitched, looking away.

What else?

"I'd like to see everyone in March and the gate shut before nightfall ..."

His gaze darted towards the adjacent forest. *Wolves – and Arthen couldn't even say the word.* Now Fran clutched the gate too, bone tired, scanning the trees, hoping against hope – and with dusk fast approaching – both Maya and his mother would just appear. But no, there was no sign, and until he knew they were safe, he would not be hiding behind any bolted gate. Could Maya have just gone home? Unlikely, given what happened. The longhouse, perhaps. Checking would eat up precious time ... But she would see it was getting late, and she would be wet and cold. She would want Ebba. Galos too ... but if she'd seen ... His hand moved to his pocket as he remembered the acorns lying on the ground. *She had seen.* He shook his head, summoning strength into his cold wet limbs. *Please, gods ... please, Arete, send help. Send HIM.*

"She's not at the grove."

Fran's heart leapt at the voice, and a sob surprised him. *Mother. Where ...?*

His mother stepped out from the trees, torn and bedraggled, but with a smile that lit the gloom. "But she was right, I did wait there until the sounds of battle died away."

In answer, he lifted her clear of the muddy lane, making sure she was real, and she was – the shield strapped across her back caught at his wrists and proved it.

"Thank the gods you're safe. I should never have left you." She gasped.

Fran shook his head. *You left to get help.* "I know why you went."

"Do you?"

"I found her."

Arthen gasped.

His mother turned towards the house. Fran followed her gaze. Light peeped from the shutters and voices broke the evening's stillness.

"Annerin, I thought it was you." Elsa appeared at the door, tripping as she ran to them. "But Maya's not here, and she's not with you ..."

Fran pushed past Arthen to help her as she righted herself then tripped again and clutched the post.

"Come. We'll work out what to do." His mother grabbed Elsa's other arm and led her back inside to the seat by the fire.

At the sight of his mother, heads turned.

"Annerin." Willett and Ebba spoke simultaneously.

Willett's face was weary and still bloodstained. "Annerin. Thank the gods," he repeated, stopping his pacing.

His mother scanned the room, her eyes lingering over the two closed cabin doors before coming to rest on Gareth. "What of the wounded?" she asked, her face grim.

"He's hurt but a little," began Ebba, following her gaze. "Galos will live. Seth's gravely ill. Raya's with him."

"Seth turned against Wyntr," Fran told his mother.

"And Gareth?" she asked.

"He killed Ileth but Wyntr wounded him."

"There's a lot of blood."

Yes, everywhere. Scarlet rags littered the floor at Gareth's side. "The sword sliced his shoulder," said Fran.

His mother took a moment to take it all in. "I've come from Mirrormantle Grove," she began eventually, plumping down on a stool.

"I took refuge there from Ileth and his men. I didn't see Wyntr, Gyll and Seth, but I feared a trap, so I stayed hidden."

"Wyntr and Gyll didn't follow you," said Willett. "They plotted other ills. Frey's gravely injured, and Elsa had a narrow escape."

Fran's mother stared at him, uncomprehending.

"Wyntr tricked everyone," Willett continued. "He accused you, but what he really wanted was the sword. He planned to take it from ... from both of you."

Fran's mind flashed back to the scene in the clearing – Wyntr dead at his feet, Gareth gasping with pain, Tom staying his hand ... A beat of disquiet sounded in his head, and he glanced up into the thatch where it steamed from the fire. *Miserable wretch, plotting all this time. Watching, waiting, flint ready to strike. Well, had it not been the confrontation with Lukas, it would've been something else.*

Fran ducked back outside to check the path. *No, no one. Just rooks gathering at the ford.*

"I'll check the clearing if you check March," he said to Willett, gesturing with the hunting horn.

Willett checked his belt and nodded. "Agreed. If she's not there, I'll come to the ford and signal you."

"You'll beat Arthen back," Fran added, recalling Arthen's warning. "Send out everyone you can to the ford with the horses and stretchers."

Willett swayed slightly. He leant on the table, muttering, "Gods help us."

Yes, you understand.

Silence enveloped the room. Elsa drifted towards sleep and Ebba, having reappeared from tending Galos in his mother's cab-in, remained on her feet, her stare encouraging Willett on his way.

Willett sighed and looked longingly towards the kettle on the hearth. He took a final swig of ale and ripped another crust of bread. "Sadly, the attack on you both also created a diversion," he told Fran's mother. "When March emptied, it gave Wyntr the opportunity to …" The rest was whispered into his mother's ear while Ebba clattered cups.

Annerin turned to Elsa. "Surely …"

"No."

"What madness made him believe such a plan would work?" his mother asked Fran and Willett, disbelief writ large on her face.

Fran, still half-focused on Elsa, shrugged. The memory of himself standing over Wyntr with the sword raised kept returning. He slipped outside again, checking the lane. *Come on Maya. Where are you?* He returned to see his mother making ready to join him.

"Maya's not wandering aimless," she pointed out. "If she did go to the grove, you need me. If we spend the night there, so be it."

"But—"

"We stay together this time. She's not wandering aimless. She's gone somewhere. We'll find her. Just like last time." His mother spoke to them all, but her eyes lingered on Gareth and her words fell into stillness.

Fran, clutching the rough-hewn door frame, and with the chill of evening on his back, felt the world shift beneath his feet.

Chapter 37

The Sword and the Water

Annerin followed Fran into the forest, the damp earth smell filling her lungs and each step bringing a fresh deluge of raindrops down on their heads. She shivered, her wet feet squelching through last season's rotting leaves.

Eventually, Fran stopped in a small clearing, took out his hunting horn and gave three long blasts, shaking the drowsy birds from their roosts, calling and flapping.

"I don't understand," she said, as the final note died away. "What if Maya's at the opposite end of the wood?"

"I'm not calling Maya."

She felt Fran's gaze on her, imploring her, it seemed, to find courage for them both. He grasped her hand.

Annerin took a deep breath, focusing on the warmth of the hand in hers. She knew the answer. Part of her had always known the answer, even before that day in the wood. The child's voice from so long ago replayed in her head. *A draygon.*

They waited until the starlings rose again from their roosts, and at last he came. The cold amber eyes stared down at her again and the forest spun.

Fran's heart slammed in his chest, his only thought to wonder how anyone could mistake this creature for a stag. An instant later, the image in front of him flickered, like a figure across the plain seen through summer's heat, revealing towering antlers where there were great scaled spikes and fans, and cloven hooves where there were sharp claws.

When the image settled, Fran looked into ancient, alien eyes but saw an echo of himself. Silently, he asked the creature if it could hear him. The great head tilted. Their exchange was unspoken, but the answers came, filling the air around their heads with the lightest puff of smoke.

"Fran, I have been able to hear you since the day you were born, but the little one you seek is in great danger. You must return to Arete for help, although Maya might, even now, be beyond our protection."

"Where is she?"

"In the water. You've seen the lake – its waters are not a safe place, and now it seems the water's made a path to reach what I hid so well, and so long ago. I don't know how. Lake Everlis is neither the beginning nor the end, and I don't know where Maya is. But come, I'll take you to Arete. Bring your mother with you. Arete is most anxious to see her again."

"Again?"

"Climb." This time the voice boomed.

He looked round at his mother to see if she too could hear it.

She nodded, and then she followed, clambering up onto the dragon's back after him.

His mother sat in front and Fran gripped her shield, in vain seeking purchase on the broad back, so she leant forwards, grasping the dragon's neck.

"You will not fall," said the voice, and he realised they were sitting in a hollow below the neck and between the huge wings.

Grasping the nearest scale, Fran lurched as the back heaved beneath him and the wings unfolded.

"He says we won't fall," whispered Fran as she turned, biting her lip. "Do you hear him?"

"I hear an echo almost beyond the reach of hearing, but it's you he's speaking to." She smiled a small hopeful smile, and the dragon broke the cover of the trees with a massive flap of his scaled wings.

They rose, the wind catching them and roaring around their heads, and the sun came back into view, massive and ruddy – a puddle of fire away to the west. The land below them stretched out, dark against the brightness of the setting sun, the stone house at the ford already tiny, and March's many lanterns and fires flickering in the distance. The vastness was overwhelming. And the smallness. Figures were dotted below, but they did not look up. Fran's head spun, and his cheek sought the rough cold of his grandfather's shield – moments stolen before the future swallowed them whole.

The dragon banked before turning towards Elden Deas and rising high over the mountain top. Lake Everlis shimmered to the south, the water as dark as molten metal where the light hit the mountainside. Below it, the forest stretched on, fringing an empty plain, while the eastern hills and fells rolled down the land, great barren knuckles of moorland with the final shafts of sunlight playing on their flanks.

"We can see the world." The wind whipped Fran's words away, although he spoke a hair's breadth from his mother's ear. Her reply was lost too, but he followed her gaze and saw their little wood and tiny home. All the distance he had ever wandered was nothing compared to what he now saw. Above them, the sky, still patched with cloud, grew diaphanous, a cover for the great wheel of the night sky. Stars twinkled into being over the moors, and away to the west, Vaden's Crown and the horseshoe of mountains it bridged fell into silhouette, heralding night. In that last light, Fran searched the far horizon, imaging the vast ocean told of in stories, but amid the blasting wind, he saw only the sun's fiery glow, and then they slowed, and the dragon set down on the hillside above the lake.

Fran climbed down first, then he helped his mother. *So familiar.* He scanned the clearing but saw no sign of Arete.

"Go," said the voice.

Fran led his mother down the steep path to the lakeside. When they reached the bottom, he looked up and saw Arete watching them from her seat on the furthest rock outside the cave mouth, her ragged dress replaced by the finest gown he had ever seen – shining lilac cloth trimmed with silver thread.

His mother gasped and took a few steps back.

"Fran, son of Edwyn, you've come back." Arete remained seated, watching him.

Raindrops hit his face, but as he glanced up at the sky, movement in the lake caught his eye. Something broke the surface, then the water began to roil and churn, throwing up spray. *Not again.* He recoiled, his innards turning liquid. He heard his mother stifle a scream.

Out in the lake, waves grew, rising and twisting as if tortured by some unseen hand, water roaring like the river in full spate, echoing round the glade, loud against the stillness of the evening. Behind them, the dragon remained poised on the hillside, riveted to the scene in the lake.

"She is coming," said the voice.

"Who?"

No answer.

"Sit down." Arete motioned him towards the adjacent rock, still wet from the day's rain. "He's right. She is coming. Perhaps we'll be able to help her."

Gingerly, Fran perched on the rock's edge. In front of them, grey shapes rose, great fists with claws, terrible heads with jaws, all instantly crashing back into the foam. Then among them was a flicker, followed by a cry. Fran, back on his feet, stepped closer, trying to see.

"It's Maya. It's Maya. Help her!" his mother screamed at Arete, running towards them across the wet pine needles.

"The water will drag me away before I can help her. You must help her yourselves but carry nothing into the water. Nothing, mind."

At the sight of Maya, white and gasping, Fran's heart lurched. He'd been carrying nothing before ... With a final glance back at the dragon, he strode into the water, only to be flung back onto the shore at Arete's feet almost immediately.

She reached out to pull him up, her grip like iron.

"Arete, what can we do?"

"You must be patient," Arete shouted above the roar, not letting go of Fran's arm. "The water is fighting to bring her here, but she carries that which wants to return to its home in the west. The object Ladon has guarded for centuries."

Ladon. Fran silently registered the name and glanced up at the dragon, who remained fixated on the water.

"Look," cried Annerin.

Only a stone's throw away, in the lake, Maya floundered among towering waves. She grasped what seemed to be yet another sword, but something else flashed into view ... another person in the water, fighting with her, dragging her back while she struggled to reach the shore.

His mother and Arete both sprang forwards, Arete releasing him and pushing him away.

"Maya. Maya!" Annerin called out, but Maya focused on Arete, who launched forwards into the shallows as if she were battling the winds of a storm.

No, roared a voice in Fran's head. *No. No.*

The mountain peak behind them shook. Arete took another step. Rocks began rolling down the hillside, and on the opposite shore, tall pines bent, their roots breaking free from the ground.

Fran went after Arete but stopped dead when he saw – standing out clearly against the waves – the figure of Wyntr snatching at Maya, reaching for the sword, his face twisted and grey. *Leave him for the birds*. Those had been Tom's words. So how could this be? If not dead, he had been severely wounded.

Maya, sword in one hand, stretched the other towards Arete's outstretched arms, but Wyntr bore down on her, and the sword appeared to weigh her, dragging her down. Across the water, a pine toppled, boughs screeching and cracking, bouncing and shaking the ground when it hit. Fran saw rather than heard Maya gasp when a wave slapped her full in the face. Spluttering, she turned away, only for Wyntr to grasp her wrist.

Arete retreated, but Fran edged forwards again. Ahead, the sword lunged and twisted in and out of the water. They made an even match, the little girl and the wounded man; time slowed, Maya fighting to bring the sword to shore, and Wyntr trying to wrestle it from her. Fran stalled, a wave buckling his legs and dragging him under. Gasping, he got to his knees, only to be felled again. He blinked away water.

The sword came into view above the waves for the third time, and a sudden warm wind whipped overhead as Ladon took off from the hillside and flew at Maya. He snatched her round the waist with one claw, the other clamping around the sword. It dragged Wyntr clear of the water too, but he let go, falling and instantly vanishing beneath a great wave that rose then descended batlike on its prey.

Fran crawled away, dragging himself up on one of the boulders.

Arete slumped down at the cave mouth as the water calmed and the roar subsided.

Maya lay nearby, wet to the skin and colourless, on the spot where Ladon had set her down. For the briefest moment, her eyes locked with his. The sword she had fought so hard to hold lay beside her; it bore a black rose on its hilt. *Vaden's sword.*

His mother ran to her, wild-eyed. "She's alive."

Maya stirred, bemused at the scene around her.

The sound of pine branches snapping beneath the weight of the fallen trunk echoed across the water, and the ripples sent out rings, already fading into the new silence. A shower of pebbles rattled down the hillside, loosened by the dragon. *Ladon.* Fran repeated the name to himself again, but it seemed familiar already. As if in answer, a puff of smoke settled over them, and Fran beckoned his mother to sit by him. Soon, he found himself drifting off to sleep in his usual spot in the cave.

Twilight followed, and Ladon lit a fire that would burn through the night before he settled down near Fran and Annerin, his tail curving round to encompass Arete and Maya where they slept. One gold-flecked eye stayed open, watching the sword. Above, a faint ribbon and bright triangle of stars twinkled into being beyond the sparse pines and joined the hosts of other stars gathering overhead.

Chapter 38

Gifts

Night-time passed, and cool morning light filled the glade. Maya sat up, her aching heart bemused by the sight of dragon, lake and mountains. Behind her, in the cave mouth, embers winked orange in the fire's ash, next to which slept a huge wildcat, its grey-speckled flank peacefully rising and falling and shaggy paws stretching to reveal wicked talons. Beyond the cat, there was a ledge strewn with pristine white furs, and a silken canopy of deepest blue and silver hung overhead. Opposite this bed, a great pair of antlers adorned the wall, and a wide curved ledge formed a seat, around which were scattered furs of many different hues, including some with stripes and spots. On the walls, smaller sills cut into the rock housed coloured bottles, ornately carved wooden boxes and cooking utensils. *Magic lived here.* Sniffing back a tear, she looked down at the woman sleeping by her side and carefully brushed away a stray curl of auburn hair. *Arete.*

The woman opened one eye, then the other, and she studied Maya for a few moments, her gaze lingering on Maya's cheek where it stung from where she'd rubbed it against the tree bark. "On many a day, child, I hear your voice when I stand on the mountainside. It's always loud as thunder. And now, Maya, you're here."

"You're Arete – the ancient one."

"Then we know one another already. In this, you're ahead of most of your fellow villagers. But come. Your sister's safe at the ford ... and your father lives."

At last, the sobs broke free.

Arete pulled her close. *He lives. He lives. Hush now.*

The words, mingling with the faint scent of juniper, landed in Maya's head. At length, she pulled her face free from the bright tangle of hair and sighed.

"How is it so?" she asked.

"He's wounded, but wounds heal. He'll mend."

Maya followed Arete's gaze to where the bottles lined the sill, her last doubts fading.

Arete nodded.

Wyntr's bottle. She knew. And he ... Maya brushed away the thought. He had gone now.

"But tell me, Maya," Arete continued, her voice catching as she peered round at the sword lying next to Maya. "How did you come by this sword? It's no child's toy."

"I found it in a tomb, but I don't know how I got there. I slipped in the cave at Mirrormantle Grove, then it felt as if I fell through time and spun through water and among the stars."

"Who lay in the tomb?"

"A great, tall man. A king. The torches still flickered ... But it was a dream, because then there was nothing. Only urns and bones."

A grey heron passed overhead, alone in a cloudless sky, its body arrowlike, wings pulsing. Arete watched it pass and shook her head. "This sword has rested safe by Vaden's side for two centuries."

"I don't understand how I came by it, or how I got here."

"The sword was waiting, and somehow it found a way ... a way back. You carried something else, something precious, it seems, that wanted you to take it home."

"A bone," said Maya. "I fell over a jar in the cave. It broke, and I picked up a bone because Wyntr attacked me. Then I slipped into the water."

Arete stared out over the lake, to where the sun touched the tops of the distant pines, a tear rolling unchecked down her cheek. "Those bones had been moved, then, from the barrows to the grove."

"I don't understand."

"The water sometimes acts as a gateway. The results of a spell – probably one of my mother's. She lives with her kin in the sea but sometimes likes to travel inland. She's probably forgotten she even cast it ... But that is by the by. Ladon and I, we fought with the owner of that sword, and ... and at great cost we brought it here and gave it to Vaden to carry into battle. No enemy prevails against it. Vaden answered the call for aid and went west into Eruthin, to stand with the kings of Tiroren, Glendorrig and Bywater. You know the story, perhaps.

"This other sword, you see" – Arete gestured behind them, to a sword propped against the hillside and displaying a red rose – "was one of many ordinary swords piled together on the mountainside before the first battle in that war. Night came and our dragons came with fire and magic, forging them anew into what you now see. The red swords belonged to Glendorrig. Were you to climb one of these peaks" – here she gestured towards the Hart's Horn and Berry Drum – "you would see the place where that happened and where the beacon was lit. The Green Table Mountain marks the boundary between Glendorrig and Bywater. Way, way beyond that, you will find the Western Sea." Arete smiled down at Maya. "You would like the sea, Maya. I always did ..."

Arete paused, and Maya imagined that great stretch of country, just out of sight and reach.

"These two swords may look alike, but they are not," Arete continued, gesturing towards the sword lying beside Maya. "I hoped never to see this thing again – nor its owner."

Maya looked from one to the other. *But what of the silver sword Fran carried? To which kingdom did it belong?*

"And then there's the silver sword," Arete continued. "That too is only an image of this weapon. More powerful, yes, but still a copy. We were lucky yesterday."

"The water."

"The water brings things back to where they belong – things that matter. When you picked up Vaden's bone, it took you back to his vigil at the barrows. Then when you picked up the sword, it was drawn towards its home in the west, but you were holding it tightly and so the water brought you to me." Arete hesitated, her eyes on Maya, green eyes filled only with pain.

"Where are your family?"

"Ladon is one, although he is a dragon. We were brought up together by the sea, in the kingdom of Tiroren, in Eruthin. There were three of us, and three dragons, their eggs birth gifts from my father. My mother's in the sea. I've not seen her in fifty summers – a blink of an eye for her ... for me too, perhaps ... My father was a mortal man, but one who spoke with dragons."

Maya wanted to ask more but held her tongue, and Arete began again, telling her about Dalred and Thalia – missing for two hundred summers and winters – and poor Everlis, interred in a cave in the mountains, to which, following a rock fall, there was only one way in – through the lake. Arete explained how the water pulled, trying to take her to her sister's tomb but offering no way back.

Maya shivered, then she wondered about Arete's mother and where she might be. She had never seen the sea, let alone heard of such a being, but it sounded as if she were the most powerful one of all. A goddess, even.

"One day, Krataia and I will be friends again, but in the meantime we both guard the mountain pass from our separate homes. Now this thing has been brought here again, I don't know what we'll do. Ladon hid it well. What happened to you is most unfortunate ..."

"But the sword was so well hidden, so I think you stayed to be near us too," said Maya. For once, it was a question, but it received no answer. She reached out, wrapping her hand around Arete's slender, work-worn fingers. "And that means you're not a witch at all."

"Once I was not, but then I couldn't control the storm. It's like anger, you see."

Elin and Roe.

"The storm killed two young men, as you must know." Arete clasped Maya's hand. On the opposite shore, a deer approached the water, its ears flicking.

"If only the people of March could understand." Fran strode over, his voice ringing round the glade, making Maya jump. He leant on the nearest rock and reached out to her, frowning at the cuts on her cheek before fixing his eyes on Arete.

"But maybe they're right," Arete answered. "Maybe I have become a witch to dread."

Fran said nothing, only watching as Arete let go of Maya's hand, rose and sat on the rock opposite him. So much had been shared so freely with Maya. It was hard not to feel hurt.

Eventually, Arete broke the silence. "There's something you carry," she began. "Something I would have you give me."

"I've brought it back." Fran, having heard much of the conversation between Maya and Arete, proffered the silver sword, but Arete ignored it.

"If you remember, you already returned this to me some time ago, and I gave it to you as your own."

Fran turned away. Two young deer now grazed on the far shore – last spring's new stags. When he looked back, she was still watching him, her fingers brushing at the fabric of the new dress.

"Keep the sword. You may need it again. Besides, it's a fitting weapon for Ladon's new protégé." She gestured towards the sleeping dragon, whose bulk now blocked the head of the pass, a short distance away. "Ladon is my companion here, but as you may have overheard, it wasn't always so." The voice wavered, almost breaking. "Once, long ago, Krataia was my dragon."

And they had fallen out literally hundreds of summers ago. What madness. Why, it was worse than the situation in March. And there was someone still out there – someone they both feared enough to make them block the pass for all this time. Fran shivered, longing to escape the pool of morning shade in which they sat.

"Now Ladon favours you, it seems, but Fran, there's something else, something you carry."

There is not. Fran turned to his shield, where it leant against the rock face by his mother.

"I don't mean your shield."

"I've nothing else I can give." *Mother.* His chest tightened.

"You picked something off my shelf. Something that was not yours."

Fran froze. *The brooch.* The brooch had been in his pocket … and now it was pinned on his cloak, which was in March.

"You understand me," said Arete.

"Then it was not …"

"No, it was not yours." She repeated what she had told Maya about the water.

"I'll bring it back," muttered Fran, half recalling something – some reference to a brooch down at the ford that he had overheard and not understood.

"It would be best. But that's not all. Come, you carry two things that are precious to you in the small pocket of your tunic."

Numbly, Fran pulled out the two acorns and balanced them in his palm. His heart twisted.

"You went back for them." Maya smiled up at him. "After we threw them at you."

"I found them again," said Fran, glancing away, back to where the stags were gathering.

Arete reached out her hand. Fran placed the two acorns in it, and she walked into the cave, took down a small wooden box, placed the acorns inside, closed the lid and put the box back. Fran shrugged at Maya, and both watched Arete collect two small bottles, weighing them in her hands before returning to her seat.

"I had three of these, but one was stolen. Each holds enough to mend or cure one person." She handed them to Fran. "Take them. Use them well."

Inside the thick little bottles, liquid moved.

Maya flinched as Fran ran his thumb over the smooth shell before putting one in each pocket.

"What's the matter, Maya?"

"Wyntr took the other bottle," she replied. "He brought it to March and held it up in the square. Arthen thought it just held water."

Arete smiled. "He was right; it is water – my water. Maya, when you get back to March you must tell Arthen to restore Mirrormantle Grove, and to bury all the bones."

"I will."

"You must also take that sword." She nodded in the direction of the black one. "It spent ten winters on the wall of your longhouse, hidden in plain view, and it can do so again."

Fran weighed the sword in his hand. It felt much like the silver sword – same weight, same balance – but it was grim, grim as iron, despite its shine. Arete paled, so he set it down by the silver one, near where his mother still slept.

"Annerin, wake up," called Arete.

His mother started from her sleep.

Fran went over and knelt beside her. "It's all right, Mother."

She sat up, staring round, then she raked her fingers through her hair.

"Give your mother water."

Fran hesitated, reluctant to leave her side.

"Quickly." Arete disappeared into the cave.

Ladon stirred, his snort waking the cat, who stretched then slunk away in the opposite direction. Ladon watched it go, took in Fran at the cave mouth and closed his eye again.

His mother drained the water. "Time to be away, Fran, and get this child home." She took up her shield and put her sword in her belt.

Arete reappeared, stopping short of Fran.

"Annerin, you were the first in two hundred summers to set out willingly to visit me. I have a gift for you." She darted forwards, pushing a bundle of cloth into reluctant hands before slipping behind Fran again.

His mother's cheeks reddened, her stare fixed on Arete. Fran moved to catch the bundle, but as Annerin's fingers explored the cloth, her expression mellowed.

"You also," Arete continued, "have something which belongs to me, and which I would have you give back."

His mother's hand covered her pocket and her jaw set hard.

"Very well, as you will. It's nineteen summers since I last saw you here, but for you it's only been days. You're welcome back here when a little more time has passed."

His mother's scowl faded, and she acknowledged Arete's words with a bow of her head, then Maya took her by the hand and led her, still carrying the bundle, past Arete and into the cave.

Fran, perched on the rock beside Arete, watching the first rays of sunshine dance on the water.

"What happens now?"

"Ladon will speak with Krataia, and we will see."

"I would help you if I could." The words tumbled out, but the thought of trying to speak to Krataia as he did to Ladon turned his insides to water.

The smile that met him was sorrowful. "I believe you would, Fran, and I thank you, but you have much to occupy you at home."

"Perhaps."

"Will you go back to March?"

"No," he replied, after a moment's thought. "The forest's my home, not March."

Hearing footsteps, Fran turned and saw his mother walking out of the cave, hand in hand with Maya, attired in a new dress, its weave delicate and flawless – pale grey, *was it wool?* with a green trim – and matching apron.

Arete, smiling at his mother, held out her hands to Maya. "Well, Fran, I'll send the black sword to March with your mother. Maybe it's time she went back home."

Later that morning, Ladon took Fran, Annerin and Maya back to the ford. The thatch smoked and shutters were flung open, letting out a jumble of voices and clanging ironware. Galos and Gareth were both sitting up, and all rejoiced at the sight of Maya. When the tumult subsided, they remarked on his mother's new clothes, and Ebba's jaw dropped enough to trick even Fran into a smile.

Slipping aside, he went to Seth, who lay grey and sweating, with Raya slumped at his side. Fran administered the first of Arete's two bottles, and soon a faint wash of colour leeched back into Seth's cheeks, and a smile fought its way to his lips.

It works. Thank the gods. His thoughts turned to Frey, and the need for haste.

Both his mother and Elsa decided to accompany him to March.

"I'll walk with you, too." Gareth, whose wounds were patched, limped towards them as they made to leave.

Fran's mother paused, a rare quality of smile briefly lighting her face. Behind the silence, the fire crackled on the hearth, and it seemed to Fran that around him, the world made a full quarter turn.

They set out along a path still muddy from yesterday's storm; he was impatient, but Elsa was slow and out of breath in the growing heat. His mother, meanwhile, gave her arm to Gareth, and the pair fell back.

When the settlement came into view, preceded by a field of smaller pyres surrounding Lukas', Fran slowed. *Not home. But Frey ...* He waited for Gareth to catch up.

The four walked together, attracting keen glances, many ice cold. Insects flashed back and forth, and behind the incessant buzz, the air hissed, like a snake poised over its prey.

Fran took Elsa's hand, while Gareth stepped forwards, straightening as he approached Ileth's widow. She waited, her face a strange mixture of resignation and grief. Ahead, on the top of March Hill, Hilda presided over a smoking fire of atonement. She watched her son, the morning sun glinting off the shield she wore strapped across her shoulders.

Fran went ahead, looking neither left nor right. He tapped on the door and, slipping inside, found Finola and Jake fretting at Frey's bedside while Cader slouched over the table. A fire made the tiny house unbearably hot. Fran showed the remaining bottle to them, and after an exchange of whispers, Jake propped up his son and Finola administered the contents.

Then they waited.

After a time, Frey's breathing evened, and he let out a small cough. Jake rushed to his side again. Frey's eyes focused on his father, and two small spots of colour appeared on his cheeks. They were followed by the ghost of a smile as his gaze drifted from his mother to Cader, then to Elsa, and he drifted into a quiet sleep.

Later that day, Galos, Ebba and Maya made their way home, and the happy news of both Seth and Frey's recoveries spread around March; it was a glimmer of hope on a day when so many pyres were to be lit.

Days rumbled on, and at the suggestion of Vanna and Arthen, who had never, either publicly or privately, agreed on anything before, Hilda moved in with Raya, and Gareth took over his father's home, and his place beside Galos, to lead March. His eye, however, was always directed towards the ford, and he wandered there so often that even the gossips tired. As a gesture of welcome, he gave Annerin and Fran the repaired roundhouse at the edge of the square, and Annerin gave him the black sword to again hang in the longhouse – a gift to him as well as a peace offering to March.

When the harvest was in, and autumn came, Fran and Elsa celebrated their betrothal. High above them, on the shores of Lake Everlis, Arete rose from her fireside. She lifted a small box down from a sill in the cave, opened it, took out two browning acorns and weighed them in her hand before returning them and sitting with Ladon and the cat in the evening sun.

Acknowledgements

Writing a novel is never an easy thing ... Like the journeys in this book, it's a long and winding road. My thanks go to all those who have helped and supported me along the way.

To the writing community at large for advice and positivity; to my beta readers, one and all; to Hazel Hitchins for unwavering support and early edits; to Victoria Seymour for editing and proofreading; to Matisse Jeffery for cover design; and to my daughters for supplying the interior artwork.

The British landscape, explored on so many family days out, has been my inspiration for the settings in this novel, and for this I owe my parents a debt of gratitude that can only be repaid by passing on the baton to my own children. Cue another hiking expedition that proves to be longer and steeper than expected!

My last and biggest thank you goes to my darling husband and children, for being there every step of the way, and for being wonderful and always believing in me, and to Todd, who sat patiently beside me through countless hours of writing and editing.

www.ingramcontent.com/pod-product-compliance
Ingram Content Group UK Ltd.
Pitfield, Milton Keynes, MK11 3LW, UK
UKHW040044230225
455421UK00004B/85